Praise for Robert Crais

'A thrill-a-minute read. Crais is on top form, which, believe me, is about as good as it gets. Don't miss it'
Independent on Sunday

'Opens like a champagne cork popping and never lets up. What follows is a nerve-racking, switchbacking tale of guilt and redemption. It's so good it gives you goose bumps' *Evening Standard*

'A dark introspective thriller . . . Fast action, false clues and sharp dialogue . . . gripping' *Literary Review*

'Yet more tough, cracking stuff from Crais, who returns to form by giving his best characters, Elvis Cole and Joe Pike, plenty of lethal action' *Daily Mirror*

'In Los Angeles, a city not entirely devoid of fictional private eyes, Robert Crais' combative, edgy Elvis Cole continues to be up there with the best of them . . . the climax and denouement are terrific' *The Times*

'Crais is in top form . . . a first-rate puzzle, with many twists and nothing quite as it seems' *Sunday Telegraph*

Robert Crais is the author of seventeen novels, including the international bestsellers *The Forgotten Man, The Last Detective, Demolition Angel* and the Edgar-nominated *L.A. Requiem*. He has two additional Edgar nominations as well as Anthony and Macavity awards for his series of Elvis Cole and Joe Pike crime novels. Crais has also written for acclaimed television shows such as *L.A. Law* and *Hill Street Blues*. *Hostage* has been made into a major motion picture featuring Bruce Willis. He lives in Los Angeles. Visit his website at www.robertcrais.com.

By Robert Crais

The Monkey's Raincoat
Stalking the Angel
Lullaby Town
Free Fall
Voodoo River
Sunset Express
Indigo Slam
L.A. Requiem
Demolition Angel
Hostage
The Last Detective
The Forgotten Man
The Two Minute Rule
The Watchman
Chasing Darkness
The First Rule
The Sentry

the first rule

ROBERT CRAIS

An Orion paperback

First published in Great Britain in 2010
by Orion
This paperback edition published in 2011
by Orion Books Ltd,
Orion House, 5 Upper St Martin's Lane,
London WC2H 9EA

An Hachette UK company

1 3 5 7 9 10 8 6 4 2

A CIP catalogue record for this book
is available from the British Library.

ISBN 978-1-4091-1823-7

Printed and bound in Great Britain
by Clays Ltd, St Ives plc

The Orion Publishing Group's policy is to use papers
that are natural, renewable and recyclable products and
made from wood grown in sustainable forests. The logging
and manufacturing processes are expected to conform to
the environmental regulations of the country of origin.

www.orionbooks.co.uk

for my friend,

Harlan Ellison,

whose work, more than any other,
brought me to this place.

ACKNOWLEDGMENTS

Pat Crais, Aaron Priest, Neil Nyren, Ivan Held, and Tim Hely Hutchinson. Jon Wood, Susan Lamb, and Malcolm Edwards. Eileen Hutton. Mark and Diane, for taking the Egg. Gregg and Delinah. Jeffrey Lane – because he's cool. Frank, Toni. Bill Tanner, Brad Johnson, Lynne Limp. Damon and Kate, as always. The Plum Brothers: Alan 'Night Train' Brennert, William F. 'Slow Hand' Wu, Michael 'Bardwulf' Toman, and Michael 'Fastball' Cassutt. Otto. Shelby Rotolo. Eileen Bickham – because I care. Chip, Gene, Roger, and Joe – now I know. Stan Robinson. Gregory Frost. Tim Campbell. Lois, Vic, Coop, Biljon, Mike A, and Mike B. Jerry. April. Don Westlake. Betsy Little, Steve Volpe.

All of them helped.

The organized criminal gangs from the fifteen republics of the former Soviet Union are governed by what they call the *Vorovskoy Zakon* – the thieves' code – which is comprised of eighteen written rules. The first rule is this:

> *A thief must forsake his mother, father, brothers, and sisters.*
> *He must not have a family – no wife, no children.*
> *We are his family.*

If any of the eighteen rules are broken, the punishment is death.

Gotta do that right thing
Please
Please
Please
Someone be that hard thing
For me

— DECONSTRUCTED CHILD

FRANK MEYER CLOSED HIS COMPUTER as the early winter darkness fell over his home in Westwood, California, not far from the UCLA campus. Westwood was an affluent area on the Westside of Los Angeles, resting between Beverly Hills and Brentwood in a twine of gracious residential streets and comfortable, well-to-do homes. Frank Meyer – more surprised about it than anyone else, considering his background – lived in such a home.

Work finished, Frank settled back in his home office, listening to his sons crash through the far side of the house like baby rhinos. They made him happy, and so did the rich scent of braising beef that promised stew or *boeuf bourguignon*, which he never pronounced correctly but loved to eat. Voices came from the family room, too far away to make out the program, but almost certainly the sound of a game show on television. Cindy hated the nightly news.

Frank smiled because Cindy didn't much care for

game shows, either, but she liked the background sound of the TV when she cooked. Cindy had her ways, that was for sure, and her ways had changed his life. Here he was with a lovely home, a growing business, and a wonderful family – all of it owed to his wife.

Frank teared up, thinking how much he owed that woman. Frank was like that, sentimental and emotional, and had always been that way. As Cindy liked to say, Frank Meyer was just a big softy, which is why she fell in love with him.

Frank worked hard to live up to her expectations, and considered it a privilege – beginning eleven years ago when he realized he loved her and committed to reinventing himself. He was now a successful importer of garments from Asia and Africa, which he resold to wholesale chains throughout the United States. He was forty-three years old, still fit and strong, though not so much as in the old days. Okay, well – he was getting fat, but between his business and the kids, Frank hadn't touched the weights in years, and rarely used the treadmill. When he did, his efforts lacked the zeal that had burned fever-hot in his earlier life.

Frank didn't miss that life, never once, and if he sometimes missed the men with whom he had shared it, he kept those feelings to himself and did not begrudge his wife. He had re-created himself, and, by a miracle, his efforts had paid off. Cindy. The kids. The home they had made. Frank was still thinking about these changes when Cindy appeared at the door, giving him a lopsided, sexy grin.

'Hey, bud. You hungry?'

'Just finishing up. What am I smelling? It's fabulous.'

Pounding footsteps, then Little Frank, ten years old and showing the square, chunky build of his father, caught the doorjamb beside his mother to stop himself, stopping so fast his younger brother, Joey, six and just as square, crashed into Little Frank's back.

Little Frank shouted, 'Meat!'

Joey screamed, 'Ketchup!'

Cindy said, 'Meat and ketchup. What could be better?'

Frank pushed back his chair, and stood.

'Nothing. I'm dying for meat and ketchup.'

She rolled her eyes and turned back toward the kitchen.

'You've got five, big guy. I'll hose off these monsters. Wash up and join us.'

The boys made exaggerated screams as they raced away, passing Ana, who appeared behind Cindy. Ana was their nanny, a nice girl who had been with them almost six months. She had bright blue eyes, high cheekbones, and was a fantastic help with the kids. Another perk of Frank's increasing success.

Ana said, 'I'm going to feed the baby now, Cindy. You need anything?'

'We've got it under control. You go ahead.'

Ana looked in at Frank.

'Frank? Anything I can do?'

'I'm good, hon. Thanks. I'll be along in a minute.'

Frank finished putting away his paperwork, then pulled the shades before joining his family for dinner. His office, with its window facing the nighttime street, was now closed against the darkness. Frank Meyer had no reason to suspect that something unspeakable was about to happen.

AS FRANK ENJOYED DINNER with his family, a black-on-black Cadillac Escalade slow-rolled onto his street from Wilshire Boulevard, the Escalade boosted earlier that day from a shopping center in Long Beach, Moon Williams swapping the plates with an identical black Escalade they found outside a gentlemen's club in Torrance. This was their third time around the block, clocking the street for pedestrians, witnesses, and civilians in parked cars.

This time around, the rear windows drooped like sleepy eyes, and street lights died one by one, Jamal shooting them out with a .22-caliber pellet pistol.

Darkness followed the Escalade like a rising tide.

Four men in the vehicle, black cutouts in the shadowed interior, Moon driving, Moon's boy Lil Tai riding shotgun, Jamal in back with the Russian. Moon, eyes flicking between the houses and the white boy, wasn't sure if the foreigner was a Russian or not. What with all the Eastern Bloc assholes runnin' around, boy coulda been Armenian, Lithuanian, or a muthuh-fuckin' Transylvanian vampire, and Moon couldn't tell'm apart. All Moon knew, he was makin' more cash since hookin' up with the foreign muthuhfucka chillin' behind him than any time in his life.

Still, Moon didn't like him back there, money or not. Didn't want that creepy, glassy-eyed muthuhfucka behind him. All these months, this was the first time the fucka had come with them. Moon didn't like that, either.

Moon said, 'You sure now, homeboy? That house right there?'

'Same as last time we passed, the one like a church.'

Moon clocked a nice house with a steep roof and these gargoyle-lookin' things up on the eaves. The street was wide, and lined with houses all set back on big sloping lawns. These homes, you'd find lawyers, business-people, the occasional dilettante drug dealer.

Lil Tai twisted around to grin at the white boy.

'How much money we gettin' this time?'

'Much money. Much.'

Jamal licked his lips, makin' a smile wide as a piano.

'Taste the money. Feel it right on my skin, all dirty and nasty.'

Moon said, 'We gettin' that shit.'

Moon killed the headlights and pulled into the drive, the four doors opening as soon as he cut the engine, the four of them stepping out. The Escalade's interior lights had been removed, so nothing lit up. Only sound was Lil Tai's eighteen-pound sledge, clunking the rocker panel as he got out.

They went directly to the front door, Jamal first,

Moon going last, walking backward to make sure no one was watching. Jamal popped the entry lights, just reached up and broke'm with his fingers, pop, pop, pop. Moon pressed a folded towel over the dead bolt to dull the sound, and Lil Tai hit that shit with the hammer as hard as he could.

FRANK AND CINDY WERE CLEARING the table when a crash jolted their home as if a car had slammed through the front door. Joey was watching the Lakers in the family room and Little Frank had just gone up to his room. When Frank heard the crash, he believed his older son had knocked over the grandfather clock in the front entry. Little Frank had been known to climb the clock to reach the second-floor landing, and, even though it was anchored for earthquake safety, Frank had warned the boys it could fall.

Cindy startled at the noise, and Joey ran to his mother. Frank put down the plates, and was already hurrying toward the sound.

'Frankie! Son, are you all right – ?'

They had only taken a step when four armed men rushed in, moving with the loose organization of men who had done this before.

Frank Meyer had faced high-speed, violent entries before, and had known how to react, but those situations had been in his former life. Now, eleven years and too many long days at a desk later, Frank was behind the play.

Four-man team. Gloves. Nine-millimeter pistols.

First man through had average height, espresso skin, and heavy braids to his shoulders. Frank knew he was the team leader because he acted like the leader, his eyes directing the play. A shorter man followed, angry and nervous, with a black bandanna capping his head, shoulder to shoulder with a bruiser showing tight cornrows and gold in his teeth, moving like he enjoyed being big. The fourth man was a step behind, moving more like an observer than part of the action. White, and big, almost as big as the bruiser, with a bowling-ball head, wide-set eyes, and thin sideburns that ran down his jaw like needles.

Two seconds, they fanned through the rooms. A second behind, Frank realized they were a home invasion crew. He felt the buzz-rush of excitement that had always sparked through him during an engagement, then remembered he was an out-of-shape businessman with a family to protect. Frank raised his hands, shuffling sideways to place himself between the men and his wife.

'Take what you want. Take it and leave. We won't give you any trouble.'

The leader came directly to Frank, holding his pistol high and sideways like an idiot in a movie, bugging his eyes to show Frank he was fierce.

'Goddamn right, muthuhfucka. Where is it?'

Without waiting for an answer, he slapped Frank with the pistol. Cindy shouted, but Frank had been hit harder plenty of times. He waved toward his wife, trying to calm her.

'I'm okay. It's okay, Cin, we're gonna be fine.'

'Gonna be dead, you don't do what I say!'

He dug the pistol hard into Frank's cheek, but Frank was watching the others. The bruiser and the smaller man split apart, the bruiser charging to the French doors to check out the back, the little guy throwing open cabinets and doors, both of them shouting and cursing. Their movements were fast. Fast into the house. Fast into Frank's face. Fast through the rooms. Fast to drive the play, and loud to increase the confusion. Only the man with the strange sideburns moved slowly, floating outside the perimeter as if with a private agenda.

Frank knew from experience it wasn't enough to follow the play; you had to be ahead of the action to survive. Frank tried to buy himself time to catch up.

'My wallet's in my office. I've got three or four hundred dollars –'

The leader hit Frank again.

'You take me a fool, muthuhfuckin' wallet?'

'We use credit cards –'

Hit him again. Harder.

The man with the sideburns finally stepped out of the background, appearing at the table.

'See the plates? More people are here. We must look for the others.'

Frank was surprised by the accent. He thought it was Polish, but couldn't be sure.

The man with the accent disappeared into the kitchen just as the bruiser charged out of the family room to Cindy and Joey. He held his pistol to Cindy's temple, shouting at Frank in his rage.

'You want this bitch dead? You want me to put this pipe right in her mouth? You want her to suck on *this*?'

The leader slapped Frank again.

'You think he don't mean it?'

The bruiser suddenly backhanded Cindy with his pistol, splashing a red streamer from her cheek. Joey screamed, and Frank Meyer suddenly knew what to do.

The man with Frank was watching the action when Frank grabbed his gun hand, rolled his wrist to lock the man's arm, and jointed his elbow. Frank had been out of the life for years, but the moves were burned into his muscle memory from a thousand hours of training. He had to neutralize his captor, strip the weapon as he levered the man down, recover with the pistol in a combat grip, put two into the big man who had Cindy, then turn, acquire, and double-tap whoever was in his field of fire. Frank Meyer had gone automatic. The moves flowed out ahead of the play exactly as he had trained for them, and, back in the day, he could have completed the sequence in less than a second. But Frank was still fumbling with the pistol when three bullets slammed into him, the last shot hitting the heavy vertebra in Frank's lower back, putting him down.

Frank opened his mouth, but only a hiss escaped. Cindy and Joey screamed, and Frank fought to rise with the fierce will of the warrior he had been, but will was not enough.

The man with the accent said, 'I hear someone. In the back.'

A shadow moved past, but Frank couldn't see.

The leader appeared overhead, cradling his broken arm. Huge shimmering tears dripped from his eyes and fell in slow motion like rain from his braids.

He said, 'I'm gonna get me that money.'

He turned away toward Cindy.

Frank's world grew dark, and all he had left were feelings of failure and shame. He knew he was dying, exactly the way he had always thought he would die, only not here, and not now. All of that should have been behind him.

He tried to reach for his wife, but could not.

He wanted to touch her, but could not.

He wanted to protect her, but had not.

His index finger was the only part of him that moved.

Twitching as if with a life of its own.

His trigger finger.

Pulling at empty air.

OUTSIDE, WITH ITS SHADES DRAWN, the Meyer house appeared peaceful. Heavy walls muffled most of the sounds within, and traffic noise from nearby Wilshire Boulevard was loud enough to mask the rest. Those screams which could be heard might have been from a home theater, a nice Surround Sound system.

Cars passed, some leaving home to go out for the evening, others returning home after a long day at the office.

The dull thump of a gunshot within the house was muted and unnatural. A Lexus sedan passed, but with its windows up and an iPod playlist rocking the exquisitely engineered vehicle, the driver heard nothing. She did not slow.

Another thump pounded within the house a few moments later, accompanied by a flash like distant lightning behind the shades.

More flashes followed.

Then more.

You become responsible,
forever,
for what you have tamed.

– ANTOINE DE SAINT-EXUPÉRY,
1900–1944, Free French warrior and aviator
who also typed

Part One
Professionals

1

AT TEN FOURTEEN the following morning, approximately fifteen hours after the murders, helicopters were dark stars over the Meyer house when LAPD Detective-Sergeant Jack Terrio threaded his way through the tangle of marked and unmarked police vehicles, SID wagons, and vans from the Medical Examiner's office. He phoned his task force partner, Louis Deets, as he approached the house. Deets had been at the scene for an hour.

'I'm here.'

'Meet you at the front door. You gotta see this.'

'Hang on – any word on the wit?'

A slim possibility existed for a witness – an Anglo female had been found alive by the first responders and identified as the Meyers' nanny.

Deets said, 'Not so hot. They brought her over to the Medical Center, but she's circling the drain. In the face, Jackie. One in the face, one in the chest.'

'Hold a good thought. We need a break.'

'Maybe we got one. You gotta see.'

Terrio snapped his phone closed, annoyed with Deets and with the dead-end case. A home invasion crew had been hitting upscale homes in West L.A. and the Encino hills for the past three months, and this was likely their seventh score. All of the robberies had taken place between the dinner hour and eleven P.M. Two of the homes had been unoccupied at the time of entry, but, as with the Meyer home, the other four homes had been occupied. A litter of nine-millimeter cartridge casings and bodies had been left behind, but nothing else – no prints, DNA, video, or witnesses. Until now, and she was going to die.

When Terrio reached the plastic screen that had been erected to block the front door from prying cameras, he waited for Deets. Across the street, he recognized two squats from the Chief's office, huddled up with a woman who looked like a Fed. The squats saw him looking, and turned away.

Terrio thought, 'Crap. Now what?'

She was maybe five six, and sturdy with that gymed-out carriage Feds have when they're trying to move up the food chain to Washington. Navy blazer over outlet-store jeans. Wraparound shades. A little slit mouth that probably hadn't smiled in a month.

Deets came up behind him.

'You gotta see this.'

Terrio nodded toward the woman.

'Who's that with the squats?'

Deets squinted at the woman, then shook his head.

'I've been inside. It's a mess in there, man, but you gotta see. C'mon, put on your booties –'

They were required to wear paper booties at the scene so as not to contaminate the evidence.

Deets ducked behind the screen without waiting, so Terrio hurried to catch up, steeling himself for what he was about to see. Even after eighteen years on the job and hundreds of murder cases, the sight of blood and rent human flesh left him queasy. Embarrassed by what he considered a lack of professionalism, Terrio stared at Deets's back as he followed him past the criminalists and West L.A. Homicide detectives who currently filled the house, not wanting to see the blood or the gore until absolutely necessary.

They reached a large, open dining area where a coroner investigator was photographing the crumpled form of an adult white male.

Deets said, 'Okay we touch the body?'

'Sure. I'm good.'

'Can I have one of those wet-wipes?'

The CI gave Deets a wet-wipe, then stepped to the side, giving them room.

The male victim's shirt had been cut away so the CI could work on the body. Deets pulled on a pair of latex gloves, then glanced at Terrio. The body was lying in an irregular pool of blood almost six feet across.

'Be careful of the blood.'

'I can see fine from here. I'm not stepping in that mess.'

Deets lifted the man's arm, cleaned a smear of blood

off the shoulder with the wet-wipe, then held the arm for Terrio to see.

'What do you think? Look familiar?'

Lividity had mottled the skin with purple and black bruising, but Terrio could still make out the tattoo. He felt a low dread of recognition.

'I've seen this before.'

'Yeah. That's what I thought.'

'Does he have one on the other arm, too?'

'One on each side. Matching.'

Deets lowered the arm, then stepped away from the body. He peeled off the latex gloves.

'Only one guy I know of has tats like this. He used to be a cop here. LAPD.'

A blocky, bright red arrow had been inked onto the outside of Frank Meyer's shoulder. It pointed forward.

Terrio's head was racing.

'This is good, Lou. This gives us a direction. We just gotta figure out what to do about him.'

The woman's voice cut through behind them.

'About who?'

Terrio turned, and there she was, the woman and the two squats. Wraparounds hiding her eyes. Mouth so tight she looked like she had steel teeth.

The woman stepped forward, and didn't seem to care if she stepped in the blood or not.

'I asked a question, Sergeant. Do about who?'

Terrio glanced at the arrow again, then gave her the answer.

'Joe Pike.'

2

FIRST TIME JOE PIKE saw the tattooed woman, she was struggling up the eastern ridge of Runyon Canyon, Pike running down, both of them blowing steam in the chill before dawn. The eastern trail was steep; a series of slopes and terraces that stepped from the apartment-lined neighborhoods at the base of the canyon to Mulholland Drive at the top of the Hollywood Hills. Seeing her in the murky light that first morning, the young woman appeared to be wearing tights, but as she drew closer, Pike realized her legs were sleeved with elaborate tattoos. More ink decorated her arms, and metal studs lined her ears, nose, and lips. Pike had only two tattoos. A red arrow on the outside of each deltoid, both pointing forward.

Pike saw her two or three times each week after that, sometimes in the early-morning dark, other times later, when the sun was bright and the park was crowded. They had never exchanged more than a word or two.

The day Pike learned about Frank and Cindy Meyer, he and the tattooed woman left the park together, jogging easily past the small homes north of Hollywood Boulevard with their whispers of faded dreams. They had not run together, but she had been at the bottom when he finished, and fell in beside him. Pike wondered if she had planned it that way, and was thinking about it when he saw the first man.

The first man waited beneath a jacaranda tree on the opposite side of the street, jeans, sunglasses, knit shirt tight at the shoulders. He openly stared as Pike passed, then fell in behind at a casual jog, three or four car lengths back.

The second man was leaning against a car with his arms crossed. He watched Pike and the woman pass, then he, too, fell in behind. Pike knew they were plainclothes police officers, so he decided to give himself room. He grunted a good-bye, and picked up his pace.

The woman said, 'See you next time.'

As Pike drifted to the center of the street, a blue sedan pulled out from a cross street two blocks behind. One block ahead, a tan sedan pulled from the curb, boxing him in. Two men were in the front seat of the tan car, with a woman in back on the passenger side. Pike saw her turn to see him. Short brown hair. Wraparound sunglasses. Frown. The man in the passenger seat dangled a badge out the open window, letting Pike see.

Pike eased to a stop. The sedans and trailing officers

22

stopped when Pike stopped, everyone keeping their distance.

The tattooed woman realized something was happening, and nervously danced on her toes.

'Dude, what is this?'

'Keep going.'

She didn't keep going. She edged toward the nearest house, clearly frightened as she glanced from car to car.

'I don't like this. You want me to get help?'

'They're police. They just want to talk to me.'

If they wanted to arrest him, they wouldn't have approached in the middle of a residential street. If they wanted to kill him, they would have already tried.

The man with the badge got out of the lead car. He was balding, with a thin mustache that was too dark for the rest of his hair. His driver got out, too, a younger man with bright eyes. The woman remained in the car, twisted around to watch. She was on her cell phone. Pike wondered what she was saying.

The man with the badge said, 'Jack Terrio, LAPD. This is Lou Deets. Okay if we come over there?'

They knew who he was, and so did the officers who had established a perimeter behind the two sedans. They had blocked the street and were rerouting traffic onto the cross streets.

'Sure.'

Pike unshouldered his rucksack. He ran with a weighted ruck, and also wore a fanny pack, a sleeveless gray sweatshirt, New Balance running shoes, blue shorts, and government-issue sunglasses. The sweatshirt was dark with sweat.

When Terrio and Deets reached him, Deets stood to the side.

'That's some nice ink you have there, Pike, the red arrows. Don't see many like that, do we, boss?'

Terrio ignored him.

'You armed?'

'Gun's in the fanny pack. With the license.'

Deets toed the ruck.

'What's in there, a rocket launcher?'

'Flour.'

'No shit. You gonna bake me a cake?'

Deets fingered open the ruck, then frowned.

'He's got four ten-pound bags of flour in here.'

'That's what he told you, didn't he? C'mon, let's stay on topic.'

Terrio put away his badge.

'Don't touch the fanny pack, okay?'

Pike nodded.

'You know a man name of Frank Meyer?'

A chill spread through Pike's belly. He had not seen Frank Meyer in years, though he frequently thought about him, and now his name hung in the mid-morning air like a frosty ghost. Pike glanced at their car. The woman was still watching, and still on the phone, as if she were reporting his reaction.

'What happened?'

Deets said, 'Have you seen him in the past week or so?'

'Not in a long time. Ten years, maybe.'

'What if I told you I have a witness who claims you were with Meyer recently?'

Pike studied Deets for a moment, and read he was lying. Pike turned back to Terrio.

'You want to play games, I'll keep running.'

'No games. Meyer and his family were murdered in their home two nights ago. The boys and the wife were executed. A woman we've identified as their nanny survived, but she's in a coma.'

No part of Joe Pike moved except for the rise and fall of his chest until he glanced at the tattooed woman. An older woman in a dingy robe had come out of her house, and the two of them were watching from the door.

Deets said, 'That your girlfriend?'

'I don't know who she is.'

Pike faced Terrio again.

'I didn't kill them.'

'Don't think you did. We believe a professional home invasion crew killed them. We believe that same crew has hit six other homes in the past three months, murdering a total of eleven people.'

Pike knew where they were going.

'You don't have any suspects.'

'Nothing. No prints, pix, or witnesses. We don't have any idea who's doing this, so we started looking at the victims.'

Deets said, 'And guess what, Pike? Turns out we found something the first six have in common. Three were drug traffickers, one was a pornographer who laundered money for the Israeli mob, and two were jewelry merchants who fenced stolen goods. The first six were as dirty as yesterday's socks, so now we're seeing what's up with Meyer.'

'Frank wasn't a criminal.'

'You can't know that.'

'Frank had an import business. He sold clothes.'

Terrio fingered a photograph from his jacket. The picture showed Frank, Pike, and a chemical-company executive named Delroy Spence in the El Salvadoran jungle. The air had smelled of rotten fish and burning oil when the picture was taken. The temperature had been one hundred twelve degrees. Spence was dirty, lice-ridden, and wearing the remains of a tattered blue business suit. Meyer and Pike were wearing T-shirts, faded utility pants, and M4 rifles slung on their arms. Meyer and Spence were both smiling, though they were smiling for different reasons. Spence was smiling because Pike, Meyer, and a man named Lonny Tang had just rescued him after two months of captivity at the hands of a band of narco-terrorists. Meyer was smiling because he had just cracked a joke about retiring to get married. Meyer looked like he was fourteen years old.

'What does this have to do with now?'

'You and Meyer were mercenaries.'

'So?'

Terrio studied the picture. He flexed it back and forth.

'He's all over the world in shitholes like this, hanging out with the wrong kind of people. Maybe he started importing more than clothes.'

'Not Frank.'

'No? None of his friends or neighbors knew what he used to do. Not one of the people we interviewed. This little picture is the only thing from those days we found in his house. Why do you think that is?'

'Cindy didn't approve.'

'Whether she approved or not, the man kept secrets. Maybe he wasn't the man you thought.'

'I can't help you.'

Terrio slipped the picture into his pocket.

'This home invasion crew doesn't pick homes at random. They don't drive around, and say, hey, that one looks good. Sooner or later, we're going to learn Meyer had something they wanted – dope, cash, maybe the ayatollah's secret jewels.'

'Frank sold clothes.'

Terrio glanced at Deets, then returned to the tan sedan without another word. Deets didn't follow.

Deets said, 'So you haven't seen this guy in ten years?'

'No.'

'Why is that? You have a falling-out?'

Pike thought how best to answer, but most of it wasn't their business.

'Like I said, his wife.'

'But it was your picture he kept. And your tattoos. What's up with that, Pike? Some kind of unit thing?'

Pike didn't understand.

'The arrows?'

'Yeah, here and here, like you.'

On the day Frank's contract expired and he left the contract service for good, Frank Meyer had no tattoos.

Pike said, 'I don't know what you're talking about.'

Deets made a stiff smile, then lowered his voice.

'I never met someone who's killed as many people as you, still walking free.'

Pike watched Deets walk away. Terrio was already in the car. Deets walked around to the far side, and got in behind the wheel. The woman in the backseat was talking to Terrio. They drove away. The plain-clothes officers followed. The neighborhood returned to normal.

Everything was normal except Frank Meyer was dead.

The tattooed woman trotted up, excited and anxious.

'Dude, that was crazy. What did they want?'

'A friend of mine was murdered.'

'Oh, shit, I'm sorry. That's awful. They think you did it?'

'Nothing like that.'

She made a ragged laugh, nervous at the edges.

'Dude, listen, they *do*. I'm tellin' you, man, those cats were scared of you.'

'Maybe.'

'I'm not.'

The tattooed woman punched him in the arm. It was the first time she had touched him. Pike studied her for a moment, then shouldered his ruck.

'You don't know me.'

Pike settled the pack, and continued his run.

3

WHEN PIKE REACHED HIS JEEP, he drove directly to Frank Meyer's home. Pike had lied to Terrio. He had seen Frank three years ago, though they had not spoken. A mutual friend told Pike about Frank's new house in Westwood, so Pike cruised by. Pike also cruised by the little ranch home Frank and Cindy owned in Studio City a few years before that. Frank Meyer had been on Pike's team, so Pike liked to make sure he was doing okay even though the two hadn't spoken in years.

The Westwood house was taped off as an active crime scene, though the crush of lookie-loos and newspeople that would have been present the day before were gone. A black-and-white radio car was out front, along with two SID wagons, an unmarked sedan, and a single TV news van. Two female officers posted to protect the scene were slumped in the radio car, bored out of their minds with nothing to do except listen to their iPods.

Pike parked a block behind their car, then studied Frank Meyer's house. He wanted to know how Frank died, and was thinking he would break in later that night when a tall, thin criminalist named John Chen came down the drive to an SID wagon. Chen was a friend. Pike would have called Chen anyway, but Chen being here was a stroke of good fortune that would save time.

Chen's vehicle was directly in front of the radio car. If Chen left, Pike would follow. If Chen returned to the house, Pike would wait.

Pike was waiting to see what Chen would do when his phone rang. The caller ID read *John Chen*.

Pike said, 'Hello, John.'

Chen was a paranoid. Even though he was alone in his vehicle his voice was guarded, as if he was worried about being overheard.

'Joe, it's me, John Chen. I'm at a murder scene in Westwood. The police are coming to –'

'I'm behind you, John.'

'What?'

'Look behind you.'

Chen emerged from his wagon. He stared at the radio car as if the officers would jump out to arrest him.

Pike said, 'Farther back. I'm on the next block.'

Chen finally saw him, then shriveled back into his wagon.

'Did the police already come see you?'

'A detective named Terrio.'

'I was calling to warn you, bro. They found a picture

of you with the vic. I'm sorry, man. I only heard about it this morning.'

'I want to see what happened in there.'

Chen hesitated again.

'It's a mess.'

Chen, warning that he would see something awful, but Pike had seen awful things before.

Chen sighed.

'Okay, listen – two dicks from West L.A. are inside. I don't know how long they'll be.'

'I'll wait.'

'They might be here all day.'

'I'll wait.'

'All right. Okay. I'll call when it's clear.'

Pike could tell Chen wasn't comfortable with him being out here, but Pike didn't care about that or how long he might have to wait. Chen reemerged from his wagon and slouched back to the house, shooting nervous glances at Pike over his shoulder.

Pike got out of his Jeep, pulled on a pair of spare jeans and a plain green windbreaker so he would be less memorable, then climbed back behind the wheel. He studied Frank's house. A sloping front lawn led to a two-story brick home with a steep slate roof, surrounded by elm trees and feathery hedges. The house looked stable, traditional, and strong, and was suited to the Frank Pike knew. Pike liked that. Frank had done all right for himself.

After a while, a man and woman who were likely the West L.A. detectives came down the drive, got into the unmarked sedan, and drove away. Chen called as Pike watched them.

'You still out there?'

'Yes.'

'I'll come get you. We won't have much time.'

Pike met Chen on the sidewalk, then followed him to the house. The two uniforms appeared to be dozing, and no one was visible in the media van. Neither of them spoke until they reached the front door, when Chen handed Pike a pair of blue paper booties.

'Gotta put these over your shoes, okay?'

They slipped on the booties, then stepped into a large circular entry with a winding staircase up to the second floor. A towering grandfather clock stood guard at the stair, standing tall over a rusty crust of blood footprints that dotted the floor.

Pike felt odd, entering Frank's home, as if he were intruding into a place where it was understood he would never be welcomed. He had glimpsed Frank's life from the outside, but never from within. He had never met Cindy, or the boys, and now here he was in their home. Pike heard movement upstairs, and Chen glanced toward the sound.

'That's another criminalist, Amy Slovak. She'll be up there a while.'

Pike followed Chen through the entry to a large, open family room adjoining a dining area. An irregular pool of drying blood covered the floor midway between the dining table and the hall. Bright green yarn had been stretched from the blood pool to two metal stands in the living room, two strands to one of the stands, a single strand to the other. These stands marked the probable location of the shooters. A jumble of footprints crossed and crisscrossed the drying pool where one or more of the shooters had walked through the blood. A second, smaller stain was visible across the family room.

Chen nodded toward the big stain at their feet.

'Mr. Meyer was here. His wife and one of the boys there by the French doors. The nanny was in her room. I can give you a pretty good take on how it unfolded.'

A blue three-ring binder was open on a nearby table where Chen had been making sketches. He flipped to a scaled floor plan showing the location and position of the bodies, along with recovered shell casings.

'The family was probably having dinner when the shooters broke in. You saw the door. Bam, they scared the shit out of everybody. Meyer probably advanced on them, brief struggle, boom, boom – he had cuts on his face like they hit him with a hard object, probably a gun – and that's when they killed him.'

Pike studied the three strands of yarn.

'They shot him three times?'

'Yeah, once high on his hip, once in the side, and once in his back. Two shooters, like they were trying to put him down fast. This suggests he was fighting. The others were shot once in the forehead at close range, which suggests a deliberate execution.'

The others. Cindy and the boys.

The ugly stain where Meyer bled out looked like

the Salton Sea. Meyer had been a good fighter. He had superb training and great instincts, else Pike would never have made him part of his team.

'How many men all together?'

'Four, which makes this one a little different. The earlier invasions, there were only three guys. They added a fourth.'

'Four guns?'

'Looks like, but we're still running the casings and bullets. It's the shoe prints. We've got four distinct shoe prints.'

Pike glanced at the black smudges on door jambs and handles.

'Fingerprints?'

'Gloves. We didn't get anything from the earlier crime scenes, either. No identifying prints, no DNA, no nothing except the shoes. C'mon, I'll show you where we found the nanny.'

Chen led Pike across the dining room, through the kitchen, then past the laundry room to a tiny bedroom where the door and jamb were split.

'See how they crunched the door? It was locked. She was probably trying to hide.'

Chen glanced at his notes.

'Ana Markovic, age twenty. Two shots close range, one in the face, one in the chest, two casings here in the room. Both nine-millimeter. Did I mention that?'

'No.'

'These guys used nines. All the bullets and casings we found – nines.'

The room was a small place to die, filled by a bed and a table, with only a casement window for light. Pictures of a smiling young woman hugging Frank's boys were taped over the desk, part of a birthday card the kids had made of construction paper. *We love Ana.*

Pike said, 'Her?'

'Uh-huh. An *au pair.*'

Smears of blood on the floor and the door indicated she tried to crawl away after being shot.

Pike said, 'Did she describe them?'

'Uh-uh. She was unconscious when the uniforms found her. They got her over to UCLA, but she's not going to make it.'

Pike stared at the streaks of blood. It was easy to imagine her outstretched hand.

'Does Terrio have any suspects?'

'No one we've identified. If he has someone from the other side, I couldn't tell you. They haven't issued any warrants.'

SID was the science side. The other side was shoe leather – whatever detectives turned from informants and witnesses.

'How many people have they killed?'

'Four. If the nanny dies, five.'

'Not here, John. All together.'

'Eleven. Hey, that's why they set up a task force. They're using divisional dicks from all over the city.'

Chen suddenly glanced at his watch, looking uncomfortable.

'Listen, I gotta get busy. Those dicks are coming back.'

Pike followed Chen back to the dining room, but he still wasn't ready to leave.

Pike said, 'Let me see the pictures.'

Criminalists, coroner investigators, and homicide detectives photo-documented everything. Chen would have photographed the scene before he made the sketches.

'Bro, these people were your friends. You sure?'

'Let me see.'

Chen went to his case and returned with a black digital camera. He scrolled through the images until he found what he wanted, then held it so Pike could see.

The image was tiny, but Pike saw Frank splayed on the floor. He was on his back, his left leg straight and right leg cocked to the side, floating in a pool of deep red that shined with the flash. Pike had wanted to see if the red arrows were inked on his arms like Deets said, but Frank was wearing a long-sleeved shirt, rolled to his forearms.

'I want to see his face. Can you zoom it?'

Chen adjusted the picture, then held out the camera again. Frank was cut beneath his right eye in two places, indicating he had been hit more than once. Pike wondered if Frank had been trying to disarm the man or men closest to him when the men across the room shot him.

Pike said, 'Was a time, he would have beat them.'

Chen said, 'What?'

Pike felt embarrassed for saying it, so he didn't answer.

'You want to see the wife and kids?'

'No.'

Chen looked relieved.

'You knew him pretty well?'

'Yes.'

'What was he holding?'

'Frank wasn't a criminal.'

'All the other vics in the string were dirty. That's part of the pattern.'

'Not Frank.'

Chen read something in Pike's voice.

'Sorry. They probably made a mistake. Assholes like this, they probably hit the wrong house.'

'Yes,' Pike said. 'They made a mistake.'

'Listen, I gotta get back to work. I gotta get you outta here.'

Pike followed the hall back to the front door, but he did not immediately leave. On the way in, they had passed what appeared to be a home office.

Photographs of Frank and his family hung on the walls. Movie posters from *The Magnificent Seven*, *Shane*, and the original *Star Wars*, Frank's three favorite films. Frank used to joke he was a Jedi. He called Pike Yoda.

Pike studied the pictures, comparing the Frank he had known with the Frank who had lived in this house. When Pike met Frank for the first time, Frank was fresh out of eight years in the Marine Corps, having seen service in Central America and the Middle East. Frank had been young and lean, but had the chunky build of a kid who would put on weight quickly if he stopped working out. The Frank in these pictures had gained weight, but looked happy and safe.

Pike found a picture of Frank and Cindy, then moved to a picture of Frank and Cindy with the two boys. Cindy was squat and sturdy, with short brown hair, happy eyes, and a crooked nose that made her pretty. Pike studied more pictures. The two boys, then the four of them together, father, mother, children, family.

Pike moved through the office until he came to a space on a shelf with an empty frame. The frame was the right size for the El Salvador picture.

Pike took a breath, let it out, then found Chen back in the dining room.

'Show me his family.'

'You want to see what they did to his wife and his kids?'

Pike wanted to see. He wanted to fix them in his mind, and have them close when he found the men who killed them.

4

PIKE LIVED ALONE IN a two-bedroom condo in Culver City. He drove home, then stripped and showered away the sweat. He let hot water beat into him, then turned on the cold. Pike didn't flinch when the icy water fired his skin. He rubbed the cold over his face and scalp, and stayed in the cold much longer than the hot, then toweled himself off.

Before he dressed, he looked at himself in the mirror. Pike was six foot one. He weighed two hundred five pounds. He had been shot seven times, hit by shrapnel on fourteen separate occasions, and stabbed or cut eleven times. Scars from the wounds and resulting surgeries mapped his body like roads that always came back to the same place. Pike knew exactly which scars had been earned when he worked with Frank Meyer.

Pike leaned close to the mirror, examining each eye. Left eye, right eye. The scleras were clear and bright, the irises a deep, liquid blue. The skin surrounding the eyes was lined from squinting into too many suns. Pike's eyes were sensitive to light, but his visual acuity was amazing. 20/11 in his left eye, 20/12 in his right. They had loved that in sniper school.

Pike dressed, then put on his sunglasses.

'Yoda.'

Lunch was leftover Thai food nuked in the microwave. Tofu, cabbage, broccoli, and rice. He drank a liter of water, then washed the one plate and fork while thinking about what he had learned from Chen and Terrio, and how he could use it.

Jumping Pike in broad daylight on a residential street to ask a few questions was a panic move. This confirmed that after three months, seven invasions, and eleven homicides, Terrio had not developed enough evidence to initiate an arrest. But a lack of proof did not necessarily mean a lack of suspects or usable information, what Chen had called 'shoe leather' information. Professional home invasion crews almost always comprised career criminals who did violent crime for a living. If caught, they would be off the streets for the period of their incarceration, but would almost always commit more crimes when released. Experienced investigators like Terrio knew this, and would compare the date of the original robbery to release dates of criminals with a similar history, trying to identify high-probability suspects. Pike wanted to know what they had.

Pike went upstairs to his bedroom closet, opened his safe, and took out a list of telephone numbers. The numbers were not written as numbers, but as an alphanumeric code. Pike found the number he wanted, then brought it downstairs, sat on the floor with his back to the wall, and made the call.

Jon Stone answered on the second ring, the sound of old-school N.W.A. pounding loud behind him. Stone must have recognized Pike's number on the caller ID.

'Well. Look who it is.'

'Got a couple of questions.'

'How much will you pay for a couple of answers?'

Jon Stone was a talent agent for professional military contractors. Stone used to be a PMC himself, but now placed talent with the large private military corporations and security firms favored by Washington and corporate America. Safer that way, and much more profitable.

Pike didn't respond, and after a while the N.W.A. was turned down.

Stone said, 'Tell you what, let's table that for now. You go ahead, ask, we'll see what develops.'

'Remember Frank Meyer?'

'Fearless Frank, my man on the tanks? Sure.'

'Has Frank been working?'

'Frank was one of your guys. You tell me.'

'Has he been on the market?'

'He retired ten years ago, at least.'

'So you haven't heard any rumors?'

'Like what?'

'Like Frank getting involved with people you wouldn't expect.'

Jon snorted.

'Fearless Frank? Get control of yourself.'

'He didn't like being called Fearless Frank. It made him uncomfortable.'

Stone lapsed into silence, probably embarrassed, and Pike went on.

'Less than two hours ago, a police detective named Terrio told me Frank was dirty. He believes Frank was using his import business for something illegal.'

'Why was a cop talking about Frank?'

'Frank and his family were murdered.'

Stone was silent for a time, and when he spoke again, his voice was low.

'For real?'

'A robbery crew broke into their home two nights ago. Frank, his wife, their kids. They zero in on targets with a cash payoff – dope dealers, money launderers, like that. Frank wasn't their first.'

'I'll ask around, I guess. I can't believe Frank went wrong, but I'll ask.'

'Another thing. You have juice with Fugitive Section or Special Investigations?'

Now Stone grew wary.

'Why?'

'You know why, Jon. If Terrio's task force has any suspects, Fugitive Section or SIS will be trying to find them. I want to know what they have.'

Fugitive Section detectives specialized in tracking down and apprehending wanted felons in high-risk situations. Special Investigation Section were elite operators who ran long-term, covert surveillance on criminals suspected of committing violent serial crime. With their expertise, skill, and experience, retired Fugitive Section and SIS operators commanded top dollar at private security firms, and Jon Stone had placed more than a few into fat corporate jobs.

Stone hesitated, and Pike listened to the N.W.A. tracks behind him, back in the day before Ice Cube went legit.

'C'mon, Jon. You have ins with those guys.'

Stone cleared his throat, sounding uncomfortable.

'I might have a friend who has a friend. I'm just saying, is all.'

'I need this information before they make an arrest.'

Stone lapsed into another silence, and now seemed thoughtful when he spoke.

'I guess you would, then, Joseph.'

'Frank was one of my guys.'

'Listen, that business about Frank, I have an idea. Ask Lonny. Lonny might know.'

Lonny Tang. The man who had taken the picture in El Salvador. Thirteen days later, on a job in Kuwait, Frank Meyer would save Lonny Tang's life on what would turn out to be Lonny's last job.

Pike said, 'Why would Lonny know?'

'Frank kept in touch with him. You didn't know? He sent Lonny Christmas cards, stuff like that. I'll bet you ten bucks his wife never knew.'

Pike didn't respond because Pike hadn't known, either. He hadn't spoken with Lonny in years, and

Frank even longer. Stone went on, finishing his idea.

'If Frank was mixed up in something, he'd tell Lonny if he was gonna tell anyone.'

'That's a good idea, asking Lonny. I will.'

'You gotta set it up through his lawyer. You want the number?'

'I have it.'

'I'll let you know about the other thing after I talk to my guys.'

'Thanks, Jon. How much do I owe you?'

Stone cranked up the N.W.A. Something about guns in Compton. Something about making a muthuh-fucka pay.

'Forget it. Frank was one of my guys, too.'

Pike lowered the phone, thought over what he needed to do, then raised the phone again. Pike owned a small gun shop not far from his condo. He had five employees who were expecting him that afternoon.

'Gun shop. This is Sheila. May I help you?'

Sheila Lambert was a retired FBI agent who worked part-time at the store.

'Me. Everything good?'

'Yeah, we're groovy. What's up?'

'I won't be in this afternoon. That okay?'

'Not a problem. You wanna speak with Ronnie?'

Ronnie managed Pike's store.

'Just pass the word. If he needs me, I'm on the cell.'

'Roger that.'

Pike hung up, cleared two other appointments he had that afternoon, then called Lonny Tang's attorney, a man named Carson Epp.

Pike said, 'I need to speak with him. Can you set it up?'

'How soon?'

'Soon. It's a family emergency.'

'May I tell him what this is about?'

Pike decided Lonny should hear about Frank from him, and not Epp or someone else. Lonny had been one of Pike's guys, too.

'Frank the Tank.'

'Frank the Tank?'

'He'll know. Let me give you my cell.'

Pike gave him his number, then lowered the phone, thinking he couldn't wait for Stone to come up with something Terrio might or might not have developed. He wondered if Ana Markovic was still alive, and if she had managed to speak. Chen said she hadn't, but Chen was only repeating what he had heard from the cops, and the cops would have left as soon as a doctor told them she was not going to wake up. Pike wanted to talk to the nurses. Even unconscious, she might have mumbled something after the cops were gone. A word or a name could give him an edge. Pike wanted the edge.

Pike changed into a pale blue dress shirt to make himself presentable, then bought a bouquet of daisies and drove to the hospital.

5

THE INTENSIVE CARE UNIT was on the sixth floor of the UCLA Medical Center. Pike stepped out of the elevator and followed signs to an octagonal command post at the end of a hall lined by glass-walled rooms. Curtains could be pulled for privacy, but most of the rooms were open so the staff could see the patients from the hall.

Pike walked the length of the hall checking for officers, but any officers who had been present were gone. He returned to the nurses' station, and waited until a harried female nurse turned to him. Her name tag read BARBARA FARNHAM.

'May I help you?'

Pike and his dress shirt held out the flowers.

'Ana Markovic.'

The nurse's expression softened when she saw the daisies.

'I'm sorry. Are you a relative?'

'I know the family.'

'We limit our visitors in ICU, only one person at a time, and then only for a few minutes. Her sister's here now, but I'm sure she wouldn't mind.'

Pike nodded.

'Room twelve, but you can't leave the flowers. If a patient has an allergic reaction, it could weaken their immune system.'

Pike had expected this, and handed over the flowers. The nurse admired them as she placed them on the counter.

'Pretty. I like daisies. You can pick them up when you leave or we can send them to another part of the hospital. We usually send them to Maternity.'

'Before I see her, I'd like to speak with her primary nurse. Is that possible?'

'Well, that's all of us, really. We work as a team.'

'The police told me she wasn't able to make a statement when they found her. I was wondering if she came around after surgery.'

'No, I'm sorry, she hasn't.'

'I don't mean a conversation. Maybe she mumbled a name. Said something that might help the police.'

The nurse looked sympathetic.

'You'll understand when you see her. She's unconscious and completely uncommunicative.'

'Would you ask the other nurses?'

'I'll ask, but I'm sure she hasn't spoken.'

A light mounted outside a nearby door came on, drawing the nurse's attention.

'Room twelve. Only for a few minutes, all right?'

The nurse hurried away, so Pike went down the hall to room twelve. Like the other rooms, the door was open and the drape pulled back so the nurses could see the patient. Pike expected to find the sister, but room twelve was empty except for the bandaged figure in the bed.

Pike hesitated at the door, wondering how far he should take this, then went to the bed. The left side of Ana's face and head were hidden beneath heavy bandages, but the right half of her face was visible. She seemed to be trying to open her eye. Her eyelid would lift, the eye beneath would drift and roll, then the eyelid would close.

Pike knew she had not spoken as soon as he saw her, and thought it unlikely she would regain consciousness. The shape of the bandage on her head suggested a bullet had entered beneath her left eye, angling away from the midline. The way the visible part of her face was swollen and discolored suggested bone fragments from the maxilla had exploded into her sinuses, mouth, and eye like shrapnel. The pain would have been excruciating. Pike lifted the sheet enough to see the incisions taped across her chest and abdomen, which were still orange from the Betadine solution used to clean the area. He lowered the sheet, and tucked it beneath her. The upper chest wound had done the most damage. The bullet had likely deflected off her ribs or clavicle, and punched down through the diaphragm into her abdomen. Between the time she was shot and the time she was wheeled into surgery, her left lung had collapsed, the chest cavity had filled with blood, and the blood had drained through the diaphragm into her abdomen. As she lost blood, her blood pressure dropped until it was so low her organs began shutting down, like a car engine without enough oil. A car engine without oil will run, but the engine will damage itself. Let it run long enough, you can replenish the oil all you want, but the damage will have been done, and the engine will die. Ana Markovic had bled out internally, and now she was dying.

Pike had seen men die this way before, and knew if this young woman was ever going to offer what she had seen, she would have to offer it soon.

Pike said, 'Ana?'

Her visible eye flagged, rolled, drooped.

Pike touched her cheek.

'Ana, we need your help.'

The eye rolled, then drooped again, an autonomic move without conscious thought.

Pike took her hand. He stroked it, then pinched the soft flesh between her thumb and index finger.

'What did they look like?'

She did not respond.

'Who shot you?'

A rigid female voice cut him from behind.

'Move away from her.'

Pike calmly turned. A woman in her late twenties who was probably the sister stood framed in the door. Eyes like flint chips, black hair pulled tight, and a pronounced East European accent.

Pike said, 'I was trying to wake her.'

'Leave go her hand, and move away.'

She wore a suede jacket over designer jeans and cradled an oversized leather shoulder bag with one hand. The other hand was inside the bag, and ominously still.

Pike placed Ana's hand on the bed.

'I'm sorry. I came to see if she was awake. The Meyers were friends of mine.'

The woman's eyes narrowed suspiciously.

'The people she worked for?'

'Frank and Cindy. Ana cared for their boys.'

'You know Ana?'

'We never met, no.'

The woman didn't soften in any way Pike could see. Her eyes charted his face, his build, his shades, and cropped warrior hair. She didn't like what she saw. Not even the shirt.

She stepped aside to clear the door.

'You should leave now. They don't like the visitors.'

Her hand stayed in the purse.

Pike said, 'Has she said anything that could help us?'

'Us. Now you are the police?'

'I misspoke. A name. A word. Something that could identify the people who did this.'

'I think you go. She tells us who did this thing, I will tell the police.'

Pike considered her for a moment, then went to the door.

'I understand. I'm sorry about your sister.'

The woman edged further to the side as Pike left. He glanced back, and saw her watching from the door as if sizing him for a coffin. He glanced again when he reached the nurses' station, but this time she was gone.

Pike waited at the station until Barbara Farnham returned, then asked if she had checked with the other nurses. She had, but all of them had responded the same. Ana Markovic had made no sounds, nor shown any signs of recovery.

'I'm sorry, but you've seen her. I wish I could be more optimistic for you.'

'Thanks for checking.'

When Pike reached the elevator, Ana's sister was waiting. He nodded, but she looked away. The elevator arrived with three other people aboard, so they rode down in silence, Pike on one side, Ana's sister on the other.

The sister exited the elevator first, but stopped at a lobby newsstand as Pike continued to the parking structure. He saw her watching as he passed, and caught her reflection in a wall of glass when she followed him.

Pike crossed to the parking garage, then stopped on the ground floor for the elevator. Pike always took the stairs no matter how many flights he had to climb, but now he waited for the elevator. He was not surprised when Ana's sister stepped up beside him.

This time, she made a tight smile.

'We are destined to see each other.'

Pike said, 'Yes.'

The elevator was empty when it opened. No one else waited to board. Pike held the door, letting her go first. The woman stepped aboard, and moved to the back corner. Pike followed her, as certain of what she was about to do as if he could see it on a Sunset Boulevard billboard. Her hand was still in her purse.

Pike said, 'Which level?'

'Three.'

As the doors closed, her hand came out of the purse with a small black gun that Pike twisted away even before she raised it. She swung at him, trying to hit, but Pike caught her arm, careful not to break it. She tried to knee him, but he leaned in just enough to pin her with his hip. He pulled the button to stop the elevator. A loud buzzer went off, but not for long.

'I didn't come here to hurt her.'

She was trapped. Breathing hard, eyes cut to slits, she looked like she wanted to rip his throat with her teeth.

Pike said, 'Calm down. Look.'

Keeping her pinned, he one-handed the clip from the pistol, and jacked the slide to clear the chamber. A nice little Ruger .380.

Pike kept his voice calm and measured.

'You see? I wasn't one of the men who killed them.'

He stepped away, raising his hands.

'Frank Meyer was my friend.'

Pike held out the unloaded gun.

'You see?'

She straightened herself, maybe embarrassed, but maybe not altogether convinced. She clutched the gun with both hands, her back pressed to the wall.

'How did you find her?'

'The police told me.'

'Those bastards might find her, too. What if they come to kill her?'

'So you're standing guard?'

'They leave her here with no one! I do what I have to do.'

Pike's phone vibrated, so loud in the closed space she glanced toward his pocket. Pike would have ignored it, but he was expecting Carson Epp, and that's who it was. Pike took the call, staring at her as he spoke.

'Pike.'

'I will have Lonny on the line in twenty minutes. Will you be able to take it?'

'Yes.'

'Twenty.'

Pike returned the phone to his pocket, then tipped his head at her pistol.

'Put it away.'

She put the Ruger into her purse. Pike added the clip and the loose cartridge, then offered his hand.

'My name is Pike.'

She stared at him, the dark eyes remaining suspicious.

Her cheekbones were high and prominent, her cheeks were lean, and a small scar capped the bridge of her nose where she had been cut as a child. Pike's hand had been cooked dark by the sun, but her skin was pale as milk.

She gripped his hand quickly.

Pale and warm, but hard underneath.

She said, 'Rina.'

'Karina.'

'Yes.'

'Russian?'

'Serbian.'

'Leave the gun home. They won't come here. Their risk would be larger than the chance she could identify them. They know that, so they won't take the chance. The police know the same thing, which is why they didn't post a guard.'

Her eyes narrowed again, mapping him like before.

'You are not a policeman?'

'Frank was my friend.'

The elevator buzzed again, anxious to move.

Pike said, 'Which floor?'

'Here. I am not parked in this building.'

Pike reached for the button to open the door.

'When we got on, what were you going to do, shoot me?'

'I thought you might be one of them. If you were, then, yes, I would have shot you.'

Pike opened the door. A round man got on as Rina Markovic stepped off.

She said, 'Perhaps someone will find these bastards, yes?'

'Someone will find them. Yes.'

She studied him for a moment as if taking his measure, and Pike thought her eyes were haunted.

'I am sorry for your friend. I think many families have been lost by this.'

She walked away as the door closed. Pike took the elevator up to his Jeep. He took off the blue dress shirt, slipped on the sleeveless gray sweatshirt, then wound his way down to the exit.

Eight minutes later, he was in a Best Buy parking lot when Lonny Tang called.

6

PIKE WAS WATCHING UCLA students cut between cars on their way home from campus, not far from Frank Meyer's home, when his phone finally vibrated, three minutes late.

Pike said, 'I'm here.'

Carson Epp said, 'Lonny, can you hear him okay?'

Lonny's voice was high-pitched and soft.

'Yeah, I hear him fine. Hey, Joe.'

Epp said, 'I'm going to hang up now. That will leave the two of you on the line. Lonny, when you're finished, just hang up. I'll check back with you to make sure everything is all right.'

'Okay. Thanks, Carson.'

'Righto, then.'

Pike heard a click as Epp left the line, then the hush of Lonny Tang's voice.

'Must be bad, you calling like this.'

Pike didn't know how else to say it, so he gave it to Lonny head-on.

'Frank's dead. He was murdered two nights ago. Frank and his family.'

Lonny was silent on the other end, but then Pike heard a gentle sobbing. Pike let him cry. If any of them had a right to cry, it was Lonny.

Lonny said, 'Sorry. I don't mean to carry on.'

'It's okay.'

Lonny got himself together and cleared his throat.

'Thanks for letting me know. I appreciate it, Joe. The bastard who did it, they get him?'

'Not yet. The police think it's a home invasion crew. Frank's house was the seventh home they've hit.'

Lonny cleared his throat again.

'Okay, well, I don't know what to say. When they get these pricks, will you let me know?'

'I have to ask you something.'

'What's that?'

'This crew, they work on good intelligence. Their first six targets were all people like dope dealers and money cleaners. You see where I'm going?'

'Frank had an import business. He imported clothes.'

'If Frank was importing something else, he was in business with someone who gave him up. That person knows who killed him.'

'You think I'm holding out on you, Joe?'

'I don't know.'

'This is Frank, man. Are you serious?'

'Did he tell you something I should know?'

Lonny was quiet for a while, breathing, and his voice was calm.

'He came to my trial. Not every day, but a couple of times. This once, I asked him if he was sorry he saved me, you know – because if he hadn't saved me, those men I murdered would still be alive. So I asked if he regretted it. He told me guys like us had each other's back, so he had my back. He didn't have any choice.'

'Way it was, Lonny. What would you expect him to say?'

'I know. I just wanted to hear it, I guess, that I still meant something to someone, and wasn't just a murdering piece of shit.'

Pike remained silent, which spurred Lonny to laugh.

'Thanks for chiming in there, boss. Appreciate the support.'

Lonny suddenly burst out laughing, but the laughter shivered into a sob.

Lonny said, 'Shit. I'm sorry.'

'C'mon, Lonny, yes or no. Did Frank tell you he was into something? Maybe ask about certain people or say something that left you wondering?'

'You think if I could help get the pricks who killed him, I wouldn't be all over it? I'd kill those fuckers myself.'

'You're sure?'

'Yes. He was the same Frank we knew. Being an Eagle Scout was in his frakkin' DNA.'

Pike felt the tightness in his chest ease, feeling a sense of relief.

'Okay, Lon. That's what I thought, but I had to be sure. You're the only one he stayed in contact with.'

'I know. She drove a hard bargain, that girl.'

Cindy.

Pike was finished. He wanted to hang up, but he hadn't spoken with Lonny in a long time, and now he felt guilty. Lonny Tang had been one of his guys for eleven years, on and off, until Lonny got hurt.

Pike asked the obvious.

'How you doing in there?'

'You get used to it. Thirteen years to go, I'm on the beach with a smile.'

'You need anything?'

'Nah. I get all the free meds and medical care I need. I crap blue nuggets and can't eat spicy foods, but other than that I'm fine.'

On the day Frank Meyer saved Lonny Tang's life, an RPG explosion sent a rock the size of a golf ball through Lonny Tang's abdomen. Lonny lost his left kidney, a foot of large intestine, two feet of small intestine, his spleen, part of his liver, half of his stomach, and his health. He was left with a growing addiction to painkillers and no way to pay for them. The Percocets led to harder drugs, and finally to a bar in Long Beach, which Lonny robbed. When two longshoremen tried to stop him, Lonny shot and killed the bar's owner and an innocent bystander. Lonny Tang was arrested less than three hours later, passed out in his car after scoring enough dope to deaden the pain. He was tried on two counts of first-degree

60

murder, convicted, and was currently serving twenty-five years to life at the California State Prison in Corcoran.

Pike didn't know what else to say, so he decided to tie off the conversation.

'Lonny, listen, the police are investigating Frank –'

'They're not going to find anything.'

'When they go through his phone records, they'll see he talked to you.'

'I don't care. I'll tell'm just what I told you.'

'Tell them whatever you want about Frank. Don't tell them about me.'

'You didn't call me. My lawyer called.'

'That's right.'

'You going after these people?'

'I gotta get going.'

'I hear you, brother.'

Pike was about to hang up when he remembered something else.

'Lonny, you there?'

'I'm here. Where else am I going?'

'One more thing. The police told me Frank had my ink.'

'You didn't know?'

'No.'

'That was years ago, man. This time he came to visit, he showed me. He'd just had'm done.'

'The arrows.'

'Big ol' red arrows like yours. Cindy was livid. She damn near threw him out of the house.'

Lonny laughed, but Pike felt embarrassed.

'He say anything?'

'Why he got them?'

'Yeah.'

'Remember all the shit she gave him about being a contractor, and how she wouldn't marry him unless he settled down?'

'Sure.'

'The rest of us were all over him to dump her – what, you're going to give this chick your balls? But Frank said you told him to go for it. Told him, if he wanted that kind of life, he had to make it happen. He really appreciated that, Joe. It was like you gave him permission.'

Pike considered that for a moment.

'Was he happy?'

'Yeah, brother. Hell, yeah, he was happy. It was like he woke up in someone else's life. What's the word? He was content, man.'

Pike said, 'Good.'

'Said somethin' weird, though. Said he'd wake up sometimes, scared God was going to realize he made a mistake, say, "Hey, that's not your life, Frank, you belong back in the shit," and take everything away. He was joking when he said it, but still.'

Pike didn't respond, thinking that sounded like something Frank would say.

'You think that's what happened? God realized he made a mistake?'

'Someone down here made the mistake, Lonny.'

'I hear you. Joe? Thanks for calling about Frankie. I don't get many calls.'

'I have to go.'

'Joe?'

'I gotta get going.'

'You were a good leader. You really took care of us, man. I'm sorry I let you down.'

Pike closed his phone.

7

THE EARLY-EVENING SKY PURPLED as Pike turned toward Frank Meyer's house for the second time that day. He drove slowly, buying time for the twilight sky to darken. Pike loved the night. Had since he was a boy, hiding in the woods from his raging father; loved it all the more as a young combat Marine on long-range patrols, then again when he was a police officer. Pike felt safe in the darkness. Hidden, and free.

Frank's house was dark when Pike drove past. The bright yellow tape across the door was now ochre in the gloomy light, and the SID wagons and criminalists were gone. A radio car remained out front, but Pike noted the windows were up and the glass was smoked. Pike recognized the car as a scarecrow vehicle, left to discourage intruders, but posted without a crew. This made Pike's task easier.

Pike circled the block, then parked in the deep shadow of a maple tree two houses away. He moved quickly and without hesitation, sliding out of his Jeep and into a row of hedges. He crossed the neighbor's yard, then hoisted himself over a wall. He followed the side of Frank's garage into the backyard, then stood for a moment, listening. The neighborhood was alive with normal sounds – cars shortcutting to Beverly Glen on their way home to the Valley, a watchful owl in the maple tree over Frank's pool, a faraway siren.

Pike went to the edge of the pool, smelling the chlorine, then touched the water. Cold. He went to the French doors, popped a pane near the handle, and stepped into the deeper black of the family room. Pike listened again, then turned on a small flashlight that produced a dim red light. He covered the lens with his fingers, letting out only enough light to reveal the room. His hand glowed as if filled with fire.

The heart-shaped stain where Cindy Meyer and her younger son died was a darker smudge on the dark floor, one murky red over another. Pike studied it for a moment, but Pike wasn't looking for clues. He was looking for Frank.

Pike circled the family room, the dining room, and the kitchen, moving as silent as smoke. He noted the furniture, toys, and magazines as if each was a page in the book of the family's life, helping to build their story.

A hall led to the master bedroom, which was large and spacious. Photographs of the kids and Frank and Cindy dotted the walls like memories captured in time. An antique desk sat opposite a king-sized bed with a padded headboard, a plaque on the desk reading: *Empress of the World*. Cindy's desk, where she had paid bills or helped with the business.

Something about the bed bothered Pike, and then he realized the bed was made. The family room and Frank's office had been upended, but the bed here in the master was undisturbed. It had likely been made that morning, and was still waiting for a bedtime that would never come. This suggested the home invaders had either been frightened away before searching the master, or had found what they wanted. Pike concluded there was no way to know, and that John Chen might be right. The invaders could have realized they hit the wrong house, but by then they had killed Frank, so they killed everyone else to get rid of the witnesses.

Pike played the red light over Cindy's desk, and saw more snapshots. Frank and the kids. An older couple who might have been Cindy's parents. And then Pike found the picture he was looking for. He had not known he was searching for it, but felt a sense of completion when he saw it. The snapshot showed Frank in a swimming pool with one of the boys. Frank had heaved his son into the air amid a geyser of water, both of them laughing, Frank's arms extended. This picture was the only photograph of all the photos that showed the blocky red arrows inked onto his deltoids. Pointing forward, just as the arrows on Pike's delts pointed forward. Identical.

Pike studied the picture for a long while before he returned it to the desk and left the bedroom. He moved back along the hall, thinking how different his own home was from the home that Frank Meyer built. Pike's furnishings were minimal, and the walls were bare. Pike did not have a family, so he had no pictures of family on the walls, and he did not keep pictures of his friends. Pike's life had led to blank walls, and now he wondered if his walls would ever be filled.

When Pike reached the entry, the outside of the house lit up like a blinding sun. Vengeful bright light poured around curtains and shades, ignited the cracks in the broken door, and streaked through the windows. Pike closed his hand over the tiny red light, and waited.

A patrol car was spotlighting the house. They had probably been instructed to cruise by every half hour or so. Pike was calm. Neither his breathing nor his heart rate increased. The light worked over the house, probing the hedges and side gates for three or four minutes. Then the light died as abruptly as it appeared.

Pike followed his crimson light upstairs.

The house seemed even more quiet on the second floor, where a stain on the carpet marked the older son's murder. Little Frank. Pike counted the years back to a deadly night on the far side of the world when Frank told Pike that Cindy was pregnant.

That time, they were protecting a collective of villages in Central Africa. A group called the Lord's Resistance Army had been kidnapping teenage girls they raped and sold as slaves. Pike brought over

Frank, Jon Stone, a Brit named Colin Chandler, Lonny Tang, and an ex–Special Forces soldier from Alabama named Jameson Wallace. They were tracking the LRA to recover sixteen kidnapped girls when Frank told him that his girlfriend, Cindy, was pregnant. Frank wanted to marry her, but Cindy had stunned him with an ultimatum – she wanted no part of his dangerous life or the dangerous people with whom he worked, so either Frank would leave his current life and friends behind, or Cindy would never see him again. Frank had been shattered, torn between his love for Cindy and his loyalty to his friends. He had talked to Pike almost three hours that night, then the next, and the next.

Pike closed his eyes, and felt the carpet beneath his feet, the chill air, the empty silence. He opened his eyes, and stared at the terrible stain. Even in the bad light, he could see where fibers had been clipped by the criminalists.

Those African nights led through the intervening years like a twisting tunnel through time to this spot on the floor. Pike covered the red light, turning the world black.

He went downstairs to Frank's office.

The drapes had been left open by the SID crews, so the office was bright with outside light. Pike turned off his red flash. He sat at Frank's desk with his back to the window. Frank the Tank's desk. A long way from Africa.

*

THE NIGHT IN AFRICA when Frank decided to change his life, he had thirty-one days remaining on his contract, but was still thirteen days from earning his nickname. Two days after Africa, Joe, Frank, and Lonny Tang flew to El Salvador. Frank had not been able to reach Cindy until they landed in Central America, but that's when he told her. She wanted him to fly home immediately, but Frank explained he had made a commitment for the duration of his contract, and would honor that commitment. Cindy didn't like it, but agreed. Joe and his guys spent five days in El Salvador, then flew to Kuwait.

It was a British contract, providing security for French, Italian, and British journalists. That particular job was to transport two BBC journalists and a two-person camera crew inland to a small village over the mountains called Jublaban, untouched and well away from hostile forces.

Pike was responsible for three different groups of journalists that day, so he split his crew, giving the Jublaban run to Lonny, Frank, Colin Chandler, and an ex–French Foreign Legion trooper named Durand Galatoise. Two Land Rovers, two operators per Rover, the journalists divided between them. A fast thirty-two miles over the mountains, leave in the morning, back after lunch. Durand Galatoise packed two bottles of Chablis because one of the journalists had a nasty smile.

They left at eight that morning, Lonny and Frank in the lead truck, Chandler and Galatoise in trail, and reached Jublaban without incident. There to do a story on rural medical care, the journalists were interviewing Jublaban's only physician when an incoming RPG hit the second Rover, flipping it onto its side. The operators and journalists immediately came under small-arms fire.

Galatoise was killed within the first sixty seconds, the remaining Rover was hit, then Lonny Tang caught the piece of shrapnel that tore him inside out. Frank and Chandler realized they were facing eight or ten men, then noticed an approaching nightmare: Four armored vehicles and two full-sized battle tanks were rumbling toward them across the desert. With both Rovers disabled, the operators and their journalists were trapped.

Frank pushed Lonny Tang's intestines back into his body, then wrapped him with pressure bandages and belts to keep him together. While Chandler laid down cover fire, Frank ran to his burning Rover for radios, more ammunition, and a .50-caliber Barrett rifle they used for sniper suppression. The Barrett, a beast of a rifle that weighed over thirty pounds, could punch through engine blocks at more than a mile.

Chandler herded the journalists to a more defensible location, but Lonny Tang could not be moved. Frank stashed him in a stone hut, then moved forward with the Barrett gun. Frank later said he was crying during the entire firefight; blubbering like a baby, he would say, running, then firing, then running again.

Pike heard much of it through his radio, with

Chandler broadcasting a play-by-play as Pike coordinated a rescue mission with a British air controller.

Frank Meyer fought on like that for almost thirty minutes, running and gunning with the Barrett even when the tanks and armored vehicles crunched into the village, Frank banging away like a lunatic to draw them from Lonny Tang.

Everyone later assumed the big boomers turned back into the desert after they picked up their troops, but Colin Chandler and the BBC journalists reported that a young American named Frank Meyer had shot it out toe-to-toe with four armored vehicles and two heavy tanks, and driven the bastards away.

Frank's contract expired five days later. He wept when he shook Pike's hand for the last time, boarded an airplane, and that had been that, changing one life for another.

Pike officially retired from contract work sixty-two days later, and maybe Frank's decision had something to do with Pike's decision, though Pike never thought so. Pike had told Frank to do it. Build the family he wanted. Leave the past. Always move forward.

PIKE WAS STILL AT Frank's desk when his cell vibrated, there in the cool blue light.

Stone said, 'All right, listen. They're watching a guy named Rahmi Johnson. Been on him for almost a month. I've got an address here for you.'

'If they're on him, he didn't murder Frank.'

'Rahmi isn't the suspect. Cops think his cousin

might be involved, a dude named Jamal Johnson.'

'Might be, or is?'

'Gotta have proof for it, but he looks pretty good. Check it out. Jamal was released from Soledad two weeks before the first score. He crashed with Rahmi when he got out, but moved out three days after the score. Four days after the second score, Jamal dropped by with a sixty-inch plasma to thank Rahmi for putting him up. A week after the third score, Jamal tools up in a brand-new black-on-black Malibu with custom rims. He gives the car to Rahmi, too. Can you imagine? My guy's telling me this, I'm thinking, shit, I wish this asshole was my cousin, too.'

Stone broke out laughing, but the laughter was too loud and too long. Stone had been drinking.

Pike said, 'Where's Jamal?'

'Nobody knows, bro. That's why they're sitting on Rahmi.'

'Maybe Rahmi knows. Have they asked him?'

'They did, and that's where they fucked up. Rolled by something like two months ago, when Jamal was first identified as a person of interest. Heard he was crashing with Rahmi, so they went by. Rahmi played stupid, but you know he warned Jamal the second those cops were out the door. That's when Jamal dropped off the map.'

Pike thought about it. Thought how he would play it.

'They should ask him again.'

Stone laughed.

'Well, they're cops, not you. That timeline business,

that's not proof, but it's convincing. They don't want to arrest the guy, they want to follow him. They want to catch him in the act or clear him, one way or the other.'

'So SIS is covering Rahmi, hoping Jamal will come around again.'

'They got nothing else, man. Jamal's their only good suspect.'

Pike grunted. SIS was good. They were patient hunters. They would shadow their target for weeks like invisible men, but Pike didn't want to wait that long. Stone was right. The police were trying to build a case, but Pike didn't care about a case. His needs were simpler.

'What's that address?'

Stone cleared his throat, suddenly uncomfortable.

'Okay, now listen, we can't have any blowback here. You go barging in and it comes back to me, the SIS guys will know who gave them up. You ruin their play, my guy is fucked.'

'No blowback. They'll never see me.'

Stone laughed again, still too loud and too long, and now more than a little nervous.

'Only you could say that, Pike, talking about SIS. Jesus Christ, bro, only you.'

Stone was giving Pike the address when light exploded into the office, so bright the walls and furniture were white with glare. Pike, still in the chair with his back to the window, did not move. The patrol car had returned.

Pike said, 'Sh.'

'What's wrong?'

An enormous blue shadow crossed the office wall as if someone had moved in front of the light. Pike heard faint radio calls, and listened for approaching footsteps.

Stone's tiny voice came from the phone.

'You sound weird, man. Where are you?'

Pike whispered, as still as a fish at the bottom of a pond.

'Frank's. The police are outside.'

'You break in?'

'Sh.'

The light swung away, moving to another part of the house like an animal tracking a scent.

'What the fuck are you doing at Frank's?'

'I wanted to see what his life was like.'

'You're a strange cat. I mean, really.'

The light snapped off. The yard plunged into darkness. The radio chatter faded. The patrol car rolled on.

Pike said, 'Okay.'

'Hey, is it nice?'

'What?'

'Frank's house. Does he have a nice place?'

'Yes.'

'Fancy?'

'Not like you mean. It's a good family home.'

Pike heard Stone swallow. Heard the glass tink the phone.

'You think it's true, he went bad?'

'Chen thinks the people who did this got the wrong house.'

'Like, what, they got confused about which house they wanted to rob?'

'It happens.'

'What do you think?'

'Doesn't matter.'

'No. No, it surely doesn't.'

Stone made a deep sigh. Pike thought it might have been a sob, but then Stone had another sip of whatever he was sipping, and went on.

'Assholes like this, they go in these houses, right house, wrong house, murder people like they were nothing, probably sleep like a baby after it's over. How many times have they done this?'

'Frank was the seventh.'

'You see? This is my point. Six times before, they got away clean. Murdered some poor bastard, and there have been no consequences. Hence, these people do not fear the dead. They LOVE the dead, Joe, because the dead – and I apologize if my assessment here seems harsh – but, the dead have not been effective when it comes to consequence and retribution.'

'What are you drinking?'

'Scotch. I am drinking scotch in honor of our friend Frank. I would rather rip off a twenty-one-gun salute out in the backyard, but my neighbors prefer the drinking. Where was I?'

'Consequence and retribution.'

'Right –'

Jon Stone was grieving, so Pike let him continue.

'But then . . . then they hit Frank the Tank, them not knowing he was Frank the Tank, them thinking he was just another ordinary dead guy without recourse to consequence. So dig this – and this is my favorite part – those assholes are somewhere right now, shootin' up, corn-holing each other, whatever – they are somewhere *right now*, and they do not know a shit storm is on the horizon, and it is coming for them.'

Pike said, 'Jon? Do you have photographs on your walls?'

'What, like naked chicks?'

'Pictures of your family. Friends.'

'Shit, yeah. I take pictures of everything. I got pictures of fuckin' human heads. Why?'

'No reason.'

'Hey, man. Those fuckers. Those fucks fucked the pooch this time, didn't they, fuckin' with Frank?'

'Get some sleep.'

'I want in on this, bro. I mean it. Whatever.'

'Get some sleep.'

'I'll call Colin. Colin will be on the first plane.'

'Don't call Colin.'

'Wallace would come.'

'Don't.'

'Fuck it. Hey, Joe? Joe, you there?'

'What?'

Stone was silent for so long Pike thought he had fallen asleep.

'Jon?'

'None of us had families. You never married. Lonny, Colin, not them, either. Wallace got divorced. I've been married six fuckin' times, man, what does that tell you? None of us had kids.'

Pike didn't know what to say, but maybe Stone voiced it for him, soft, and hoarse from the booze.

'I really wanted Frank to make it. Not just for him.'

Pike closed his phone.

He sat in Frank's office for almost an hour, alone with himself and the silence, then walked back along the hall to Cindy's desk. He took the framed picture of Frank in the pool, tucked it into his pocket, then let himself out the way he had entered, and drove home for the night.

They call this the city
The city of angels
All I see is death-dealin' dangers.

— Tattooed Beach Sluts

Part Two
The First Rule

8

PIKE RETURNED HOME AFTER leaving Frank's house and found a message waiting from Elvis Cole, who was Pike's friend and partner in a detective agency. Pike listened while he drank a bottle of water.

Cole said, 'Hey. A cop named Terrio came by the office today, asking about you and someone named Frank Meyer. Felt like he was fishing, but he also said this guy Meyer was murdered. Call me.'

Pike deleted the message, then looked up Rahmi's address on his computer. He was hungry, he wanted to exercise and return Cole's call, but he needed to keep moving. Movement meant progress, and progress meant finding the men who killed Frank.

The Google Maps feature was like having a spy satellite. Pike typed in Rahmi's address, and there it was – all of Compton spread out thousands of feet below. Pike zoomed in for a closer look, then went to the street view, which allowed him to see Rahmi's building as if he were standing in the street. Faded paint. Dying grass. Big Wheel on its side. The Google pictures had been taken on a bright, sunny day, and might have been taken months ago, but they were a good place to start.

Rahmi Johnson lived in a green two-story apartment building 1.67 miles north of the Artesia Freeway in Compton. His building was shaped like a shoe box, with three units on bottom, three on top, and a flat, featureless roof. Rahmi had the center ground-floor apartment. Single-family homes and similar buildings lined Rahmi's side of the street, set on lots so narrow that some of the homes were turned sideways. Rahmi's building was sideways. Almost every yard was protected by short chain-link fences, and almost every house had security bars on its windows. The opposite side of the street was lined by single-story commercial buildings.

Because of the sideways orientation, the side of Rahmi's building faced the street and the front of the building faced the next-door neighbor's property. Residents entered through a chain-link gate, passed the Big Wheel, then went along the length of their building to reach their apartments. This sideways orientation made it difficult for Pike to see Rahmi's door from the street. He considered this, and knew the police would have the same problem.

Pike was studying the buildings surrounding Rahmi's apartment house when his cell phone rang. He saw it was John Chen, and took the call.

'Yes.'

'We confirmed a fourth gun to go with the fourth set of shoe prints. Three of the four guns were used in the earlier murders, but the fourth gun was not. That fourth gun showed casings in the nanny's room and the family room.'

'How many?'

'Three. The fourth gunman shot Frank Meyer once, and put both bullets in the girl – Ana Markovic. We're still matching the other bullets and casings, but that's the prelim. I thought you'd want to know.'

'Thanks.'

Pike put down the phone, and thought about the fourth shooter. The new guy. Someone who had not taken part in the earlier invasions, but had gone to Frank's house. Pike wondered why a fourth man had joined the crew. Had the original three members known about Frank's background, and expected more resistance?

Pike finally put it out of his head, and returned to his computer. He studied Rahmi's building, then the surrounding structures and the commercial properties across the street. He noticed that both sides of the street were lined with parked cars, then went back to the overhead view and realized why. Neither Rahmi's building nor the other small apartment buildings had driveways or spaces for off-street parking; residents parked on the street. This meant Rahmi's new Malibu would probably be parked in front of his building.

No building in the area was more than two stories, and most were only a single story. With no overlooking vantage point, the spotter would have to be close. The high density of residents, the on-street parking, and the long-term nature of the surveillance meant the spotter was housed in a nearby building. You couldn't park a Crown Vic out front for three weeks and expect the neighbors not to notice. Ditto repair vans, delivery trucks, and phony cable trucks. After forty-five minutes of studying the area, Pike believed the surveillance options for SIS were limited. He had a pretty good idea where they would place their spotters, and also how he could reach Rahmi without being seen. He would have to see the area at night and during the day to be sure, but he knew what he had to do.

Pike changed into his workout gear, stretched to warm himself, then eased into the meditative state he always found through yoga. He moved slowly, and with great regard, working deeply through asanas from hatha yoga. He breathed, and felt himself settle. His heart rate slowed. Forty-two beats per minute. His blood pressure, one hundred over sixty. Peace came with certainty, and Pike was certain.

When Pike finished, he eased awake like a bubble rising to the surface of a great flat pond. Dinner was rice and red beans mixed with grilled corn and eggplant; the rice and beans he had made, the corn and eggplant were from a restaurant. After dinner, he showered, cleaned himself, then dressed in briefs and a T-shirt. He returned Cole's call, but Cole didn't pick up, so he left a message.

Pike poured a finger of scotch in a short glass, then

shut the lights. He sat on his couch, alone in the dark, listening to water burble in the black granite meditation fountain. Listening to the water, it was easy to imagine he was in a natural world where wild things lived. He sipped the scotch, and listened.

After a while, Pike went upstairs to bed. The mattress was hard, but he liked it that way. He was asleep almost at once. Pike fell asleep easily. Staying asleep was difficult.

His eyes opened two hours later, and Joe Pike was awake. He blinked at the darkness, and knew sleep was done. He remembered no dreams, but his T-shirt was damp with sweat.

Pike rolled out of bed, dressed, got together his things, then drove south to Compton across a landscape brilliant with unwavering lights.

9

PIKE KNEW RAHMI was home the first and only time he drove past in his Jeep because the shiny black Malibu was wedged to the curb. Three in the morning on a weeknight, traffic was nonexistent and the streets were dead. Pike pulled his jacket collar high, his cap low, and slumped behind the wheel. Everyone else in the world might be sleeping, but SIS would be watching. One pass, they would ignore him. Two passes, they would wonder. A third pass, they would likely call in a radio car to see what was going on.

Pike drove to a well-lit, twenty-four-hour Mobil station by the freeway, parked, then called a cab service. While he waited for the cab, he went inside. The attendant was a middle-aged Latin guy with a weak chin who looked scared even though he was behind an inch and a half of bulletproof glass. As soon as Pike walked in, the attendant's right hand went under the counter.

'Engine trouble. I'm going to leave my Jeep here for a while. Okay?'

Pike held up a twenty-dollar bill, then slipped it under the glass. The attendant didn't touch it.

'Ain't nothin' bad in there, is it?'

'Bad?'

'Like . . . bad?'

Dope or a body.

Pike said, 'Engine trouble. I'll be back.'

The attendant took the twenty with his left hand. He never revealed his right. Pike wondered how many times he had been held up.

Pike went outside and stood in the vapor light breathing cold mist until a lime green cab showed up. It appeared lavender in the silky light.

The cab driver was a young African-American with suspicious eyes, who did a double take when he saw his fare was a white man.

He said, 'Car trouble?'

'I have a friend nearby. You can take me to her place.'

'Ah.'

Her. A woman made everything better.

Pike gave the nearest major intersection, but not Rahmi's address. Pike didn't want the cabbie to know it if he was later questioned. When they reached Rahmi's street, Pike told him to cruise the block.

Pike said, 'Go slow. I'll know it when I see it.'

'I thought you knew this girl.'

'It's been a while.'

The SIS spotters would be watching the cab. This time of morning, they didn't have anything else to watch. Pike slumped in the shadows of the backseat as they passed Rahmi's building. The SIS spotters would be on alert now, but Pike wanted to see how Rahmi's apartment was lit. The lighting was crucial in helping Pike determine where the spotters were hiding, and in planning how to defeat them.

Pike said, 'Slower.'

The cab slowed even more. The watch officer was likely keying his radio or kicking his partner, saying they might have something here.

The entry side of Rahmi's building was lit by six yellow bulbs, one outside each of the three doors on the ground level, but only one outside a door on the second floor. The others appeared to be out. Pike was more interested in the back of the building than the front. The Google images showed the back of Rahmi's building was very close to the neighboring home, and now Pike saw the area caught only a small amount of reflected glow from the neighbor's porch. This was good for Pike. The heavy shadows, along with the distance from the street and the narrow separation between the two buildings, meant the area behind Rahmi's apartment was a tunnel of darkness. Pike would be able to disappear into the tunnel.

The cabbie said, 'Which one?'

'Don't see it. Let's try the next block.'

Pike had the cabbie slow in front of two more buildings to throw off the spotters, then headed back to his Jeep. During his days as a combat Marine, the helicopter pilots used the same technique when inserting troops into enemy territory. They didn't just fly in, drop off Marines, and leave. Instead, the pilots made three or four false inserts along with the real drop to mask the true drop point. If it worked in hostile jungles, it would work in South Central Los Angeles.

Pike took another cab past the apartment just before dawn to check the lighting again from the opposite direction, and made six more cab rides before noon, different cabs each time, twice having the cabs stop nearby so he could study the street. One of the cabbies asked if he was looking for a woman, another stared at him in the rearview with marble eyes, finally saying, 'You down here to kill a man?'

They were parked outside a different apartment house on the next block. Pike now believed the primary SIS spotter was located in one of two commercial buildings directly across from Rahmi's building. The only other building with a view of Rahmi's door was the house it faced, but Pike had seen a tall, thin woman herd three children out of the house for school. The two commercial buildings were the only remaining possibilities. SIS wanted to see Rahmi's door. They would want to see who entered, and who left, and with the bad angles this meant they had to be directly across the street in one of two places. Pike hadn't found their exact location, but he now believed it wasn't necessary.

The cabbie said, 'I don't want no shootin' in this cab. Don't you be gettin' me involved in some crime.'

'I'm cool.'

'You don't look cool. You look so hot a man could fry just bein' next to you.'

Pike said, 'Sh.'

'Just sayin', is all.'

Pike pushed a twenty-dollar bill onto the man's shoulder. The cabbie grunted like he was the world's biggest fool, but the bill disappeared.

Rahmi's Malibu was parked outside his building almost directly in front of the chain-link gate. Tuxedo black with double-chrome dubs covering the wheels that probably retailed at two thousand dollars each. Every time Rahmi drove away, SIS would follow. They would have placed a GPS locator on the car, and they would use at least three vehicles to maintain contact. Their cars would be nearby and ready to roll.

The Malibu was Pike's key. SIS had to watch Rahmi's apartment, but Pike only needed to watch the Malibu, and a place to hide without being seen.

The driver made a loud sigh.

'Ain't you seen enough?'

Pike said, 'Let's go.'

Pike picked up his Jeep, then drove north into East L.A. A friend of his had a parking lot there, where he kept vehicles he rented to film companies. Vintage cars, mostly, but also specialty vehicles like dune buggies, decommissioned police cruisers, and customized hot rods. Pike rented a taco truck with faded paint, a heavy skin of dust, and a cracked window. A flowing blue legend was emblazoned along the side: ANTONIO'S MOTORIZED RESTAURANT –

HOME OF THE BBQ TACO! The legend was faded, too.

Pike put it on his credit card, left his Jeep, then drove the taco truck back to Compton. He parked three blocks from Rahmi's on the opposite side of the street in front of what appeared to be a tow yard and a row of abandoned storefronts.

Pike shut the engine, cracked open the windows for air, then moved back into the kitchen bay where he would be hidden from people on the street. Three blocks away, the SIS spotters would ignore him. They were too busy watching Rahmi's apartment.

Pike couldn't see the apartment, but he had a good view of the Malibu, and the Malibu was all he needed.

Pike settled in. He breathed. He waited for something to happen.

10

AT EIGHT-FIFTY THAT NIGHT, the Malibu pulled away, came toward Pike until the first cross street, then stopped before making the turn. The light was poor, but the black-on-black Malibu gleamed beautifully and the polished chrome dubs glittered.

Pike watched.

A dark blue Neon approached on the cross street as the Malibu signaled to turn. The Neon was dirty, and missing the left front hubcap. When the Malibu turned, the Neon continued across the intersection behind it. Pike figured the Neon was SIS, and at least two other vehicles were maneuvering into surrounding positions.

Pike waited another five minutes before he slipped out of the taco truck. No lights came on when he opened and closed the door.

When Rahmi left his apartment, the spotters would have radioed the officers in their nearby cars, and the drivers would have scrambled to get into position. After that it was their show. For the first time in hours, the spotters would relax. They would kick back, check email, call their significant others, get some exercise. They wouldn't be staring at Rahmi Johnson's door because Rahmi was gone.

Pike trotted up to the same intersection, then rounded the corner to the next street and vaulted a fence into the yard butting the back side of Rahmi's building. A dog barked, mincing and scraping at the door of the neighbor's house, but Pike slid past the door and lifted himself over another chain-link fence directly behind Rahmi's apartment.

Pike stood in the shadows, waiting to see if someone would turn on a light. The little dog continued barking, but a woman in the house shouted, and after a few seconds the barking stopped. Pike got to work.

Each of the apartments had only a single window on the back of the building, one of those high, small windows you find in bathrooms, but the windows were caged by iron bars. Rahmi's window and the window in the street-side apartment were lit, but the rear apartment was dark. Pike wondered if it was filled with SIS operators.

The bathroom door was open. The bathroom light was off, but lights and the television were on in the outer room. The television being on, Pike figured Rahmi would return soon, but couldn't be sure.

Pike examined the security bars. The bars were not individual bars, but a single cage formed of vertical rods welded to a frame like a catcher's mask. More expensive security systems were hinged on one side, but these bars had been installed on the cheap and were likely against the building code. Pike ran his fingers along the bottom frame plate and found four screws. The owner had probably sunk wood screws through the stucco into the studs. They would be difficult to break, but not impossible.

Pike had come prepared with a pry bar. He jimmied the pry bar under the frame, used his SOG knife to pop the heads off the screws, then levered the cage from the window. Pike placed it on the ground, pushed open the window, then lifted himself through.

Rahmi had a studio apartment, with the bath in one corner sharing a wall with his kitchen. The furnishings were ratty and cheap, with a threadbare couch fronting a discolored coffee table, a couple of bean-bag chairs pimpled with stains, and a gray comforter suggesting the couch did double duty as a bed. The sixty-inch flat-screen hung opposite the couch like a glittering jewel, as out of place as a human head. Cables bled down the wall to a stack of components, then vined along the floor to a series of speakers. Rahmi had Surround Sound.

Pike wanted to turn off the lights and mute the television, but if the police were watching and listening, they would wonder what happened. The police had almost certainly been inside the apartment, and probably left a listening device. Pike didn't want them listening when Rahmi came home.

Pike put away the pry bar and knife, and took out a

small RF scanner about the size and shape of an iPod. Pike used it often in his security work. If the scanner picked up an RF signal, which pretty much all eavesdropping bugs emitted, a red light would glow.

Pike swept the main room, the kitchen, and finally the bath, then checked the big-screen components and furniture without finding anything. Pike considered the air conditioner wedged in the window. If the device was in the AC and someone turned it on, you wouldn't be able to hear anything, but he checked it anyway. Nothing. Then he studied the shades covering the windows. The rollers were dingy and fuzzy with dust and spiderwebs. Pike scanned them, and found the bug on the second roller. It was the size of an earbud and stuck to the roller's bracket with a piece of earthquake putty. Pike gently removed it and placed it on the floor behind the door. This would be his position when Rahmi came home.

Pike put away the scanner, but continued his search. He found a nine-millimeter Smith and Wesson wedged between the cushions on the couch, a blue glass bong the length of a nightstick on the floor, and a baggie containing two joints and a small quantity of loose marijuana. A smaller glass rock pipe was in a wicker basket, along with a plastic bag containing three balls of rock cocaine and assorted pills. Pike unloaded the nine-millimeter, pocketed the bullets, then tucked the gun under his belt. He found nothing else of interest, so he returned to his position behind the door. Rahmi might be back in five minutes or five days, but Pike would wait. Pike was good at waiting.

Twenty-five minutes later, Pike heard the chain-link gate, and drew Rahmi's pistol.

Three locks were built into the door. Someone unlocked them one by one, and then the door swung in. Pike stepped on the bug as the door opened. Rahmi Johnson entered carrying a white paper bag, closed the door, and saw Pike just as Pike hit him with the pistol. The police would have resumed their watchful positions and would be wondering why the sound went dead, but would assume the closing door had somehow knocked it loose.

Rahmi raised his hands for protection, but didn't get them up fast enough. Pike hit him a second time, and Rahmi staggered sideways. Tacos spilled out of the bag, smelling of grease and chili sauce.

Pike twisted Rahmi's arm behind his back, clipped his knees, and rode him down.

Rahmi said, 'Bro, hey, the fuck?'

Pike held the gun out.

'See?'

Rahmi probably thought Pike was a cop, the white facedown here in Compton.

'What you want, man? I ain't done nuthin'.' Pike tapped him again.

'Sh.'

Pike muted the television, then went through Rahmi's pockets. He found a cell phone, a fold of cash, a pack of Parliaments, and a yellow Bic lighter.

No wallet. He pulled Rahmi to his feet and pushed him to the couch.

'Sit.'

Rahmi sat, glaring at Pike like a sullen teenager. Rahmi was trying to read him, trying to figure out who Pike was and what was in store. Pike understood he looked like a cop, but he didn't want Rahmi to think he was a cop.

Pike stuffed Rahmi's cash into his pocket, and Rahmi jerked forward.

'Yo! That's my money, muthuhfucka!'

'Not anymore. Jamal owes me cash.'

'You a cop?'

'Where's Jamal?'

'I don't know where Jamal is. Shit.'

'Jamal has my money. I'll get it from him, or from you.'

'I don't know you, man. I don't know nuthin' 'bout no money.'

Rahmi wet his lips, thinking if Pike wasn't a cop, maybe it wasn't as bad as he thought, but Pike wanted him to think it was worse.

Pike threw the cell phone at him, so hard Rahmi caught it to protect himself.

'Call him.'

'Man, I ain't seen Jamal since visiting day. He in prison.'

Pike swung the Smith backhand, hitting the sixty-inch plasma dead in the center of the screen. The safety glass split, and multicolored blocks danced and shimmered where the image had been. Rahmi lunged up from the couch, eyes trembling like runny eggs.

Pike aimed the Smith at Rahmi's forehead and thumbed back the hammer.

'Call.'

'I'll call. I'll call all you want, but we ain't gonna get no answer. I been leavin' messages. His message box full.'

Rahmi fumbled with the phone, then held it out for Pike to see.

'Here. Listen here. You'll see. I called him right now.'

Pike held out his free hand, and Rahmi tossed the phone over. Pike caught it to hear a computer voice say the recipient's message box was full.

Pike ended the connection, then brought up the call log. The last call out showed as *Jamal*. Pike closed the phone, then put it into his pocket. He would go through the other numbers later.

'Where is he?'

'I don't know where he is. Layin' up with some ho, I imagine. Maybe in Vegas.'

'He told me he was crashing here. How else would I have your address?'

Now Rahmi appeared confused, as if he thought all this might be possible, but wasn't sure how.

'Man, that was weeks ago. I don't know where he cribs now. He don't tell me, and I don't wanna know.'

'Why not?'

'Aw, man, you know. The police came around looking, so he's gotta stay low. He didn't say where he went and I didn't ask. If I don't know, I can't say.'

Pike decided Rahmi was telling the truth, but Jamal was only one of the people he wanted to find.

'When's the last time you spoke?'

'Few days, I guess. Maybe a week.'

'What did you talk about?'

'Just talkin' shit. This cop show I'm watching on DVD, *The Shield*. That shit is righteous, here on the sixty-inch. We talkin' about *The Shield*. Jamal say up there in Soledad, they all into *The Shield*.'

'I think you're lying. I think he left my money with you, and you spent it.'

Pike aimed the Smith at Rahmi's left eye. Rahmi held up a hand as if he could ward off the bullet.

'That's crazy. I don't know nuthin' 'bout no money.'

'He tell you I was coming?'

'He ain't said nuthin' 'bout no money, you, or anything else. How much he owe you?'

'Thirty-two thousand dollars. I'm getting it from him, or you.'

'I ain't got no thirty-two kay.'

'You were driving it. Now I'm driving it.'

Rahmi blinked at what was left of his big-screen television, then slumped in defeat.

'Nigga, please, whatever passed between you and Jamal, I got no part in that. Jamal, he gave me these things 'cause he doin' so well. We family, dog.'

'How'd he get to be doing so well?'

'He got in with a good crew.'

'Who? Maybe I can find him through them.'

'Jamal never told me no names.'

'He never told you I'd come for my money, either. I think he stole it from me. I think this stuff is mine.'

Pike raised the gun again, and this time Rahmi pleaded.

'It's true, bro. They hooked up with this Serbian cat, lays off one fat score after another. They makin' the bank!'

Pike lowered the gun.

'Serbian.'

'They in with this dude set'm up with the scores. Tell'm who to hit, they split the cash. He say it the easiest money he ever made.'

'He said Serbian? Not Russian or Armenian?'

'What difference it make? How's a brother know the difference?'

'What was the name?'

'Just some Serbian muthuhfucka, that's all.'

Ana Markovic was from Serbia. Dying in the hospital with her sister standing guard.

Pike studied Rahmi, but wasn't really looking at Rahmi. He thought for a moment, then went to the bag of tacos. He stepped on it. Crunch.

Rahmi looked pained.

'Muthuhfuckin' dinner, muthuhfucka. Why you do a mean-hearted thing like that?'

Pike picked up Rahmi's keys, then tossed them to him.

'Get some more tacos.'

'What?'

Pike held up the fold of bills.

'Take your car. Go get more tacos.'

Rahmi wet his lips as if he was expecting a trick, then snatched the bills and went to the door.

'How you know Jamal?'

'He murdered me.'

Rahmi froze with his hand on the knob.

Pike said, 'You see Jamal before I find him, tell him Frank Meyer is coming.'

Rahmi let himself out.

Pike stood by the door, listening. He heard the gate. He heard the Malibu rumble, and the tires screech. Just as before, the SIS detail would scramble to follow.

Pike slipped out the bathroom window, and returned to the night.

11

PIKE RETURNED TO UCLA the next morning. When he stepped off the elevator onto the ICU floor, he saw Rina outside her sister's door with a doctor and two nurses. Pike stepped back onto the elevator and rode down to the lobby. He wanted to speak with her alone.

Pike repositioned his Jeep so he could watch the lobby entrance, then turned on the phone he had taken from Rahmi Johnson. He had bought a power cord for the phone on the way to the hospital. Pike wanted to keep the phone charged in case Jamal called his cousin.

Pike scrolled through the list until he reached Jamal's number, then pressed the button to dial. Pike had called the number twice last night, and now again, but the response was the same. A female computer voice came on, informing Pike that Jamal's message box was full.

Pike put away the phone, then stared at the lobby.

He was prepared to wait as long as necessary, but Rina emerged a few minutes later. Same jeans and jacket as yesterday. Same shoulder bag clutched to her chest.

Pike moved through a row of cars as she crossed into the parking lot. She walked fast, with hard, clipped steps, as if she wanted to cover as much ground as possible.

She didn't see Pike until he stepped from between the cars, then she gasped.

Pike said, 'Do you know who did this?'

'Of course not. How could I know?'

'Is that why you're afraid? You know who did this?'

She edged away, keeping the purse close.

'I don't know what you are saying. Of course I don't know. The police are looking.'

Pike stepped in front of her.

'The people who shot her were sent by a Serbian.'

'And this means what? Please –'

She tried to get around him, but Pike caught her arm.

'The crew who shot your sister bought the score from a Serbian gangster. They bought information about a house where your sister worked. And now here you are, afraid, with the gun.'

She glared at his hand, then drew herself up.

'Leave go of me.'

Pike let go because he saw her look past him. Pike drifted to the side, and saw a large, burly man approaching. He was jumbo large, with sloping shoulders, a big gut, and a dark, unshaven face. His beard was thick enough to grind marble.

He stopped when Pike turned, still two rows away, and said something Pike did not understand. Rina answered in the same language.

'My friend, Yanni. He see you grab me. I tell him we're fine.'

Yanni was probably six five and weighed three hundred pounds. He was scowling at Pike like a Balkan grizzly, but Pike wasn't impressed. Size meant little.

Pike turned back to the woman.

'If you know who did this, tell me. I can protect you better than him.'

Rina stepped back.

'I don't know what you mean, Serbian gangster.'

'How did Frank and Cindy meet your sister? How did she get the job with them?'

'I don't know.'

'Did someone you know recommend her to them?'

She moved farther away.

'If you think you know something, you should tell the police.'

'Who are you afraid of?'

She studied him a long time, then shook her head.

'Ana is dead now. I have much to do.'

She turned and walked past Yanni, the two of them exchanging words Pike could not understand. She walked quickly, as if she still had all the ground to cover but was falling behind. Yanni continued scowling, but now his scowl seemed sad.

Pike returned to his Jeep. He watched them cross

the parking lot to a small white Toyota. The woman got in behind the wheel.

Pike let them gain ground before he followed them, creeping along several cars back through the ugly Westwood Village traffic, then onto the freeway. He kept the Toyota in sight, rolling north into the San Fernando Valley, then east to Studio City. Pike worked closer when they left the freeway, following them into a residential area between the L.A. River channel and Ventura Boulevard, and then into the parking lot of a large apartment complex. It was one of those complexes with gated entries and visitor parking, and lots of used brick and trees.

Pike parked at the curb and followed her on foot, staying along the edge of the building. He stopped when her brake lights flared. Yanni got out, spoke with her for a moment through the open window, then climbed into a metallic tan F-150 pickup truck. The Toyota continued into the residents' parking lot.

Pike noted the F-150's license plate, but stayed back until Yanni drove away, then jumped the gate into the parking structure. He continued along the line of parked vehicles until he found Rina's Toyota parked in a space marked 2205. Pike thought it likely that 2205 would also be Rina's apartment number.

Pike returned to his Jeep, wrote down the various license plates and numbers before he forgot them, then phoned a friend.

Pike was good at some things, but not so good at others. He wanted information about Ana and Rina

Markovic, and on the phone numbers in Rahmi Johnson's phone. Pike was a warrior. He could hunt, stalk, and defeat an enemy in almost any environment, but detective work required relationships Pike did not possess.

A man answered on the second ring.

'Elvis Cole Detective Agency. We find more for less. Check our prices.'

Pike said, 'I need your help.'

12
ELVIS COLE

ELVIS COLE PUT DOWN the phone, feeling even more concerned than he was before Pike called. Cole couldn't count the times Pike had saved his life, or the endless moments of silence they had shared when just being with someone who has seen the same horrible things you have seen was the last best way to survive. But he could count on one hand the times Joe Pike had asked for help.

Cole hadn't felt right since Detective-Sergeant Jack Terrio hit him with questions he couldn't answer about a multiple homicide he knew nothing about, and now Cole was irritated he had to wait to find out what was going on. As usual, Pike hadn't explained anything over the phone. Just said he was on his way, and hung up. Ever the mannered conversationalist.

The Elvis Cole Detective Agency maintained a two-office suite four flights above Santa Monica Boulevard. The selling point had been the balcony. Cole could step outside on a clear day and see all the way down Santa Monica to the sea. Sometimes, the seagulls flew inland, floating in the air like white porcelain kites, blinking at him with beady eyes. Sometimes, the woman in the next suite stepped onto her balcony to sun herself. Her selection of bikinis was impressive.

Cole's name was on the door, but Joe Pike was his partner, as well as his friend. They bought the agency the same year Pike left the LAPD and Cole was licensed by the state of California as a private investigator.

That morning, the sky was milky, but bright, cool, but not chilly, and the French doors were open so Cole could enjoy the air. Cole was wearing a killer Jams World aloha shirt (colors for the day: sunburst and lime), khaki cargo pants, and an Italian suede shoulder holster of impeccable design, said holster currently gunless. Cole was wearing the holster in hopes the woman next door would emerge in her latest bikini, see it, and swoon, but so far, Cole was zero for two: no woman, no swooning.

Twenty minutes later, Cole was balancing his checkbook when Pike arrived. Cole didn't hear the door open or close. This was just how Pike moved. As if he was so used to moving quietly he no longer touched the earth.

Cole pushed the checkbook aside, letting Pike see his irritation.

'So I'm sitting here, the door opens, and these cops walk in, badge, badge, badge. Three of them, so I know it's important. They say, what do I know about Frank Meyer? I say, who? They say, Meyer was a merc with your boy Pike. I say, okay, and? They say, Meyer and his family were shot to death. I don't know what to say to that, but that's when the alpha cop, a guy named Terrio, asked what I knew about your personal relationship with Meyer, and whether you had a business relationship. I said, brother, I have never heard that name before.'

Cole watched as Pike settled into a spot against the wall. Pike rarely sat when he was at their office. He leaned against the wall.

Pike said, 'No reason you would. Frank was one of my guys. From before.'

'Terrio told me they had reason to believe this crew hit Meyer because he had cash or drugs at his home.'

'Terrio's wrong. He believes the other six victims were crooked, so he's gunning for Frank.'

Cole frowned, feeling even less in the know.

'Other six?'

'Frank's home was the seventh hit in a string. Same crew, working the Westside and Encino. They've been ripping off criminals.'

'Terrio left out that part. So did the paper.'

After Terrio left, Cole had searched the L.A. *Times* website and local news stations for their coverage of the murders. The *Times* had provided the most information, describing Frank Meyer as a successful, self-made businessman. No mention was made of his past as a professional military contractor, but maybe that hadn't been known at the time the article was written. A detective named Stan Watts was quoted, saying he believed a professional home invasion crew numbering between three and four men entered the home between eight and ten P.M., with robbery as the likely motive. Watts provided no details about what might have been stolen.

Cole had printed out the article, and now pushed it toward Pike, but Pike didn't look at it.

Cole said, 'If Terrio's wrong, then what did these people go there to steal?'

Pike took a sheet of notepaper and a cell phone from his pocket, and placed them on Cole's desk.

'I found a connection Terrio doesn't know about.'

Cole listened as Pike told him about a recently released criminal named Jamal Johnson and his cousin, Rahmi. Pike told him about a new Malibu, and that Jamal told Rahmi his crew bought scores from someone in the Serbian mob. Pike was in the middle of telling it when Cole raised a hand, stopping him.

'Waitaminute. SIS is watching this guy, and you broke into his place?'

'Yes.'

'That's insane.'

Pike tossed the phone to Cole.

'Rahmi's phone. Jamal's number is in the memory. Maybe you could ID the service provider, and backtrace Jamal's call list. We might be able to find him through his friends.'

Cole put the phone aside, and picked up the note.

'I'll see what I can do. How are these people connected?'

'Ana Markovic was the Meyers' nanny. She died this morning. Rina was her sister. She has a friend called Yanni. I'm not sure how he spells it. Rina was at the hospital before her sister died. She was standing guard because she believed the people who shot her sister might come around to finish the job.'

'You think she knows something?'

'They're Serbian. Rahmi says his cousin hooked up with a Serbian gangster. What are the odds?'

Cole thought about it. Los Angeles has always had a small Serbian population, but, just as the Russian and Armenian populations increased after the Soviet Union collapsed, the Serbian and expatriate Yugoslavian populations shot up after the conflicts in the nineties. Criminals and organized gangsters arrived along with everyone else, and L.A. now had significant numbers of criminal gang sets from all over Eastern Europe. But even with the increasing populations, the numbers of East Europeans remained statistically small. A Latin, African-American, or Anglo connection would have meant nothing. A Balkan connection in Westwood was worth checking out.

Cole placed the note with the phone.

'Your pal Rina, you think she'd talk to me?'

'No.'

Cole stared at the information Pike had cribbed onto the sheet. It wasn't much.

'Where did Ana live?'

'With Frank.'

'Maybe she had another place for the weekends.'

'I don't know.'

'I guess you and I aren't up to speed on the nanny lifestyle.'

'No.'

The classic Pike conversation.

'What I'm getting at here is that talking to people who knew this girl might be a good place to start. I'll need the names of her friends, maybe some phone numbers, things like that. If the sister won't talk to us, can we get into the crime scene?'

'I'll take care of it. Also, John Chen is on the SID team. He's running the physical evidence.'

Cole nodded. Chen was good, and Chen had worked with them before. Cole would call him after Pike left.

Two seagulls appeared in the empty blue nothing outside the glass. Cole watched them float on their invisible sea, tiny heads turning. One of them suddenly dropped out of sight. His partner watched the other fall, then folded his wings and followed.

Cole said, 'And Terrio doesn't know about Jamal and the Serbian connection?'

'No.'

'You going to tell him?'

'No. I want to find them before the police.'

Pike was staring at him, but his face was as empty of expression as always, the dark glasses like two black holes cut into space. The stillness in Pike was amazing.

Cole looked for the gulls again, but they were still gone. The winter sky was a milky blue, just edging into gray from the haze. Cole got up, went around his desk to the little fridge under the Pinocchio clock, and took out a bottle of water. He offered it to Pike. Pike shook his head once. Cole brought it back to his desk.

Cole glanced at the news story again, the one Pike had not touched. The second paragraph, where the names of the murdered victims were given. Frank, Cindy, Frank, Jr., Joe. The youngest was Joey. Executed. The word chosen by the journalist to describe what had happened. *Executed.* Cole had not stopped thinking about that word since he read the story. He knew better, but the writer was good. She had burned a few words onto a blank page, forcing Cole and her other readers to imagine the scene, and there it was. A black steel muzzle to the head. Clenched eyes, tears squeezing through stitched lids, maybe the sobbing and screaming, and the short, sharp *BAM* that ends all of it. The sobbing stops, the face grows serene as its lines relax in death, and all that remains is the mother's screams. Cindy would have been last. Cole folded the article and pushed it aside, wondering the thing he had been wondering since reading the article yesterday – whether or not the youngest boy, Joey, had been named after Pike.

Who was Frank Meyer?

One of my guys.

Cole had learned enough over the years to know what was meant. Pike had been able to hand-pick his guys, which meant he chose people he respected. Then, because they were Pike's guys, he would have arranged for their gear, and meals, and equipment, made sure they were paid on time, that their contracts were honored, and that they were properly equipped for the job at hand. He would have taken care of them, and they would have taken care of him, and he would not have let them sell their lives cheaply.

Who was Frank Meyer?

One of my guys.

Cole said, 'I don't need to hide from what you're going to do. You haven't done it yet. Maybe things will change. Maybe the police will find them first.'

Pike said, 'Mm.'

Cole studied Pike, and thought that Pike was studying him back, but maybe Pike was just looking. Cole never knew what Pike was thinking. Maybe Pike was just waiting for Cole to say something. Pike was very patient.

Cole said, 'I want you to hear this, and think about it. I don't think Terrio is necessarily wrong. If I were him, I would be looking at Meyer, too. What if it turns out Frank isn't the man you knew? What if Terrio's right?'

The flat black lenses seemed to bore into Cole as if they were portholes into another dimension.

'He's still one of my guys.'

The seagulls reappeared, drawing Cole's eye. They hung in the air, tiny heads flicking left and right as they glanced at each other. Then, as one, the two birds looked at Cole. They stared with their merciless eyes, then banked away. Gone.

Cole said, 'You see that?'

But when Cole looked over, Pike was gone, too.

13

TWO MEN AND A WOMAN in dark blue business suits were walking up Frank's drive when Pike cruised past. A senior uniformed officer with the stars on her collar that marked her as a deputy chief was gesturing as the three civilians followed. Downtown brass giving a few big-shots the tour.

A single black-and-white command car was parked at the curb, indicating the officer had driven the civilians herself. No other official vehicles were present. Three days after the murders, the lab rats had found everything there was to find. Pike knew the house would remain sealed until the science people were certain they wouldn't need additional samples. When they gave the okay, the detectives would release the house to Frank and Cindy's estate, and someone would notify Ana Markovic's family that they could claim her possessions. Pike wondered if Ana's parents lived in Serbia, and if they had been notified. He wondered if they were flying in to claim their daughter's body, and whether they could afford it.

Pike circled a nearby park, slowly winding his way back to Frank's. He approached from the opposite direction this time, and parked two blocks up the street with an easy, eyes-forward view of the command car.

The senior officer and her guests stayed inside for forty-two minutes. This was much longer than Pike would have expected, but then they came back down the drive, climbed into the command car, and drove away.

Pike waited five minutes, then pulled forward to park across from Frank's. An older woman with white hair was walking a little white dog. The dog was short, and old, with a heavy body and eyes that had been playful before they were tired. Pike let them pass, then walked up Frank's drive, and entered through the side gate as he had two nights before.

Someone had taped a piece of cardboard over the broken pane in the French door. Pike pushed the cardboard aside and let himself in. After four days, the blood pooled on the floors had soured and mildewed. Pike ignored the smell, and went to Ana Markovic's room.

The handmade Valentine poster made by Frank's boys, the posters of European soccer players, the tiny desk with its clutter of magazines and laptop computer all remained as Pike remembered. The screen saver was still playing – a young Hawaiian surf stud riding a wave that swallowed him, only to be resurrected and swallowed again in an endless loop. Pike closed the screen, unplugged the power cord, and placed the computer by the door. He searched through the drawers and clutter, hoping for some kind of address book or cell phone, but found neither. Instead, he found a high school yearbook and some birthday and holiday cards. He put the cards in the yearbook, and the yearbook with the computer.

Pike was bothered by the absence of a phone. He looked under and around the desk, then pulled a mound of sheets and a comforter from the bed. He found rumpled clothes, two open boxes of cookies, an open box of Pampers, some magazines, three partially consumed bottles of water, a paperback novel about vampires, an unopened bag of Peanut M&M's, and a single unused tampon still in its wrapper. He found the messy clutter of a young woman who liked to shove everything in the corner, but no phone. Pike lifted the mattress. Nothing.

Pike realized he had not found a purse or wallet, either. It occurred to him that her phone had probably been in her purse, and the paramedics might have taken her purse along when they rushed her to the hospital. Pike made a mental note to tell Cole. Cole could check to see if this was what happened, and whether or not the hospital still had the purse in their possession.

The tiny room held a closet smaller than a phone booth. The bathroom was across the hall. Pike went through the closet first, then the bath. The closet floor was deep with clothes, shoes, and an empty backpack. A corkboard had been tacked to the inside of the door and was covered with snapshots, cards, pictures cut from magazines, ticket stubs, and drawings. Ana was in most of the pictures, but not all, posing with people her own age, everyone smiling or mugging for the camera. Most of them had probably been taken in the past couple of years, and a few had writing. *Luv, Krissy. You da bomb! BFF!* Like that.

Pike didn't take them all. He selected pictures that appeared the most recent, and those with handwritten notes and names, and tucked them into the yearbook. He had just crossed the hall into the bathroom when he heard a car door. He picked up the computer and yearbook, hurried to the front of the house, and saw two unmarked Crown Vics. Terrio and Deets were already out of their car, and two more detectives were climbing out of the second car. Terrio and Deets went to Pike's Jeep, then scowled toward the house.

Pike left the way he had entered, went around to the side of the house, then slipped through the hedges to the wall. He didn't go over. He stripped a .25 caliber Beretta from his ankle and a Colt .357 Python from his waist, then chinned himself up to see what was on the other side. He dropped the computer, yearbook, and guns into a soft cushion of calla lilies, then let himself out the side gate onto the drive.

Terrio and the others were halfway up the drive when Pike stepped out, letting them see him.

Terrio said, 'You forget what that yellow tape means?'

'I wanted to see what happened.'

'You have no business seeing what happened. Did you enter the premises?'

'Yes.'

'Why?'

'To see.'

Deets grinned at the other detectives.

'I like it. We have breaking and entering, illegal entry, interfering with a lawful investigation. How about adding burglary, Pike? Did you take anything?'

Pike spread his arms, offering to let them search.

'See for yourself.'

Deets moved behind Pike.

'Good idea. I've heard about this guy, Jack. Never know what he might be packing.'

The younger detective ran his hands over Pike's legs, pockets, and belt line, but his grin collapsed when he found nothing.

Terrio didn't look so happy about it, either, but he tipped his head toward the house, speaking to the other detectives.

'I'll catch up with you. I'm going to walk Mr. Pike to his car.'

Terrio didn't say anything more until they reached the street. He leaned against Pike's Jeep. This bothered Pike, but he didn't object.

Terrio studied Frank's house for a moment.

'Why'd you come here?'

'To see. Like I told you.'

'That why you went to the hospital?'

Pike wondered how Terrio knew.

'That's right.'

'The girl died this morning. That makes twelve homicides. If you think I'm spending all my resources digging up dirt on your friend, you're wrong.'

Pike didn't respond. He figured Terrio would make his point soon enough.

'I've got the mayor, the police commissioner, and the brass on my arm. I've got a rising body count, and no certain suspects. If you know something that could help, you should tell me.'

'Can't help you.'

Terrio stared at Pike for a moment, then laughed.

'Sure. Sure you can't. You're here because you want to see.'

Pike's cell phone buzzed. It buzzed so loudly that Terrio stepped away from the Jeep.

'Why don't you get it, Pike? Might be important.'

Pike didn't move. The buzzing stopped when the call went to voice mail.

Terrio said, 'Get out of here.'

Pike watched him head toward the house. Pike knew Terrio would glance back when he reached Frank's door, so he got into his Jeep and pulled away. He drove far enough so he couldn't be seen from Frank's house, then jogged back through the neighbor's yard to the calla lily bed, recovered his guns and the things he had taken, and walked away.

14

PIKE DROVE TO THE far side of the park before he pulled over to check his phone. Cole had left a message, asking him to call.

When Cole answered, Pike said, 'Me.'

'You wanted to know how a gangster could be connected to the nanny?'

Cole was being dramatic, and continued without waiting for an answer.

'Here's a hint. Your girl Rina works for the Serbian mob.'

'Ana's sister.'

'That's right. Her sister is the connection.'

Pike watched the children in the park. He watched the toddlers run with short, awkward steps, and little ones try to stack blocks, and fail, because their tiny hands were too small to hold the blocks well.

'You've been on this less than two hours.'

'Am I not the World's Greatest Detective?'

Pike glanced at his watch.

'Ninety-two minutes.'

'Karina Markovic, also known as Karen Mark, age twenty-six, arrested twice for prostitution, once for assault, and once for robbery – a john claimed she stole his wallet. Total jail time served is nine days. She was busted in a Serbian sex crib up in the Valley. She's been in this country for at least eight years, and she's probably here illegally.'

The San Fernando Valley was the porn capital of the world, and the Russian gangs discovered it as soon as they arrived. The sex trade was an easy moneymaker, but American women were difficult to control, so the Russians brought Russian girls over, and each new wave of East European gang sets followed the pattern – from the Ukrainians to the Armenians to the Serbs.

Pike said, 'Does she have warrants?'

'None at this time, but that doesn't mean there won't be. Her license plate came back as inactive, which means the plate is not in active registration through the DMV.'

'Her car is stolen.'

'Stolen, or built from stripped parts. The Eastern Bloc gangs are into that – they build them from stolen parts, and ship them home. She might not know it was stolen. She might not even know the plate is no good. But the apartment address you gave me? Definitely not hers. The registered tenant is one Janic-with-a-J Pevich.'

Cole pronounced Janic with a *y*. Yanni.

'He have a record?'

'Nothing that I found, but the day is young.'

Pike lowered the phone, but did not move. He watched the children playing, and thought that now he understood why Rina Markovic was armed and afraid. The Serbian mob owned her, and someone in the Serbian mob had killed her sister. Pike wondered if this was the fourth man.

Either way, Rina knew who pulled the trigger.

Pike made his way toward Yanni's apartment, wondering if Rina was there or if she had already moved on. Pike wasn't worried about it. Even if she had gone, he could make Yanni tell him where to find her.

Pike cruised through the small visitors' parking lot where Yanni's truck had been parked before, but now it was gone. He took a space at the end of the lot, and tucked the Python under his belt. He didn't bother to hide the pry bar.

Pike waited until two joggers passed, then hopped the gate into the residents' parking lot. Rina Markovic's car was still in the parking spot for apartment 2205.

Pike left the parking garage like any other resident and made his way along a sidewalk between the buildings. The grounds were large, with eight separate three-story buildings laid out like four 'equals' signs end to end in a line. The buildings followed a curve of land between the river channel and a residential street, and were pleasantly shaded with tall gray eucalyptus trees and thick oleanders. Pike searched almost ten minutes before he realized the apartment number wasn't 2205, but was apartment 205 in building number 2. He found the apartment in the second-to-last building.

It was quiet at the rear buildings, with all the daytime activity around the pool and up front by the mailboxes and parking garages.

Pike climbed a flight of stairs, found 205, and listened at the door. The apartment was silent, so he covered the peephole and knocked. When no one answered, he knocked again, harder, but still heard nothing.

Pike checked the area to make sure no one was watching, then wedged the end of the pry bar into the jamb where the dead bolt was seated. The door had more play than he expected, so Pike pressed harder, and realized the dead bolt wasn't locked. He gave the pry bar a hard shove, and the jamb gave at the knob lock. Pike stepped inside, then closed the door, having to force it past the splintered jamb.

Pike found himself in a small, simply furnished apartment that was dim because of the pulled curtains. He was in the living room, facing an open kitchen to his right and a bedroom to his left. The kitchen and bedroom were separated by a door that was probably a bathroom. The bedroom door was open, but the bathroom door was closed. The shower was running.

Pike drew the Python as he crossed to the bedroom. He made sure the bedroom was empty, then moved to the kitchen as the shower stopped. Quick glance into the kitchen, then he turned toward the bathroom, waiting, the gun hanging along his leg.

The door opened an inch, then suddenly opened wider with a billow of steamy air. Rina came out with her eyes down, vigorously toweling her hair. She was naked, with very white skin and a fleshy body. In the instant before she realized she was not alone, Pike studied her, seeing that corded pink scars crisscrossed her belly as if she had been clawed. The scars were so deep they puckered, and Pike knew by their faded color they were old.

Then she saw him. She shrieked and lurched sideways, bunching the towel to cover herself.

Pike raised the gun enough to make sure she saw it, but did not point it at her.

'Who killed them?'

She was as still as an ice sculpture. Her white face paled to translucence, her gaunt cheeks and hollow eyes highlighted by points of blue. She stood with the towel, water leaking across her shoulders and down her legs.

Pike said, 'Who?'

'Get out of here. I will call the police.'

'Who?'

'You are insane. I will scream.'

She glanced at the door just as Pike heard the knob, and Yanni stepped through carrying what looked like a large gym bag. He was so big he filled the door, and had to tip sideways to enter.

A scowl flickered on the big man's face even as he dropped the bag and charged. Rina shouted something in the other language, but Pike simply waited as he watched Yanni come.

Yanni came hard and large the way big men do, trusting his size to do everything for him, so Pike knew Yanni had never been properly trained. He came in with his arms up and out, planning to drive Pike into the wall. Pike was so far ahead of the play he saw the steps of what was about to happen as if they were preordained.

He let Yanni reach him, then pushed Yanni's hand down to hook his arm. Pike dropped under and brought the arm with him, rolling the big man over his hip, and put Yanni flat on his back. Pike hit him on the forehead with the Python. Pike hit him again, harder, and this time the skin split deep and Yanni's eyes turned glassy.

It took less than two seconds, but when Pike glanced up Rina was already in the bedroom.

He reached her as she turned from the bed with the pistol, caught it, and twisted it away. She didn't quit easily. She punched at him and tried to claw his eyes as Pike dragged her backward to the living room so she could see Yanni. Her elbows cut into him, and she stomped at his feet and made grunting noises while trying to rake his eyes.

Pike said, 'Stop.'

Yanni was still down, blinking in confusion at the blood filling his eyes.

'I know you know. The mob owns you. You know who did this.'

She fought even harder, whipping her head from side to side. She was strong. Muscles like rope under the pale skin.

Pike squeezed so tight that something in her cracked. He hammered back the Python.

'I won't ask you again.'

'Yes.'

'Yes what?'

'I *know*. I know who killed them. I know who did this.'

'Who?'

'My husband.'

Pike held her trapped in his arm, the water from her hair soaking into his skin, her chest heaving.

15

PIKE TOLD HER TO wrap herself in the towel, then put her on the couch. She glanced at Yanni, still flat on his back.

'What about him?'

'He's bleeding.'

'We should do something.'

'After you tell me.'

She didn't like that, and said something to Yanni in Serbian.

Pike said, 'English.'

Yanni rubbed stupidly at his face, smearing the blood on his arm. Pike slipped her pistol into his pocket, then positioned himself so he could see both of them at the same time. If Yanni tried to get up, Pike wanted to know.

Pike said, 'Who's your husband?'

'Michael Darko. You know this name?'

'No. He's a thief?'

She smirked, as if Pike was an idiot. She was cool

and aloof, even naked on the couch with Yanni bleeding on the floor.

'Please. He is a boss of thieves.'

'Okay, the boss. Was he your boss when you were arrested for prostitution?'

A tint of pink colored her cheeks.

'Yes. He bring me here to America. I work for him then.'

'Okay, the boss of thieves is a pimp. This boss sent a crew to Frank's house?'

'Yes.'

'Did he go with them?'

'Maybe he go, maybe not. I was not there.'

'What did he go there to steal?'

'My baby.'

Her answer hung in the air like a frozen moment, as surprising as if they had gone to steal a nuclear bomb. Pike stared at her, thinking about what she had said, her gaunt face as smooth as porcelain, her eyes as hard as marble.

'Frank and Cindy had your baby?'

'My sister. I give him to my sister when I find out Michael is going to take him. I hide him with her until we can leave.'

Pike tried to get his head around it. Then he remembered seeing the box of Pampers in Ana's room. He had seen it, but thought nothing of it because it was just another box. There had been no crib, or bassinet, or baby food – just the one box of Pampers.

'A baby.'

'Yes.'

'How old?'

'Ten months.'

She sat up straighter, pulling her shoulders back and chest out.

'I look good, yes? I do much hard work.'

'Michael and his crew, they've invaded six other homes. They've killed other people. He have kids in those places, too?'

Her eyes flashed, angry.

'I don't know nothing about other things. All I know is this. Michael want his child. He take him back to Serbia.'

Terrio hadn't mentioned a kidnapping. Neither had Chen or anyone else, and then Pike realized why.

'You didn't tell the police, did you?'

'Of course not. They cannot help me.'

Of course not.

Yanni was waking up. He touched his face, then looked at the blood on his palm as if he wasn't quite sure what it was. Pike moved the gun toward him.

'This one your boyfriend?'

'No. He want to be, but, no. I hide with him when I hear Michael wants the baby, but then I get scared and I have much to do, so I give the baby to Ana.'

Yanni stirred. A knee came up, then he rolled onto his side, trying to rise.

Pike said, 'Tell him to stay down.'

'In English?'

'In whatever he understands. Tell him if he gets up, I'll shoot him.'

'Would you?'

'Yes.'

She spoke the language, and Yanni turned toward Pike. Pike showed him the gun. Yanni sighed, then rested his head on the floor. His face was a mess.

Pike said, 'I want to be clear. Your husband, this guy Michael Darko, he went to Frank's house to steal his kid from your sister?'

'Yes.'

There it was. Michael Darko was the fourth man.

'What happened that night, it had nothing to do with Frank. It was all about taking your kid.'

'Michael is going back to Serbia. He wants to raise his son there. Me, he wants to kill.'

'Why?'

'I am nothing. Do you see? A whore he made pregnant. He does not want his son to be the child of a whore.'

'So he murdered your sister and an entire family?'

'My sister was nothing to him. Your friends, nothing. I am nothing, too. He will kill me if he can. He will kill you, too.'

Pike said, 'We'll see.'

He closed his eyes and saw the bodies: Frank, Cindy, Little Frank, Joe. He saw the oily, irregular pools of blood. The Day-Glo green yarn that traced the bullets' paths.

Collateral damage.

Bystanders in a domestic dispute.

Pike took a slow breath, and felt as if his world had

gently shifted. He ran a hand over his head, the short hair stiff and hard. Everything realigned itself into a more comfortable and familiar arrangement, but Frank and his family were still dead. Someone had violated their home. Someone had hurt them. Someone would pay.

Pike considered the woman on the couch, and realized Frank had not been expecting what happened.

'You didn't warn them. Frank didn't know this lunatic was after your kid.'

She glanced away for the first time, not quite so cold or aloof.

'No. We lie to them.'

She said it that simply. No, we lie to them. Then she went on.

'We tell them I have emergency. Is just for a few days, and the lady there, she is nice. I was making arrangements for to get to Seattle. A few days, that's all, then we will go to Seattle. No one know Ana work for these people. How could he find out?'

Collateral damage.

Frank, Cindy, the boys. At least in the desert, Frank had seen the tanks coming.

'Stay on the couch.'

Pike went into the kitchen. He found ice in the freezer, and plastic trash bags under the sink. He cracked a tray of cubes into a trash bag, then dropped it on Yanni.

'Put this on your face. Tell him to put it on his face.'

Yanni said, 'I know what you say.'

Pike stepped around him and returned to the woman. He thought about putting his pistol away, but decided to keep it out.

'Is Darko still in Los Angeles?'

'I think yes. It is hard to know.'

Pike wasn't thrilled by her uncertainty, but at least she seemed willing to cooperate.

'Let's say he is. If he's here, where can I find him?'

'I don't know. If I knew where he was I would have the boy, yes? I would shoot him, and take back the boy.'

'Where does he live?'

'I don't know. He move a lot.'

'How can you not know where your husband lives?'

She closed her eyes. Her hard face softened, but the corners of her mouth seemed bitter.

'He has not been my husband for many months.'

Pike thought about it, then waved the gun at her belly.

'He do that?'

She looked down and opened the towel, not giving a thought that she was naked. Or maybe she had. Her pale body looked softer now; her belly creased awkwardly at the scars because she was seated. Her breasts were small, but firm. She was a good-looking woman. A little too hard and cold, but maybe that came from the belly. These weren't surgical scars. Someone had wanted to hurt her, and had likely been trying to kill her. Pike wondered who, and why, and how long ago it had happened. She had been cut deep, and the cuts had hurt. Pike liked it that she wasn't self-conscious about the scars.

She considered herself before closing the towel.

'No, not Michael. He make me pregnant after the scars. They turned him on.'

'You have a picture of him?'

'No. He does not have his picture taken. He has no pictures.'

'How about a phone?'

'No.'

Pike frowned. Everything was no.

'What if the kid got sick? What if you needed something?'

'These things are paid for. There are other people I tell.'

She shrugged like Pike was an idiot for not knowing the ways of the world.

Pike thought hard, trying to come at it from a different direction. Either she was lying, or she knew almost nothing about him.

'Where would he take the kid?'

'Serbia.'

'Not Serbia. Now. Before he goes to Serbia. He has to keep a ten-month-old baby somewhere. '

'A woman, I think, but there are many such women. Michael is not going to change the diaper. He is not going to wake all night to feed.'

'Another whore?'

Her eyes flashed, and Pike felt bad for saying it so harshly. He asked again.

'Does he have a girlfriend? Is he living with another woman?'

'I don't know. I am going to find out.'

Pike studied her. She was going to find out. She was going to take back her child. She.

'It was a mistake not to tell the police. You still can. You should.'

Yanni mumbled something in Serbian, but Rina snapped back, cutting him off.

Pike said, 'English.'

'What will they do, deport me? I have been arrested many times. I am not here with the papers.'

'They won't ask if you're a citizen. And they won't care about your record. Your child was kidnapped. The kidnappers murdered five people. Michael's crew has murdered twelve people, altogether. That's what the police care about.'

'You don't know anything.'

'I know the police. I used to be a policeman.'

The remains of her smile grew nasty.

'Well, let me ask you this, Mr. Policeman-used-to-be. When I find this man, you think the police will let me shoot him in the head? That is what I am going to do.'

Pike thought, this woman means it.

Rina seemed to read his thoughts, and the sharp smile grew edges.

'This is how we do it, old-school, where I am from. Do you see?'

'Are all Serbian women like you?'

'Yes.'

Pike glanced at Yanni, still with the bag of ice on his face. Yanni nodded.

Pike looked back at the woman.

'Maybe you should come with me. I can put you someplace safe.'

'I don't know nothing about you, and I got a lot of work to do. I will stay with my friend.'

Pike holstered the Python. He took her Ruger from his pocket. It wasn't a fancy gun, but it was serviceable and deadly. He took out the magazine, then worked the slide to unload the chamber just as he had at the hospital. He thumbed the loose cartridge into the magazine, then tossed the gun and magazine onto the couch. They bounced against her thigh.

She said, 'You aren't going to call the police?'

'No. I'm going to help you.'

When he took out his cell phone, Rina jumped up.

'You say no police!'

'I'm not calling the police.'

Pike called Elvis Cole.

16

MICHAEL DARKO. Pike now had a name, but he knew nothing about Michael Darko, and needed to know more. It was important to understand the enemy before you engaged him, and impossible to find him without knowing his patterns and needs.

When Cole arrived, Yanni was seated on a dinette chair, holding a bloody towel to his head. Rina was dressed, but the Ruger was still by her on the couch. Pike introduced them by pointing at each and saying their names.

Cole eyed Yanni, then the gun, then Rina. Rina eyed him back, cool and suspicious.

'What is this one, another used-to-be policeman?'

'He's a private investigator. He's good at finding people.'

'Then let him get started. We have wasted much time.'

Cole took a seat near the couch as Pike sketched out everything Rina had told him about Darko, how the baby came to be with Ana, the kidnapping, and Rina's intention to take back her child. When Pike was recounting that part of it, Cole looked over at Rina. When Cole looked, she tapped the pistol nestled against her leg.

Cole said, 'What's your son's name?'

'*Petar*. Peter.'

'You have a picture?'

Pike thought her face darkened, but she stared at Cole glumly until Yanni mumbled something in Serbian.

Pike said, 'English. I'm not going to tell you again.'

Rina pushed up from the couch.

'Yes, I have picture.'

She went into the bedroom, dug through her bag, then returned with a snapshot. It showed a smiling baby with wispy red hair. The baby was on a green carpet, reaching toward the camera. Pike didn't know much about babies, but this one didn't look ten months old.

She said, 'When I leave apartment, I leave fast. This is only picture I have. You cannot have it.'

Pike said, 'He doesn't look almost a year old.'

She scowled like he was an idiot.

'You are stupid? He is ten months and three days now. In picture, he is six months, one week, and one day. Is only picture I have.'

Cole arched his eyebrows at Pike.

'What's wrong with you? Can't you tell how old a baby is?'

Pike wasn't sure if Cole was joking or not. Cole turned back to the woman.

'I can scan a copy on my computer, and give this one back. Would that be okay?'

She seemed to think about it, then nodded.

'That would be okay.'

Cole put the picture aside, and turned back to ask more questions.

'Why did you have to leave so fast?'

'Michael was coming.'

'For Peter.'

'Michael say he want the boy, I say no, he say ha. I know what Michael thinks. He kill me, he take the boy, he pretend the whore-mother never exist.'

'So you stashed Peter with your sister while you went to find a place to live in Seattle.'

'Yes.'

'How did Michael find them?'

'I don't know.'

'Would Ana have called him, maybe trying to work things out for you?'

Rina laughed, but it was bitter and wise.

'She would never do that. She is scared of these people. I keep her away from all that.'

Cole glanced at Pike, not understanding.

'These people?'

Yanni spoke again, and another brief, incomprehensible conversation ensued. Pike stood, and Yanni immediately raised both hands.

'She means the thieves. Ana is little girl when they

come. Rina keep Ana away from these men.'

Rina was nodding, her eyes narrowed and hard, and then she picked up where Yanni left off.

'She is not to be a whore. She is not to work for Michael. I make her go to school, and have normal friends in her life, and to be a good girl.'

Pike said, 'You protected her.'

Rina glanced out the window.

'Not so well.'

Cole cleared his throat, pulling them back.

'Who knew Ana had the baby?'

'No one.'

'Yanni knew.'

Yanni raised his hands again and shook his head.

'I not tell anyone. I am with Rina every minute.'

Rina made an impatient wave.

'Yanni is good. I don't know how Michael find her there. I cannot understand.'

Cole said, 'Let's get back to Michael. This guy is your husband, but you don't know where he lives?'

'Nobody knows. That is how he makes his life.'

'No address, no picture, not even a phone?'

'He get new phone every week. The numbers change. What do you want me to say?'

Rina scowled at Pike.

'When is he going to start all this finding he is so good at?'

Pike said, 'Michael hides. We get that. But you know more about him than anyone else here. We need information so we have something to work with.'

She spread her hands.

'I am anxious to get started.'

Cole said, 'Who are his friends?'

'He has no friends.'

'Where does his family live?'

'Serbia.'

'I meant his relatives here.'

'He leave them all in Serbia.'

'Okay. What about *your* friends? Maybe one of them can help us find Michael.'

'I have no friends. They are all afraid of Michael.'

Cole looked over at Pike again.

'I can't write fast enough to keep up.'

Rina squinted at him.

'Is the great finder of people making fun of me?'

Pike cleared his throat.

'We need some names. Who does Michael work with? Who works for him? Even if you don't know them, you must've heard the names mentioned, time to time.'

Rina frowned at Yanni as if looking for guidance. Yanni glanced at Pike, afraid to say anything. Pike nodded, giving permission. They had a brief conversation that sounded more like an argument, and then they both started spitting out names. The names were difficult to understand, and even more difficult to spell, but Cole scratched them into his notebook.

When Cole finished with the names, he looked up, and seemed hopeful.

'Has Darko ever been arrested? Here in L.A.?'

'I don't know. I don't think so, but I don't know. He has been here much longer than me.'

Cole glanced over at Pike, arching his eyebrows again.

'Keep your fingers crossed on that one. I'll check out Darko and these other guys, see if they're in the system. If Darko's been arrested, we might get lucky here. The one person you can't lie to about where you live or what you own is the bail bondsman.'

Pike knew this to be true from his time as an officer. Criminals lie to everyone about everything. They would give phony names, ages, and addresses to the police, the courts, each other, and even their own lawyers, but they could not lie to a bail bondsman. A bondsman would not post a bond without collateral, and if a bondsman could not confirm that the applicant legally owned what he claimed to own, that applicant stayed in jail.

Cole continued the questioning, but she didn't know very much more. Darko paid for everything in cash, used no credit cards that were not stolen, and made Rina pay all the bills for herself and the baby from her own checking account, which he then reimbursed in cash. Phones changed, addresses changed, locations changed, and cars changed. He was a man who left no trails and lived a hidden life.

Pike said, 'How were you planning to find him?'

She shrugged as if there were only one way, and they should have gotten around to it sooner.

'I would watch for the money.'

Cole and Pike traded a glance, then Cole turned back to her.

'How does he make his money?'

'Sex. He has the girls. He has the people who steal the big trucks –'

'Hijackers? Trucks filled with TVs, clothes, things like that?'

'Yes. He has the people who steal the credit card information. He sells the bad gasoline. He has the strip clubs and bars.'

Pike said, 'You know where these places are?'

'Some. I mostly know the girls.'

Cole glanced up from his notes.

'You know where he keeps the girls?'

'I don't know to say the address. I can show you.'

Now Cole glanced over, and this time he stood. Pike followed him to the far side of the room, where Cole lowered his voice. Both Rina and Yanni were watching.

'Did you find anything of her sister's?'

Pike told him what he found – the laptop, the year-book, a few other things. All out in the Jeep.

Cole said, 'Good. I want to check out her story. Just because she tells us this stuff doesn't make it real.'

'I'll put everything in your car when I leave.'

'Also, I want to see what I can find out about this guy, Darko. If she's giving it to us straight about him, then I probably know someone on LAPD who can help.'

Pike knew someone, too, though not on LAPD, and

now Pike wanted to see him.

From the couch, Rina said, 'I don't like all these whispers.'

Pike turned to face her.

'You're going to take a ride with him. Show him whatever you know about Darko's businesses, and answer his questions.'

'Where are you going? What are you going to do?'

'I'm going to answer his questions, too.'

Pike glanced at Cole.

'You good?'

'Living the dream.'

Pike let himself out.

17

PIKE PLACED THE LAPTOP and other things he had taken from Ana's room in Cole's car, then headed back to his Jeep. As he was crossing the visitors' parking lot, a brown Nissan Sentra slowed by the entrance. Two Latin men in the front seats turned to check out the parking lot, and seemed to be looking at Pike's Jeep. Then the driver saw Pike. There was a slight hesitation, then the driver gestured angrily at his passenger, making as if they were in the middle of an argument and seeing Pike hadn't meant anything. Then the Sentra sped up and was gone.

Maybe it was something, but maybe not.

Troops in the desert called it spider-sense, after the movies about the Marvel comic book character, Spider-Man, how he senses something bad before it happens.

Pike's spider-sense tingled, but then the Sentra was gone. He tried to remember if he had seen a brown Sentra with two Latin guys earlier, but nothing came to mind.

Pike was in no hurry to leave. If the Sentra was waiting around the corner to follow him, they might get tired of waiting and come back to see what he was doing. Then Pike would have them.

Pike spent the next few minutes thinking about Michael Darko. Learning that Darko belonged to an EEOC gang set was a major break, mostly because it gave Pike direction. Los Angeles held the second largest collection of East European gangsters in the United States, most of whom were Russian. The fifteen republics of the former Soviet Union had all contributed gang sets to what most cops called Russian Organized Crime, whether they originally came from Russia or not. The Odessa Mafia was the largest set in L.A., followed by the Armenians, but smaller sets from Romania, Uzbekistan, Azerbaijan, Chechnya, and the rest of Eastern Europe had been arriving for years. Most had been criminals back in their home states, but some had done other things.

Pike called Jon Stone.

'How's your head?'

'Bugger off. My head's fine, bro. That's just another night for me.'

'Is Gregor still in L.A.?'

'It's George. He's George Smith now. You have to be careful with his name.'

'I remember. Is he here?'

'Got a new place over on La Brea. What do you want with George?'

'He might be able to help.'

'This thing with Frank?'

'An EOC gang is involved.'

'No shit?'

'Yes.'

Stone was silent for a moment, then gave Pike an address.

'Take your time getting there, okay? I'll talk to him first. You walk in cold, he might get the wrong idea.'

'I understand.'

La Brea Avenue starts at the foot of the Hollywood Hills, and runs south through the city to the Hollywood Park racetrack. A ten-block stretch of its length between Melrose and Wilshire was known as decorators' row because it was lined with everything from high-end custom furniture boutiques to Middle Eastern rug merchants to designer lighting and antique shops. The people who owned the stores came from all over the world, and sold to customers from all over the world, but not all of them were what they seemed.

Pike found a spot for his Jeep outside a flower shop a block south of Beverly Boulevard. Pike had watched for the Sentra on a meandering drive from the Valley, and now he checked for the Sentra again when he got out of his Jeep. The Sentra had probably been nothing more than two guys who thought they saw something they didn't, but Pike still had the creeped-out sensation of crosshairs on his back.

Pike didn't go into the florist. He walked south one and a half blocks to an antique-lighting store. The store was narrow, with so many ceiling lights and wall sconces filling the window that the place looked like a secondhand junk store. A chime tinkled when Pike entered.

The interior of the shop was as cluttered as the window; the walls festooned with sconces, and chandeliers and pendant lamps dripping from the ceiling like moss. Lamps of different sizes sprouted from every available surface like tropical plants in a jungle.

A man's voice said, 'Hello, Joseph.'

Took Pike a moment to find him, hidden behind the lamps like a hunter hidden by undergrowth.

'Gregor.'

'It's George now, please. Remember?'

'Sure. I'm sorry.'

George Smith materialized from between the lamps. Pike hadn't seen him in years, but he looked the same – shorter than Pike, and not as muscular, but with the sleek, strong build of a surfer, a surfer's tan, and pale blue eyes. George was one of the deadliest human beings Pike knew. A gifted sniper. An immaculate assassin.

George was Gregor Suvorov in those days, but had changed his name when he moved to Los Angeles. George Smith sounded as if he had grown up in Modesto, having what broadcasters called a 'general American' accent, but Gregor Suvorov had grown up in Odessa, Ukraine, where he enlisted in the Army of the Russian Federation, and spent a dozen years in the Russian Special Purpose Regiment known as the Spetsnaz GRU – the Russian version of the U.S.

Army's Special Forces – which was run by the KGB. The KGB gave special schooling to their brightest troopers, and Gregor was exceptionally bright. Hence, his fluency with English.

After combat tours in Chechnya and Afghanistan, he cashed in to the private contractor market, enjoyed his newfound money and freedoms, and opted for even more. He moved to Los Angeles, where he enjoyed the sun, sold collectible lamps, and worked for the Odessa Mafia.

George offered his hand, and Pike took it. Warm iron. George smiling, welcoming Pike into his store.

'Man, it's been forever. You good?'

'Good.'

'I was surprised when Jon called. But pleased. Watch your head. That's a deco Tiffany, circa 1923. Eight thousand to the trade.'

Pike dipped sideways to avoid the light. Despite being filled with lamps, the shop was dingy and dim, with shadows lurking in the corners. George probably liked it that way.

Pike said, 'Business good?'

'Excellent, thank you. I wish I had come to America sooner. I should have been born here, man. I'm telling you!'

'Not the lamp business. Your other business.'

'I knew what you meant. That business is good, too, both here and abroad.'

George still accepted special assignments outside of the Odessa work if the price was right, though his clients these days were almost always governments or political agencies. No one else could afford him.

Pike followed George to a desk at the rear of the shop where they could sit.

'Jon tell you why I'm here?'

'Yeah. Listen, I'm sorry about Frank. Really. I never met the dude, but I've heard good things.'

'You still involved with Odessa?'

George's smile flashed again.

'You wouldn't mind a quick scan, would you? Would that be all right?'

Pike spread his hands, saying scan all you want.

George took an RF scanner similar to the one Pike owned from his desk, and ran it over Pike from his sunglasses to his shoes. Pike didn't object. He would have been surprised if George hadn't checked him. When George was satisfied, he put the scanner away.

'Old habits.'

'No problem.'

'Would you like a cup of tea? I have the black tea. From Georgia. Not your Georgia – ours.'

Pike didn't want his tea and didn't want to chat.

'I'm good. You still in with the ROC, George?'

George pursed his lips. Annoyed. The deadliest man Pike knew was pissy.

'It's Odessa, and I'm not *in* with them. I'm not a *member*. I consult on a freelance basis. I'm my own boss.'

This seemed important to George, so Pike nodded.

'I understand.'

'That being said, if you want to discuss Odessa business, I can't.'

'I don't care about Odessa. I want to know about the Serbs.'

'So Jon told me. A hard people. Very tough. I fought them in Chechnya.'

'Not there. Here. Can you talk about the gang sets here in Los Angeles?'

George nodded, but a vagueness came to his eyes as if he had suddenly noticed something a thousand yards away.

'Shouldn't be a problem. They do their thing, Odessa is something else. Like with the Armenians. The same, but different.'

'You know of a Michael Darko?'

George rocked back in his chair, the body language telling Pike that George was uncomfortable talking about Darko.

'He killed your friend, Frank Meyer?'

'Looks that way.'

George grunted.

'I know who he is. A hard man.'

'What does hard mean?'

'You understand the word, *pakhan*?'

'No.'

'A boss. Middle management for now, but he's on the way up. These people aren't given their promotions, they take them. Like cannibals eating each other.'

Pike saw disdain in the pale eyes, and realized

George felt superior to the gangsters who employed him. Maybe this was why he was adamant that Pike understand he was an independent contractor, and not part of Odessa. All of them might be killers, but George had come out of Spetsnaz – the rest were just animals.

'What kind of crime does he do?'

'A finger in many pies, like all these guys. Girls and sex, hijacking, extorting his own people. He's aggressive, and trying to expand. Quick with the trigger.'

George made a pistol with his hand and pulled the trigger.

Pike said, 'Know where I can find him?'

'I don't.'

'A place of business? He must have some kind of front operation. He'd need that for taxes.'

'I'm sure he must, but this man is just a name to me. Like I said, different circles. I'm a lamp salesman.'

A lamp salesman who could put a bullet through your head from a thousand meters away. Then George continued.

'They have a nickname for him, the Shark. Did you know this?'

'No.'

'Could they be more dramatic? The Shark. He probably made this up for himself.'

George made quote marks in the air when he said 'the Shark,' and rolled his eyes.

'He is the Shark because he never stops moving, and he moves so no one can find him. This is not a loved man, even among the Serb sets.'

Pike grunted, now understanding why Rina didn't know where to find him. So far, her descriptions of Michael Darko matched with Gregor's.

Pike said, 'He's been using a home invasion crew to take out his competition. He used the same crew on Frank. I want to find them, and I want to find him.'

George laughed, full-bodied and deep.

'You got part of that wrong, buddy. He isn't taking out his competition. He's ripping off his partners. Why do you think this asshole has to keep moving?'

'You know about this?'

'Enough to keep tabs. If he wants to rip off his own business partners, good riddance. If he sends a crew to Odessa, they'll have to deal with me.'

Pike wondered if Darko was ripping off his partners because he was returning to Europe – get some quick cash, grab his kid, go.

'The tabs you keep include his crew?'

George shrugged, no big deal.

'Bangers from Compton.'

'Jamal Johnson?'

'Never heard of him.'

'A Compton offender who's come into recent wealth.'

'Is he a Crip?'

'I don't know.'

'A D-Block Crip called Moon Williams runs Darko's crew. Another dramatic name. Darko feeds him the targets. Williams splits the take.'

Pike felt a burn of excitement, as if he had taken a step closer.

'Moon Williams. You sure?'

George cupped a hand behind his ear as if he was listening.

'The KGB is everywhere. Also, Mr. Moon has been making much money recently, too. He spends it in a club owned by Odessa. Cristal champagne, the finest rock, and beautiful Russian women. He loves the Russian women. He loves to tell them what a badazz life-takin' nigga he is.'

George burst out laughing again, an obvious glee in his eyes. For George, people like Moon Williams were here so he would always have targets.

Pike said, 'Uh-huh. Does the KGB know where I can find him?'

George considered Joe for a moment, then lifted his desk phone, and punched in a number. George spoke Russian to whoever answered, and had a back-and-forth conversation that lasted several minutes. George was silent for a while in the middle of the conversation as if he had been put on hold. During that silence, he gazed at Pike with his pale blue eyes empty, never once blinking. Then he came back to life, whispered a single word in Russian, and hung up. When he looked at Pike again, he was somber.

'Jon told me you and Frank were close.'

'Yes.'

'So you have business with Mr. Darko.'

'If he's good for Frank's death, yes. Is that a problem?'

'So long as you stay with the Serbian sets, go with God, my friend.'

'More than one gun was fired that night.'

'I understand. Odessa won't like losing Mr. Williams. These girls go to work on him, he's an outrageous source of information.'

'I'm not asking permission, George.'

George smiled at the phone.

'That's probably the best way.'

George told him where to find Moon Williams, then stood to indicate their meeting was over.

They shook again, and Pike looked around the store. The lamps were old, and ornate, and each had been lovingly and delicately restored.

Pike said, 'Why lamps?'

George smiled softly, and now it was filled with warmth and sadness, and, Pike thought, more than a little loss.

'Oh, Joseph. There is so much darkness in the world. Why not bring light?'

Pike nodded.

'*Udachi*, my friend. Good luck.'

When Pike reached the door, he glanced back, but George was hidden by the lamps, wrapped in so many shadows the light could not reach him.

18

EVEN WITH HIS SUNGLASSES, Pike squinted against the glare, scanning the cars parked along both sides of La Brea. He stood with his back to George's door, searching until he was satisfied, then walked up the street to his Jeep. No Sentra.

Pike located Moon Williams's address on his Thomas Guide map, then pulled into traffic.

According to George, Earvin 'Moon' Williams was a D-Block Crip banger with a harsh reputation, two felony strikes, and five 187s tattooed in a neat column on his right forearm. Moon bragged to the Russian strippers that each 187 represented a body he knew for sure he put in the morgue, not the people he cut, stabbed, hit with a brick, beat down, or wounded – just the muthafuckas he saw die with his own eyes. Leaving some muthafucka hopping around in a pool of blood or screaming like a bitch didn't count, he told the strippers. Shooting into a crowd of people on a porch didn't count either. Moon had to see the bitch die with his own eyes or he didn't claim the credit. Moon Williams, he told these girls, was a fearless, heartless, stone-cold killer.

Operatives of the Odessa Mafia, who followed him home on at least three occasions, twice without his knowledge and once to sell him drugs, determined that the stone-cold killer lived with his grandmother, a woman named Mildred Gertie Williams, who the killer called Maw-Maw.

Pike found the address in a weathered residential neighborhood in Willowbrook, just north of Compton, at the bottom of a freeway off-ramp. A small stucco house had probably sat on the property at one time, just like all the other houses lining the street, but at some point the original house had likely burned, and now a double-wide mobile home sat on blocks in its place, with four ancient Airstream trailers shoehorned behind it. Pike figured the no-doubt-illegal trailer park was how Mildred Williams paid her bills.

The trailers might have been nice at one time, but now they were faded and scabbed with freeway dust. The double-wide had a small porch set up with a sun awning and potted plants, but shriveled brown threads were all that remained of the plants, and the yard had gone over to sand, dirt, and litter blown down from the freeway. The litter hugged the inevitable chain-link fence as if trying to escape.

Pike turned around on the next block, then pulled to the curb. Three girls on bikes pedaled past, swung around hard in the middle of the street, and rode past again. Eyeing the white man. They probably thought he was a cop.

Pike watched the mobile homes for a few minutes, but saw no signs of activity. An ancient Buick Riviera was illegally parked alongside the fence, so wide it covered the sidewalk. Pike didn't necessarily expect to find anyone home, but he wanted to confirm that Moon still lived here. If so, he would wait until Moon returned, then use him to reach Darko.

Pike took out his phone and called Jamal again. He got the computer once more. Jamal's mailbox was still full.

The girls rode past again, slower, and this time Pike rolled down the window. The first girl wore a blue short-sleeved shirt, the second a baggy white T-shirt, and the third was wearing a red sweatshirt. Red, white, and blue. Pike wondered if they had planned it that way.

'Need some help, ladies. You live on this street, or you just passing through?'

The girl in blue turned in a slow, curious circle. The girl in white slowed, but the red kept going. She didn't stop until she reached the corner.

The blue girl said, 'Are you a policeman?'

'No. I'm a salesman.'

The girl laughed.

'You're a plainclothes policeman. My Uncle Davis is a plainclothes officer, so I know. Also, you're white. We don't get many white people except for the police.'

Pike said, 'Do you know Ms. Mildred Gertie Williams, up there in the trailers?'

The girl said, 'You here for Moon?'

Just like that.

Pike said, 'Yes.'

'I live right over there, that yellow house? Uncle Davis warned us about that Moon Williams. He said don't never go over there and stay away from those boys. He said if that Moon ever makes a problem, we should call him right away.'

Pike tipped his head toward the other girls.

'Those your sisters?'

'No, sir. That's Lureen and Jonelle. They're my friends.'

'Which one of those trailers does Ms. Williams live in?'

'The one up front. That's the big one.'

'Does Moon live with her?'

'He's in the back trailer, the one with the dogs.'

Pike hadn't seen dogs when he passed the yard.

'He has dogs?'

'Those pit bull dogs. Those dogs are mean. Uncle Davis told my mama if she ever saw those dogs running loose, she had to call him right away.'

'You know who lives in the other trailers?'

She screwed up her face, then shook her head.

'Was a lady in one and Jonelle's cousin lived there for a while, but they moved out after Moon came home.'

Moon had brought a blight to the neighborhood.

'What's your name, blue girl?'

'I'm not supposed to tell my name to strange adults.'

Uncle Davis again.

'You probably shouldn't be talking to strangers, either.'

'I'm not stupid. You get out of that car, I'll ride away as fast as I can. Lureen and Jonelle over there, they'll call my Uncle Davis, then you'll see.'

'One more thing. Have you seen Ms. Williams or Moon today?'

She circled a couple of times, thinking, then shook her head.

'No, I sure haven't. I haven't been down that way today. I was at school, and then I was at Jonelle's, and Lureen just came over so we're going to her house.'

Pike said, 'Okay, then. You have a nice time at Lureen's.'

'You watch out for those dogs.'

Pike decided he didn't have much time as the three girls rode away. They would probably tell Lureen's mother, and Lureen's mother would probably call the blue girl's mother, who would call Uncle Davis. Uncle Davis would probably send a patrol car by to take a look.

Pike waited until the girls disappeared, then idled forward and parked alongside the Riviera. The edge of Mildred's yard butted against city property where the off-ramp looped down from the freeway, and the rear of the property backed against what appeared to be a large storage facility. Pike saw no dogs, though the last trailer was surrounded by its own taller fence. Pike slipped his .45 Kimber under his belt at the small of his back, clipped the Python to his belt under his sweatshirt, then hopped the first fence into Mildred Williams's yard.

Pike went to the big double-wide, listened at the door, then went to the nearest window. The freeway was loud, which made listening difficult. He stretched on his toes to peek inside, and saw a basic living room with an old-fashioned console television. The room was neat, clean, and the television was off. Pike angled his head, trying to see through an interior door when a gray-and-white cat jumped against the window. The cat cried at him through the glass as if it was lonely and wanted to escape.

Pike returned to the door. He tapped three times, then decided Ms. Williams had probably gone out.

Pike drew the Python as he moved to the second trailer, and let it dangle down along his leg. The second and third trailers were both empty, the tenants long since gone to escape Moon and his crew.

The fourth trailer sat by itself against a wall of ragged oleanders, caged by a six-foot chain-link fence. A gate in the center of the fence was latched but not locked. There wasn't much of a yard. Just a few feet of dirt on either side of the Airstream and a few feet behind. Two large metal bowls were under the trailer, one filled with water. A chain stretched from the tow hitch to disappear behind the trailer. It was the kind of chain used for a strong, aggressive dog, but Pike could not see what was attached to the other end.

Pike stood at the fence, listening. The trailer was still. Windows closed. No voices or music.

Pike made a *tsk, tsk, tsk* sound.

A dog inside the trailer barked. Not behind, inside.

Pike lowered himself into a push-up position, trying to see what was behind the trailer by looking under it, but accumulated junk and dead weeds blocked his view. He made the tsking sound again, and the dog inside barked. One dog inside.

The blue girl said Moon had dogs – more than one.

Pike let himself through the gate, ready to step back if an animal charged, but nothing moved. The dog inside was barking so loudly, Pike doubted Moon or anyone else was home. He latched the gate, then took a roundabout route to see behind the trailer, and that's when he saw the dog. A ragged male pit bull lay on its side, two legs stiff in the air. The dog's head was matted with dried blood and swarming with black bottle flies, but the dog wasn't the only dead thing behind the trailer. An African-American man was sprawled a few feet beyond the dog, his face covered with so many ants they looked like a second skin. The smell followed an instant later, strong enough to make Pike's eyes water.

Pike checked the body, but found no identification. He had been shot twice in the back. A black nine-millimeter Ruger pistol lay in the dirt by his hand.

Pike left the man and the gun, and went to the

window. The barking inside grew louder as he approached, then abruptly stopped.

The old Airstream was much smaller than the double-wide. It contained only three small rooms – a kitchenette, a living room, and a single bedroom with a bath. Pike looked into the kitchen first, saw nothing, then looked into the living room.

The inside pit bull had stopped barking because it was eating. The dog tore a strip of flesh from a man's neck, gulped the meat down, then lapped at the wound. The dog's face and chest were matted with blood, and its feet were red boots. A second male body was half on a couch and half on the floor. The flesh on the second man's left forearm had been partially eaten, but his right forearm was intact. The numbers tattooed there were easy to read.

187
187
187
187
187

One for each of the people he put in the ground.
Pike said, 'Good night, Moon.'

19

PIKE STOOD AT THE WINDOW, deciding what he needed to do. He wouldn't leave the dog trapped in the trailer, and he wouldn't leave the bodies where the red, white, and blue girls could find them. Pike would call the police, but he wanted to search the premises first. While Pike was thinking, the dog stopped lapping the blood and looked at him. It cocked its head, squinting as if it couldn't see so well, and wagged its tail. Then a fire grew in its eyes, and it lunged against the window.

Pike said, 'Let's hope I don't have to kill you.'

Pike wasn't afraid of the dog, but the trick would be controlling the animal without harming it.

Pike found a length of two-by-four by the double-wide. He unclipped the chain from the tow hitch, fashioned a noose, then looped it around the two-by-four. The dog tracked Pike's location by sound, and followed him around the inside of the trailer, barking and snarling.

When Pike approached the trailer's door, the dog slammed into the interior side like a linebacker.

Pike said, 'Easy.'

The door was hinged to open out, which Pike figured would work to his advantage. He pressed his shoulder against the door, unshipped the latch, and the big dog immediately tried to push the door open.

Pike let it open enough to offer the end of the two-by-four. The dog crunched into the wood, shaking its head as if trying to break a smaller dog's back. Pike let the noose slip off the board over the dog's head, then pulled the noose tight, and dragged the dog out of the trailer. The dog spit out the two-by-four and lunged, so Pike lifted its front legs off the ground. The pit twisted and snapped, streamers of drool flying. The dog wasn't trying to get away; it was trying to bite.

He worked the dog to the tow hitch, and wrapped the chain so the dog's head was held close to the steel. The dog's head and shoulders were blistered with scars, its nubby ears were shredded, and the left eye was milky. Mangy scabs covered its rump. A fight dog, tossed in the pit with similar dogs because Moon and his friends dug watching them rip each other apart. The dog licked the dried blood on its muzzle.

Pike said, 'Guess you had the last laugh.'

Pike entered the trailer, picking a careful path around tendrils of blood that spread from the bodies. The chemical stink of decay gases, dog shit, and spoiled human meat was terrible. Pike pulled on a pair of latex gloves, then noticed that Williams's right elbow appeared injured. The inside of the elbow above the 187s was badly discolored, showing a prominent lump under the skin as if Williams had two elbows instead of one. Pike felt the lump and realized it was bone. Moon's elbow had been broken.

Pike thought Frank Meyer might have done the deed, and the corner of his mouth twitched, Pike's version of a smile.

Pike searched Williams first, and found a nine-millimeter Glock in Williams's back pocket. Pike checked the chamber, then the magazine, and counted thirteen cartridges in a magazine designed to hold seventeen. With one remaining in the chamber, this meant three shots could have been fired. Pike wondered if the bullets found in Frank's house had come from this gun. SID would test-fire the weapon, and run a comparison, and then they would know. Pike put the clip back into the gun, and the gun in Moon's pocket.

Moon's remaining pockets produced a wallet, a ring of keys, a blue bandanna, a pack of Kools, two joints, a pink Bic lighter, and a PayDay candy bar. The wallet contained three hundred forty-two dollars, seven Visa cards in seven different names (none of them Earvin Williams), and no driver's license. Pike examined the keys, and found one with worn teeth bearing the Buick emblem. He kept the keys.

The second body yielded another nine-millimeter Glock, this one missing two bullets. Elsewhere on the body, Pike found eighty-six dollars, a pack of Salem

Lights, a stick of Juicy Fruit, and another set of keys, but no wallet or cell phone. Neither Moon nor the man outside had cell phones, either, which made it three for three.

Pike moved to the door for some fresh air, and looked back at the scene. Open beer bottles, two crack pipes on a wide ceramic ashtray, and a plastic baggie of rock – these guys were chilling when they were shot, and Moon had been trying to dull the pain of his damaged elbow. Moon had been shot twice in the face. The other man had been shot once in the chest and once in the head. Both were armed, but neither had drawn their weapons, suggesting they had been caught off guard by someone they knew. The third man probably bailed when the shooting started, but was chased down outside and shot.

Pike studied the floor, wondering if the murders had been committed by more than one person. The dog had been trapped for days, endlessly moving from door to windows, in and out of each room, and on the furniture. Blood, dog crap, and piss were smeared everywhere, obliterating any footprints.

Pike found three shell casings. He examined each one without touching it, noting that all three were nine-millimeter casings. He wondered if the bullets in Moon and his friends would match the bullets in Frank, and if Michael Darko had killed them.

Pike quickly searched the rest of the trailer, but found no evidence that a baby had been present. He decided to check the Buick, but when he stepped outside and saw the dog, he stopped. The pit bull made a low, huffing bark, then pawed the earth. Its tongue lolled like a strip of purple liver.

Pike pulled the metal water pan from beneath the trailer, found a hose, then set the pan at the dog's feet. The dog strained to drink, but the lead was too short, so Pike played out enough chain for the dog to reach the water. The dog slurped noisily, splashing most of the water out of the pan.

Pike laid a hand on the dog's hard back, and the dog spun fast as a striking snake, exploding out of the water as it went for Pike's throat. The dog was fast, but Pike was faster, one instant beside the dog, the next a pace away, just out of reach. The dog clamped its jaws in a frenzy.

Pike felt no fear or anger at the dog. He simply got the hose, and refilled the bowl from a safe distance. He figured the animal had been beaten regularly to make it mean. Wasn't the dog's fault. Even now, the dog tried so hard to reach him that its neck bulged over the chain and its eyes rolled with rage.

Pike said, 'It's okay, buddy. I understand.'

The dog strained even harder to bite him.

Pike went to the Riviera.

Moon's key opened the Riviera perfectly, but Pike did not get in. He pulled on a fresh pair of latex gloves, then searched the glove box and under the front buckets, hoping for a cell phone or some hard link to Michael Darko.

He found it on the backseat, as alien to the car's

cracked, filthy interior as a perfect white rose – a baby's bib. Made of a soft white cloth with a pattern of blue bunnies. Orange and green stains streaked the front. Pike felt the supple material, and knew the bib had been in the car only a few days. He held it to his nose, and knew the stains were recent. The orange smelled of apricots, the green of peas.

Pike folded the bib into a square and tucked it into his pocket, wondering what Moon Williams had done with the baby. Then Pike remembered Moon's grandmother. The freeway noise was loud, but multiple gunshots had been fired. The woman should have heard. Her grandson and the other two bodies had been here for at least three days. She would have discovered them.

Pike locked the Riviera and went to the double-wide. This time he didn't knock.

The gray-and-white cat raced out when he opened the door, and the same terrible smell seared his throat. The living room was neat and orderly the way he had seen it through the window, but as soon as he entered he saw the broken door at the end of the hall, and heard the cheery, upbeat melody of game-show music. Pike found Ms. Mildred Gertie Williams dead on her bedroom floor. A small television on her dresser was showing a rerun of Bob Barker's *The Price Is Right*. Ms. Williams was wearing pajamas, a thin robe, and furry pink slippers, and had been shot twice in the body and once in the forehead. She had been shot in the left hand, too, but the bullet had entered the palm and exited the back of her hand, making a through-and-through defensive wound. She had been trying to ward off the shooter or begging for her life when the shooter fired, shooting through her hand.

Pike turned off the television. Her bed was rumpled and unmade, with a TV remote by the pillows. She was probably watching TV when she heard the shots, and got up to see what happened. Pike pictured her standing as she would have been before she was murdered. He placed himself where the shooter would have stood, made a gun of his hand, and aimed. The spent casings would have ejected to the right, so he looked right, and found them between the wall and an overstuffed chair. Two nine-millimeters, same brand as the casings in Moon's trailer.

Pike stood over Mildred Williams, her face now misshapen and rimed with blood. Framed pictures of children lined the dresser, smiling gap-toothed boys and girls, one of whom was probably Moon.

Pike studied the pictures. He said nothing, but thought, this is how your love was repaid.

Pike left her as he found her, went outside, and sat in one of the lawn chairs under the awning. The air was good and cool, and not filled with death. Pike exhaled with his diaphragm, pushing out the bad stuff. If death was in him, he wanted to get rid of it.

Pike phoned John Chen, who answered from the lab at SID in a hushed, paranoid whisper.

'I can't talk. They're all around me.'

'Just listen. In a couple of hours, SID will roll to a

murder site in Willowbrook. They'll find three deceased males, a deceased female, three nine-millimeter pistols, and spent casings from a fourth gun.'

Chen's voice grew even softer.

'Holy Christ, did you kill them?'

'Comp their guns with the casings and bullets you have from the Meyer house. They're going to match.'

'Holy Christ again! You got the crew who killed the Meyers?'

'The spent casings in Willowbrook will probably match with the casings you found in Ana Markovic's room. The man who killed Ana probably committed the Willowbrook murders.'

'The fourth man?'

'Yes.'

'Waitaminute. You're saying one of their own guys killed them?'

'Yes.'

Pike broke the connection, then phoned Elvis Cole.

'It's me. You alone?'

'Yeah. I'm at the office. Just dropped her off.'

'She have anything?'

'She showed me three condo complexes and gave me a lecture on how Darko runs his call-girl business, but whether it's true or helps us, I don't know. I'm having a title and document search run, but I won't have the results until later. I'm about to get started on her sister.'

'You won't need to trace Rahmi's calls.'

'You found Jamal?'

Pike did not mention George Smith by name, but described how someone with inside information connected Michael Darko with a D-Block Crip named Moon Williams, who lived down in Willowbrook. Then Pike described what he found.

'You think they were killed the same night Meyer was murdered?'

'Within hours. We'll know if these are the same guns when Chen runs the comps, but they're going to match.'

Pike told him about the bib.

Cole said, 'But why would Darko kill them after they delivered his kid?'

'Maybe they didn't deliver the kid. Maybe they tried to hold him up for a bigger payoff, or maybe he just wanted to get rid of the witnesses.'

Cole said, 'What are you going to do?'

'Call the police. I can't leave these people like this. Little kids live around here. They might find the bodies.'

Even as Pike said it, the pit bull growled, and Pike saw two L.A. County sheriff's cruisers coming toward him up the street. An unmarked car was behind them.

Pike said, 'Looks like I won't have to call. The sheriffs are rolling up now.'

'How did the cops get there?'

'Cars.'

'You know what I mean.'

'I don't know. I'm wondering that myself.'

A third cruiser appeared from the opposite direction,

the three of them blocking his Jeep. Uniformed deps and the plainclothes people climbed out of their vehicles, and no one seemed in much of a hurry. Almost as if they knew what they'd find. Pike found that curious.

Pike started to end the call, then remembered the bib in his pocket.

'Don't tell her what I found here, okay? I want to tell her.'

'Whatever you want.'

'I have to go.'

Pike put away his phone, but stayed in the chair, and raised his hands. The deputies saw him, and an older dep with gray hair and a hard face approached the gate.

'You Joe Pike?'

'I am. I was just about to call you.'

'Sure, you were. That's what they all say.'

The deputy drew his gun, and then the other deps fanned out along the fence, and they drew down on him, too.

The dep said, 'You're under arrest. You do anything with those hands other than keep them up, I'll shoot you out of that chair.'

The pit bull went into a frenzy, trying to break free. Pike didn't move. He studied the two plainclothes cops who got out of the unmarked car. Middle-aged Latin guys. They looked familiar, and then he realized where he had seen them before. The last time he saw them, they were driving a Sentra.

20
ELVIS COLE

ANA MARKOVIC GRADUATED FROM the East Valley Arts and Sciences High School in Glendale two years earlier. Cole knew this from the yearbook Pike took from her room. First thing Cole did, he found her picture among the senior class – a thin girl with bright features, a large nose, and two monster zits on her chin. She had tried to cover them with makeup, but they were so inflamed they had burst through. Ana had probably been mortified.

Cole thought she kinda looked like Rina, but many people kinda looked like someone else.

The yearbook stated that Ana's class consisted of 1,284 graduating seniors, most of whom, Cole thought, had written an inscription in Ana's book. The yearbook's inside covers were dense with notes and signatures, mostly from girls, telling Ana to remember what great times they had or teasing her about boys she had liked, everyone promising everyone else they would be best friends forever.

Pike had tucked three snapshots in the yearbook. One showed Ana with Frank Meyer's two little boys, so Cole put it aside. The second showed Ana with two girlfriends, the three of them on a soccer field, arms around each other with huge, happy smiles. In this picture, one of the girls had short black hair with purple highlights, and the other was a tall girl with long, sandy brown hair, milky skin, and freckles. The third photo showed Ana and the brown-haired girl at what appeared to be a Halloween party. They wore identical flapper costumes, and had struck a funny pose with their splayed hands framing their faces like a couple of jazz-era dancers.

The background in the soccer field picture suggested a school campus, so Cole went back to the yearbook. He started at the beginning of the 1,284 senior class pictures and scanned the rows of portraits, hoping to get lucky. He did. The brown-haired girl was named Sarah Manning.

Cole phoned Information, and asked if they had a listing for that name in Glendale. He was hoping to get lucky again, but this time he wasn't.

'I'm sorry, sir. We have no listing by that name.'

'What about Burbank and North Hollywood?'

Burbank and North Hollywood were next to Glendale.

'Sorry, sir. I already checked.'

Cole put the yearbook aside and examined Ana's computer. It was an inexpensive PC that took forever to boot up, but the desktop finally appeared, revealing several neatly arranged rows of icons. Cole studied the icons for an address book, and found something called *Speed Dial*. He typed in *Sarah Manning*, clicked *Search*, and there she was.

Cole said, 'The World's Greatest Detective strikes again.'

The entry for Sarah Manning showed an address in Glendale, an 818 phone number, and a gmail Internet address. Cole almost never called in advance. People tended to hang up on him, and never returned his calls, but driving to Glendale to find out Sarah Manning had moved didn't appeal to him. For all he knew, she was pulling a tour in Afghanistan.

He called the number, and was surprised when she answered.

'Hello?'

'Sarah Manning?'

'Yes, who is this, please?'

She sounded breathy, as if she was in a hurry. It occurred to him she might not know that Ana Markovic had been murdered, but she did, and didn't seem particularly upset.

Cole said, 'I'd like to sit down with you for a few minutes, Sarah. I have some questions about Ana.'

'I don't know. I'm at school.'

'East Valley High?'

'Cal State Northridge. High school was two years ago.'

'Sorry. This won't take long, but it's important. I understand you were close with her.'

'Did they catch the people who did it?'

'Not yet. That's why I need your help.'

She was slow to answer, as if she had to think about it.

'Well, okay, like what?'

'In person is better.'

'I'm really busy.'

Cole studied the picture of Ana and Sarah in the flapper outfits. Cole didn't want to ask about prostitute sisters and Serbian mobsters over the phone, especially since these things might turn out to be lies.

'It's important, Sarah. You're on campus? I can be there in fifteen minutes.'

'Well, I guess so. I'll have to cut class.'

Like it was the end of the world.

Sarah described a coffee shop on Reseda Boulevard not far from campus, and told him she would meet him in twenty minutes. Cole hung up before she could change her mind.

Twenty-two minutes later, he found her seated at an outside table. She was wearing pale blue shorts, a white T-shirt, and sandals. Her hair was shorter than in the high school picture, but otherwise she looked the same.

'Sarah?'

Cole gave her his best smile and offered his hand. She took it, but was clearly uncomfortable. He nodded toward the deli.

'Would you like something?'

'This is just weird, that's all. I don't know what I can tell you.'

'Well, let's see where the answers take us. When was the last time you spoke with her?'

She thought for a moment, then shook her head.

'A year. Maybe more than a year. We kinda drifted apart.'

'But you were close in high school?'

'Since seventh grade. We all came from different elementaries. We were the three musketeers.'

Cole flashed on the picture of the three girls on the soccer field.

'Who was the third?'

'Lisa Topping. I thought about Lisa while I was waiting. You should talk to Lisa. They stayed in touch.'

'Black hair, purple highlights?'

Sarah cocked her head, and seemed engaged for the first time.

'Yeah. How'd you know?'

'Ana had a picture of the three of you in her room. She had a picture of you and her dressed like flappers, too. That's how I found your name.'

Sarah stared at him for a moment, then looked away. She blinked several times, and her eyes grew pink.

Cole said, 'You sure I can't get you something? Water?'

She shook her head, glancing away as if eye contact was painful.

'No, I'm just – I don't know –'

She suddenly reached into her purse and came out with her cell phone. She punched in a number, then held the phone to her ear. Voice mail.

'Hey, honey, it's me. There's this guy here, his name's Elvis Cole and I guess he's working with the police or something, he wants to know about Ana. Call him, okay –'

She covered her phone.

'What's your number?'

Cole told her, and she repeated it. Then she put away her phone.

'She'll call. It's her you should talk to.'

'Purple hair.'

'Not anymore, but yeah. She goes to school in New York, but they stayed in touch.'

She seemed sad when she said it, and Cole wondered why.

'Great. I will. But you're here, and you've known her since the seventh grade, too, so I'll bet you can help. My understanding is she lived with her sister. Is that right?'

Sarah nodded, but stared at the street.

'That's right. Her parents were dead. They died when she was little. Back in Serbia.'

'Uh-huh. And what was her sister's name?'

Cole made as if he was poised to take notes. He had two objectives. He wanted to see if Rina's story checked out, and, if so, he was hoping to learn something that might help find Darko.

Sarah said, 'Rina. I think her full name was Karina, with a *K*, but we called her Rina.'

So far so good.

'You knew the sister?'

'Well, yeah. They lived together. Kinda.'

'What's the "kinda" mean?'

Sarah suddenly shifted, and grew irritated.

'Dude, I'm not an idiot. I know you know. Rina was a prostitute. That's how she paid the rent.'

Cole put down his pen.

'Did everyone know?'

'Ohmigod, no. Just me and Lisa, and we had to swear. Rina didn't want anyone to know. She didn't even want Ana to know, and Ana only told us because she had to tell *someone*. It was demented.'

'Her sister being a prostitute.'

'Yes! I mean, we were kids. We thought it was cool, like this glammy, sexy Hollywood thing. But it was creepy. After a while when you thought about it, it was just gross.'

She wet her lips and looked away again, and Cole sensed this was probably why they had grown apart.

'Did Rina see clients at home while Ana was there? Is that what you mean?'

'No, nothing like that. She would go away for a few days. I guess she worked at one of those places. She would go away for a few days, and then she would come back.'

Sarah made an exaggerated shiver.

'Yuck.'

Cole wondered how many people knew, and how far word had spread.

'Did you and Lisa tell anyone?'

Sarah glanced away again, and it took her a while to answer.

'We wouldn't do that to her. She was our friend.'

'You ever hear them mention the name Michael Darko?'

'I don't know. Who's Michael Darko?'

'How about where she worked, or who she worked for? You remember anything like that?'

'Nothing to remember. Rina wouldn't tell her anything about that part of her life. She absolutely refused to discuss it. Forget about us. She didn't even know we knew. She wouldn't tell Ana. It was like an open secret they had. Ana knew, but they didn't talk about it.'

'How did Ana know if Rina wouldn't talk about it?'

'Rina got arrested. Ana always thought Rina was a waitress or something until this time Rina called her from jail. Ana got really scared. That wasn't until, like, ninth grade. I wanted to tell my mom and dad, but Ana totally freaked out. She made me swear. She said she'd never speak to me again if I told. So she came over and stayed with me for a couple of days like nothing was wrong – just like a regular sleepover. That's how we explained it. Then she stayed with Lisa. She was really scared, 'cause she didn't know what was going to happen, like, what if Rina went to prison? What would she do?'

Cole counted backward to ninth grade, and compared it with Rina's arrest record. The year matched with the date of her first arrest.

Cole sighed. Ninth grade meant she would have been fourteen. A fourteen-year-old girl home alone, not knowing whether her only family and sole support was ever coming back. She would have been terrified.

'And nobody knew? Just you and Lisa.'

Sarah glanced away again, nodding.

'What about the other Serbian kids? Who were her Serbian friends?'

'She didn't have any. Rina wouldn't let her. Rina wouldn't even tell her about the people they left behind.'

'So all she had was you.'

Sarah nodded again, looking lonely and lost.

Cole tried to read her, and thought he understood what she was feeling, both then and now.

He said, 'Hcy.'

She glanced over, then quickly away.

'Sounds like Rina was trying to protect her. I think you were trying to protect her, too.'

She didn't look at him, but he could see her pink eyes fill.

'I should've told someone. We should have told.'

'You didn't know, Sarah. None of us ever know. We just try to do our best.'

'She might be alive.'

Sarah Manning stood and walked away without looking back. Cole watched her go, hoping, for her sake, that she was wrong.

21

PIKE WATCHED THE TWO LATIN COPS. They stayed in the street, one making a short phone call while the other spoke with a dep. They did not approach Pike or acknowledge him, though the shorter of the two circled Pike's Jeep before rejoining his friend. They left the scene while Pike was being searched.

The senior dep was named McKerrick. While his officers spread through the trailers, McKerrick placed Pike under arrest, cuffed him, and went through his pockets.

McKerrick said, 'Christ, man, you're an arsenal.'

He placed the things he found in a green evidence bag. These included Pike's watch, wallet, weapons, and cell phone, but not the baby's bib. McKerrick probably thought this was Pike's handkerchief, and the stains were snot.

At no time did McKerrick Mirandize Pike, or question him. Nothing about the bodies, or why Pike was there, or anything else. Pike found this curious. He also wondered how the two Latin guys had followed him since he left Yanni's apartment. Even if they had run a split-team tail, Pike was certain he hadn't been followed. He found this curious, too.

When the search was complete, McKerrick walked Pike to a sheriff's car, placed him in the backseat, then climbed in behind the wheel.

As they drove away, Pike looked back at the dog. The dog watched him go.

Willowbrook was not technically part of Los Angeles. It was an unincorporated area, and used the Los Angeles County Sheriff's Department as its policing agent. Pike expected McKerrick to bring him to the nearest sheriff's station, which was the Century Station just off the Century Freeway in Lynwood, but when they climbed onto the freeway, McKerrick headed away from the station. Pike found this curious, too.

Twenty minutes later, they pulled off the freeway into downtown L.A., and Pike knew where they were going.

McKerrick reached for his radio mike, and spoke two words.

'Three minutes.'

McKerrick brought him to Parker Center, the Los Angeles Police Department headquarters. They drove around the side of the building to the processing entrance, where three uniformed LAPD officers were waiting. Two men and a woman, all in their late twenties, with short hair and freshly polished shoes.

The female officer opened the door, and gave him two more words.

'Get out.'

The lead officer was a rangy, athletic guy with spiky blond hair and buff shoulders. He steered Pike by the upper arm. They brought Pike inside without processing him, directed him onto an elevator, then up to the fourth floor. The fourth floor was special. Robbery Special. Rape Special. Homicide Special. The three divisions of the Robbery-Homicide Division. Terrio and his task force would live on the fourth floor.

'Gotta pee?'

'No.'

When the elevator opened, the officer carrying the evidence bag split off, and the other two steered Pike along an ugly beige hall to an interview room. Pike had been on the fourth floor before, and in their interview rooms. It was one of the smaller rooms, sporting the same bad paint, bad flooring, and cruddy walls as the rest of the building. A small table jutted from the wall, with a cheap plastic chair on either side.

The lead officer uncuffed Pike, then re-cuffed his right hand to a steel bar built into the table. When he had Pike locked down, he stepped back, but didn't leave. The female officer waited in the door.

He said, 'Joe Pike.'

Pike looked at him.

'I've been hearing stories about you since I came on the job. You don't look like so much.'

A video camera was bolted to the wall in the corner

up by the ceiling. The interview room didn't have a two-way mirror; just the camera with its microphone.

Pike studied the officer for a moment, then tipped his head toward the camera. The two officers followed his gaze. When the male officer saw the camera, he turned red, realizing a senior officer might be watching him act like an ass. They stepped out, and closed the door.

Pike looked around. The interview room smelled of cigarettes. Even though smoking was not allowed in city buildings, the last suspect had probably been a smoker, or the last detective. The table and the wall beside the table were covered with a jigsaw of scribbles, drawings, gouges, stains, and jailhouse slogans, most of it cut so deep into the Formica it could not be erased. *Biggie. ThugLife. LAPD187. OJWUZHERE.*

Pike considered the camera, and wondered if Terrio was watching. They would probably let him wait for a while, but Pike didn't mind. He took a slow, deep breath, paused, then emptied his lungs, taking exactly as long to exhale as to inhale. He focused on the camera. He emptied his mind of everything except the camera, and breathed. There was just Pike and the camera and whoever was on the other side of the camera. Then there was just Pike and the camera. And then only Pike. After a few breaths, he felt himself float, his chest expanding and contracting with the rhythm of the sea. His heart rate slowed. Time slowed. Then Pike simply was. Pike had spent days like this, waiting for the perfect shot in places that were not as comfortable as an LAPD interview room.

Pike pondered why they had pulled him in, and what they expected to learn. He knew they weren't going to charge him with anything because they had not Mirandized him, and had bypassed the normal booking procedure. Hence, they wanted to talk, but the question was why? He also wondered why they bounced him at Williams's home. If they were on him all day, they could have bounced him at any time, yet they waited until he found Williams.

Pike was still pondering these things two hours later when Terrio and Deets came in. Pike saw them as if he were hovering at the bottom of a deep, clear pond, and rose through the water to join them. Maybe now he would get answers.

Terrio unlocked the cuff from the metal bar, then from Pike's wrist. He pocketed the handcuffs, then took the remaining chair. Deets leaned into the corner and crossed his arms. There was a carefulness to his expression that Pike thought was composed.

Terrio said, 'Okay, listen. You are not under arrest. You don't have to talk to us. I'm hoping you will, but you don't have to. If you want a lawyer, here –'

Terrio took out a cell phone, slid it across the table – '– you can use this. We'll wait.'

Pike flicked it back.

'I'm good.'

Deets in his corner, chin down, looked up from under his brow.

'Did you kill those people?'

'No.'

'You know who did?'

'Not yet.'

Terrio pushed closer to the table.

'What were you doing down there?'

Down there. As if Willowbrook was another world.

'I was looking for a two-time felon named Earvin Williams. Williams might have participated in or had knowledge of Frank's murder.'

'Why did you think Williams was involved?'

'Williams was a D-Block Crip. He put together a crew of his homies, some of whom have shown a sudden increase in personal wealth.'

Terrio arched his eyebrows.

'You know other D-Blocks who were involved?'

'Jamal Johnson.'

Terrio turned white, and Deets snapped a glance as fast as a nail gun.

'How do you know about Jamal Johnson?'

'His cousin, Rahmi.'

'No way. SIS is on Rahmi Johnson. They're on him right now. You couldn't have spoken with him.'

Pike shrugged, believe what you want.

'Williams and Johnson were both D-Block. I don't know about the other guy. Was Johnson one of the vics?'

Deets said, 'Screw that, Pike. We ask, you answer. This isn't a conversation.'

Terrio held up a hand, cutting him off.

'Johnson was confirmed as one of the vics.'

'Who was the third male?'

'Samuel "Lil Tai" Renfro. He goes back to the D-Block with Williams and Johnson. How was it you came to believe this is the crew who hit Meyer's home?'

Terrio was staring at Pike so intently that he looked as if he might tip out of the chair. That's when Pike realized that Jamal Johnson had still been only a suspect, and Williams hadn't even been on their radar. They had not asked how Williams was involved, but why Pike thought he was involved. They hadn't brought Pike in to find out what he knew – they wanted to know how he knew it.

Pike said, 'I came to believe Williams was running the crew. We'll know for sure after you run their guns.'

Deets shook his head.

'There is no *we* here. No *we*.'

The hand again.

Terrio said, 'We have no physical evidence tying these people with what happened to Meyer or the earlier six robberies.'

'You do now. Run their guns.'

'How did you come to identify Williams as a person of interest?'

'Sources.'

Deets glared at the camera.

'This is bullshit.'

Terrio slipped a spiral notepad from his pocket, and read an address.

'One of these sources live in Studio City?'

Pike didn't respond. He was at Yanni's apartment building in Studio City when he first saw the Sentra.

'How about on La Brea just south of Melrose? Maybe we'll find one of your sources there, too.'

Terrio slipped the pad back into his pocket, then leaned forward again.

'Who killed these people?'

'Don't know.'

'Do you care?'

'No.'

Deets made a 'ha,' then pushed from the corner.

'You would have popped them yourself, Pike. If you'd found those dudes alive, you would have fed them to the dogs just like the sonofabitch who left them there.'

Pike shifted his gaze to Deets.

'Not the lady.'

Terrio leaned back in his chair, studying Pike as he tapped the table.

'These three idiots – Williams, Johnson, and Renfro – they weren't in this alone. Someone was pointing them in the right direction. You and I on the same page with that?'

'Yes.'

'Your sources tell you who they were working for?'

Pike studied Terrio for a moment, then glanced at the camera. Something about Terrio's inflection suggested he already knew, and wanted to find out if Pike knew as well.

'Williams was working for a Serbian OC gangster named Michael Darko. Darko or someone working for Darko probably killed Williams and his crew.'

Terrio and Deets stared at him, and for a few seconds the interview room was quiet. Then a large, balding deputy chief opened the door. Darko was the magic word.

'Jack, let's clear the room, please.'

Terrio and Deets left without a word. The chief followed them, and the woman Pike had seen in the backseat of Terrio's car on the day they told him about Frank entered and closed the door. Blue blazer over a white shirt. Dark gray slacks. An angry slash for a mouth.

She studied Pike as if he were a lab specimen, then glanced up at the camera, hanging patiently from the ceiling. She went to the camera, unplugged it, then turned back to Pike.

She held up a federal badge.

'Kelly Walsh. I'm with the ATF. Do you remember me?'

Pike nodded.

'Good. Now that we've met, you're going to do exactly what I say.'

As if she had no doubt it was so.

Part Three
It's Personal

22

KELLY WALSH STOOD twelve inches from the table, close enough so he was forced to look up, but not so close as to touch the table. Pike recognized this as a controlling technique. By assuming a superior position she hoped to create a sense of authority. Like unplugging the camera. She was demonstrating she had the power to do as she wished, even at Parker Center.

Pike thought it was all a bit obvious.

Then she said, 'Was Frank Meyer smuggling guns?'

This was the first time one of them asked a question that surprised him.

'No.'

'You sure?'

'Yes.'

'Sure sure? Or you just want to believe he wasn't?'

Pike didn't like this business about guns. He studied her face, trying to read her. Her eyes were light brown, almost hazel, but not. A vertical line cut the skin between her eyebrows, matched by a scar on her upper lip. No laugh lines, but no frown lines, either. Pike didn't like her certainty.

'How did you find me?'

She made an offhand shrug, her face as flat as a Texas highway, ignoring his question.

'Okay, you're sure. Personally, I don't know, but I need a reason Darko killed him, and that one makes sense.'

'Guns.'

She pointed at herself.

'ATF. The *F* is for firearms.'

She studied him a moment longer, then cocked her head.

'You don't know about the guns. You're just in this to get some payback. Okay, I get it. That's who you are.'

Pike knew she was trying to decide what to tell him, and how to play him. Same things he was thinking about her.

'Terrio lied about our not having anything that ties Williams to the earlier six invasions. We found a woman's bracelet in his grandmother's trailer that puts him with the Escalante invasion, and an antique Japanese sword that puts him with the Gelber invasion. We'll probably find something in Renfro's crib, too. The gun comps will be the icing, but these boys are our killers.'

Pike knew that Escalante was the second of the six previous home invasion/homicides. Gelber was the fifth.

'If you found these things only now, then you didn't know Williams was involved.'

'No. Turns out Johnson was living with Renfro. That's why no one could find him. Except for you. You did a good job there, Pike, finding these guys so fast. We hadn't even come up with names for these guys, but you found them. I like that a lot.'

She reached into her inside jacket pocket, and fingered out a four-by-six-inch photograph. Pike saw a clean-cut African-American man, early thirties, high and tight hair, and a tasteful gold stud in his left ear.

'Special Agent Jordan Brant. Jordie was one of my undercovers. He was murdered twenty-three days ago trying to identify a takeover crew employed by one Michael Darko. This is Darko.'

She produced a second picture, this one showing a big man in his late thirties with wide-set eyes in a round face. He had black hair pulled into a short ponytail, a thick mustache, and long, thin sideburns. The man who would not let himself be photographed had been captured on a security camera at the Bob Hope Airport in Burbank.

Pike stared at the picture, and Walsh read the stare. Walsh smiled for the first time, but it was nasty and mean.

'Yeah, baby, that's him. Killed your boy, Frank. Killed those little kids. The young one, Joey? Was he named after you?'

Pike sat back, and said nothing.

'You know where he is?'

'Not yet.'

'Jordie was found behind an abandoned Chevron station in Willowbrook. They used a box cutter on him. Wife and a child. You can relate to that, right? Me losing my guy. You losing your guy.'

'You believe Williams killed him?'

'Considering that Williams and his crew were Willowbrook homies, I'd say yes, but all we knew at the time is that a Crip set was involved. Jordie was trying to identify them.'

She returned the pictures to her pocket.

'What does this have to do with guns?'

'Darko works for a man named Milos Jakovich. Also known as Mickey Jack and Jack Mills.'

She arched her eyebrows, the arch asking if he recognized the names. Pike shook his head, so she explained.

'Jakovich heads up the original Serb set here in L.A. – the first of the old bosses to come over in the nineties. Think Don Corleone in his later years, but meaner. Jakovich is bringing in three thousand Chinese-made AK-47 assault rifles.'

The number stopped Pike. He tried to read if she was lying, but decided she was telling the truth.

'Three thousand.'

'Full-auto combat rigs that pirates stole from the North Koreans. So if Darko sends his killers to murder a man who used to be a professional mercenary, and who probably knows how to buy and sell weapons anywhere in the world, pardon me if I see a connection.'

Pike took a breath. A new element had entered the field, and now Pike felt a stab of doubt. He felt bad for having it, as if he were betraying Frank's memory.

'Frank wouldn't do that.'

'Tell you what? Let me figure out whether he would, since that happens to be my job. Here's what's more important – you're going to help me get those guns.'

Walsh moved for the first time. She leaned forward, resting her hands on the table.

'Darko works for Jakovich, but he's trying to take over the deal, pick his own buyer, and force a regime change. Old school out, new school in. That buys me time to find the guns, but if you keep dogging this guy, and he feels the heat –'

She snapped her fingers.

'Poof! The guns disappear, and they could be anywhere – Miami, Chicago, Brooklyn. So – first – you're going to drop your search-and-destroy.'

She didn't give Pike time to respond, but pushed on, leaning even closer.

'These East European sets, if these bastards didn't know you in the old country, they don't talk to you, and they haven't been in this country long enough for us to develop informants. My guy died trying to bust that lock, Pike, but you – I think you have someone inside with the Serbs. So – second – I want your contact.'

This was why she bounced him. Pike still didn't know how they made him at the trailers, but Williams was the break point. A Crip connected to Darko. When Pike reached Williams, Walsh must have realized he had inside help, and triggered the bust. She was with Terrio and Deets on the day they made such a big show telling him about Frank, and now he wondered if she was behind it, and if she had been using him to get inside from the beginning.

Pike thought it through, wondering if someone as far down the food chain as a prostitute would have information about an important deal. It was doubtful, but Rina might be able to find out.

Pike said, 'I'll see.'

Walsh shook her head.

'You don't understand. We have three thousand automatic weapons coming into this country, so I am not asking you. You *will* put me together with your informant.'

'I hear what you're saying, Walsh. This isn't lost on me.'

'That isn't the right answer.'

'I told you I would talk to my source. I will, but there's a risk. I didn't know about these guns. If I bring it up now, and word gets to Darko, you're in the weeds.'

Walsh glared, but only for a moment, as Pike went on.

'There are people in the EOC community who know I'm on the hunt, and they know why. They won't be spooked by a civilian working out a grudge. It's something they understand.'

Walsh showed her palms, shaking her head to stop him.

'Don't even think about it, Pike. Don't go there. I am not going to allow you to murder this man.'

'I suddenly stop, the people who know are left hanging. They want things in this, too. That's why they're helping me. If I go back with this gun thing, and tell them I'm talking to you, they'll disappear as fast as your guns.'

Now Walsh didn't seem so confident.

'What are you saying?'

'You don't have someone inside – I do. They're inside – and they want me to find Darko – badly. Whatever I learn, I will pass back to you, and I can start by giving you something right now – Darko is going back to Europe.'

She stared at him, and now her tanned face paled. Pike read her apprehension in how she shifted, a subtle step to the side as if she felt her own private earthquake. She glanced at her watch as if she wanted to note the time she learned this thing for the official record.

'Is this bullshit?'

'It's what I was told.'

She shifted again.

'When?'

'Don't know.'

'Why is he going back?'

'Don't know. Maybe his deal is closing. Maybe he wants to go back after it's finished.'

Pike decided he could not mention the child, or

Rina, or the true reason Darko sent his killers to Frank Meyer's home. Not without Rina's permission.

Walsh's face hardened as she struggled with the new information. She stared through him as she wrestled with her options, not liking any of them. When she spoke again, her voice was soft.

'I can take you out of the play. You don't want that.'

'No. I want Darko.'

Her eyes refocused. On him.

'I've got three thousand weapons being brought into this country by a foreign national. That's a terrorist act. By the law as written in the Homeland Security Act, I could make you disappear. No trial, no lawyers, no bail – just gone. Look me in the eye, Pike –'

She stared at him, letting him see.

'If I lose those weapons because I couldn't find them, I can live with it, but I am not going to trade the guns for Darko. Do you understand that?'

'Yes.'

'I want him, but on my terms, not yours, alive, so I can testify against him in open court. So Jordie Brant's wife can sit in the front row, and watch this piece of shit squirm. So she can take the stand during sentencing, and tell this piece of shit how much he hurt her, and how much he took from their child. I want that, Pike, just like you want what you want, and I will have it. Guns or not, the only way you're leaving here is if you agree.'

Pike studied her face, and knew she meant it. He nodded.

'Okay.'

'You agree? Darko is mine?'

'Yes.'

She put out her hand, he took it, and, for a moment, she did not let go.

She said, 'If you kill him, I swear to God I will devote the rest of my life to putting you in jail.'

'I won't kill him.'

She walked him downstairs herself. His Jeep was waiting. So were his weapons.

23

PIKE TURNED OFF HIS CELL PHONE as soon as he was alone. He stopped at the first large shopping mall he reached, cruised up to the top floor of the parking structure, then down, looking for tails. He found none, but he had found none before. He still didn't understand how they followed him.

Pike left the parking lot the way he entered, and backtracked three blocks. He reversed course again, clocking the cars he passed, but found nothing suspicious.

Returning to the mall, he parked on the second floor of the parking structure, then inspected the underside of the Jeep. He found nothing, but still wasn't satisfied.

He cleaned himself as best he could, then went into the mall. He bought a throwaway cell phone, extra batteries, and a prepaid calling card good for two hours. Seated on a bench outside a kitchen store, Pike spent ten minutes activating the phone and loading the prepaid calling time, then called Elvis Cole.

Cole's phone rang four times, a long time for Cole because he didn't recognize the incoming number.

'Elvis Cole.'

'It's me. Where's Rina?'

'With Yanni. I brought her back after our tour.'

'Do me a favor, and go get them. The ATF knows I was at their building, and suspects I was seeing a source. They want the source.'

Cole made a soft whistle.

'How do you know?'

'I just spent three hours with them.'

Pike sketched out what he found at Willowbrook, what happened when Walsh had him picked him up, and the information she gave him about Darko.

'This is no longer about some gangster murdering people in their homes – they're bringing three thousand Kalashnikovs into the country. That's why the Feds are involved.'

Cole said, 'I'll get them. You want me to bring them to my place?'

'For now. I'll have a place for them by the time I get there.'

Pike phoned Jon Stone next. Stone's phone rang five times before his voice mail answered, and Pike waited for the beep.

'It's Pike. You there?'

Stone answered, talking loud over Nine Inch Nails.

'Fuck, man, I didn't recognize the number.'

'Someone's been able to find me without following

me, Jon. That's why I'm using a different phone. I think the Jeep might be bad.'

Nine Inch Nails vanished.

'You driving it now?'

'Yes.'

'Don't come here. I'll meet you.'

Twenty minutes later, Pike arrived at a car wash on Santa Monica Boulevard in West Hollywood, and pulled around back to the detailing bays as Stone had instructed. In the rear of the car wash, they couldn't be seen from the street.

Stone's black Rover was in one of the bays, and two young Latin men were detailing a black Porsche in another. Stone was with them, laughing about something when he saw Pike arrive. He pointed at the empty bay on the far side of his Rover, and that's where Pike parked. One of the young men was sleeved out with gang tats. Neither looked over as Pike climbed from his Jeep.

Stone opened the back of his Rover and took out a long aluminum tube with a movable mirror jointed to a pod containing sensors and antennas. Jon's security work often required him to scan for explosives and multiplatform surveillance devices. Jon was a pro, and had the equipment to accomplish his mission.

He swept the pod under the Jeep, talking to Pike as he watched a dial in the handle.

'You find these fucks?'

'Found the crew. They were dead.'

'No shit. Who bagged them?'

'Their boss.'

'No honor among scumbags. What was the butcher's bill?'

'Three. Their boss is still up, but these three are down. One more to go.'

Stone paused between the Jeep's headlights, and studied the dial. After a moment, he continued on around the Jeep, making a full sweep of the vehicle until he returned to the front end. Then he put the pole aside, and wiggled under the engine.

'Here you go.'

He rolled to his feet, and showed Pike a small gray box the size of a pack of cigarettes.

'GPS locator. High-end piece made by Raytheon under an NSA contract. This is top-dollar equipment. Federal?'

'ATF.'

Stone grinned.

'Right now, there's an agent with a laptop staring at a real-time map overlay. X marks the spot, bro – right here at the car wash on Santa Monica Boulevard.'

He tossed it to Pike.

'Three choices – kill it, toss it, or – my personal favorite – tack it to a FedEx truck and let'm watch it roll all over town.'

Pike didn't want Walsh to know he found it or had even thought to look for it, but he didn't want her watching his path. If he put it on another vehicle, she would realize what he had done within a matter of hours. Pike tossed it back.

'Kill it, and I need you to do something else.'

'For Frank?'

'Yes.'

'I'm there.'

Pike told him about the guns – three thousand Chinese AKs stolen from the North Koreans.

Pike said, 'Jakovich didn't steal them. He bought them from someone. See what you can find out.'

Stone hesitated.

'About Frank?'

'About the guns. Frank didn't have anything to do with this.'

Stone hesitated again, but made a slow nod.

'I know a guy who knows a guy, but I want a piece of the hunt. I'll help, but I want some trigger time. For Frank.'

'You got it.'

24

PIKE DROVE TO COLE'S HOUSE when he left the car wash, climbing the narrow canyon roads to the top of the hills, then along Woodrow Wilson Drive through a heavily wooded canyon. He decided Walsh had planted the locator on his Jeep the day they stopped him at Runyon Canyon. Maybe that was why they stopped him the way they did, to keep him clear of the Jeep until they finished installing the locator.

Pike wondered now if she bugged him to follow his own investigation, or because she believed Frank was involved with the guns. There would have been no reason for her to believe Pike was involved in an arms deal, but maybe she knew something Pike didn't yet know.

The sky was deep purple when Pike pulled up in front of Cole's A-frame and let himself into the kitchen. Pike liked Cole's home, and had helped Cole maintain it over the years whenever Cole needed a hand painting, roofing, or staining the deck. Perched high in the canyons where it was surrounded by trees,

Cole's rustic A-frame felt removed from the city. Pike took a bottle of water from Cole's fridge. A dish of cat food sat on the floor beside a small bowl of water. The house smelled of eucalyptus, wild fennel, and the flora that grew on the canyon's steep slopes.

Cole, Rina, and Yanni were in the living room, watching the news. Rina's bag was on the floor at her feet, along with a bag that probably belonged to Yanni. They glanced over when Pike entered, and Cole muted the sound. Yanni's face was purple where Pike hit him.

Rina squinted at Pike as if she were sizing him up for target practice, then waved toward Cole.

'We are not going to stay here. It smells like cats.'

Cole arched his eyebrows, the arch saying, You see what it's like?

Pike motioned Cole over.

'See you a minute?'

When Cole joined him, Pike lowered his voice.

'You were going to check out her story. What do you think?'

Cole glanced at Rina and Yanni to make sure they couldn't hear, then shrugged.

'I located one of Ana's friends, and have a call into another. Everything checked. Rina spent the 90210 years protecting her sister. Kept Ana completely away from this stuff, just like she said.'

Rina stood, then raised her voice.

'I don't like this whispering. I told you already once. Yanni and I, we are going to go.'

Pike said, 'Yanni's building is being watched by the police. You shouldn't go back.'

Yanni mumbled something in Serbian, and Rina chattered something back.

She said, 'The police don't care about Yanni. Why would they watch?'

'They followed me earlier today. They know I'm trying to find Darko, so now they believe someone in Yanni's complex has information about him. They will look for that person.'

Rina and Yanni launched into more Serbian, and Yanni didn't look happy. Cole turned away as if he had heard enough foreign-language conversations to last a lifetime.

'You want something to eat?'

'Not yet. Did you find anything running the check on Darko's condominiums?'

'Yeah. They're not his condos – not in his name or any name I've been able to connect to him. This guy is hidden, man – he does not exist, so he's almost certainly here illegally.'

Cole ticked off the points.

'No one named Michael Darko appears in the DMV, the Social Security rolls, or the California state tax rolls. No one by that name has an account with any of the major credit card companies, the public utilities here in Los Angeles County, the telephone company, or any of the major cell service providers. Michael Darko has no criminal record that I've been able to find.'

Rina said, 'In Serbia. In Serbia, he was arrested. This I know.'

Pike thought over what George told him about how the old-school Serb gangsters tried to instill fear by creating a myth for themselves. The Shark. Here, then gone, like an imagined man. A monster his men talked about, but never saw.

Pike shrugged.

'He's just another turd.'

Cole said, 'A smart turd. His hookers rent their condos in their own names. Darko supplies them with a credit and rental history so they look good on the application, and kicks back cash to cover their rent, but they have to write the checks. Same with their phones, and other expenses. Everything is in their names, and they pay the bills. That way he avoids a paper trail to the girls.'

Rina said, 'Yes. That is why we follow the money. The money will give us the man.'

Cole nodded.

'He has women spread from Glendale to Sherman Oaks. A collector stops by every day to pick up their cash.'

Pike glanced at Rina.

'You know the man who picks up the money?'

'I will know him to see him unless the man change. He will be there between four and six. This is always the way. The girls, they have their money from the night before, but their money from the day is better.'

Pike said, 'Will he know how to find Darko?'

She shook her head, making the expression she made when she thought Pike was a moron.

'No, no, no. He is an outcast.'

Pike and Cole traded a look, not understanding.

'Why is he an outcast? He's being punished?'

Rina had a brief conversation with Yanni. When they stopped speaking Serbian, she tried to explain.

'Outcast is like someone learning.'

Cole said, 'Starting at the bottom?'

'Yes! The men who want to be accepted, but must prove themselves. The *pakhan* is the boss – that is Michael. Below him, his close friends are what we call the authorities. These are the men who make sure everyone do what Michael say.'

Pike said, 'Enforcers.'

'Yes. They make the men obey. The men, they are the ones who do the work and earn the money. The outcasts help the men.'

'Okay, so the guy who collects the money, he's an errand boy. He brings the money to Michael?'

'He brings it to his boss. Michael does not touch the money.'

Cole said, 'Then how do we find Michael?'

She thought for a moment, then glanced at Yanni. Yanni mumbled some more, and Rina shrugged.

'Depends on who the boss is. If boss is authority man, then maybe he know. If boss is only one of the men, then no. We won't know until we see. Is like a sergeant, and Michael is a colonel. The sergeant does not talk to the colonel. He talks to the captain.'

Pike looked at Cole.

'Maybe there's a way to turn this around. Maybe we can make Darko find us.'

'Steal the money?'

'Follow these people from business to business, and hit him. Hit him so hard he has no other choice.'

Cole thought for a moment, then nodded.

'Sounds like a plan. You ready for something to eat?'

Cole stepped past him into the kitchen. Pike looked at Rina and Yanni. They whispered to each other in Serbian, and then Rina glanced over.

'We will go to motel. Here smells like cats. It is making me ill.'

Pike said, 'Eat. I have a place you can stay. We'll go after dinner.'

He took his new phone and stepped out onto Cole's deck.

25

THE NIGHT AIR WAS CLEAR, and chill, and the canyon below Cole's home was quiet of man-made sounds. A wooden deck jutted from the back of Cole's house, hanging out over the night-filled canyon like a diving board to nowhere. Pike went to the rail. The air felt good, and its clarity seemed to magnify the lights that fell away to the city. Out here on the deck, at the edge of the glow from within Cole's home, Pike enjoyed the solitude.

He turned to face Cole's home, and leaned into the rail, the wide glass face of the house an invisible wall. Rina and Yanni were still huddled together on the couch, and occasionally glancing outside. Cole was in the kitchen, busy with cooking.

Pike fished out the new phone, and called George Smith. He did not want to call, but he had to warn George about Walsh.

George answered on the first ring, his voice as American as a Modesto car salesman.

'This is George. Who's calling, please?'

'Williams was dead. Williams, and two of his crew. Jamal Johnson and Samuel Renfro.'

George laughed.

'Well, there you go. Justice is swift.'

'Wasn't me. Someone killed them the same night they murdered Frank.'

'Ah, are you asking if I knew? I did not.'

'Not asking. I thought you should know in case your friends in Odessa ask.'

'Then muchas gracias.'

'Something else you should know. The ATF was tracking my vehicle when I came by this morning. They might come around, knocking on doors.'

George was silent for several seconds, and when he spoke, the Modesto tone was edged with something dark.

'You brought them to my store?'

'I don't know. They were tracking my vehicle. They know where I parked, and how long I parked there. I don't know if they had eyeballs on me or not.'

Another moment's silence.

'Where did you park?'

'A block north.'

Another moment.

'There are many shops within a block of my place.'

Pike didn't bother to say anything. George was shaking the facts to see if he could live with them, just as a terrier shakes a rat.

Inside, Rina stood. She peered outside, trying to find Pike at the edge of the light, then said something to Yanni. Yanni gestured as if he were getting impatient with her, and wanted to leave.

George said, 'Why might they knock on doors, Joseph?'

'Darko. They know I have inside information on the Serbians. They want my source. They'll probably retrace my route today, trying to locate everyone I spoke with.'

George suddenly laughed, giving it his best Modesto twang.

'Why, hell, George Smith ain't some Bosnian refugee. If they come around, I'll tell'm you wanted a lamp. I'll bet I can sell them a nice little sconce. Might even give them a discount.'

George laughed again, and now Rina came around the couch and was heading for the deck. Pike would have to go, but he needed a favor from George.

'One more thing.'

'I'm listening.'

'I'm going to hit Darko's business, and I want him to know it's me. Maybe some people at Odessa can drop my name in the Eastern Bloc neighborhoods.'

'This would put a target on your chest.'

'Yes.'

George made a little sigh.

'Well, we do what we do.'

George hung up as Rina opened the door. She stepped out onto the deck as Pike put away his phone.

She said, 'It's dark out here. Why do you stand in the dark?'

Pike hesitated, wondering whether he should tell her what he had found in Willowbrook, and finally decided he should. He had been feeling the bib in his pocket as if it were a living thing, alive and pulsing, and wanting to come out.

'Darko's crew is dead.'

She visibly stiffened, then joined him at the rail.

'You found them?'

'Yes. Men named Jamal Johnson and Moon Williams. Have you heard of them?'

She shook her head.

'Samuel Renfro?'

She shook her head again.

'They were killed the same night they took your son and murdered my friends.'

Her mouth shrunk to a tight knot, and her eyes turned watchful.

'Were Michael or my boy with them?'

'No. But I found this.'

Pike took the bib from his pocket, and once more marveled at its softness. As soon as he opened it, he smelled the apricots, even in the rich night air.

Rina took it, and seemed to marvel at it just as Pike had marveled at it.

'But nothing to say where's the baby?'

'No. I'm sorry, but no.'

Her face folded into a frown, and she turned to face the canyon. Pike decided to feel her out about Jakovich.

'I found another line I can follow – a man named

Milos Jakovich. Do you know who he is?'

She stared into the dark for a moment, then shrugged.

'The old one. Michael, he work for him.'

'Do they have business together?'

'I do not know. The blood is not good.'

'They don't like each other?'

'I don't think so. Michael never tell me these things, but I hear. Like with his business. I am just whore.'

She turned back toward the canyon, and Pike felt uncomfortable.

'Maybe Jakovich or someone who works for Jakovich knows how to find Michael.'

'I don't know those people.'

'Is there someone you could ask?'

She worried the inside of her cheek, then shrugged again.

'It is like a different family. I would be scared, I think.'

Pike let it go, thinking she was probably right in being scared. If Jakovich and Darko were in some kind of war, she might find herself in jeopardy from both sides.

Pike said, 'It's okay. Forget it.'

'I will do it if you wish.'

'Forget it.'

They stood in silence, then she leaned over the rail to peer down into the black canyon.

She said, 'It is so dark.'

Pike didn't answer.

'Do you have children?'

Pike shook his head.

'You should have children. You should make plenty of babies, and be a strong father.'

Pike didn't answer again.

Rina held the bib to her nose, and Pike could feel her draw in the deep apricot smell and the scent of her child. She touched her belly where the knife wounds had scarred, as if the pain she felt then and now were linked, and he wanted to touch that place, too, but didn't.

Pike said, 'We'll find him.'

'Yes. I know we will find him.'

Rina leaned into him, and gazed up with shadowed eyes that seemed to be searching.

'I would be with you. It is okay.'

'You don't have to be with me.'

'Whatever you like, I will do.'

Pike turned away.

'Get your bag. I have a place where the two of you can stay.'

Pike went out without eating, and took them away.

26

THE NEXT MORNING, Pike had Cole take him to check out the building in Sherman Oaks. It was a modern, three-story structure a few blocks south of Ventura Boulevard, across from a gourmet food store.

Pike said, 'How many prostitutes does he have in there?'

'She says he had four, two on the top floor and two on the second, but that could have changed.'

'The pickup happens between four and six?'

'Yeah, but that's only approximate. These people aren't running an airline. We should set up early, plan on staying late, and be ready to wait a few days.'

Pike expected no less.

'It's hunting.'

'Yes. It's hunting.'

They circled the building to see the surrounding residential streets, and finished their tour in the food store's parking lot. Pike noted the proximity to entrance and exit ramps for both the San Diego and

Ventura Freeways. The location had been chosen so customers could be given easy directions. The prostitutes who worked here saw customers who came to them, and were known as in-call girls. Safer for the girls, and with a lower overhead for Darko. Out-call girls needed drivers and bodyguards.

Pike said, 'How many stops does he make before here?'

'Three. Darko has buildings in Glendale, Valley Village, and this one. This was always the last stop.'

'So he should be carrying the full day's take.'

'Should be. If this is still the last stop.'

Pike was going to steal the money. That was the plan. He was going to steal Darko's money, and leave the pickup man so scared he would run straight to his bosses. Then Pike would take whatever his bosses had, too.

Pike said, 'I've seen enough. Let's go.'

They would need Rina to identify the bag man, so Pike picked her up a little while later. He had brought them to an empty guesthouse a few blocks south of the Sunset Strip the night before. It was small, but nice, with a lovely courtyard and neighbors who wouldn't pry. Pike had used it before.

Rina was waiting on the street when he arrived. Yanni's truck was parked at the curb.

She said, 'Yanni want to come.'

Pike looked past her, and saw Yanni in the courtyard.

'No Yanni. Forget it.'

She barked something in Serbian, and Yanni gave Pike the finger.

Pike brought her to Cole's, where they reviewed the plans and maps of the location with Jon Stone. When Stone first arrived, Rina squinted at him, and tugged at Pike's arm.

'Who is this?'

'A friend. He was a friend of Frank's, too.'

'I don't trust these people I don't know. I would rather have Yanni.'

'Not for this, you wouldn't.'

At one-thirty that afternoon, they climbed into their cars and returned to Sherman Oaks, Pike and Rina in his Jeep, Cole in his Corvette, and Stone in his Rover. They looked like a caravan winding their way along the spine of the mountains.

When they reached the market, Pike and Cole turned into the parking lot, but Stone continued past, moving to set up on one of the nearby residential streets. Pike found a parking spot in one of the middle rows facing the apartment building's entry, and Cole parked three spaces away.

Pike said, 'You need to use the bathroom?'

'No, I am fine.'

'The guy who's coming to pick up the money, does he know you?'

'I don't know. Probably he would know me, yes.'

'Then let's get squared away. Get in the backseat. You won't be as easy to see in back.'

She looked at him as if he was an idiot.

'It's only two o'clock.'

'I know. But we want to be prepared in case he comes early.'

She gripped her big purse. The one with the gun.

'I don't care if he see me or not.'

'I care. Get in the back.'

She scowled again, but got out, and climbed into the backseat. Pike adjusted the mirror so he could see her.

'Can you see the entry?'

'Yes.'

'Watch.'

'It's only two o'clock. Will be hours before he come.'

'Watch.'

He expected her to fidget or try to make conversation, but she didn't. She sat behind him, a second presence in the car, quiet and still, watching.

They watched for an hour and ten minutes, silent, as people came and went around them, parking, backing out, pushing buggies filled high with groceries. Rina did not move or speak for the entire time, but then she suddenly pulled herself forward, and pointed past his chin.

'That window on the top floor, on the side there away from the freeway. That was mine.'

Then she settled back and said nothing more.

Pike studied her in the rearview, but only for a moment. He didn't want her to catch him staring.

An hour and twenty minutes later, she abruptly

pulled herself forward again.

'That girl. She is one of the girls there. In the green.'

A young woman in black spandex shorts and a lime green top came around the corner and went to the glass door. Her dark hair was pulled back into a sleek ponytail, and a large gym bag was slung over her shoulder. On her way back from the gym. She was lean and fit, but her breasts were too large to be natural. She looked very young.

Rina said, 'You see? I know this girl when they bring her here. They make her waitress, and then she dance.'

'Stripper.'

'Yes. And this.'

The girl let herself into the lobby, then pushed a button for the elevator.

Fifteen minutes later, Rina pulled forward again.

'There. In the black car.'

A black BMW convertible turned off Sepulveda and crept past the building as if looking for a parking place. The driver was a white male in his twenties with a thick neck and long, limp hair. He wore a white shirt with the sleeves rolled, a day-old beard, and mirrored sunglasses.

Pike hit the speed dial for Cole.

Three cars away, Cole glanced over as he raised his phone.

'What's up?'

'The black convertible.'

Cole glanced at the street.

'I'll get Jon.'

Pike lowered the phone, but didn't end the call. Cole was using a second phone to put Stone in the loop. They had planned on multiple phones to maintain constant contact.

The BMW reached the stop sign, but instead of circling the building to park on the street, the driver turned into the parking lot.

'Get down.'

Rina slumped down in her seat without question, but lifted her head enough to see.

The Beemer passed behind Pike's Jeep and Cole's Corvette, then turned onto the next row and parked by the sidewalk. The driver got out, stepped over a low hedge, then crossed the street. Pike made him for his late twenties, maybe average in height but with a heavy frame. He looked like a hitter, and probably thought he was good at it. He let himself into the building with his own key.

Pike said, 'Here's where you leave.'

Rina went directly to Cole's Corvette, and got in as they had planned.She did not dawdle, stare, or draw attention to herself. Pike liked that about her.

Cole's voice came from the phone.

'You want Jon to come in?'

'I'm good. Get her gone.'

Cole backed away, and cruised out of the parking lot.

The bagman was inside for less than ten minutes. For him, picking up cash from four prostitutes was just another stop in a day filled with stops – something to be accomplished quickly, and without wasted energy. The girls probably felt the same.

When the man emerged from the building, Pike stepped out of the Jeep, but hung back to be sure he was returning to his car. When the man angled toward the Beemer, Pike made as if he was heading for a nearby car, but Darko's boy never once looked at him. He passed in front of Pike within ten feet and swung around the Beemer's rear end. As he opened the door, Pike closed the gap. When the bagman slid in behind the wheel, Pike came up along the passenger's side, and lifted himself over the door and into the passenger's seat.

The man lurched in surprise, but by then it was too late. Pike showed him the .357, down low so no one could see.

'Sh.'

The man's eyes went wide as oncoming headlights, but he was a burly guy who was used to muscling people. He lunged for Pike's gun, but Pike rolled his hands down and away with a minor *wing chunz* deflection, and snapped the Python up hard into the bottom of the man's chin, popping his jaw like a rat trap. The Python flicked again, and this time Pike hit him in the Adam's apple.

The bagman clutched at his throat, choking. His face turned bright red.

Pike took the key from his hand, fit it into the ignition, the convertible top. He had to keep the button depressed throughout the process, but that was okay. His arm was a steel bar with his tattoo in the bagman's face. Pike wanted him to see the red arrow.

Pike didn't move or speak until the top was in place and the windows were closed, and neither did the bagman. He was too busy trying to breathe.

Pike said, 'Grab the wheel. Both hands.'

He grabbed the wheel.

'Try to escape, I'll kill you. Try to grab this weapon again, I'll kill you. Do you understand?'

'This is a mistake, my man. I don't know what you –'

Pike backfisted him hard on his temple, striking so fast the man had no time to react. His head bounced off the window, and Pike caught him again on the rebound. The second backfist made his eyes flag.

Pike jerked him upright, then dug his thumb into a nerve bundle between the man's ribs. The man moaned, and pushed weakly at Pike's hand, so Pike hit him again. The man covered his head.

Pike said, 'Grab the wheel. Grab it.'

The man grabbed the wheel with both hands.

'Try to escape, I'll kill you. Try to take this weapon again, I will kill you. Do you understand what I'm saying?'

'Jesus, stop hitting me. Please –'

'If you let go of the wheel again, I'll kill you. Do you understand?'

'Yes.'

The man's knuckles turned white as he tightened his grip. Blood from his mouth dripped onto his shirt, and the corner of his eye at his temple was swelling.

Pike said, 'What's your name?'

'Vasa.'

'I'm going to search you, Vasa. Don't let go of the wheel. Do not resist.'

Pike went through Vasa's pockets, finding a black ostrich wallet, a Nokia cell phone, and four thin vinyl billfolds.

Pike said, 'One from each girl?'

'Yes.'

'They have the money ready? You stop by, they give it to you?'

'You know who this belongs to?'

'Me.'

Pike thumbed through the bills, mostly hundreds and twenties, and counted out thirty-eight hundred. He tucked the money into his pocket.

'Where's the rest?'

Vasa blinked at him.

'What rest? That's it.'

Pike stared into Vasa's eyes, and finally Vasa sighed.

'Under the seat.'

Pike found another seventy-three hundred dollars under the seat, and added it to the cash in his pocket. That made eleven thousand, one hundred dollars of Darko's money.

Pike studied Vasa. He stared at Vasa so long, the man turned away.

'Why are you staring at me? Who are you?'

'My name is Pike. Say it.'

'You are Pike?'

'Say the name. Say it.'

'Pike. I say it. You are Pike.'

'Look at me.'

Vasa cringed as if he was certain Pike would hit him again.

Pike touched the arrow on the outside of his arm.

'See this?'

Vasa nodded.

'Tell me you see it.'

'I see it.'

'Where is Michael Darko?'

Vasa's eyes grew into saucers again.

'I don't know. How would I know?'

'Call him.'

'I don't have his number. He is the boss. Why are you taking his money? This is crazy. He will kill you for taking his money.'

Pike studied Vasa a moment longer.

'Tell Darko I'm coming.'

Pike got out, taking the money, the wallet, the keys, and the cell phone.

Vasa said, 'What am I supposed to do without my keys?'

Pike returned to his Jeep, and circled the parking lot until he pulled up behind the Beemer. He wanted Vasa to see his Jeep, too. He motioned for Vasa to roll down his window.

Inside the BMW, Vasa couldn't roll down the window without the keys, so he opened the door.

Pike tossed out his keys, then drove away.

Pike drove exactly two blocks, then pulled to the curb, and lifted his cell phone.

'What's he doing?'

'Getting on the freeway. Jon's three cars behind him, and I'm behind Jon.'

Pike pushed hard to catch up.

27

THEY FOLLOWED THE BEEMER east across the bottom of the San Fernando Valley, Pike watching Cole and Jon Stone take turns behind the Beemer. The BMW drove steadily, in no great hurry to get where it was going. Vasa probably wasn't looking forward to explaining what happened to Darko's money.

They stayed on the Ventura Freeway past the Hollywood split, but took the first exit, climbing up Vineland past the aging shopping centers and strip malls of North Hollywood. Cole tightened up on the Beemer when they left the freeway, and Jon fell back. Ten minutes later, Cole once more spoke in Pike's ear.

'Blinker. We're turning up ahead on Victory.'

Neither Pike nor Stone responded.

Three minutes later, Cole spoke again.

'Turning again. A place called the Glo-Room. We're going past to the first cross street.'

Jon Stone said, 'Sweet. Strippers.'

Two blocks ahead, Pike caught a glimpse of the BMW turning, and spoke to Cole.

'Does she know the place?'

'She's heard of it, but never been here. It's one of the places she told me about.'

When Pike passed, he glimpsed Vasa's convertible parked in a narrow parking lot alongside a black single-story building. A marquee sign jutted out from the front of the building, saying GLO-ROOM GENTLEMEN'S CLUB – AMATEUR NITE WED. Pike continued past to the first cross street, where the other two cars were waiting. Cole and Rina were already waiting in Stone's Rover. Pike pulled in behind them, parked, then climbed into the Rover's front passenger seat. Stone immediately turned down an alley to circle around behind the bar. The alley ran between the shops and stores that lined the main street and a long row of additional parking spaces and Dumpster bins.

Pike said, 'Stop short.'

Stone stopped three doors away, parking behind a pet store. A white delivery van was parked behind the Glo-Room, though the only person they saw was a middle-aged Latin man in a stained white T-shirt. He was standing between the truck and the building, smoking.

Pike turned in his seat so he could see Rina.

'Darko owns this place?'

'One of his men own it, but, yes, it will belong to Michael. The other men run it, but Michael he get the money.'

'You know the people who work here?'

She shook her head, then shrugged.

'No, I don't think so. I know of this place, but I never been here. Michael, he have three or four places like this. Maybe more.'

They started rolling again, and drifted past the delivery truck. They drove all the way to the next cross street, turned around, and came back from the opposite direction. They stopped with an easy view of the side lot and delivery truck. A back door used for deliveries and service help was cracked open on the alley, but the white van blocked the building's interior from view. The BMW was parked outside a door on the side of the building, which appeared to be the bar's main entrance. A dark gray Audi sedan and a silver Mercedes were parked near the Beemer, and now three men were standing outside the door. Two of the three were large guys wearing loose shirts that hung over their bellies. The third man was younger, with hard, muscular shoulders.

Pike turned enough to see Rina.

'Know them?'

'That one in the middle, maybe I seen him before, but maybe not. Other two, no, for sure.'

The one in the middle wore gold chains, and appeared to be the focus of attention.

Stone said, 'You see it?'

Pike nodded.

Rina said, 'See what?'

Cole said, 'The muscle has a gun in his belt.'

The three men finished their conversation, then the two big men went into the bar, and the muscular guy walked back to the delivery van. He slapped the side twice, then stepped away as the van's rear door opened. A burly guy with a monumental belly climbed out, showing a mat of dark hair on his arms and neck. He hoisted three cases of Budweiser, and brought them into the bar. The muscular guy leaned into the van, came out with three more cases, and followed him inside.

Rina said, 'They steal the beer to sell, you see? He buy some, but he have people who steal.'

This fit with what George described. Darko resold merchandise stolen by hijack crews. Alcohol went to his clubs. Everything else went to fences and flea markets.

Pike tapped Jon's leg, and Jon rolled on, cruising back to their cars. Everything moved quickly after their brief reconnoiter, which was how Pike liked it. Speed was good. In armed confrontations, speed was the difference between life and death.

Cole immediately put Rina in his car and left the area. Stone motored away, but would circle the block to approach from the front. Pike returned to his Jeep, immediately pulled into the alley, and parked behind the bar. By the time he got back, the van and the back door were both closed, but the door was unlocked.

Pike hit the speed dial on his phone for Jon Stone, and Stone answered with a single word.

'Go.'

Pike closed his phone, stepped inside, and found himself in a hall crowded with stacked boxes. A larder to his left was filled with more beer, tap kegs, booze, and other supplies, and a tiny food and dish-washing area was to his right. The Latin guy who had been smoking out in the alley glanced at him with tired eyes from an industrial-sized dishwasher. Pike stepped into the door, and spoke quietly.

'Police. We're going to arrest everyone here, but you can go. Walk away now.'

One look at Pike, the man did not hesitate. He put down his towel, squeezed past, and immediately left the building. Pike locked the door behind him.

Farther along the hall was a small dressing room for the dancers, a couple of restrooms, and a swing-ing door. The restrooms and dressing room were all empty. The dressing room smelled of mildew. Pike heard voices coming from the front of the club, but no music or other sounds.

Pike pushed through the swinging door. The lights were on, the stage was empty, and the music was off. The three men from the parking lot were crowded around a bar table with a fourth man and Vasa, who was holding a wet towel to his face. The furry man was behind the bar, maneuvering a beer keg into place. Pike had entered so quietly the men at the tables did not hear him, but the furry man caught the movement, and stood.

He said, 'We're closed. You'll have to leave.'

The men at the tables all looked over, and Vasa saw

Pike. He lurched to his feet as if someone had kicked him.

'That's him. The fuckin' guy –'

The four men at the tables didn't move. The muscular guy didn't reach for his gun. They sat perfectly still.

Pike said, 'I'm looking for Michael Darko.'

The oldest was a heavy man with large bones, thick wrists, and small eyes. Three of the four wore short-sleeved shirts, two showing skin that had been inked up with Eastern Bloc prison tats back in the old country.

The oldest man said, 'I have never heard of this man. You have come to the wrong place.'

Two vinyl billfolds identical to the ones Pike took from Vasa were on the bar, along with a brown leather briefcase. Just sitting there, as if someone was in the middle of business when Vasa rushed in to tell his story. Pike moved toward the bar, and the muscular man stood.

He said, 'Get the fuck out of here.'

When Pike reached the end of the bar, the furry man behind the bar shoved the beer keg aside and charged. He threw up his forearms like an offensive lineman blocking a defensive back, but Pike slipped to the side, pushed the man's elbow down and away, caught his head, and rolled him into the floor. Third of a second once contact was made, and Pike was on his feet, watching the muscular man rush toward him in slow motion as the three other men, even more slowly, jumped to their feet.

The muscular man reached under his shirt even as he pushed past the tables. Pike did not try to stop the gun; he rolled his hand under the man's wrist, drove the man's arm over and back, and pulled him backward and down. Pike had the gun before the man slammed into the floor, and hit him on the forehead with it two hard times, even as Jon Stone's voice cut through the gloom.

'Freeze, motherfuckers!'

The three men at the tables, on their feet now, raised their hands.

Jon stood just inside the door with an M4 carbine, painted up nicely in desert camo. Never taking his eyes from the men, Stone closed and locked the door, sealing the building. He grinned at Pike.

'Always wanted to say that.'

Pike checked the man's pistol, then went through his pockets.

The man with the gold chains said, 'What is it you want?'

Stone stepped forward, the grin suddenly gone, all fierce lines in full-on combat mode.

'Shut it, bitch. You will not speak unless spoken to.'

Pike found a wallet, keys, and cell phone, then stood away. He waved toward the floor with the pistol.

'Knees. Fingers laced behind your head.'

Stone kicked the nearest man down, and the others hurried into position.

Pike returned to the man with the enormous belly.

His eyes were open, but unfocused, and he made no move to rise. Pike came away with a neat little .40-caliber pistol. He put everything on the bar with the vinyl billfolds, then returned to Stone's prisoners, and searched them as well. None were armed, and none spoke while he went through their pockets, collecting their things.

When Pike finished, he returned to the bar and checked the vinyl billfolds. They were filled with cash. He opened the briefcase. More cash, a metal skimmer used to steal credit card information, and what looked like business papers. He put the two pistols and the other things he had taken from the men into the briefcase, closed it, then carried it back to the men. They watched him the way a cat trapped by a window watches a bird.

Pike said, 'Darko?'

The older man shook his head.

'You are making a mistake.'

Behind them, Stone's voice was soft.

'Maybe these fuckers were there that night. Maybe one of them gunned Frank.'

Pike said, 'Vasa, do you remember my name?'

'You are Pike.'

The older man said, 'You are dead man.'

Stone snapped the M4 into the back of his head. The man fell like a bag of wet towels and did not move. Vasa and the other man stared at his unconscious form for a moment, and now their eyes were frightened.

Pike dangled the briefcase, showing them.

'Everything Darko owns is mine. Darko is mine. This bar is mine. If you're here when I come back, I'll kill you.'

The other big man, the one still awake, squinted as if Pike was hidden by fog.

'You are insane.'

'Close this place now. Lock it. Tell him I'm coming.'

Pike left with the briefcase, and Stone followed him out. They went directly to Pike's Jeep, then drove around the corner to Stone's Rover. When they stopped, Stone opened the briefcase. He pushed the cash packs aside, and frowned.

'Hey, what is this shit?'

Pike fingered through the pages, clocking the columns of numbers organized by business, and realized what they had.

'Our next targets.'

He opened his phone to call Cole.

28

THEY MET BACK AT Cole's house to go through the papers. Rina recognized them immediately.

'They are gas stations.'

Stone said, 'What the fuck?'

Cole thought the pages were bookkeeping ledgers, accounting for income from All-American Best Price Gas, Down Home Petroleum, and Super Star Service.

Cole said, 'Super Star Service is right down the hill in Hollywood. One of those indie places.'

Rina nodded.

'You see? He make much money there. Very much. Maybe more than anywhere else.'

Stone said, 'Bullshit. How much dough can he make selling gas?'

'You are an idiot. He not make the money selling gas. He steals the credit card information.'

Cole said, 'It's a skimmer rip-off. He's doing credit card fraud.'

Cole explained how it worked. Darko's people

connected a skimmer sleeve to the card reader inside each gas pump, along with an altered keypad over the pump's actual keypad. This allowed them to collect credit card and PIN information every time a customer swiped a credit card or used a debit card to pay for gas. Darko's fraud crew then used this information to create new credit and debit cards, with which they could drain the victims' debit accounts or run up huge charges before the victims or credit card companies froze the accounts.

'Each of these skimmers is worth anywhere from a hundred thousand to one-fifty a month in goods and cash, times however many skimmers he has in the three stations.'

Now Jon Stone made a little whistle, and laughed.

'Pretty soon you're talking real money.'

Then he frowned.

'But waitaminute – if there's no cash, what are we gonna steal?'

Pike said, 'His machines.'

Cole nodded.

'Bust them right out of the pumps. Pop out the skimmers and keypads, he's bleeding way bigger money than he earns from his prostitutes.'

Stone said, 'Busting shit up. Now you're talking, bro. Let's get it going.'

Pike stopped him.

'Tomorrow. We want to pace it out, give him time to hear about what happened today, let him get angry about it. Tomorrow, we take him down one by one, pace it out over the day.'

'And sooner or later the enforcers show up.'

'That's the idea.'

This was called baiting the enemy – Pike would pattern his actions to create an expectation, forcing the enemy to act on that expectation.

Later, Pike drove Rina back to the guesthouse. They rode in silence most of the way, she on her side of the Jeep, he on his. Up on Sunset, the kids were already lined up outside the Roxy, but Rina didn't look. She stared out the window, thoughtful.

Yanni's truck was at the curb when they pulled up.

Pike said, 'You're not coming tomorrow. No need for it. I'll let you know what happened after.'

He thought she would object, but she didn't. She studied him for a moment, and made no move to open the door.

'This is very much that you do. For this, I thank you.'

'Not just for you. For Frank and for myself, too.'

'Yes, I know.'

She wet her lips. She stared down the length of the street into the dark. Two people walked along the broken sidewalk, enjoying an after-dinner stroll.

Pike said, 'You should go in.'

'Come in with me. I would like it.'

'No.'

'Yanni will leave. I will tell him. He doesn't care.'

'No.'

The hurt came to her eyes.

'You don't want to lay with a whore.'

'Go in, Rina.'

She considered him for a moment, then leaned across the console and kissed him on the cheek. It was a quick kiss, and then she was gone.

Pike didn't go home. He cruised the length of the Strip, taking it slow, then turned up Fairfax to Hollywood, then up again into the residential streets at the base of the canyon.

The park was closed at night, but Pike left his Jeep and walked up the quiet streets. The air was rich with winter jasmine, and cold, and grew even colder as Pike squeezed around the gate and entered the park.

The canyon was his. Nothing and no one else moved.

Pike climbed the steep fire road, rising above the city, walking, then walking faster, then jogging. The ravines were pooled with ink shadows, and the shadows enveloped him, but Pike did not slow. The brittle walls above him, the ragged brush and withered trees beside him, and the plunging slope below were sensed more than seen, but the invisible brush teamed with moving life.

Coyotes sang in the ridges, and eyes watched him. Eyes that blinked, and vanished, and reappeared, pacing him in the scrub.

Pike followed the road up, winding along the ravine to the end of the ridge where the lights of the city spread out before him. Pike listened, and enjoyed the crisp air. He smelled the rough earth, and jasmine and sage, but the strong scent of apricot overpowered everything else, and was sweet in the raw night.

He heard a whisper of movement, and metallic red eyes hovered in space, watching. A second pair of eyes joined the first. Pike ignored them.

The canyon was his. He did not reach home until just after sunrise, but even then did not sleep.

29

ALL-AMERICAN BEST PRICE GAS was a ragged dump in Tarzana. Six pumps, no service bays, little mini-mart with a middle-aged Latina holed up behind a wall of bulletproof glass.

Cole and Stone went in first, Cole scouting the surroundings, Stone pretending to put air in his tires while he checked out the people in and around the station. Pike waited two blocks away until they called. Pike heard them through his Bluetooth earbud, which he would wear while he did what he had to do, Cole and Stone providing security.

Cole told him about the woman.

'One female. Strictly counter personnel.'

Pike didn't like the idea of terrorizing an innocent woman.

'Will we have a problem with her calling the police?'

'Rina said no. These places get held up like any other gas station, so the employees are schooled to call their manager, not the police. That's the front man who runs it for Darko.'

Stone, who was conferenced in, spoke up.

'That's all well and good, but what if she's got a shotgun behind the counter?'

'Rina said no. Listen, they're selling diluted gas and they have skimmers on all the pumps. They don't want the police sniffing around.'

Stone said, 'Maybe Rina should rob the place.'

Pike said, 'I'm rolling.'

Pike pulled up to the pumps outside the mini-mart, giving the woman inside a clear view of his Jeep. He wanted her able to describe it accurately.

Pike went inside, and immediately saw a security camera hanging from the ceiling behind the glass. He wondered if it worked, then decided this didn't matter. He gave the woman his name and told her he was there to give Mr. Darko a message.

She looked confused.

'Who's Mr. Darko?'

'Doesn't matter. He'll still get the message.'

'You don't want gas?'

'No. I'm going to adjust the pumps.'

'They didn't tell me about this.'

'Mr. Darko will explain.'

The emergency cutoff switch for the pumps was on the wall outside the door. Pike cut the power, then pry-barred the cover off each pump register. They didn't come easily, leaving the metal bent. The woman behind the glass expressed no surprise when she saw what he was doing. She simply picked up her phone as if something like this happened three or four times each day, and made a calm call.

Six pumps, two sides to each pump, twelve card readers.

The skimmer sleeves were obvious, having been fixed around the white plastic reader track with duct tape. Every time a customer slipped a credit or debit card into the reader, the card also tracked through the skimmer, which read all the same information, storing it in a green circuit board wired to the sleeve. Pike tore off the sleeves and circuit boards, and stowed them in a plastic bag. He left the pump registers broken and open.

A woman driving a silver Lexus SUV pulled up while Pike was working.

He said, 'The pumps are being serviced.'

She drove away.

Eight minutes later, the skimmers were stripped from the pumps and Pike was finished.

They could wait around to see who would show up, but Pike wanted to maintain the pressure. He wanted to flush them into his sights.

They took a long break for breakfast, and hit the next station three hours later. Down Home Petroleum (proudly independent!) was a cheesy little station in North Hollywood that was older and smaller than the All-American Best Price, and so dirty it looked like a smudge.

Cole and Stone rolled in first, just as they had

before, and this time it was Stone who spoke in his ear.

'Two dudes inside, bro.'

'Soldiers?'

'Dunno. Young, white, and skinny, but that doesn't mean they aren't packing.'

Cole, listening in on the conference, said, 'Surrounding streets clear.'

'I'm in.'

Pike rolled, once more pulling up to the pumps.

The Down Home was too low-rent for a glass barrier. A tall Anglo kid sat behind a counter, unshaven, shaggy, and looking as if he'd rather be having surgery. Had a friend keeping him company. A shorter, stockier guy about the same age kicked back in a chair propped against the wall. Pike heard them talking when he entered, and recognized accents similar to Rina's, though not as pronounced. A flicker of recognition flashed in their eyes when he mentioned Darko, and the kid behind the counter raised his hands.

'Hey, man, I just work here.'

His friend smiled stupidly, incredulous.

'Dude. Are you *robbing* us?'

The counter kid glared lasers at the friend.

'Shut up before you get us killed.'

Civilians, or so far out of the loop they might as well have been.

Six pumps, twelve skimmers, eight keypads rigged to steal PIN numbers. Pike figured they knew the pumps were rigged, or knew enough to guess, but neither tried to interfere. Pike was gone in seven minutes, and met up with Cole and Stone at the Studio City park.

When Stone saw the number of skimmers Pike had collected, he whistled.

'Man, we should bill LAPD for this.'

They killed the next two hours at Cole's house, then rolled down through the canyons to Hollywood. Super Star Service was located on a seedy part of Western Avenue, just north of Sunset. It was smaller than the Tarzana station, having only four pumps split between two pump islands, and shared its property with a taco stand. The stand was doing a vigorous business.

As Pike waited for Cole and Stone to recon the area, it occurred to him this was their last target. If Darko's enforcers didn't show, they would have to come up with something else. That's when Cole spoke in his ear.

'Well, Joseph, I think we have company.'

'What do you see?'

'Dark blue Navigator parked across the street and a silver BMW alongside a little taco stand they have here.'

Stone's voice came in.

'I make two men in the Beemer, and at least two in the Nav.'

Pike said, 'What about the station personnel?'

Cole again.

'One male at the counter, but he's nothing like the

last kids. This guy's all sharp corners. I don't think you get out of the car this time.'

'No?'

'These boys are ready. I don't know if they'll try to take you here or follow you out, but I say we don't give them the chance. Come in. Let them see you. Then leave. Make them follow you. Don't give them another choice.'

'Rog. I'm rolling.'

Pike slipped his .357 from its holster, and set it between his legs.

Pike approached the station slowly, seeing both the Navigator and the BMW in his peripheral vision without looking directly at them. They had to believe he did not suspect they were waiting.

Elvis said, 'Looking good.'

Stone echoed him.

'All good.'

Pike eased into the station, but stopped short of the pumps. He counted to ten, then slowly turned back to the street and out into traffic. He didn't speed away, didn't punch it, and never once looked in his mirror.

Cole said, 'Here we go. Nav's pulling out.'

Pike glanced in his rearview and saw the dark blue Navigator swing through a hard one-eighty, looping into the gas station and out, jumping into traffic four or five cars behind him. The BMW followed the Navigator, cutting across oncoming traffic as the oncoming cars jammed their brakes and fired off their horns.

Stone said, 'Groovy. This is gonna be like shooting fish, bro.'

Pike's mouth twitched.

'Shoot them later. Right now, watch them.'

30

PIKE DIDN'T WANT THEM to realize he knew they were behind him, so he didn't speed up when he decided to lose them, he slowed down. Pike led them into a bottleneck where construction had forced three lanes of traffic into two. When Pike popped out the other side, they were trapped by the quicksand of congestion. Pike simply drove away, and waited at a nearby IHOP.

A few minutes later, Cole reported.

'The one dude jumped out and chased after you on foot. That didn't work so well.'

'What are they doing?'

'They split up. I'm with the Navigator, northbound on Vine. Jon's with the Beemer.'

Stone said, 'Beemer's north on Gower. We're probably heading for the same place.'

Pike said, 'I'll catch up.'

This was what Pike wanted. The authority men had sent the enforcers, and now the enforcers had to explain how they blew it. They would lead Pike to an authority man, and might even lead him to Darko.

Pike caught sight of Stone's Rover at the bottom of Laurel Canyon, just as it turned past a pair of pretentious Greek columns to enter the Mount Olympus planned development.

Cole, three cars ahead of Stone and already climbing the side of the canyon, called again to warn that their caravan would stand out in the residential neighborhood.

Cole said, 'I'm approaching a construction site here on the right. Let's dump two of these cars.'

'Rog.'

Pike sped up, trying to close the distance. He and Cole left their cars at the construction site and jumped into Stone's Rover. Stone barreled away, hurrying to make up lost ground before they lost their targets.

Palatial homes of dubious architecture lined the steep streets, none of them worthy of the Greek gods the streets were named for. Mount Olympus led to Oceanus, then to Hercules and Achilles. They climbed hard, catching glimpses of the cars they followed higher on the mountain.

They reached the crest of the ridge, rounded a tight curve, and saw the Navigator and Beemer parked outside a dark gray home on the downhill side of the street. The cars were empty, suggesting the occupants were inside the house. Like every other home in Mount Olympus, the house was set on the curb with almost no setback. Low-slung and contemporary, the face of the house was a windowless, monolithic wall with a buffed-steel entry and a matching three-car garage. Gates and walls on either side of the house blocked any view to the rear.

Stone said, 'Darko, baby. I can smell him.'

'Drive past, and drop me in front of the next house.'

Jon slowed enough for Pike to slide out. Pike glanced at the surrounding houses to see if anyone was watching, but all of the homes were still, and closed to the world.

Pike walked back to the gray house's mailbox and found a thin stack of magazines and envelopes. He shuffled through, and saw that everything was addressed to someone named Emile Grebner.

Pike returned the mail, then set off after the Rover. It had turned around at the far intersection and was waiting at the curb.

As he walked, Pike phoned George Smith. George recognized the incoming number this time, and answered right away.

'My friends tell me you're a one-man wrecking crew.'

'Your KGB friends?'

'Odessa is loving this. One of the brothers has a competing service station business with Mr. Darko's operation.'

'I'm not doing this for Odessa.'

'It never hurts to be liked, my friend.'

'What does the KGB know about Emile Grebner?'

'Grebner –'

George thought for a moment.

'If this is the same Grebner, he works with Darko, yes. I do not recall his first name.'

'An authority man?'

George laughed.

'That's what they call them. You'll be speaking Serbian soon. Maybe Russian.'

'Meaning Grebner and Darko are tight?'

'Darko will have three or four like Grebner, each running three or four cells of their own down at the street level – the people who do the crime. Secrecy is everything with people from our part of the world, my man. They may not even know each other.'

The old KGB and Communist Party had been organized the same way as far back as Lenin, and Pike knew the earliest Soviet gangs had adopted the same system when the Party tried unsuccessfully to put them out of business. The Soviet gangs had outlasted the old Party members, and had spread their system throughout Eastern Europe and, now, America.

'A cell system.'

'Yes. Like these gas stations you hammered – they're probably Grebner's responsibility, so you're his problem to handle. Is that how you know him? He sent people for you?'

'That's how I know him.'

'Pity for them.'

Pike put away his phone as he reached the Rover.

Stone said, 'Casa Darko?'

'Not Darko.'

Pike slipped into the Rover, and filled them in on what he had learned from George Smith. As he went through it, the front door opened and the two big men from the Navigator came out. They didn't look happy, with the guy in front bitching out his friend, probably blaming him for their troubles. The Navigator squealed away in a wide, screaming U-turn.

Stone laughed.

'I guess those boys need their assholes stitched.'

Pike said, 'How many were in the Beemer, Jon?'

'Two. Coupla pussies. I could tell by the way they drove.'

Stone said things like that.

Pike wondered if Darko was holed up with Grebner. Pike thought this unlikely, but knew it was possible. There might be only one or two men inside, but there could be a dozen, or a family with children.

Cole said, 'So what are we going to do?'

'Take a look. Me and you. Jon, you're outta here. Let us know if someone comes.'

As Cole and Pike slipped out, Stone said, 'Want the M4? It's ideal for urban assault.'

Cole frowned at Stone.

'You have an M4?'

'Shit, yeah, man. Suppressed. Frangible bullets so you don't kill a buncha people in the next house. Straight from the Delta Armory.'

Cole looked at Pike.

'Is he kidding?'

'Let's go.'

Pike jogged away, and Cole fell in behind him. They slowed as they neared the house, then lingered at the nearest side gate to let a car pass. Neither spoke, and neither needed to. Pike had been on missions as long as a week, and never uttered a word.

Pike went over first. He landed softly, then slipped along the side of the house without waiting. When he reached the corner, Cole was at his shoulder.

The backyard was small, but designed for sophisticated entertaining, with an outdoor bar, cabana seating around an elevated fire pit, and an infinity pool that stretched into space. The view past the pool encompassed the entire Los Angeles basin from downtown to the Pacific, and south all the way to Long Beach. The waterline at the edge of the pool seemed to simply stop, hanging at the edge of the sky. Views like this were why they called the development Mount Olympus.

Pike heard the steady drone of faraway voices, and realized he was hearing the television. ESPN, someone going on about the Lakers.

Cole touched Pike's shoulder, and pointed. The service walk ran behind the bar to an area walled off for the pool equipment. Cole touched his shoulder again, then pointed at his own eyes, telling Pike the pool equipment would be a good vantage point.

Pike slipped past the bar to the pool, and squeezed in behind the pool equipment. Cole joined him a moment later.

The entire back of Emile Grebner's house was

open. Floor-to-ceiling glass sliders had been pushed into pockets, erasing the line between inside and out, and opening the house to air and light. Two younger men and a shorter, bulky man in his fifties were in the living room, but none of them were Michael Darko. The older man wore only baggy sweatpants cut at the knee, exposing a chest and back matted with gray hair. He was doing all the talking, so Pike decided he was Grebner. Grebner was angry, and making a big production of waving his hands.

One of the younger men made the mistake of speaking, and Grebner slapped him. The slap almost knocked him down, and the younger man scurried away. He came outside, where he lit a cigarette, and leaned against the bar. Sullen.

Grebner finally ran out of gas. He picked up a phone to make a call, and the other young man hurried into the kitchen. Grebner threw down the phone, then stalked into a bathroom off the living room. He slammed the door.

When the door slammed, the man at the bar held up his middle finger.

Pike touched Cole, then pointed at the man in the kitchen – that man is yours. He touched himself, then pointed at the man by the bar – that one is mine.

Cole nodded, Pike returned his nod, and both moved without hesitation, Pike moving first to clear a path for Cole.

Pike slipped up behind the man at the bar, hooked his left arm around the man's neck, and lifted.

Pike said, 'Sh.'

A shape flickered at the edge of Pike's peripheral vision as Cole passed, but Pike was focused on his target. The man struggled, but Pike lifted him higher, compressing the carotid artery to cut off the blood to his brain, and in a few seconds the man went to sleep. Pike laid him behind the bar, and bound his hands behind his back with a plasti-cuff.

Pike glimpsed Cole putting the other man down as he moved for the living room. He reached the bathroom and placed himself behind the door only a second before it opened, and Grebner stepped out.

Pike slapped him behind the right ear with the .357, and Grebner pitched forward. He hit the terrazzo hard on his hip, but didn't go all the way down, crabbing away on his ass until he bumped into the wall. Pike hadn't wanted him out. Pike wanted him awake.

Cole stepped out of the kitchen, glancing at Grebner but otherwise ignoring him.

'I'll clear the house.'

Cole disappeared, leaving Grebner to Pike. You never knew – someone could be hiding in a closet.

Pike looked at Grebner. Grebner's eyes went to the Python, to Pike's arms, to Pike.

'Who the fuck are you?'

Pike opened his phone.

'We're good.'

Stone said, 'I'm here if you need me, cocked and locked, brother man.'

Pike returned the phone to his pocket.

Grebner said, 'I'm talkin' to you, you better stop this.'

Pike could see he was scared, which was good. Outside, Cole dragged the man behind the bar out into the open. He tied the man's ankles, then headed toward the kitchen.

Grebner shook his head.

'You got no idea, I am telling you. No idea what kind of hell you have unleashed.'

Pike said, 'Stand up.'

Grebner shuffled warily to his feet. Pike turned him around, tied off his hands, then pushed him back to the floor. Grebner squinted at Pike, trying to read him, but saw only the mirrored surface of Pike's sunglasses – blue bug eyes in an expressionless face. Pike knew Grebner would find this unnerving. Like Walsh when she had him at Parker Center, he was psyching the edge.

'Where's Darko?'

'Kiss my ass.'

Pike hit him again. The barrel of the .357 caught him high on the temple and split the skin.

'Darko?'

Grebner made a low growling sound, and shook his head, spreading blood over his face.

'I know you want Darko. You been telling everyone you want Darko. Here, you can call him –'

Grebner tipped his head toward the couch.

'Get the phone. You see the phone there on the couch? Get it. Scroll for Michael. Call him.'

Pike saw the phone. He picked it up, then scrolled through the directory until he found the name.

Grebner said, 'Go ahead. You see the number there? Write it down, you want. Call him.'

Outside, Cole dragged the man from the kitchen next to his friend. Both men were now awake, and bound hand and foot. Cole hurried away to another part of the house, his gun out and ready.

Pike called the number, and reached a female computer voice.

'Enter your callback number at the tone, followed by the pound sign.'

A paging system. Pike hung up when the tone sounded, and brought up the phone's call list. The call list revealed the same number had been dialed a few minutes earlier, which would have been the call Grebner placed before he went to the bathroom. Grebner was telling the truth.

Pike slipped the phone into his pocket, then went back to Grebner.

'Where is he?'

Grebner glanced at the pocket.

'There. This is where Michael is. You page him, and he calls. He lives there in the phone. He's in your pocket.'

Pike holstered the .357, then squatted so he and Grebner were only a few inches apart.

Pike said, 'This will hurt.'

Pike dug the point of his thumb behind Grebner's right collarbone, probing for a bundle of nerves. He

found it, and pinched the bundle into the bone. Grebner flinched, and tightened against the wall. Pike
pinched harder, crushing the bundle. Grebner's entire
body stiffened like a drawn bow, and he made the low
growl again, straining to stand up to the pain.

Pike let go.

'It will hurt worse the next time.'

Grebner sucked deep breaths, and shook his head
to gather himself. A spray of fine blood speckled the
wall.

'I know you want Darko, but what are you doing
here, man? You want some money? I can give you
money.'

Pike dug at the nerve again, and this time Grebner
screamed. His face went bloodred to purple, and he
kicked spastically, but Pike held him down. And then
released the pressure.

'Not money. Darko.'

Grebner sobbed, still shaking his head.

'I do not know. I call him. I call the number. That
is all I know. He tells no one his whereabouts for this
very reason. You can beat me all you like, but I cannot
say. You are not the first who wants to find him.'

'Jakovich?'

Grebner's eyes narrowed as if Pike had finally
surprised him. He glanced at his men and then toward
the front door, almost as if he couldn't believe he was
in this position and if he only pretended hard enough
Pike would go away.

'You got no idea what you are saying.'

'How about if I say, "Kalashnikov"?'

Grebner slowly opened his mouth, staring as if Pike were mystical.

'How can you know these things?'

'Are the rifles in Los Angeles?'

Grebner did not answer. He was still trying to figure out how Pike knew.

Pike reached for his shoulder, and Grebner jerked.

'Yes! Yes, this is what I hear. I don't *know* this – I don't *see* them – but this is what I am told.'

As Grebner answered, Cole reappeared, now carrying a grocery bag tucked under his arm. He motioned Pike over, and spoke so Grebner couldn't hear.

'The guns are here?'

'That's what he says.'

'How about Darko? He have a location?'

'He has a pager number. That's it.'

Cole patted the bag.

'I scooped some billing records and files, but it's lame. I don't know if this will help.'

Pike and Cole returned to Grebner, who was watching them like a cornered rat would watch circling dogs.

Pike said, 'Where are the guns?'

'How would I know? The old one. He has them.'

'Jakovich.'

'You do this for the guns? You want to steal them, buy them, what? Who are you working for?'

'Frank Meyer.'

'I don't know a Frank Meyer. Who's that?'

'Darko sent a crew to a house in Westwood almost a week ago. Do you know about that?'

'Of course, I know. This was Frank Meyer's house?'

'Frank, his wife Cindy, their two little boys. Darko's crew murdered them after his son was snatched.'

Now Grebner's eyes narrowed again.

'Michael's son?'

Pike nodded, but this seemed to confuse Grebner even more.

'Michael has no children. This was the old man's child he took.'

Cole and Pike shared a glance, then Cole took the picture of Rina's son from his pocket and held it out. The baby with the wispy red hair.

'Peter. *Petar*. Is this the kid you're talking about?'

'I have not seen the child. All I know is what Michael tell me.'

'Which is what?'

'Michael took the child to get the guns. He thinks he can force the old man to make a deal, but the old man is crazy like these old fucks back home. He went insane.'

'So now they're at war.'

Grebner laughed.

'You would have to be Serbian to understand. This is beyond war. The old man, he tells Michael he will kill the child himself. The old one will kill his own child to show he has no weakness, and cannot be threatened, and he will kill Michael. Do you understand what I am telling you? This whole mess has blown up in Michael's face.'

Cole said, 'Jakovich's child? Not Michael's.'

'Yes.'

'Who's the mother?'

'Who can say? I don't know these people.'

'How many children does Michael have?'

'Some? Many? None? You think we go on picnics? I never see Michael with anyone but whores.'

The phone in Pike's pocket rang with a high-pitched jangle that made Grebner jump. Grebner's phone.

Pike glanced at the incoming number, but it was only a number and meant nothing. Pike answered, but said nothing. The person on the other side was silent. Pike heard breathing, then the person hung up.

Pike slipped the phone into his pocket, and saw that Grebner was smiling, his teeth filmed with blood.

Grebner said, 'This will be Michael, yes?'

'Probably.'

'I am sorry for your friend, Frank Meyer, but he should not have involved himself in our affairs. Neither should you. We are terrible enemies.'

Pike studied him for a moment, then glanced at Cole, whose eyes were wide, the eyes saying, What in hell just happened here?

Pike said, 'We're done. I'll be right behind you.'

Cole headed for the front door, and Pike turned back to Grebner. When Cole was gone, Pike drew the .357 and thumbed back the hammer. The locking steel spring was a breaking bone in the quiet house. Grebner, eyebrows lurching, wet his lips and breathed faster.

Pike touched the muzzle to Grebner's head. Grebner clenched his eyes, then opened them, wide and glistening, dancing like moths trying to escape a glass.

Pike said, 'Where did Jakovich get the guns?'

'I got no idea. I don't know.'

'Was Frank involved?'

'What? Who?'

Grebner was so scared he had already lost the name.

'The man who owned the house. Frank Meyer. Was he involved in the deal for the guns?'

'I don't know. How could I know?'

'What did Darko tell you?'

'He said nothing about this Frank Meyer. He told me he knew where the old man had his son. That's all he said.'

Pike pressed the muzzle into Grebner's head. It would leave a perfect, circular mark.

'Did he tell you why the child was with the Meyers?'

'No, just he was going to get the old man's boy. That is what he say.'

'Darko went with the crew to the Westwood house?'

'That's what he say. To make sure they not fuck it up. Please –'

Pike looked out over the white terrazzo floor and the fine white furniture and beyond the two trussed men with their frightened, watching eyes, to the infinite, hazy sky. Knowing was good.

'Deliver a message.'

Grebner opened his eyes. He had expected Pike to kill him.

'Tell Michael nothing he does or can do will stop me.'

Grebner slowly nodded, staring into Pike's invisible eyes.

'I think maybe you are a terrible enemy, too.'

Pike holstered his gun and left.

31

PIKE FLAGGED JON TO pick them up, Cole tugging his arm as soon as they were out of the house.

'Refresh my memory. Whose kid is this we've been trying to find?'

'Your memory's fine. She said Darko is the father.'

'Only Darko tells this guy that Jakovich is the father.'

'Yes.'

'I don't get it. Everything she told us checked out when I spoke with Ana's friend.'

In the car, Pike explained about Grebner as they drove down the hill, and asked Jon to stay at the scene to follow Grebner in case he left for a face-to-face with Darko. Stone told him it would be no problem, then had a few questions.

Stone said, 'This guy Grebner, was he in on killing Frank?'

'No. Says he knew about it, but it was Darko's play.'

'So he didn't know if Frank was involved?'

Pike realized Stone was staring at him, and realized why.

'He doesn't know if Frank had anything to do with the guns or not. He doesn't think so, but he doesn't know.'

Cole said, 'The guns are in Los Angeles, and Jakovich has them. Way these people keep secrets, Darko may not even know how he got them. He just wants them.'

Stone didn't say any more. They drove the rest of the way down in silence, but Stone was likely thinking much the same things as Pike. The field of fire was growing confused. Rina hid her baby with her sister to keep him from Michael, or Jakovich hid his child with Ana or Frank for the same reason, which meant Jakovich had a relationship with Rina's sister or with Frank. Frank and his family were either innocent collateral damage, or Frank was somehow involved with Jakovich in the acquisition of three thousand automatic weapons. Pike thought about these things, but didn't try to get his head around everything at once. Pike knew how to remain calm during the chaos of combat. He had been trained for it, and had survived withering fire in overwhelming combat situations dozens of times. He had learned to keep his head by thinking about one thing at a time. Access the situation, plan a single action, then commit yourself to that action. A war is won one maneuver at a time.

Pike said, 'Let's talk to Rina again.'

They took their own vehicles to the guesthouse while Jon Stone returned to Grebner's. The drive to the guesthouse at the far end of the Sunset Strip took only minutes, and then they cruised along the narrow, sun-dappled street to the rental property. Yanni's truck was gone, and Pike immediately sensed they would find the house empty.

Pike waited for Cole at the gate, then eased along the stubby drive past the front home into the tiny courtyard. All of it vibed deserted and creepy, and when Pike glanced at Cole again, he saw that Cole had his gun out, dangling along his leg.

Pike tried the knob, found it unlocked, and went in with Cole behind him. The little guesthouse was cool and pleasant, and smelled of the vining roses.

The single studio was empty. The bathroom door was open, but the light within it out. Pike called anyway.

'Rina?'

'They're gone. Look. Their things are gone.'

Cole set the bag on the dinette table.

'I'll see if this stuff gives us anything.'

Cole dumped the contents of the bag, then began organizing a jumble of phones, wallets, and papers.

Pike phoned Walsh as Cole worked, putting the phone on speaker so Cole could hear. When Walsh realized the call was from Pike, she seemed distant and wary.

'Where are you?'

'Doing what I told you I'd do.'

'You were supposed to keep me advised. I want to know what you're doing.'

Pike knew she was trying to bait him into admitting he found the bug, so he ignored her.

'The guns are in Los Angeles.'

'Where?'

'Don't know, but the deal is close. I have some information I need to confirm.'

'Don't just leave me hanging. *Where are those guns?*'

'Jakovich has them. That's all I know. You want me to leave it at that?'

'No.'

She sounded defeated, as if needing Pike's help left her depressed.

'Does Jakovich have any children?'

'What does that have to do with anything?'

'Michael Darko caused a one-year-old male child to be kidnapped, and I have conflicting information about the child's identity.'

'Jakovich is an old man.'

'Doesn't mean he can't have a baby.'

'Jesus, Pike, I don't know. So what if he does?'

'One of my sources tells me the child is Darko's child. The other says Jakovich is the father. If Darko kidnapped this kid to force the old man's hand, it's blown up in his face. This source tells me the old man has ramped up the war, which means he could unload the guns faster just to get rid of them.'

'Okay, wait – how has he ramped up the war?'

'He's vowed to kill the kid himself. This takes the child off the table as a bargaining chip, and sends a message to the other Serb sets. The source told me they're big on messages.'

Pike heard Walsh take a deep breath.

'Is this source reliable?'

'I had a gun to his head, Walsh. How reliable could he be? That's why I'm calling you – to see if any of this is possible.'

She breathed again, and then her voice was thoughtful.

'*Vorovskoy Zakon*. You know what that is?'

Pike glanced at Cole, but Cole shook his head.

'No.'

'Started with the Russian gangs back in the old Soviet Union, but it's all through the East European gangs now.'

'What is it?'

'It translates as 'thieves in law.' *Vory v Zakone*. What they call the thieves' code. These people live by eighteen rules, Pike – actual written rules, kind of like a guidebook for assholes. The first rule – rule number one – is that their families don't matter. Mom, dad, the brother, sis – those people do not matter. They are not supposed to have wives or children. It's actually written like that, Pike. I've read it with my own eyes.'

Pike thought about Rina.

'What about girlfriends?'

'Girlfriends are fine. Have all the girlfriends you

want, but marriage is out. These guys swear a blood oath on this crap, and I have interrogated enough of them to tell you they mean it. So if you're asking me whether Jakovich would sacrifice his own child, I have to say yes. They have these rules, and the rules are enforced. If the rules are broken, the punishment is death. I'm not shitting you. The old *pakhan*s take this stuff seriously.'

Pike nodded, thinking about a man who could do such a thing, and then he continued.

'I need to know about Darko, too. If the child is Darko's, then my other source is solid. If not, then not, and that business I told you about Darko leaving the country is probably wrong.'

'I'll check with Interpol. They might have something on Jakovich, but I can already tell you we don't have the information on Darko. You're on your own with Darko.'

'Okay. Let me know.'

She said, 'Pike?'

Pike waited.

'Don't get second thoughts about killing him. Don't make that mistake. Darko is mine.'

Pike said, '*Sh.*'

He hung up as Cole glanced up from the things he had spread onthe table.

Cole said, 'I think we have something.'

Pike went to see, thinking he had rules of his own.

32

JON STONE

JON STONE DROPPED OFF Pike and his buddy at their cars, then drove back up the hill, but he didn't return to his observation point. He would in a few minutes, but he wanted to take care of something first.

He parked outside Grebner's house, noting that half the vehicles at the surrounding homes were Rovers just like his, and that almost all of them were black, also like his. He counted two white Rovers, and a silver, but all the others were black. Parking in this neighborhood was like hiding a tree in the forest.

Jon got out, went around to the rear, and opened the hatch. He dug around in his gearbox, selecting a sweet little nine-millimeter Sig he had rebuilt himself, along with its matching suppressor tube, which he had also built. He screwed the suppressor in place, checked to make sure no one was watching, then closed up his Rover and let himself into Grebner's house.

Stone figured the three turds Pike described would still be trying to get loose, and, sure enough, there they were, the two outside, and the older turd there in the living room – Grebner.

Grebner was on his feet, stumbling around in a circle as he tried to see his back in a mirror. He had scored a pair of scissors, and was trying to cut the plastic ties binding his wrists.

When Jon walked in, Grebner looked over, saw the Sig, and froze like a stiff.

Jon said, 'That guy who was here, with the dark glasses? He's the nice one.'

Stone stripped the scissors from Grebner's hand, kicked his legs out from under him, and dropped him to the terrazzo.

Stone said, 'Watch.'

The two men outside saw him coming and tried to roll away, over and over like a couple of glowworms. One of them was barking in Serbian, but the other just kept rolling. Jon had to hand it to the guy.

Jon grabbed the barker by the feet, dragged him to the pool, and pushed him in. The other one managed to wedge himself against the bar by the time Jon caught him. Jon dragged him back to the pool, and tossed him in, too. They were splashing around like a couple of beached fish, and breathing about as well.

Grebner managed to gain his feet again, and ran to the front door, but lost a lot of time fumbling with the lock. Jon had locked it when he entered. Jon caught him at the door, dropped him to the ground again, then dragged him back to the living room. Dude slid easily across the terrazzo.

Jon said, 'This is a lovely home, by the way. Wonderful view. Nice clean design. I have an interest in residential architecture.'

Jon bellied him out, then lifted his head by the hair so he could see the splashing.

'See that? They're drowning. If those boys had the proper training, if they were true elite killers, they'd know what to do. That boy who was just in here? Sunglasses? He'd know what to do. Me, you could drop me in there like that, wouldn't be a problem.'

Jon watched the splashing for a moment, and decided there wasn't as much now as a few moments ago.

'Only you couldn't drop me.'

Grebner said, 'I told the other one everything I know.'

'I know. I just didn't want him to have all the fun. You wanna go for a swim?'

'No!'

Jon smiled. Jon wasn't going to throw him in.

But then Jon stopped smiling.

'You got a message to deliver. I just wanted to make sure you'll deliver it in a timely fashion. You'll do that, won't you?'

'Yes!'

'I thought you might. Now let me ask you a question – does Jakovich have a buyer?'

'I don't know. Michael say no, but I don't know.'

'How about Michael? Why's he hot for so much heavy metal?'

Grebner glanced away, which meant he was thinking. Thinking was bad. Stone snapped a hard right fist into his nose. He punched him again, then a third time.

Grebner snorted out streamers of blood, now spitting the words.

'He has a deal with the Armenians. Way over market price. He can make much. Way over much.'

'How much over much?'

'Three million dollars. He think maybe more.'

Stone dropped Grebner's head. He admired the distant view for a moment, and thought, briefly, that he should probably drag those two assholes out of the pool, but then decided against it. He patted Grebner's head.

'You boys truly fucked up this time.'

Jon left the lovely house, broke down and stored his weapon, then resumed his position at the end of the street.

He took out his cell phone, and called a friend of his who often dealt in illegal arms.

'Hey, bruddah-man! What's the word on those AKs?'

Sitting there, he reminisced about the good times he had with Frank Meyer in foreign lands, and waited for something to happen.

33

COLE WENT THROUGH THE call log on Grebner's phone, examining both the incoming and outgoing calls, and made notes in a spiral notebook. When he finished, Cole brought up the most recent incoming call number on Grebner's phone, and held it out. Pike saw a number in the 818 area code.

Cole said, 'This is the call you answered when the caller hung up. The incoming number.'

'Darko.'

'I think so. This is the last outgoing call, which is the pager number programmed to Darko's name.'

Cole showed him a number with a 323 area code, then scrolled back through the outgoing call log.

'The second to last outgoing call went to the same number, which is the call we saw Grebner make before he threw the phone.'

'That's why I think it was Darko. Grebner paged him, so he was probably answering the page.'

'Uh-huh, so check it out. This particular phone

only retains the most recent twenty incoming calls and outgoing calls –'

Cole turned the tablet so Pike could see. Cole had listed the call numbers in two columns, along with the times and dates the calls were made or received. Cole had drawn an X next to almost half of the incoming numbers, indicating the calls were received from blocked numbers. Cole had drawn lines connecting three of the outgoing calls with three incoming calls. He pointed out the outgoing calls.

'Here's Grebner paging Darko. See the times?'

'Yeah.'

Cole pointed out the corresponding incoming calls.

'Okay, over here he receives an incoming call within twenty minutes of making the page. One of the call-backs was from a restricted number, but two come from the same number as the call you answered up at the house.'

'Different locations?'

'That's what I'm thinking. But why use a listed number? Twice?'

'No cell service. Nothing else available.'

Cole stared at the call lists for a moment, then picked up his phone.

'Let's see what we get.'

Cole dialed the number, then listened. He listened for a very long time before he ended the call.

'No answer. I counted twenty rings, but nada. That usually means a phone is unplugged.'

Pike said, 'Can you get an address?'

Two calls and twelve minutes later, Cole had an address. The phone number was listed to something called Diamond Reclamations in Lake View Terrace, up in the San Fernando Valley. When Cole lowered his phone, he nodded at Pike.

'It fits. Lake View is in the foothills up by Angeles Crest. Mountains mean bad cell service, so landlines are the way to go.'

Pike said, 'Good start. How about I check out Lake View, and you see what you can get from the rest of this?'

Cole pushed the papers back into the grocery bag.

'How about I try to find Rina and Yanni? There are way too many conflicting stories here –'

Cole was still talking when they heard the outside gate, and Pike went to the door. Rina stopped when she saw him, shielding the sun from her eyes with a hand. She was wearing a black T-shirt over the same jeans, the big purse slung over one shoulder, her bag slung over the opposite shoulder.

She said, 'What you find?'

'Where's Yanni?'

She scowled at him for not answering her question, then pushed past him into the guesthouse. She glanced at Cole as she put her bag on the table.

'He work for a living. They don't give him time off to help find stolen children.'

Cole said, 'Where were you?'

She upended her bag, dumping out freshly washed clothes.

'I went to wash. My clothes, they smelled like feet.'

Pike said, 'You know Emile Grebner?'

'Of course, I know. He has fucked me many times.'

She said it as matter-of-factly as if she had told them her eyes were blue or her hair black, and refolded her laundry without pausing, as if this statement had no meaning. Pike thought maybe, for her, it had none.

Cole said, 'How do you know him?'

'He have the big house in the hills, and would have girls for the parties. This was before Michael, when I was first here, fifteen, sixteen years old, I think. He like only Serbian girls, not American or Russian. He trust the Serb girls, and we speak like back home. That is where Michael first see me, up there. Why you want to know?'

'So you know he's one of Darko's authority men – a close associate?'

'I just tell you I know him. Are you not listening?'

Pike said, 'Grebner told us the baby's father is Milos Jakovich, not Darko.'

Pike watched her carefully to read her reaction. A deep frown cut lines between her eyebrows as if she was struggling with the language problem. She glanced at Cole, who was watching her just as carefully, then turned back to Pike.

'You are making this up?'

Cole said, 'We're not making it up. Are you?'

'Fuck you. You and the dog you walked in on.'

She turned back to Pike.

'This is bullshit. I know who the father is and Michael know, too. Grebner, he lies. Why he say this? Where you see him?'

Pike said, 'Grebner believes it. Darko and Jakovich are at war over some illegal arms. Rifles. Do you know anything about that?'

'Michael hate the old man, this I know, but I don't know nothing about this other thing. Why he say Michael not father?'

'Probably because this is what Michael told him. Is Jakovich the father?'

'No.'

'Could he *think* he's the father?'

She drew herself up and gazed at Cole as if he was the scum of the earth.

'His dick has never been in me.'

Cole turned red, but Rina looked back at Pike, and Pike thought her eyes were growing wet.

'This is what Michael is telling his men, that he is not the father?'

'Yes.'

'This makes no sense. Michael tells me he will take Petar back to Serbia, and will not take me. Michael is father, not this old man I have never seen. I am mother. Petar is mine.'

Cole frowned at Pike.

'This is making my head hurt.'

Rina ignored him.

'He say Michael say this terrible thing?'

'Yes.'

Her face folded as she thought about it, and she looked forlorn.

'I don't know. Maybe he tell them this to hide his shame.'

Cole crossed his arms, and leaned back, his eyes growing distant and cool.

'That the boy's mother is a whore?'

'Why else? All men are weak. You would do the same.'

'No. I wouldn't.'

'Big talk. So maybe you make me pregnant, then we'll see how big you talk, here is the mother, she is a whore.'

Cole simply stared at her, and Rina turned back to Pike.

'Does Grebner say where is my boy?'

'No.'

'Men are so weak. Take me to him. I make him say.'

'He doesn't know, but we might have a lead on Darko. Have you heard of Diamond Reclamations?'

Her face scrunched as she thought, but then she shook her head.

'No. This is a jewelry store?'

Pike said, 'We're going to find out.'

Rina shoved her clothes aside, and started for the door.

'Good. Let's find out.'

Pike stopped her.

'Not you. Me.'

Rina launched into a stream of Serbian, and kept it up as they left.

Outside, Cole said, 'What do you think she's saying?'

'No idea.'

'We probably wouldn't like it.'

'No. Probably not.'

Pike left Cole at his car, and headed for the Valley.

34
ELVIS COLE

COLE THOUGHT ABOUT YANNI as he left the guesthouse.

Janic 'Yanni' Pevich had come back clean. When Cole checked the plate Pike gave him from Yanni's F-150 pickup truck, he had learned the vehicle was registered to a Janic Pevich. The leasing office at Yanni's building confirmed the apartment was being leased to a Janic Pevich, and reported that Mr. Pevich had been an excellent tenant. Cole had then checked with a friend at LAPD's Hollywood Station, who reported that Pevich had no criminal record. Cole had related all this to Joe Pike, and let it go, but after leaving Grebner, he had begun to have second thoughts.

They now had two divergent and different stories, which meant one of the principals was lying.

Cole worked his way up Coldwater Canyon to Studio City, and returned to Yanni's apartment. Rina had said he was at work, but Cole didn't know if he was working, or care. The F-150 was missing. Cole parked in the visitors' parking lot and made his way back to Yanni's apartment.

He knocked first, then rang the bell. When no one answered, he slipped the dead bolt and let himself inside.

He said, 'Hey, Yanni, Rina's out in the car.'

Just in case.

No one answered and no one was home.

Cole locked the door behind himself, then made a quick search of Yanni's bedroom. The apartment was small, with only one bedroom, but it looked lived-in, and real. Cole searched through the bathroom, the dresser drawers, the bedroom closet, and under the bed. He found nothing unusual or incriminating, and nothing to suggest Yanni had lied. He also found nothing of a particularly personal nature, which he found odd – no pictures of family or friends, no souvenirs, and nothing to anchor a personal history. Ana Markovic had a yearbook and snapshots of her friends, but Yanni had nothing.

Cole returned to the living room, then went into the kitchen. The counter and sink were cluttered with unwashed dishes. Cole found a box of plastic baggies under the sink, then selected a glass tumbler, placed it in the bag, and let himself out. Yanni Pevich had no record, but maybe Yanni Pevich was someone else.

Cole phoned John Chen from his car, and explained the situation.

Chen said, 'How am I going to sneak it in with everyone here?'

'You'll think of something. I'm already on my way.'

'You're *coming* here?! Don't come *here*!'

'Meet me outside.'

The trip down to SID took only fifteen minutes, and John Chen had probably been waiting out front for the entire time. When Cole pulled up, Chen was hopping from foot to foot like a kid who had to pee. He relaxed when he saw the glass.

'Hey, that's a pretty good sample.'

The fingerprints were clearly defined on the glass.

'Yeah. You won't have to glue it or do anything fancy. Just tape off the prints and see what you get.'

'You want an Interpol check, too?'

'Yeah, Interpol. I'll be in my car.'

'You're going to wait?'

'I'm going to wait. How long could it take, John? Just see what you get.'

Chen scurried away. All he would have to do is dust the glass with latent powder, lift the prints with tape, then scan them into the Live Scan system. He would have a hit, or not, in minutes.

When Cole reached his car, he phoned Sarah Manning. He had not heard from the girl with the purple hair, and wished now he'd gotten her phone number. He was disappointed when Sarah's voice mail picked up.

'Hey, Sarah, it's Elvis Cole. I never heard from Lisa Topping. Would you please reconsider giving me her number? Thanks.'

Cole left his cell number, and hung up. He checked

the time. He had been waiting for only eight minutes, and Chen might get hung up forever.

Cole couldn't think of anything else to do, so he thought about Grebner. Grebner had really blind-sided them with that business about Jakovich, which seemed all the more believable because Rina had so readily admitted she knew him. They both seemed believable, but Cole knew from experience the best liars are always believable, and the very best lies were mostly the truth. Here was Grebner with his party house in the hills, and here was Rina, who claimed to have attended his parties along with other Serbian prostitutes so Grebner and his gang-set buddies could boogie with girls they trusted.

Cole wondered if there was a way he could find out if this was true, and thought he might be able to get the information from one of the other prostitutes.

Cole didn't have the files, but he had his notebook. He had copied the dates of Rina's arrests, and now he phoned the district attorney's general administration office. He worked his way through three clerks and spent almost twenty minutes on the phone before he found someone to look up the case number and identify the deputy district attorney who handled the case.

'That would be Elizabeth Sanchez.'

'Could I have her current posting and number, please?'

Deputy District Attorney Elizabeth Sanchez was currently posted to the Airport Courthouse in Playa del Rey, south of the Los Angeles International Airport.

Cole thought he would likely get a voice mail, but a woman picked up the call.

'Lauren Craig.'

'Sorry. I'm calling for Elizabeth Sanchez.'

'Hang on, I think I can –'

Cole heard her call out, then the muffled clunks of the phone being handled, and a different voice came on the line.

'Liz Sanchez.'

Cole identified himself, gave her the date and the case number, and told her he needed the names of the other prostitutes scooped up in the sting.

Sanchez laughed.

'That was almost six years ago. Wow, I was still a Grade Two. You can't really expect me to remember their names.'

'I thought it might stand out because of the nature of the arrest.'

'A vice sting?'

'A Serbian sex ring. They worked for a Serb gang set.'

'Ah. Okay, that sounds familiar. NoHo Vice took down thirteen or fourteen girls over by CBS Studio Center. A joint task force deal with OCTF.'

Organized Crime Task Force.

'That's it.'

'Serbians. Okay, sure. They had cribs all through those complexes. They had so many hookers around the pool over there it looked like the Playboy Mansion. Not that I've ever seen the mansion.'

'That's the one. I want to talk to them about events occurring on or about that time.'

Sanchez said, 'You mind if I ask what this is about?'

'A gang *pakhan* named Michael Darko. Darko heads up the set that owned these particular girls.'

Sanchez said, 'Darko.'

'Yeah. One of his lieutenants probably ran the operation, but Darko was the man. The *pakhan*. I have some questions about Darko these girls might be able to answer.'

The silence from Sanchez was thoughtful.

'I don't think that was it. I don't think that was the name.'

Now it was Cole's turn to hesitate.

'Darko?'

'Well, I'm thinking.'

'Was it Grebner? Might have been Grebner.'

'Hold on. The OC guys weren't happy with the way it turned out. The Vice coppers were fine – they took down thirteen hookers – but the OC dicks were pissed. They wanted to move up the food chain, but none of the girls would roll. I remember because the OC dicks were totally pissed off. They couldn't get the girls to roll.'

'Yeah, that would be Darko, or maybe a guy named Grebner.'

'No, I remember it now – his name was Jakovich. That's who they wanted. His set ran the girls.'

'Jakovich.'

'That's him. The OC dicks just murdered his name. Everything was Jakoffovich, Jerkoffovich, Jakobitch, like that.'

'You're telling me these prostitutes worked for Milos Jakovich.'

'Absolutely. That's why OC planned the sting. They wanted Jakovich. We had thirteen prostitutes coming out of a prelim, and none of them – not one – would roll.'

'Thanks, Liz. You've been a big help.'

Cole put down the phone. He stared at the empty sky, and knew, once more, how well some people could lie.

His phone rang, and he answered, feeling dull and slow.

A young woman's voice came from far away.

'Mr. Cole? This is Lisa Topping. Sarah Manning called. She said you want to speak with me?'

Lisa Topping was Ana's very best friend, and knew things no one else knew.

35

PIKE FOUND THE ADDRESS for Diamond Reclamations on his Thomas Guide map, then wedged the picture of the red-haired baby on his dash. He drove north on the Hollywood Freeway in silence. The creaks and whistles made by the speeding vehicle were faraway reminders of his progress. He studied the baby in brief glimpses. The kid looked nothing like Rina or Darko, but Pike had never been good at that kind of thing. Pike saw a baby, he thought the baby was either cute or not, and this kid was not a cute baby. Looking at the picture, he couldn't even tell if the child was male or female. He wondered if it would turn out to look like Jakovich.

Pike followed the Hollywood Freeway into the northeast part of the Valley, joined up with the Golden State, and dropped off less than a mile later into a flat landscape where low buildings stood guard over empty lots veined by dried weeds and crumbling concrete. Rows of faceless buildings lined the larger streets, surrounded by equally faceless tract homes, all of which were bleached by the hazy light, and perpetually powdered by dust blown down from the mountains. Telephone poles lining the streets were strung with so many cables and wires they cut the sky like spiderwebs, as if to snare the people who lived there.

Pike did not have to check the Thomas Guide again. Having seen it once, he knew the route, and skirted around the Hansen Dam Park past nurseries, outdoor storage facilities, and row after row of sun-bleached, dusty homes. He found Diamond Reclamations on a four-lane boulevard at the foot of Little Tujunga Canyon, fenced between a Mom's Basement public storage location and a stone yard where Bobcat loaders were moving slabs of limestone and marble. A huge Do-It-Yourself home improvement center sat directly across, surrounded by acres of parking and a couple of hundred parked cars. Dozens of sturdy brown men were clustered at the entrances to the Do-It-Yourself, come up from Mexico and Central America, ready and willing to work.

Pike pulled into the Do-It-Yourself center, hiding his Jeep in plain sight among the parked cars and trucks. Diamond Reclamations was a scrap-metal yard. A yellow single-story building sat at the street with eight-foot red letters painted across the front: SCRAP METAL WANTED SALVAGE AUTO PARTS STEEL. A gravel drive ran past the front building to a small parking lot. Behind the parking lot was a larger, two-story corrugated-steel building. The front building blocked most of what lay behind it from view, but Pike could see that the grounds were crowded with stacked auto chassis, rusting pipes, and other types of scrap metal. Two new sedans were parked out front on the street, and two more sedans and a large truck were in the parking lot, but the gravel drive was chained off, and a sign in the front office window read CLOSED. As Pike watched, a man in a blue shirt came out of the front office building, and crunched across the parking lot to the corrugated building. As he reached the door, he spoke to someone Pike didn't see, and then that man stepped out from behind the parked truck. He was a big man with a big gut, and thick legs to carry it. The two men laughed about something, then the man in the blue shirt went into the building. The big man studied the passing traffic, then slowly returned to his place behind the truck.

Everything about the man's body language defined him. Guard. Darko probably traveled with body-guards, and this man was likely one of his guards. Pike wondered how many more guards were inside and around the building.

Pike decided against calling their phone number again. He wondered if the phone rang in the smaller front building or the large corrugated building. Darko might be in one or the other. The man who murdered Frank and Cindy Meyer, Little Frank, and Joey.

Pike said, 'Almost there, bud.'

Three of the Latin workmen broke away from the

group by the entrance, and came toward Pike across the parking lot. They had probably been waiting for work since early that morning, and were taking a bathroom break or going for a piece of fruit.

Pike rolled down his window and motioned them over. Pike spoke Spanish pretty well, along with French, gutter German, a little Vietnamese, a little Arabic, and enough Swahili to make himself understood to most Bantu speakers.

'Excuse me. May I ask you a question?'

The three men exchanged glances before they approached, and the youngest man answered in English.

'My cousin is a very good mason, but we can also work with pipes and rough carpentry. I have three years' experience with painting and dry wall.'

They had mistaken Pike for a contractor.

Pike said, 'I'm sorry, but I am not looking for workmen. I have a question about the business across the street.'

He pointed, and all three men followed his finger.

'The scrap yard?'

'Yes. I see people and cars, but the entrance is chained. I have metal to sell, but the sign says closed. How long has it been like this?'

The three men spoke among themselves in Spanish. Pike understood most of their conversation, and gathered that all three were regulars at the home improvement center. He knew this to be true at home improvement centers, paint stores, and hardware stores throughout Los Angeles. The same workers gathered daily at the same locations, and were often met by the same contractors, landscapers, and construction foremen.

The three men reached a consensus, and the younger man finally answered.

'The people are there, but the chain is up. It has been like this three or four days.'

Since the murders in Westwood.

'Before that, the chain was down and the business open?'

'Yes, sir. Before the chain, the trucks come to bring or take the metal, but now, they no longer come. My cousin and I, we go there to see if they need good workers, but they tell us to leave. Now the chain is always up, and the trucks do not come, just the men in their nice cars.'

'The men you spoke with, they were here in the front? The little building is the office?'

Pike pointed again, and the men nodded.

'Yes, the men in there. They are not friendly.'

'This was the man in the blue shirt? I just saw him. He was the rude one?'

'There were two men, and both were rude. We see other men in the back, but we were scared to ask them.'

'Did they have Americano accents?'

'No, sir. They speak with a different flavor.'

'One more question. In the evening, do these men leave for the day?'

They had another discussion, this time with the older man doing most of the talking. Then the younger man answered.

'We cannot know. If we have no job when lunch ends, we go, but we arrive before seven in the morning, and the men are always there with cars in the lot. They must come with the sun to be here before us, but they are.'

'The nice cars?'

'*Sí*. Yes. They are very nice.'

'And they come and go during the day?'

'Sometimes. Mostly no, but sometimes. The man will take down the chain, and they go in or come out, but mostly no.'

'Sometimes different cars?'

'*Sí*. Sometimes.'

'*Muchas gracias, mis amigos.*'

Pike offered a twenty-dollar bill for their help, but the men refused and continued on their way. As they were leaving, the man in the blue shirt reappeared and returned to the front building.

Pike thought about dialing the number again to see if anyone answered, but then it occurred to him to see if the business had a second number. He opened his cell phone to call Information, but his phone could not find a signal. This confirmed the reason behind the landline.

Pike brought a handful of quarters to a pay phone hanging beside the center's entrance to make the call, and asked if they had a listing for Diamond Reclamations in Lake View Terrace. They did, and a computer voice gave him the listing. It was different from the number he had.

Pike copied the new number, then called Information again for the same listing, and asked if Diamond had more than one number. The operator now read off two numbers, and the second number was the number from Grebner's phone.

Pike thumbed in more money, and dialed the newest number. He watched the office as he dialed.

A male voice answered on the second ring, and Pike wondered if he was the man in the blue shirt. East European accent, but the accent was light.

The man was careful when he answered, as if he wasn't sure what to say.

'Hello.'

'Is this Diamond Reclamations?'

'Yes, but we are closed.'

'I have ten Crown Victorias for sale. I need to get rid of them, and I will let you have them cheap. Is there someone I can speak with about this?'

'No, I am sorry. We are closed.'

'The sign says you want metal.'

The man hung up before Pike could say more.

Pike counted to one hundred, then dialed the number again, but this time an answering machine picked up.

Pike was returning to his Jeep when a tan Ford Explorer turned onto the gravel drive, stopped at the chain, and beeped. The man in blue came out of the front building, unhooked the chain, and the Explorer pulled into the parking lot. A blond woman and a man in a black T-shirt got out of the Explorer. She was chunky and middle-aged, with hair so blond it was almost white. The man was younger, with lean muscles. He lifted a case of bottled water from the Explorer's backseat, and the woman took out a grocery bag. The groceries and water suggested people were spending much time in the building.

They were heading for the corrugated building when three men came out. The last man out held the door, but the first man was a big man who moved like he wanted to knock the woman out of his way.

The corner of Pike's mouth twitched.

The big man was Michael Darko.

36

PIKE KEPT DARKO IN sight at all times. Crossing the parking lot, moving between and around the parked vehicles, Pike did not look at anyone or anything else. Pike was locked on.

Pike slipped behind the wheel of his Jeep, lowered the sun visor, then started the engine. None of the three men looked toward the enormous Do-It-Yourself parking lot across the street. They would have seen nothing if they had. The Jeep was just another tree in a two-hundred-tree forest.

Pike used a pair of Zeiss binoculars to confirm the man was Darko. He was. Darko was thinner than in the picture Walsh showed Pike, and looked in better shape, as if he had been working out. His mustache was gone, and his hair was shorter, but the wide eyes and sharp sideburns were unmistakable. As Pike watched, Darko lit a cigarette, then waved the cigarette angrily, pacing with stop-and-go bursts in front of the two men.

Pike wondered if Darko had spoken with Grebner, and if he was preparing to change locations. If so, Pike would have to act quickly. Pike studied the three men and gauged the range at a hundred forty yards. At one hundred yards, the bullet from his .357 would drop about three and a half inches. At one-forty, the bullet would be down almost eight inches. Pike could make a center-of-mass shot, but he wasn't going to shoot. Pike wanted Rina's kid, and he wanted the truth about Frank. Darko knew the answer to these things, and Pike was certain he could make Darko talk.

Darko flicked away his cigarette and stalked back into the corrugated building. The other two men followed. Pike pulled out of the Do-It-Yourself lot like any other customer, drove two blocks, then swung around and went back to the Mom's Basement, where an eight-foot cinder-block wall separated the storage location from the scrap yard.

People who rented space drove through a security gate that required a swipe card. Behind the gate, storage units ran along the eight-foot wall like soundstages at a film studio. Some were long and low to house cars and boats, but the largest was a three-story block building at the rear of the site.

Pike clipped on his .357 Python and his .45 Kimber, pulled off his sweatshirt, then strapped into his vest. He left his Jeep at the street, scaled the gate, and trotted along the storage units built against the wall. Two older men unloading a pickup watched him pass, but Pike ignored them. He would be over the wall before they could report him.

When he was beyond the corrugated building next door, Pike hoisted himself up onto the low shed roof, then peered over the wall. Parts and pieces of deconstructed vehicles dotted the ground like squares on a checkerboard, crossed and crisscrossed by narrow paths – fenders, tops, hoods, and trunks; chassis, driveshafts, and towering stacks of wheels. Giant spools of wire were overgrown by dead weeds, sprouted during the most recent rain only to die.

Pike saw no guards or workmen, so he moved along the top of the wall to inspect the building. A single door and several casement windows were cut into the back of the corrugated building, but the windows were too high to reach and the door was so caked with dust and debris it probably would not be usable. Pike chose a path through the scrap that would allow him a view of the opposite side of the building, then dropped over the wall. He drew his Python, then slipped between the stacks of scrap, and followed the path to the far side of the yard.

From his new position, Pike saw the office, part of the gravel parking area with the chain across the drive, and the long side of the corrugated building. A row of windows ran along the upper half of the building, suggesting a series of rooms on the second floor. A single large overhead garage door was open near the rear of the building, revealing a large service bay outfitted with tools, hoists, and bins. This would be where salvaged cars and trucks were broken down into their component parts. A man sat on a lawn chair in the open door. Wires dripped from his ears to an iPod, and he was reading a newspaper. A black shotgun leaned against the wall beside him.

Pike slipped behind a row of fenders overgrown by dead weeds as tall as scarecrows. When he had a view of the service bay again, the man in the chair was now on his feet. A second man had appeared at a door, and the two were talking. The chair man picked up his shotgun to join him, and the two of them disappeared.

Pike moved fast to the building. He pressed his back flat to the wall outside the big door, then cleared the service bay and saw it was empty. Darko would either be in the rooms beyond the door or upstairs, but Pike didn't necessarily want Darko. He would have taken the chair man if the chair man had stayed, then worked his way up. Someone close to Darko would do if they could tell him what he wanted to know.

Pike stepped into the service bay when he heard the baby crying. The hiccup-y wail babies make was lost in the building, echoing through the cavernous room. Pike thought it might be coming through the far door or the walls, but then he realized it was coming from one of the windows overhead.

Pike thought through his moves. Making for Darko was the play to make, but the kid was upstairs. Crying.

Pike made his decision.

A metal stairway at the back corner of the service bay led up to the second floor. Pike made for the stairs.

37

THE STAIRWELL OPENED TO a long, narrow hall that let Pike see the length of the building. The first door in the hall was open, and the baby sounds were loud, but now Pike heard a woman's irritated voice. Pike couldn't understand her language, but he caught the harsh irritation, as if the woman had been tasked with a job she resented. Male voices came from the far end of the hall.

Pike took a breath, then slowly entered the room, moving so quietly the woman did not hear.

The woman was bouncing a baby with wispy red hair, trying to quiet him. She was facing the window, and trying to get the baby interested in something outside. A bassinet was against the wall, along with a small table spread with a sky blue blanket and a battered wooden desk. Disposable diapers and jars of baby food were stacked on the desk, along with baby wipes, cotton, and the other things babies required.

Pike made a *ss-ss-ss* sound to draw the woman's

attention. When she turned, Pike touched the gun to his lips.

'Sh.'

The woman was so still she might have stopped breathing, and her white skin paled to a sickly blue.

Pike whispered.

'Whose baby is this?'

'Milos Jakovich. Please do not kill me. I have not harmed this child. I care for him.'

She thought he was working for Jakovich, come to kill the child.

Pike said, 'Don't speak. Don't move.'

The baby frowned at Pike, its snow-white brow scrunching like a crumpled handkerchief. Its red hair was wispy and fine, and its blue eyes seemed large for its head.

Pike moved past the woman to look out the window. The drop was about fourteen feet. The impact would be similar to a hard parachute landing, but Pike could make the drop with the baby. He could cushion their impact, then make his way back over the wall.

Pike holstered the Python. He was opening the window when something thumped in the hall, and the same man who summoned the chair guard appeared, and saw him.

The man shouted, and was pulling a pistol when Pike crushed his larynx and snapped his neck.

The woman was shouting out the window, and now the baby was screaming, too, its face a vivid red. Pike pulled her backward by the hair, but he didn't have to fight her for the baby. She shoved it into his arms, and ran, stumbling down the hall. Pike took the baby back to the window, but now three men were running toward them, one of them pointing up at the window.

Pike stepped back and listened. He heard footsteps, voices, and a slamming door, but nothing on the stairs. This meant they were talking to the woman. They would spend a few minutes trying to figure out who he was and whether he was alone, and then they would come. Men would be outside to cover the window, one team would come up the far stair, and another team would come up the near stair. Then they would fight.

The baby was screaming, tiny legs kicking, miniature fists clenched for battle, tears squeezed from eyes clenched tightly closed.

Pike held up the baby so they were face-to-face.

'Boy.'

The screaming stopped, and the angry blue eyes opened to nasty slits.

The close-quarters fight would be loud and vicious, and it occurred to Pike he had to protect the kid's ears. He spotted the cotton in the baby supplies, pinched off two bits, and pushed a plug into each of the baby's ears. The baby fought fiercely and screamed even louder.

'Gonna be loud, boy. Suck it up.'

Pike heard movement in other parts of the building, and knew the fight was approaching. When it came, they would shoot to kill him, which meant he couldn't stand around with the kid. Pike jerked a blanket from the bassinet, wrapped it around the baby, then pulled a bottom drawer from the desk. He scooped out old files and paper, and placed the baby inside. The baby immediately stopped crying.

'You good?'

The baby blinked.

'Good.'

Pike closed the drawer with the baby inside, and hurried back to the door. Shooters were probably in both stairwells by now, and only seconds from making their move. They would have listened to the blond woman, made some kind of plan, and now felt confident they had Pike trapped. They were wrong. Pike attacked.

Pike crushed the near stairwell door from its jamb like a breaching charge. The two men on the stairs were caught off guard, and did not react quickly enough. Pike shot them in place, single-tapping each man in his center of mass, and immediately heard shouting below in the service bay.

Pike did not continue down because that was what the men below expected. They would cover the bottom door, thinking that Pike was trying to fight his way out. The men at the far end of the second floor would likely advance, believing they could trap Pike on the stairs.

They couldn't. Pike was already gone.

Pike did not have to think these things through because he already had. He knew the plays even before he tucked the kid in the drawer, ten steps ahead of the curve.

Bang, bang, two down, and Pike blew back up the stairs. He was braced in the doorway and ready when the door at the far end of the hall opened, and two more men charged out. Pike shot the first man, and the other fell back, kicking the door closed, leaving his partner moaning. Pike put three fast rounds into the door to keep it closed, then popped the Python's wheel and fed it a speed-loader. He didn't wait, and didn't check the downed man. He ducked through the baby's room and swung out the window. The three men seen earlier were gone, drawn inside by the gunshots and shouting.

Pike hit sand, then ran, always moving forward. Speed was everything. The men inside were confused. They didn't know where he was or how many people they faced, so Pike increased the pressure.

He slipped into the same service bay he entered earlier, only now four men were jammed at the base of the far stairwell, focused on the door. Pike shot the nearest man in the back, moved to cover, and shot a second. The remaining men fired blindly into the walls and ceiling as they fled. Pike heard fading shouts and engines rev.

A short hall led toward the front. Pike worked his way along the hall, hearing more engines, and came to a room filled with standing metal shelves, and an open door. He paused for the first time, but heard only silence, then approached the open door. The gravel parking lot was empty. Darko and his people were gone.

Pike found the front stair and hurried up to the second floor. He stepped over the dead man at the top of the stairs and moved toward the screaming. He worked his way down the hall, clearing each doorway until he was back where he started, then put away his gun and opened the drawer.

The baby looked angry as hell. The little fists swung and the legs pumped, and the red face was slick with tears.

Pike said, 'You good?'

He lifted the baby out, and snuggled it to his chest. He took out the cotton plugs. The crying and screaming stopped. The baby settled against him. Pike rubbed its back.

'That's it, buddy. I got you.'

Pike headed back along the hall to the front stair, then down, and into the parts room. Someone would have called the police, and the police would be rolling.

Pike was only five feet from the door when Rina Markovic came in from the service bay. She was holding her little black pistol, but it was her eyes that gave her away, and he knew she was Jakovich's killer. They were cold, and dull, like the eyes of fish on ice.

She said, 'You find him. Good. There is Petar. Yanni, he have Petar.'

Yanni stepped in from the gravel, muttering something in Serbian. Yanni's gun was stainless steel, and found Pike as if it could see him.

Pike knew his best chance was now, in the opening second, before they got to the killing. And as before, Pike took immediate action.

Pike spun to the left as he went for his gun, shielding the baby with his body. Pike thought he would take at least two bullets in the back before he could return fire, and either the vest would save him or it wouldn't. If those first two shots didn't kill or cripple him, he thought he could beat them even if he had to fight wounded.

Pike did not hear the shot when Yanni fired, but the bullet hit his back like a big man throwing a good hook. Pike staggered with the impact, but still managed to draw his weapon, and turned to fire when Jon Stone appeared in the door. Jon forearmed the M4 into Yanni's head, and the big man dropped as Cole hit the woman from behind, stripped her weapon, then rode her down, his own gun out, eyes crazy and wide.

Cole said, 'You all right?'

Pike checked the kid, who was screaming so hard he might have a stroke.

Petar was fine.

'We're good.'

Stone said, 'Let's get the hell out of here.'

Part Four
Guardian

38

THEY TIED OFF YANNI and Rina with plasti-cuffs, then dragged them out to the cars, working to clear the area before the police arrived. Pike had the kid, screaming like a banshee, and Rina was screaming, too.

'Is not what you think. Petar is mine. I was trying to save him –'

'Shut up.'

Stone's Rover was in the parking lot. They shoved Yanni into the rear. Cole pushed Rina into the backseat, and climbed in after her.

Pike said, 'Up in the canyon. Angeles Crest. Jon?'

'I know where.'

Cole held out his hands for the boy.

'Here, I'll take him.'

'I got him.'

'How you going to drive, just you?'

'Go.'

Stone ripped away before the door was closed, throwing up gravel and dust.

Pike ran hard to his Jeep, and saw the oncoming flashers as he pulled into traffic, heading for the mountains, the old guys at Mom's Basement watching him peel away. Three sheriff's cars flashed past a quarter mile later, so Pike pulled to the right like everyone else. The kid was scared, and screaming, and Pike felt bad for it. He repositioned the little guy on his shoulder, and patted his back.

'It's okay, buddy. Gonna be fine.'

They slipped under the Foothill Freeway, and climbed into the Little Tujunga Wash. The road rolled through the bottom of the ravine, and something about the motion settled the boy. He lifted the big head to look around.

Pike drove exactly six-point-two miles up the canyon, then turned onto a gravel road. He knew the distance because he made the drive often, coming up to the middle of nowhere to test-fire weapons he had repaired or built. He followed the gravel another two-point-three miles over a gentle rise, and saw Stone's Rover parked on the flat crest of the hill. Stone and Cole were already out. Yanni was belly-down on the ground, and Rina was cross-legged beside him, hands still cuffed behind her back.

Pike turned to join the Rover, and the rocky ground crunched beneath his tires. The earth was littered with thousands of cartridge casings. Maybe hundreds of thousands, or millions. Most so old and tarnished, their once gleaming brass was black.

Cole came over as Pike got out with the boy, and

painted him with a ragged smile.

'We could be professional babysitters. I hear there's good money in that.'

'He's loud.'

The boy arched his back again, and turned to see Cole. Cole wiggled his fingers and made a face like a fish.

'Cute kid.'

The baby broke wind.

Pike glanced at Yanni and Rina, and lowered his voice.

'Is she the mother?'

'None of that was true. They work for Jakovich. I don't know who his parents are, but she isn't the mother. Maybe Grebner was telling the truth.'

'Is Darko the father?'

'All I know is she isn't the mother. Ana told a friend named Lisa Topping that Rina couldn't have children because she was cut. That's probably why she was so protective. That's the only part of Rina's story that was true.'

Pike watched Rina while Cole described what he knew and how he knew it. Rina had told the truth about Ana and their relationship, and about being a prostitute for Serbian mobsters, but she worked for Jakovich, not Darko. Rina Markovic had lied about damn near everything, and had been good at it, mixing her lies with the truth the way all the best liars do. Pike nodded toward Yanni.

'What about him?'

'Real name is Simo Karadivik, originally from Vitez. That's Jakovich's hometown. Yanni there – Karadivik – is one of Jakovich's enforcers. He shows three arrests back in Vitez, and two under his true name since he arrived in Los Angeles. That's why nothing popped up when I ran his alias. Janic Pevich doesn't exist.'

Pike realized he had a long way to go before the kid was safe. Everything he thought he knew was lies, and the only truth seemed to be that Darko and Jakovich hated each other, and were willing to murder a ten-month-old baby to further that hate. Pike sensed this was something he could use, and stroked the baby's back.

'Is his name really Petar?'

'I don't know.'

Pike considered Rina and Yanni as he stroked the boy's back. Her legs were twitching as if a nervous fire burned in her belly. Yanni's face drooped, making him appear sleepy, but his eyes tocked from Pike to Stone to Cole like gleaming ferrets in twilight caves. They were scared. That was good. Pike wanted them scared.

The boy quivered, and, a moment later, Pike smelled a strong odor.

'He messed himself.'

'How do you know?'

'I felt it. Now I can smell it.'

Pike thought for a moment.

'We need to get some stuff for him. We have to get

something for him to eat, too. He'll get hungry.'

Cole came around and stood in Pike's line of sight, blocking his view of Rina and Yanni.

'Are you serious? We can't keep this kid.'

'I'm going to keep him until he's safe.'

'I know people in Children's Services. I'll call someone.'

'When he's safe.'

Pike rubbed the boy's back, then held him out to Cole.

'Take him, okay? He's getting cold. Get whatever he needs, and we'll hook up back at your place. You can take my Jeep. I'll ride with Jon.'

Cole glanced at Yanni and Rina, and Pike saw he was worried.

'What are you going to do with them?'

'Use them.'

'For what?'

'To meet Jakovich. I have something he wants.'

Cole considered Pike for a moment, then took the boy. Pike watched them go, not moving until the Jeep disappeared. Pike wanted Cole gone, and now he was, so Pike walked over to his prisoners. He took Yanni's arm, and Stone pitched in, and they pulled the big man into a seated position. Yanni didn't make eye contact, but Rina straightened her shoulders.

She said, 'You are making mistake. Petar is mine. Why are we tied up like this?'

Pike didn't say anything. There was no point. He had crossed paths with so many people who did and would do the most heinous atrocities that none of it left much of an impression anymore. Here was this woman, and she would have murdered a child. Here was someone named Jakovich, who had probably ordered her to do it, and Darko, the same. People willing to do this terrible thing.

Pike stretched his back where Yanni shot him. It hurt. He thought the impact had probably cracked a rib.

'Whose baby is it?'

'Is mine!'

'No, not yours.'

'I am saying the truth. What you think is happening here? Why are you acting like this?'

Stone prodded Yanni with the M4.

'Maybe because this asshole shot him.'

'That was a mistake. He got confused.'

Pike looked at Yanni.

'Was shooting me a mistake, Simo?'

Yanni's eyes fluttered at the mention of his true name.

'I get confused. Who is this Simo?'

'A soldier for Milos Jakovich. From Vitez.'

'This is not me.'

'Ran your prints, Simo. We know.'

Rina's voice grew.

'I don't know why you are saying this things. I am the mother –'

Pike drew the .357, put it to Yanni's head, and pulled the trigger. The blast echoed off the surrounding hills like a sonic boom. Rina jerked sideways, and shrieked, but Yanni simply slumped.

Jon Stone said, 'Ouch.'

Pike thumbed the hammer, but he did not have to ask Rina again. The words spewed from her like lava.

'No, no, no, no – is not mine, isn't, but is Milos's. That is why Darko take him. It is true.'

'You work for Jakovich?'

'Yes!'

'Jakovich is the father?'

'No, no! The grandfather! He is the boy's grandfather!'

These people lied so much they might not even remember the truth.

'Where's the boy's father?'

'He is dead! In Serbia! The boy is here because he has no one else. Even the mother is dead.'

The newest story rattled out, but this time Pike believed her. Milos Jakovich's actual and only son was a forty-two-year-old man who had been incarcerated in a Serbian prison. Petar had been conceived during a conjugal visit, only to have his mother die in childbirth. Two months later, the boy's father, Stevan, was murdered in his cell by a Bosnian-Croat who was serving time for the mass murder of sixty-two Bosnian Muslims at the Luka detention camp. This left Petar Jakovich as the old man's lone remaining male heir, so he had the boy shipped to the U.S.

Rina said, 'When Milos find out what Michael going to do, he say we must hide the baby. He give

Petar to me and Yanni, and I give him to Ana. Then Michael take, and Milos tell us to find the boy, and show them.'

Show them. Murder his own grandson to show them.

Stone spit in the sand.

'Father of the motherfuckin' year. You know what? I wanna cap this prick. I want to do him with a goddamned knife.'

Pike thought through what he had, and what he needed. Protect the boy. The man who killed Frank. Three thousand combat weapons. In that order.

'Where is Jakovich? Right now, where is he?'

'On his boat. He have a boat.'

'Where?'

'The marina.'

'You can reach him? Call him?'

'Yes! He is not like Michael. He does not hide.'

Pike jerked her to her feet and cut the plasti-cuffs, freeing her wrists.

'Good. We're going to see him.'

Stone said, 'Fuckin' A.'

Pike shoved her toward the Rover. He now had something that both men wanted, and a plan was coming together.

39

THE LONG DRIVE FROM Angeles Crest to Marina del Rey gave Pike time to find out what Jakovich knew. Rina had told him about Pike, and Pike's relationship with Frank Meyer, and what Pike was trying to do. Pike decided this was good. Jakovich's familiarity would make Pike's play more believable, especially with what Jon Stone had learned about the guns.

'Does he know I tracked Darko to the scrap yard?'

'Yes. I tell him after you leave.'

'Does he know you and Yanni followed me?'

'Yes. He the one tell us to go.'

Which meant Jakovich was wondering what happened, and expecting Rina to call. Considering the amount of time that had passed, he would be thinking something had gone wrong, but this was okay, too.

The condominium towers surrounding the marina grew larger as they approached, then the freeway ended, and they circled the marina past restaurants, yacht dealers, and stunning condo towers built of green glass.

Rina did not know the name of his yacht, but she knew where it was berthed.

Pike said, 'Show me.'

'How I going to show you? We out here, it in there. He have to let us in.'

The marina was surrounded by restaurants and hotels open to the public, but the yachts were protected by high fences, electric gates, and security cameras. Pathways existed outside the fence so visitors could admire the boats, but admittance required a key or a combination. Rina directed them to the far side of the marina, and onto a street with yachts on one side and apartment buildings on the other. It was like driving onto a long, narrow island, and when they reached the end of the island, they found a hotel.

She said, 'Is behind the hotel. Where they keep the big boats.'

Stone cruised through the hotel's parking lot until they found a view of the yachts. Rina searched the rows of yachts, and finally pointed.

'That one. The blue. You see it there, on the end? The dark blue.'

Stone scowled when he saw the boat.

'Piece of shit scumbag motherfucker, living in a boat like that. I'd sink that bitch right there. Put it right on the bottom.'

Pike made the boat for an eighty-footer, a fiberglass-and-steel diesel cruiser with a dark blue hull and cream decks. Boats were slipped by size, so this one was berthed with the other long yachts, near the end of the wharf with its bow to the channel. Pike didn't see anyone on Jakovich's boat, but he counted seven people moving on the boats nearby. Witnesses were good.

'Take us back to the gate, Jon.'

When they reached the gate, Pike gave Rina her phone. He had already told her what to say and how to say it.

'Remember – you're alive as long as you help me.'

Rina made the call.

'Is mc. I have to speak with him.'

They waited almost three minutes, and then she nodded. The old man had taken the phone.

'No, we did not get him. No, not Michael, either. Pike got the boy. Yes, he has the boy now, but Michael escape. You must listen –'

Pike could hear a male voice on the other side of her conversation. She talked over him to keep going.

'We are here at the gate, Milos. He is here. Pike.'

She glanced at Pike.

'He is sitting here with me. He want to see you.'

She glanced away.

'I cannot. If I say Serbian, he will kill me.'

Another glance.

'Yanni is dead.'

Pike took the phone.

'I shot him. I will do the same thing to Michael Darko, but I need your help to do it.'

The phone was silent for several seconds, but then the male voice spoke.

'Go to the gate. We will buzz you in.'

As Pike got out, Stone said, 'Sink that bitch. Put it on the bottom.'

Jon was like that.

Pike was at the gate less than thirty seconds when he heard the lock open. He let himself through, walked down a long ramp to the wharf, then followed the wharf past the row of yachts. The sky was beginning to color, but the afternoon was still bright, and people were out.

Two large men were waiting, one on a lower fantail deck that jutted from the stern, and one a short flight of steps above on an upper deck. They wore Tommy Bahama shirts and carried a lot of fat, but they looked hard, with brooding faces and dark eyes. Pike decided he would be safe as long as he stayed on deck, and in the open. No one would pull a trigger with so many people nearby, and Pike didn't think either or both men could beat him with their hands.

A balding man who appeared to be in his seventies was seated at a small round table on the upper deck. He had been a big man once, but his skin was beginning to hang like loose fabric. When Pike stopped at the stern, he motioned Pike aboard.

'Come on. Let's see what you have to say.'

His accent wasn't pronounced. Probably because he had been here longer.

Pike went aboard. The big man on the lower deck

moved to search him, but Pike pushed his hand away.

'I'm not here to shoot. If I wanted to shoot, we wouldn't have warned you.'

The big man glanced up, and the older man waved again.

'Come on. It's fine.'

Pike climbed to the upper deck, but did not join Milos Jakovich at the table, and wasn't invited. A salon behind the old man was visible through sliding glass doors. A young woman was inside watching television. Naked.

Jakovich said, 'Okay. So here we are. What is this business with Michael Darko, and why would I help you?'

Pike said, 'Three thousand Kalashnikovs.'

Jakovich tapped the table. His finger was the only part of him that moved. Tap tap tap. He shook his head.

'I don't know what you are talking about, these guns. Is this a joke?'

He was concerned that Pike was wired. Pike raised his hands to the side, holding them out.

'We have to speak plainly. Have your boy search me.'

Jakovich considered it for several seconds, then came around the table and stood very close. He searched Pike himself.

Pike said, 'One on my right hip, and another on my left ankle. You can touch them, but if you try to pull either one, I'll kill you with it.'

Jakovich leaned even closer. He smelled of cigars.

'You got some balls, saying that on my boat.'

Staying close, Jakovich moved his hands over and under Pike's clothes. He felt under Pike's arms, down the trough of Pike's spine, and into Pike's pants. His search was thorough. He felt Pike's genitals, and Pike didn't react. He worked his way down Pike's legs, inspected Pike's shoes, then returned to the table.

He said, 'Okay, we will speak plainly.'

'Do you know why I'm going to kill Michael Darko?'

'Your friend.'

'Yes. My friend and I were military contractors. Do you understand? Professional soldiers.'

'I know this. The girl, she tells me.'

'Did my friend help you buy the guns?'

The question Pike had been waiting to ask.

'I knew nothing about this man. Rina's sister, she worked for him. That is what I knew.'

'Was he helping you sell them?'

'No. I just tell you, no. I didn't know anything about these people. Not even their names.'

Pike did not show his relief. Frank was clear. Always had been, and would be.

'I didn't think so. If he was helping you, you would have had a buyer.'

Jakovich tried to act offended.

'I have many buyers.'

'If you had a buyer, the guns would be gone, and Darko would have no play to jam you. You need a buyer, but you don't know anything about the arms market. I want to buy them, and I can eliminate Darko. I can kill him for you, or I can give him to you, let you make an example of him, whatever you like.'

Milos Jakovich cleared his throat. He rubbed at his eye, then cleared his throat again.

'This isn't what I expected.'

'No. I probably know more about the guns than you. They were stolen by Indonesian pirates from a container ship bound for Pyongyang from Kowloon. They're new, fully automatic weapons, still in their wrappers, but they won't be easy to sell because of how they came to the market.'

Jakovich looked irritated.

'How do you know these things?'

'You're an amateur at this. I'm a professional. The North Koreans still want the guns, but won't pay for them – they would consider that a ransom. The Chinese want them back, but they're going to kill the people who stole them, and they've let out word that they will view anyone who buys them as an accomplice to the crime. You don't want the Chinese coming here to the marina.'

Jakovich pooched out his lips, probably imagining a Chinese invasion.

Pike said, 'I want to buy them. If you agree, I'll throw in Darko and your grandson as an incentive.'

'What kind of money are we talking about?'

'Three thousand rifles, five hundred per, that's one-point-five million, but only if they're fully automatic and free of rust and corrosion. I will check each weapon – not three or four, but all three thousand. If they're missing bolts or receivers, I'll still buy them, but at a reduced price.'

Pike never once looked away, and made his offer as businesslike as he could.

'That isn't enough.'

'It's more than you'll get. And with me, you'll get Darko.'

Jakovich wet his lips again, and Pike could see he was thinking. He was convinced Pike knew what he was talking about, but afraid. Pike's offer had surprised him, but he was desperate enough to consider it.

'You have the cash?'

'I can have it by this time tomorrow. I will show you half the money up front. You'll get the other half at the time I take delivery.'

Jakovich crossed his arms, resisting, but trying to talk himself into it.

'And how will you give me Michael?'

'He wants the rifles, too. If you make a deal with me, I'll bring Darko when I pick up the guns. I will need one of the rifles to convince him, but I won't tell him your people are waiting. Then he's yours, and your problems are over.'

Jakovich slowly decided.

'Give me your phone number. I will let you know sometime tomorrow.'

'Don't wait too late in the day. I can only get the cash during business hours.'

Pike left his cell number, then walked off the boat without looking back. He let himself through the gate and climbed back into the Rover.

Stone looked disappointed.

'I didn't hear anything blow up.'

Pike made no comment for a moment, still thinking about Jakovich and how his plan was developing. One of the first rules of combat was that all battle plans change, and the winner was usually the guy who forced the changes.

Pike said, 'Can you put your hands on a Chinese AK? New, still in the wraps?'

'Like the ones we're talking about? Sure. Plenty of AKs around.'

'Has to be Chinese. Not a sporterized gun. A battle rifle.'

Stone shrugged.

'I know a guy who knows a guy.'

'Call him. Let's go see Grebner.'

Stone made the call while he drove.

40

THERE WAS ONLY ONE guard this time, a short, muscular man who answered Grebner's door with a scowl, and never had time to speak. Pike shut off his air, disarmed him, and marched him through the house. Emile Grebner was on the toilet when Pike found him. Pike made the guard lie on his belly, and told Grebner to stay on the can. It was hard to move quickly with your pants around your ankles.

Pike said, 'Call Darko. I have the boy now, and that changes things.'

'How you mean changes?'

'I can get Milos Jakovich, and that means I can get his rifles. I will sell Jakovich to Darko for one third of the guns – two thousand rifles for him, one thousand for me.'

'You will sell him? What are you talking about?'

'It means if Darko and I can put our disagreement behind us, Darko can get rid of his competition. I wrote my phone number on the floor in your living room. Tell Darko to call.'

'These rifles, you have them?'

'Tell Darko to call. If he doesn't call, Jakovich will sell them to someone else, and he can kiss his Armenian deal good-bye.'

Pike walked out of the house, and filled Stone in as they headed for Cole's. The Jeep and Cole's Corvette were side-by-side in the carport. They parked across the drive, blocking both cars, and Pike let them in through the kitchen. Stone hung on to Rina like she might try to run.

Cole had the boy in his arms, watching the Lakers. Cole was set up nicely by the time they arrived. Food for the boy. Pampers and lotions, and a baby-sized spoon set. Pike saw the stuff in the kitchen as they entered.

Cole stood as they entered and arched his eyebrows because he expected to see four people, and Yanni was missing.

'I shot him.'

Rina said, 'I have to go to the bathroom.'

'Jon.'

Stone took her to the bathroom. He went in with her, and left the door open. She didn't complain.

Cole came over with the boy. The little kid swiveled the big head around, saw Pike, and smiled. He flapped his hands. Excited.

Cole said, 'He wants you.'

Pike took the boy, and propped him on his chest.

Cole lowered his voice so Rina wouldn't hear.

'What happened?'

Pike explained what he now believed to be the truth, and described the play he was making on Jakovich and Darko.

'I'll have to call Walsh. They'll find Yanni's car up in Lake View, so they'll know he was at the scene. When the IDs come back on the stiffs at the scrap yard, and everyone shows a gang-set connection, the police will be all over it. I'm going to need her cover, and her co-operation pulling this off.'

'I don't think she signed on for a war.'

'She signed on for three thousand combat rigs. She's going to get them, and she'll get the man who killed her agent.'

Pike jiggled the boy. The boy laughed, then pulled off Pike's sunglasses. The last person who took Pike's shades bought a three-week stay in the hospital. The boy waved them like a rattle.

Cole said, 'What about the baby?'

Pike jiggled the kid again, and let the little guy punch him. Pike was fascinated by his eyes. He wondered what the boy saw, and why he took such delight in those things.

'He needs someone who'll take care of him.'

'And that's you?'

'Not me, but someone. Everyone needs someone.'

'Even you?'

Pike studied his friend for a moment, then gently took back his glasses. He didn't put them on. The boy seemed to like him without them.

They handcuffed Rina to the bed in Cole's guest

room, then made a makeshift bassinet in the living room. The boy didn't like the food Cole bought, so they made scrambled eggs. He liked the eggs fine.

Pike phoned Kelly Walsh at ten minutes after nine that night, but kept it vague. He told her he might soon know where the guns were located, and promised to call her tomorrow. His true purpose was to make sure he could reach her in case he heard back from Jakovich or Darko. If either of them went for it, he would have to move quickly, and he would need Walsh to move quickly, too.

Later, Cole went for a run, so Pike and Stone stayed with the boy. The kid crawled around on the floor, but grew tired quickly, and seemed cranky unless Pike held him. Pike held him, and after a few minutes the boy fell asleep. Pike kept his cell phone handy, but nobody called.

Stone got shitfaced and passed out on the floor, so Pike woke him and told him to sleep in the car. Pike didn't want the snoring to disturb the boy.

Groggy, Stone said, 'I gotta go see that guy.'

Cole returned an hour later, and volunteered to watch the boy if Pike wanted to run, but the boy was still sleeping on Pike's shoulder, and Pike didn't want to disturb him.

Cole shut the lights and went up to his loft for a shower. A few minutes later, Pike heard Cole climb into bed, and the last light went off. That was it for the day. Pike listened to the house settle, and still didn't move.

Sometime after two that morning, a thin layer of clouds masked the full moon, filling the room with blue light. Pike had been holding the boy for almost three hours, neither of them moving. Then the boy squirmed, and Pike thought he might be dreaming. He mewled like a cat, then kicked as if he were about to start bawling.

Pike said, 'I got you, bud.'

The boy woke, arched his back, and saw Pike watching. He stared into Pike's eyes as if he had never seen eyes before, looking from one eye to the other, as if each view was different and fascinating.

Pike said, 'Better?'

The boy lowered his head, and after a while he snored.

Pike never moved.

The little body was solid and warm. Pike felt the boy's heartbeat, delicate and fast, and his chest move as he breathed. It felt good, holding a tiny living person.

Pike watched the night shadows play in the canyon.

The boy shifted again, and sighed, and once more opened his eyes.

Pike whispered, 'Hey.'

The boy smiled. He kicked his legs and pumped his arms with excitement.

Pike said, 'That's right.'

The boy reached a hand toward Pike, his fingers spread.

Pike touched the center of the little hand with his

index finger. The boy's hand closed on his fingertip.

Pike wiggled his finger, just a little, and the boy, still hanging on, gurgled with a sloppy smile as if Pike's finger was a wonderful toy.

Pike wiggled his finger again, and the kid gurgled again, and Pike realized the little guy was laughing. Holding tight, and laughing.

Pike whispered again.

'You're safe, boy. I won't let them hurt you.'

The feet kicked, and Pike sat, and held the little man for the rest of the night until a golden light brightened the world.

41

LATER THAT MORNING, JUST after full-up sun, Jon Stone crept into the house. He made a thumbs-up, indicating he had the rifle. Pike eased the baby onto the makeshift bed, and followed Stone out. The baby never stirred.

Outside, Stone led him behind the Rover.

'The real deal, brother. Chinese, not Russian. Fresh from the oven.'

When Stone opened the rear door, Pike saw a long, narrow cardboard box printed with Chinese characters. Stone opened it. The rifle was wrapped in a greasy plastic wrapper. Stone slid the rifle from its wrapper, and placed it on the box.

'Never been fired. The factory preservative is still on it.'

The rifle was mottled with a synthetic preservative that smelled like overripe peaches. The stock and pistol grip were made of a bright orange wood that was slick with the preservative. The Russians had gone to polymer stocks, but the Chinese still went with the wood. Pike opened the bolt to inspect the receiver and breech. They were flawless.

Stone said, 'See? Not even a nick, bro. Mint condition.'

Pike worked the bolt several times. It was sticky. You had to put a thousand rounds through these things before they loosened up, but they were damn near indestructible. He slipped the rifle back into its wrapper, and returned it to the box. A 30-round magazine in its own plastic bag was included.

'Good work, Jon. Perfect.'

They put the box into Pike's Jeep, and went back inside.

Michael Darko called at ten minutes after seven. Both the baby and Stone were sleeping, and Cole was checking on Rina. Pike was doing push-ups when the phone buzzed.

'Pike.'

'You been trying to kill me for four days. Why should I talk to you?'

'Three million dollars.'

'What are you talking about?'

'We both want the guns.'

'I want the guns. What you want, I don't care.'

'You can't get the guns. I can. My deal is in place, and you have a buyer.'

Darko hesitated.

'You are lying.'

'No, I'm not lying, but I need you to make it happen.

That's forced me to reconsider our relationship.'

'You think me a fool.'

'I have his grandson. That got you nowhere because he hates you. Me, he doesn't hate. I met him yesterday at his boat to see the guns. I did, we dealt, they're mine.'

Another hesitation.

'You saw the arms?'

'A sample. He gave it to me when we closed the deal, but now there's a way to make even more money. I'll show you. Hollywood Boulevard outside Musso's in one hour. At the curb in full view where we'll both be safe. You'll see my Jeep.'

Pike hung up. He knew he couldn't convince Darko with more talk. Darko would have to convince himself, and now he would either show or he wouldn't.

Cole was back in the living room when Pike put down the phone. Stone was still sleeping. Pike explained what he was going to do, and Cole offered to come, but Pike turned him down.

'I'll need your help later, but not now. Take care of the kid. Let Jon get some rest. I'll be back in a few minutes.'

Pike knew he should have accepted Cole's offer, but he wanted to be alone when he faced Darko. Didn't matter how many people Darko brought, or whether or not Darko tried to kill him, Pike wanted no company. He later realized this was because he had not fully decided whether to kill the man even though he had made the agreement with Walsh. He wanted his feelings and his decision to be pure.

Hollywood was only a few minutes away. Pike drove down through the canyon, and was in front of the restaurant in less than ten minutes. The commuter traffic was building, but Hollywood Boulevard was still moving well and the early hour meant most of the metered parking spots were empty. He parked in front of the restaurant under a jacaranda tree, rolled down the windows, and waited.

Twenty minutes later, a heavy young man who needed a shave came around the corner, heading toward Pike. Just another pedestrian except he was watching the Jeep. He walked past, looking to see if anyone else was inside. Pike watched him in the mirror. He continued past, and turned up the next cross street. A few minutes later, the same man and another man appeared in the mirror. They looked around at the other pedestrians and parked cars and Pike. They did this for several minutes, then the first man took out a cell phone. Pike watched him talk. He put away his phone, and moved closer, approaching Pike and the Jeep as if they were radioactive. The other man stayed on the corner.

When the first man arrived, he looked in at Pike.

'Why don't you come out here? Come stand with me.'

Pike got out, and stood with the man on the sidewalk.

A few minutes later, Michael Darko came around the corner. Pike had seen him in Lake View Terrace, but this was different. This felt more personal, and right, and Pike was glad he had come alone.

Pike stared at the man who sent Earvin Williams and his crew to Frank's house. This man's pistol had killed Ana Markovic, and fired one of the three bullets that killed Frank Meyer. Here he was, the man responsible for Frank, Cindy, Little Frank, and Joey. Pike felt very little as he considered this. He was not angry or filled with hate. More like he was an observer. Pike thought he could probably kill all three men in less than a second with his pistol. He could also kill them with his hands, though this would take longer. Pike waited until Darko arrived, then motioned toward the Jeep.

'In back. Take a look.'

'You open it.'

Pike lifted the hatch, and swung the box around so Darko could see the Chinese characters. Then he opened it, and let the weapon speak for itself. Darko leaned close, but did not touch. The smell of the preservative was strong.

Darko finally straightened.

'All right, he will make the deal with you, but still you call me.'

'He wants the money in cash. I don't have it.'

'Ah.'

'I can buy them for five hundred each – that's one-point-five million dollars. And you have a buyer in place who will pay a thousand – the Armenians.'

'But you don't have enough to buy them.'

'No. He wants half the cash before he will take me to the guns. That's seven-fifty. I thought of you. Maybe you have it, but he won't deal with you. So we partner.'

'I don't like being partners with you.'

'I don't like being partners with you, but business is business. This is why I offered a bonus.'

'Jakovich.'

'Once he sees the cash, Jakovich, the guns, and the money will be in one place. If we partner, you can be in that place, too, only he won't know it. Then you can solve your problem, we can keep all the money, and you can be the head *pakhan*.'

'So what you're saying is we will steal the guns.'

'It saves a lot of money.'

Darko studied him, and Pike knew he was considering it.

'What of your friend?'

'I miss him, but this is three million dollars, a third for me, that's a million. I don't have to like you.'

'I will think about it.'

'You're either in or you're not. If not, then I'll find another partner. Maybe Odessa.'

A flash of irritation shadowed Darko's face, but he nodded.

'All right. When it is time, call me. I will have the cash.'

Darko motioned to his men and walked away without another word.

Pike closed the Jeep, and watched them. He was

vaguely aware of the bodyguards, but they were as inconsequential as a passing thought. He focused on Darko. Darko had done these things, and now Pike had an obligation to Frank. The obligation existed because they carried each other's slack and trusted their teammates would pick them up if they fell. No one was left behind, which meant the obligation extended beyond logic and reason. It was an obligation made to the living that remained in death. Pike had spent much time thinking about these things, and decided it was a matter of karmic balance.

Pike let Darko walk away. He felt a stab of regret about the deal he made with Walsh, but he needed something from her maybe even more than he needed to kill Darko.

Pike climbed back into his Jeep, and called her as he pulled into traffic.

'I need to see you.'

'A red Jeep Cherokee was seen leaving a scrap yard in Lake View Terrace yesterday. Was that you?'

'Yes.'

'Damnit, did you kill five people up there?'

'Six. I need seven hundred fifty thousand dollars.'

'What the fuck are you doing?'

'I met Jakovich. I just left Darko. Do you want the guns or not?'

'You met with them? Face to face?'

'Do you want the guns?'

Pike was in Hollywood, she was in Glendale. They split the difference and met in a Silver Lake parking lot on Sunset Boulevard. Pike arrived first, and stayed in his Jeep until he saw her pull into the lot. She was driving a silver Accord. Her personal car. He went over and climbed into the passenger seat. The agitation in her voice on the phone was gone. She seemed cool, and removed.

'You're in deep doo-doo, buddy. The police want to arrest you, and they're blaming me for getting them involved. You want to explain how six people came to be dead?'

'They were holding Milos Jakovich's grandson hostage. Now I have him.'

'Excuse me?'

Pike told her about Petar Jakovich, and Rina and Yanni, and the rest of it. She had been completely out of the loop.

'Frank didn't have anything to do with the gun deal. Jakovich told me that himself. Frank and his family were collateral damage. Darko went in because of the nanny.'

'Ana Markovic? You're telling me those people were murdered because of a twenty-year-old nanny?'

'Her sister stashed the old man's grandson with Ana to hide him from Darko, but Darko found him anyway. Darko thought he could use the kid to force Jakovich into a deal, but he was wrong.'

'How old is this child?'

'Ten months. A baby.'

'And where is he now?'

'With me. Darko was holding him at the scrap yard, but now he's with me.'

Walsh wet her lips again, and her jaw flexed. As if there was too much information to process, and the swell was lifting her too high and too fast to catch her breath. She finally nodded.

'Okay. I'm listening.'

'Jakovich wants Darko. Darko wants the guns. I have something they both want, and I'm using it to play them against each other. I believe I can put them together with the weapons.'

'How?'

'Jakovich thinks I'm going to buy the guns, and Darko thinks we're going to steal the guns. They each think I'm going to double-cross the other.'

'Jesus, Pike, are you an adrenaline junkie or what? What's our timeline here?'

'Later today. Darko's on board. I'm waiting to hear from Jakovich. I need three things to make it happen.'

'Let's hear it.'

'I haven't been working alone. The people who are helping me, they get a pass. In writing. I get a pass, too. In writing. Absolution from any and all charges arising out of our activities in this matter, now and in the future.'

'This isn't a double-oh license to kill.'

'I'm not finished. I need seven hundred fifty thousand dollars, and I'll need it in a few hours. Darko promised to front the cash, but he may or may not deliver. If he doesn't, I can still make the play on Jakovich, but he needs to see cash.'

'Jesus. Three-quarters of a million dollars?'

'If I can't show Jakovich the cash, he won't show me the guns.'

She nodded, slowly.

'Okay. I understand. I think I can make it happen.'

'One more thing. I get the boy. You're going to supply him with a U.S. birth certificate and full citizenship, so I can place him with a family of my choosing. This placement will not be a matter of state or federal record. No record will exist that his biological family can use to find him.'

Walsh was silent on this point even longer than when he asked for a pass on the killings. She finally shook her head.

'I don't know if that's possible. I mean, even if I wanted to, I don't know if it's legal.'

'I don't care if it's legal. I just want it done.'

Walsh let out a long sigh. Her fingernail ticked on the console between them, as precise as a metronome. She finally nodded.

'I'd better get started.'

Pike returned to his Jeep and drove back to Cole's. Cole, Stone, and Pike spent the rest of the morning getting together their gear. When it happened, it would happen fast, and it started at ten minutes before noon.

Pike's cell vibrated, and now it was Jakovich.

He said, 'You have this money?'

'I can get it in four hours.'

'Cash.'

'Yes. Cash.'

'And Michael. I will want Michael.'

'If I get the guns, Michael is yours.'

'Yes, he is mine.'

'Where do I meet you?'

'Here. On the boat. I will be here.'

They agreed on a time, then Pike hung up and immediately called Kelly Walsh.

'It's on.'

42

WALSH AND FOUR AGENTS from the Bureau of Alcohol, Tobacco, and Firearms arrived at Cole's house an hour later. Two stayed with their cars, but two male agents came in with Walsh – a tough-looking Latin guy named Paul Rodriguez and a tall lanky guy named Steve Hurwitz. Hurwitz was wearing an olive green Special Response Team jumpsuit. SRT was the ATF's version of SWAT. They spread through Cole's living room with an air of watchful suspicion, as if someone might jump out of a closet. Jon Stone had brought in a large box of his surveillance gear, and Cole was helping him set up. Cole was shirtless, but had strapped on a bullet-resistant vest. Pike couldn't blame them for being wary, especially with the cash.

Seven hundred fifty thousand dollars in cash didn't take up much room. It could be packed in four shoe boxes, and fit in a single grocery bag.

Walsh carried the money in a gym bag slung over

her shoulder. The bag was smaller than Pike thought, but he could see the weight in her walk.

She hefted it onto Cole's dining room table, and opened it, letting Pike see why the package was small. The bills were in vacu-packed bricks, bound in clear plastic wrap.

She said, 'It isn't all real. Half a million is funny money we took off a drug dealer.'

Cole said, 'What if Jakovich checks?'

Hurwitz laughed.

'You'd better start running.'

Walsh placed a form on the table and handed a pen to Pike.

'You have to sign for it. If Darko delivers, don't use it, but it's the best I could do with this little time. C'mon, sign, and let's figure this out. I have a lot of people to coordinate.'

Cole said, 'Aren't you going to let him count it?'

'Stop being stupid.'

Pike signed, and pushed back the form.

Walsh said, 'Where's the girl's sister?'

Cole brought Rina from the guest room. She looked shrunken, and even more pale. Rodriguez placed her under arrest as Cole snipped off the plasti-cuffs. The agent immediately turned her around, and cuffed her again. Hurwitz repeated everything Rodriguez told her in Serbian.

Pike said, 'For what it's worth, at the end, she helped.'

'Goody for her. If she helps when it comes to

testify, it might do her some good.'

Rina looked at Pike as Rodriguez led her out, and said something in Serbian, but Pike didn't know what she said.

Hurwitz looked at him.

'You speak it?'

'No.'

'She hopes you do it for Ana.'

Walsh looked irritated, as if they were wasting time.

'What about the kid? Where is he?'

'Someplace safe.'

She started to say something, but shook her head and changed course.

'Forget it. Okay, let's go through this. What are we doing?'

Pike said, 'Jon.'

Stone held up something that looked like the GPS locator he removed from Pike's Jeep.

'Remember this?'

Walsh reddened as Stone went on.

'It's not yours. We canned the one you put on his Jeep. This one's mine. White-burst digital ceramic, no RF, will not show on airport scanners or wands. It's better than yours.'

The SRT agent laughed.

'But my dick is bigger.'

Stone ignored him.

'One on Pike, one on Cole – they're going together – and one on their vehicle, Pike's Jeep. We link through a receiver that repeats on my laptop. I can email the software to you, and slave the repeater.'

Hurwitz went to the door, and called to the agents outside.

'Carlos. Get in here, dude. We're into some technical stuff.'

Another agent trotted in on the bounce, and immediately got together with Stone. Pike went through the setup, and how he planned to bring Jakovich and Darko together with the guns. It would be up to Walsh and her people to follow in trail, and make their entrance when the guns were confirmed.

She said, 'What about Darko?'

'Elvis and I will meet him in Venice. We picked a location close to the marina.'

Walsh looked at Cole.

'Both of you?'

Pike said, 'He's going to have people. It'll look better if I have people, too.'

Cole pointed at himself.

'I'm his people.'

Pike went on with it.

'He thinks we're meeting to pick up the money. The real reason is to give him this.'

Stone showed them a handheld GPS locator.

'He thinks he's getting this to follow Joe and Elvis to the guns, but we're going to use it to follow him. You'll be able to track him, too, when you download the software.'

Carlos was grinning.

'I like it.'

Hurwitz said, 'So Venice will be our start point?'

'Only to meet Darko. From Venice, we're going to the marina. That's the true start.'

Walsh said, 'We don't know the end point. Jakovich will be taking them to the guns.'

'If he takes them out on the boat, we're screwed.'

Hurwitz wasn't thrilled, but he shrugged.

'Okay. So we trail and set up on the roll. We've done it before.'

They spent the next hour going over their plan and setting up their equipment. Stone loaded his software onto Carlos's laptop, then fit locators on Pike and Cole, one in Cole's hair, and the other on the back of Pike's belt buckle. Both Walsh and Hurwitz made multiple calls, coordinating the tactical SRT team and six additional Special Agents.

At twelve forty-five, the agents left, heading for Venice to rendezvous at their staging area. Walsh was the last agent to leave. She hung back until the others were gone, then pulled Pike aside.

She said, 'Nobody likes what happened up at Lake View, buddy. Makes me wonder what you were trying to do.'

'I told you what happened.'

'Just remember – when the shit goes down, Michael Darko belongs to me.'

At exactly one o'clock, Pike and Cole climbed into Pike's Jeep and drove down the hill. Stone had already gone. Cole made an exaggerated sigh.

'Finally. Some alone time for Dad and Dad.'

Pike didn't answer. He was thinking about the kid. They had left the boy with Cole's next-door neighbor, Grace Gonzalez, and Pike wondered how he was doing.

Michael Darko was waiting for them at the end of Market Street in Venice. Market was lined with diagonal parking spaces, and died at the Venice boardwalk, just around the corner from the Sidewalk Café. Cole suggested it because he liked the pizza, but Darko agreed because the location was busy with tourists, street performers, and locals.

Two black Beemer sedans and a black Escalade were hunkered together, taking up most of the spaces.

Cole said, 'Don't these guys know any color but black?'

Pike pulled up beside the Beemers, and got out. Cole stayed in the Jeep. As Pike got out, both Beemers opened, and Darko and three of his men emerged.

Darko stared at Cole.

'Who is this?'

'He's going to help me check the rifles. Jakovich expects it.'

Pike gave him the handheld locator and showed him how it worked. It showed a circle of green light on a map.

'This is how you follow us. See the light? That's us. Don't follow too close because Jakovich might see you. Hang back. Use this to stay with us.'

Darko and two of his men had a conversation about

the device, which Pike didn't understand, and then Darko opened the Beemer's back door. He took out a gym bag that was much larger than the one Walsh delivered.

'The money. Count it, you want.'

Banded packs of hundred-dollar bills filled the bag. Pike didn't bother to count.

'Don't need to count it. We take the guns, you're getting it back.'

Darko smiled, then winked at his friends.

'You know, this works, maybe you and me, we will do business again.'

Pike said, 'I doubt it.'

Darko was thoughtful.

'So tell me something. How are you going to deliver me to Jakovich?'

'I told him you think I'm going to sell the guns to you. I told him I would set up the meet with you, and when you showed up, his guys could kill you.'

Pike made a pistol of his hand, pointed at Darko, and pulled the trigger.

Darko seemed to realize what Pike had said, and slowly looked around at the surrounding buildings.

Pike said, 'We'd better go. He's waiting.'

Pike got back into the Jeep and headed for the marina.

43

PIKE COULD SEE THEM in the rearview, eight or ten cars back, but the three large black vehicles bunched together looked like a freight train.

Cole phoned Jon Stone and described their cars.

'Two Beemer sedans and an Escalade, all black. You reading us okay?'

Cole listened for a minute, then closed his phone.

'They're clear. We're clear. He'll pass it to Walsh.'

They drove south along the beach, then turned inland at Washington, heading for the Palawan Way marina entrance. It was close, and getting closer. The SRT and Special Agent teams were set up on both sides of Palawan Way outside the marina. At least one SRT car had taken a position inside on the island, but Pike did not look for them, and probably wouldn't have found them if he had.

They turned onto Palawan, drove to the hotel at the end of the finger, and parked in exactly the same spot Pike had parked in the day before.

Pike said, 'You ready?'

'I'm good.'

Pike called Walsh.

'We're at the gate.'

'We can see that, Pike.'

'Calling him now.'

Pike broke the connection, then called Jakovich. A man who wasn't Jakovich answered.

'Pike. For Mr. Jakovich.'

Pike expected them to buzz him in, but they didn't. The voice said, 'We'll be right out.'

Five minutes later, Milos Jakovich and his two bodyguards came through the gate. Jakovich hesitated when he saw Cole, and Pike could see he wasn't happy, but the three of them finally approached.

Jakovich said, 'Who is this?'

'He's going to help me check the weapons. If we make the deal, he'll arrange the transportation.'

Jakovich looked even less happy.

'I'm not going to stand there while you inspect three thousand rifles. It will take all night just to take them out of the crates.'

'I don't care if you wait or not, but I'm going to check them. This isn't a surprise. I told you I would.'

Jakovich was clearly irritated, and waved his hand.

'Let me see the money.'

Pike got out, and showed him Darko's gym bag.

'Seven hundred fifty.'

Jakovich rifled a few of the packs, then pulled a bill at random and examined it. He took a marker from his pocket, wrote on the bill, and studied the ink.

Cole said, 'Good thing they aren't counterfeit.'

Jakovich glanced at him, then put the bill back into the bag.

'Okay. We go.'

He raised his hand, and two dark gray Hummers rumbled out from either side of the hotel. One stopped in front of the Jeep, and the other behind, trapping it.

Jakovich said, 'We go in my cars. I like it better that way.'

Pike did not look at Cole or hesitate. He followed Jakovich to the closest Hummer. One of the bodyguards brought Cole to the second Hummer. Separation was bad, but showing fear was worse.

Pike said, 'How far?'

'Not far.'

As soon as he was in the backseat, a man in the front passenger seat pointed a pistol at him.

Jakovich said, 'We going to take your gun this time.'

The other big man patted for his guns, and immediately pulled back.

'He is wearing a vest.'

Pike said, 'Precaution.'

Jakovich tugged at his shirt.

'We take the vest. You not going to need it.'

They took his Python and the .25 he kept on his ankle, and told Pike to take off his sweatshirt. Pike unstrapped the vest, then was allowed to put on the sweatshirt. The same big man ran a wand over him, searching for RF devices. Pike kept himself relaxed, planning what he would do if they found Stone's bug. The wand moved over his shoes, then up the sides of his legs. If they found the bug, Pike knew his only chance was to acquire a weapon and exit the vehicle. He wouldn't go for the weapon that was pointed at him. If the wand beeped, he would pull the man with the wand close as a shield, then go for the wand man's weapon. He would shoot the man in the front seat first, then the wand man, then push his way out.

The wand passed over his buckle without beeping.

Point for Jon Stone.

They pulled away, and the second Hummer fell in behind.

Two points for Stone.

They followed Palawan off the finger, then circled the marina. Pike felt certain they were heading for the freeway, but the Hummers never left the marina. They circled past the green glass towers and restaurants, and kept circling until the street ended at undeveloped land. Then they turned back toward the water, following the last remaining street in the marina. They passed the final row of slips, then the last leg of the channel before it reached the ocean. Here, the channel was lined with maintenance buildings, nautical supply shops, storage facilities, and fishing and boat rental businesses.

The Hummers pulled up outside a long, low industrial building at the edge of the channel, and Jakovich opened the door.

'The guns are here.'

Pike looked around. It had taken only five minutes to reach the weapons, but there was only one road in or out. Jakovich's guards would be able to see Walsh and her backup units coming from a quarter mile away.

44

A SIGN ON THE METAL building read A. L. BARBER – DRY STORAGE. It reminded Pike of an airplane hangar, with hangar-sized doors, but now the doors were closed. Two oversized forklifts were parked nearby, along with yachts on metal frames. They were either on their way into the building or on their way out, but for now they beached in the parking lot.

A large slip cut into the dock allowed boats to be floated onto a sling. They were then lifted from the water and placed on a metal frame. The forklifts then carried them into the building for secure, long-term storage. The building was on the channel, but directly across the street the landscape was brown and ragged. A few stunted oaks and some marsh brush dotted the sandy plain, but nothing else. Pike knew Ballona Creek was somewhere on the other side, but a rise in the land blocked his view.

Jakovich said, 'I sent them all home. We have the place to ourselves.'

Cole said, 'You own it?'

'Of course.'

Jakovich unlocked the door and entered the building. Two of his men followed, but the others stayed by their cars.

Pike stopped at the door.

'You should have your men come in with us. They'll attract attention out there.'

'There is no attention to attract, and who cares? I own it. I have every right to be here.'

The lights slowly flickered to life. The ceiling was almost three stories high, and supported by parallel steel girders. A thin frame of more girders was built onto the long walls, each facing the other. They reminded Pike of the Hollywood Squares, like a tic-tac-toe board set on its side. Most of the squares were now filled with yachts, a row on the floor with a second row above.

Jakovich and his two watchdogs set off the length of the building. Cole and Pike followed, with two more guards behind them. Cole glanced at Pike, arching his eyebrows to send a message. If Darko and Walsh followed their signal to the end of the marina, a caravan of vehicles would appear.

Cole ran his hand through his hair, palming the bug. He broke it, then flicked the tiny pieces away. Pike did the same.

A metal storage container the size of a two-axle truck sat in a bay at the far end of the building. It was just sitting there, secured by a single lock. Jakovich removed the lock and pushed open the door. It scraped the concrete floor with a high squeal.

Jakovich said, 'There.'

Wooden crates stamped with Chinese characters filled the container. Pike knew from their size each crate would contain ten rifles. Three hundred crates. Jakovich mumbled something, and one of his goons pulled out a crate. It hit the floor with a bang that cracked the wood. Each rifle weighed about nine pounds. Ninety pounds. Three hundred crates, twenty-seven thousand pounds.

Jakovich toed the crate.

'You want to inspect, you better get started. You gonna be here forever.'

Pike opened the crate. Cardboard boxes matching Jon's box were packed inside. Pike tore open the cardboard and slid out the rifle in its plastic wrapper.

'Forget it. We don't need to inspect.'

'You like my rifles?'

'Yes.'

'Good. So do I. I'm going to keep them. I'm going to keep your money, too.'

He made a little finger wave, and the watchdogs drew their guns.

Pike felt Cole move more than saw him, shifting to the side, and Pike shook his head.

'You're giving up Darko?'

'I will get Darko on my own. This way, I get three-quarters of a million dollars.'

'Let me ask you something. Everything Rina told

365

you about me, you think I'd give you seven hundred fifty thousand in cash, and come here unprotected?'

Jakovich reached under his shirt, and came out with a small black pistol.

'Yes, I think maybe you did. Now we'll take you for a boat ride. Show you the sights.'

He was saying something in Serbian when a voice outside shouted, followed by a soft pop like a champagne cork. The two guards closest to the door turned toward the sound. Pike didn't know if it was Darko or Walsh, and did not wait to find out. Jakovich shouted at his men, and Pike instantly moved. He stepped into Jakovich, stripped his pistol, and shot the two closest guards. They dropped their guns when they fell, and Cole scooped up the nearest. Pike locked his arm around Jakovich's neck, and fell back, using him as a shield.

'There a way out behind us?'

'I'm looking.'

Three loud bangs echoed through the building, and three men ran through the far door. They stopped long enough to fire several shots, then noticed the two men Pike shot, and then they saw Pike holding Jakovich. Jakovich shouted something, but Pike cut off his wind before he finished. The men disappeared between the yachts as more men came through the door.

Cole shouted, 'Back here. The big doors –'

The gunfire out front exploded into a firefight. Bullets snapped through the thin metal walls as if they were tissue, and plunked into the yachts. Pike dragged Jakovich to the doors, then pushed him away to help Cole open the doors. Outside, they saw a confused group of men running and gunning between Jakovich's Hummers and Darko's black cars.

Cole said, 'This is a clusterfuck.'

'Here comes Walsh.'

An SRT wagon appeared at the far turn, followed by several unmarked cars.

Pike turned to look for Jakovich just as two men ran into the building. The first man was Michael Darko. He stopped just inside the door, saw Jakovich, and shot him. He ran closer, and shot him twice more. He shouted something in Serbian, and shot Jakovich a fourth time. Then he saw Pike, and Michael Darko gave a big smile.

'We got this bastard. You had a good plan.'

He would have stood over Frank Meyer exactly like that. Pike saw him shooting Frank in exactly the same way.

Pike raised his gun, and shot the man who had run in with Darko. Darko stood slack-jawed for a moment, as if he didn't understand, then lifted his gun and fired.

Pike pushed Cole out, and followed, ducking behind the big door as the SRT teams identified themselves over their P.A. systems and demanded that everyone surrender. Two or three might have surrendered, but the gunfire continued.

Cole said, 'He's out the side door. He's running.'

Darko.

Pike ran hard along the front of the building through the chaos of the fight. The SRT operators and arriving ATF agents were spreading along a perimeter, taking men into custody.

Pike ran past them.

He reached the corner of the building, and saw Darko halfway down its length, far beyond the action. Pike started after him. Darko suddenly turned toward the street. He saw Pike following, and popped off two shots, but Pike didn't slow.

Darko ran across the street, jumped high onto the chain-link fence, and clawed his way over. He dropped into the sandy brush, staggered to his feet, and fired three more shots. One of his bullets sparked off the tarmac at Pike's feet, but Pike kept running.

He heard Kelly Walsh shouting behind him.

'Stop it, Pike! You stop! He's mine!'

Pike ignored her.

He hit the fence at a hard run, and crashed down into dead scrub that tore into his skin. Pike couldn't see Darko or hear him, so he traced the fence until he found the spot where Darko climbed over. The signs were easy to follow, even as Hurwitz's voice echoed over the P.A.

'Stand down, Pike. We are moving into the area. We'll get him. Now stand down.'

Pike picked up his pace.

The footprints and trail scuffs led up a low rise, then down into a depression overgrown with chaparral and sage. Pike pushed through the hard scrub, so thick and dense he was unable to see anything except the ground at his feet.

The chaparral thinned as the ground rose, and tabled out into a small clearing. Darko's footprints continued across. Pike paused to scan the far side of the rise for movement. Ballona Creek was visible about three hundred yards ahead. It was a wide creek with concrete walls, and a current that pushed to the sea. They were very close to the ocean. If Darko made it to the creek, there was a good chance he could escape.

Pike set off across the clearing, pushing even faster.

Pike was less than halfway across when Michael Darko exploded from a ball of chaparral, and crashed into him. He had circled back to wait in the brush, and had done a good job of it.

Darko was a heavy man, and strong, but Pike spun with the contact and pushed him past. Darko staggered sideways, then caught his balance. He was winded and out of shape, and breathing hard to show it. He wasn't holding a gun. Dropped it, fighting his way through the brush.

Pike said, 'No gun?'

Darko stared at Pike's gun, still sucking wind like a bellows.

Pike tossed the pistol to the ground at Darko's feet. 'How about now?'

Darko dropped for the gun. His hand was on the grip when Pike hit him with a roundhouse kick that snapped his humerus like a wet stick. He made a deep grunt, then Pike caught him from the other side on the outside of his knee, and swept his legs from under him. Darko landed on his side, then rolled onto his back.

The pistol was next to him, but Darko made no move for it.

Pike was staring at him when the brush moved, and Elvis Cole stepped out. Cole took in the scene, then moved a little closer.

'You got him. We're done here, Joe.'

Pike picked up the gun. He held it with a relaxed grip and jiggled it, still looking at Darko.

Cole said, 'You good?'

Pike didn't know if he was good or not. He thought maybe he was, but wasn't sure.

Cole said, 'It's over.'

More crashing came up the hill, then Walsh burst into the clearing. She had her service piece, and immediately beaded up on Pike.

'Put it down! Move away from him and put it down, Pike. Do it!'

Pike jiggled the gun again.

Cole slowly stepped between them, putting himself in front of her gun.

'Take it easy, Walsh. We're cool.'

She angled sideways to see her target.

'He's mine, goddamnit! You step away from there, Pike! That bastard is *mine*!'

Pike tossed the little pistol toward her. It landed in the sand.

Pike glanced down at Darko again, but saw Frank and Cindy. Frank, Cindy, and their two little boys.

Cole stepped up beside him, and put a hand on Pike's shoulder.

'We're done. You got him.'

Pike followed his friend out of the brush.

Part Five
Rest

45

CINDY'S SISTER ARRANGED THE memorial. She did not know Pike, Jon Stone, or Frank's friends from that earlier time, so Pike was not invited. Cole saw a notice for the memorial when he read the Meyer family's obituary. The obituary was published as a sidebar to a longer article in the *Los Angeles Times* about East European gang wars, the death of Milos Jakovich, and the conviction and sentencing of Michael Darko to three consecutive life sentences for the murders of Earvin Williams, Jamal Johnson, and Samuel Renfro, as well as the murders they committed on Darko's behalf. Darko did not stand trial. He accepted a plea agreement that let him escape the death penalty. The obituary noted that a memorial for the Meyers would be held at the United Methodist church in Westwood on an upcoming Sunday.

Cole pointed out the memorial.

'You should go.'

'I don't know.'

Pike told Jon Stone about it, and asked if he would go, but Stone refused, not because he didn't care about Frank, but because he hated funerals. They made him depressed, and he always showed up drunk.

Pike decided to go. He wore a black suit over a black shirt and black silk tie. Frank, Cindy, Little Frank, and Joey were represented by poster-sized photographs set up on easels, along with an enormous blowup of a family portrait.

The people in attendance were mostly Cindy's family, but a significant number were people who knew the Meyers from school, their business, and church. Two cousins from Frank's side showed up, both listless men with scabbed hands and coarse skin who looked like they worked hard for a living. They attended only because they brought Frank's mother – an overweight woman of meager means who had difficulty walking. She sat in a front pew with the two awkward cousins as if she was out of place, and knew it. Her clothes were cheap, and her hair was bad, and when the memorial was over she would go back to her trailer in San Bernardino.

Pike introduced himself, and shook her hand.

'Frank was my friend. We were in the service together.'

'This is so terrible. I don't know what I'm going to do.'

'I'm sorry about your son.'

'I don't know what I'm going to do.'

Pike shook other hands. When people asked, he

told them he knew Frank from the service, but didn't say where or when, and provided no details. These people knew the Frank they wanted to know, and the Frank that Frank and Cindy wanted them to know. Pike was fine with it.

Pike left in the middle of the service, and drove to Frank's house. The yellow tape was down, and someone had replaced the broken front door. A For Sale sign had sprouted on the front lawn.

Pike took off his jacket and tie, then rolled his sleeves. He let himself through the side gate, walked around to the back, then stood beneath the huge maple tree beside the still pool. The relatives would be through the house soon, dividing and sharing the mementos, deciding what to do with the possessions. Pike went to the French doors, but did not enter. He had what he wanted. He peered into Frank's house, then faced the pool and the trees. It was easy to imagine Frank tossing his sons in the air, but imagining it didn't make him hurt less.

Pike returned to his Jeep, and turned toward the ocean. He followed Sunset Boulevard west, through Brentwood and the Palisades to the Pacific Coast Highway, then up the coast toward Malibu. The ocean was gray, and crowded with sailboats and surfers, come out on the weekend to play.

Pike turned up into Malibu Canyon, and drove for a while, leaving the people and houses behind. He found a gravel fire road, and drove until he came to a bluff deep in the hills with no one else around. Pike shut off his Jeep, then got out and stood on the earth.

One night four men Frank Meyer did not know and to whom he had no connection entered his home. They killed Frank, his family, and everything he held dear. Frank was left with nothing except how he lived, and how he died.

Frank Meyer's fingerprints were found on Earvin 'Moon' Williams's pistol. A postmortem examination of Williams's elbow revealed that the ulnar collateral ligament was ruptured, along with cracks in both the ulna and radius in the forearm. The break in the radius bone was of the 'green wood' variety, and damaged the surrounding tissue so severely that blood pooled in the joint until the time of Williams's death. This was how Pike wanted to remember his friend. Chubby, out of shape, and a dozen years out of the game, Frank had moved to defend his family, engaged a superior force, and lost his life in the effort. Frank the Tank to the end.

Pike returned to the Jeep and opened a gun case on the backseat. He took out his pistol and three speed-loaders, two of which were already charged with six bullets, and one which was only half loaded.

Pike raised the Python, fired six times, then re-loaded. He fired six more shots, reloaded, then did it again, and finally a last time, firing only three shots. Twenty-one shots, in all.

'Good-bye, Frank.'

Pike put his gun away, and drove the long road home.

46

THREE WEEKS LATER, one day after they removed the cast from his arm, Michael Darko scowled at the flat, dry fields as they approached Corcoran, California, and thought, This must be the far side of the moon. Darko was surprised that morning when he was herded onto a bus and told he was being relocated to Corcoran State Prison. Darko had spent the past two weeks at Terminal Island, a federal facility he thought would be his home for the next many years. He asked why he was being transferred, but no one offered an answer.

Another inmate on the ride up told him Corcoran was a very bad place with many dangerous people, but now, after four hours in the bus and seeing the prison in the distance, Darko was not so much scared that this place would be dangerous, but disappointed because it was ugly.

After what he had known in Bosnia, American prisons and American prisoners did not frighten him, just as American policemen did not frighten him. Michael Darko had come from a dangerous place, and was, himself, a dangerous man.

Even as the prison grew in the van's dusty windows, Darko was planning to establish contact with other East European inmates, and forge relationships with the Aryan Brotherhood. Many of these associations were already in place, and would be useful in building an empire.

Ten minutes later, the van entered the facility through a rolling gate, then drove into a small parking area where several guards waited. Darko and the two inmates sharing the ride had to wait for the guards to enter the van and unlock them. Each of the three were wearing hand and ankle restraints, and had been locked to separate seats well out of reach of each other. This was done because violent inmates often tried to kill, maim, fornicate with, and sometimes eat each other on the long drive up to nowhere.

The guards entered the van one by one, unhooked an inmate, and walked him off – one guard per inmate. Darko was taken off last. He gave his guard a merciless leer.

'Home, sweet home! It is a beautiful place, is it not?'

The guard had seen tough-guy swagger before, and paid no attention.

The three new inmates were herded through the admitting process. They were stripped, searched, probed, and X-rayed, then were fingerprinted, photographed, and had a DNA sample removed and recorded. They were sprayed with de-louser, made to shower, and given new clothes and shoes. The clothes and shoes they were wearing when they arrived were discarded. The allowable possessions transferred with them were inspected, logged into their records, and returned.

The admission process took forty minutes, during which the chief guard-of-the-watch lectured them on the dos and don'ts of Corcoran, read them a set of written rules, and issued their housing assignments.

Michael Darko was assigned a cell in Level Three Housing, a facility for homicidal offenders capable of self-restraint. Two guards walked him to his new home, turned him over to yet more guards, who processed him into their facility. He was then given fresh bedding, and led to his cell.

He arrived during the afternoon break, a time at which the cells on the main block were open, and main block prisoners were allowed to mingle in the common areas.

The two guards brought Darko to his cell and pointed out a sheetless bunk.

'This side. Your bunkie's a brother named Nathaniel Adama-bey. Calls himself a Moor. He's in for two homicides, but he ain't so bad.'

'I am sure we will become great friends.'

'I'm sure you will.'

The guards left, and Darko turned to his bunk. He unrolled the mattress, straightened it, then picked up his sheet. It was coarse, and stiff with plenty of starch. Darko hated making a bed, and wished he had one of his whores to take care of it. Then he chuckled. Maybe he would make this Nathaniel Adama-bey his whore, and then Nathaniel could do it.

Darko unfolded the sheet, and shook it into the air to open it. The sheet billowed out, and floated for a moment like a great white bubble. The bubble was still in the air when Michael Darko slammed face-first into the wall, breaking his nose. Then an arm as hard as steel locked around his throat, and something stung his back like an angry wasp, low on his side over his kidney – *stickstickstick, stickstickstick, stickstickstick* – a sharp pricking that happened too fast to hurt, and moved from his side to his ribs – *stickstickstick, stickstickstick.*

Michael Darko tried to rise, but the man kept him off balance – *stickstickstick* – until a hissing, hot breath scalded his ear.

'Don't die yet, not yet.'

Darko was flipped over. He saw a short Asian man with tremendous shoulders and arms, whose face was dimpled with scars as if from horrible wounds. Michael Darko tried to raise his hands, but couldn't. He tried to defend himself, but was beyond all that. The man's arm moved as furiously as a needle on a sewing machine – *stickstickstick, stickstickstick* – punching Darko in the chest with an ice pick.

Michael Darko watched himself being killed.

The man suddenly grabbed Darko's face, and leaned

close with his rage, close enough for a kiss.

'You're gonna meet Frank Meyer, you piece of shit. Tell'm Lonny sends his love.'

The man shoved the ice pick hard into Darko's chest, all the way to the hilt, and abruptly walked away.

Michael Darko looked down at the handle, protruding from his chest. He wanted to pull it out, but his hands wouldn't move. Darko slid off his bunk into his sheet, and the folds draped over him like a shawl. His back and chest felt as if ants were migrating under his skin, and seemed to be swelling. Darko tried to call for help, but could not find the breath. He could not breathe. He felt light-headed, and cold, and afraid.

The white sheet grew red.

47

TRAFFIC AT A STANDSTILL. Late afternoon. Someone lost control of his vehicle, and now the southbound 405 was a parking lot. Kelly Walsh didn't mind. Windows up, AC blowing, the horns outside muted. CD player. She touched the replay button, and the backup singers began their soothing riff – dum, dum, dum, dundee, doo-wah – and Roy Orbison kissed her heart with longing and pain.

Only the lonely.

Walsh had listened to the song four times in a row, and was now on her fifth; trapped on the stalled freeway in a cocoon of melancholy.

Walsh missed him terribly, Special Agent Jordan Brant, killed in the line of duty, one of her guys, and could not escape the guilt that she had failed him, then, and even now.

Michael Darko had cut a deal, which meant there had been no trial. Walsh knew she should be happy, but Jordie Brant's wife lost the chance to confront her husband's killer, and Walsh herself lost the righteous vengeance of offering the testimony to nail Darko's conviction. The lack of closure left her feeling as if Jordie remained unavenged, and that she had somehow failed him again. And lost him again.

They're gone forever.

As she sat there, listening to Roy, her cell phone buzzed. Walsh checked the incoming ID, then stopped the music to answer.

'Kelly Walsh.'

'Have you heard?'

'I get promoted?'

'Better. Michael Darko was murdered.'

Walsh was caught off guard and left feeling surprised. She had expected this call sooner or later, but not this soon, and not today. A mixture of warmth and fear blossomed in her belly.

She said, 'Couldn't happen to a nicer guy.'

'These things happen.'

'Yes. Yes, they do. They know who did it?'

'Uh-uh. Someone got in his cell during a free period. No video, either. The DVR was down.'

Walsh kept the smile from her voice.

'No shit. That's a bad break. How'd they kill him?'

'Looks like an ice pick or a screwdriver. Stuck him sixty-two times.'

Walsh smiled a warm, soft smile all the way from Jordie Brant's grave.

'Thanks for letting me know. Sounds like someone had a serious mad-on for this prick.'

'No kidding. Hope that dude doesn't get mad at me.'

Walsh laughed politely, then closed her phone. She sat in silence for a moment, feeling her spirits lighten. Walsh had called in big favors to have Darko transferred to Corcoran, and would owe a big favor in return, but Special Agent Kelly Walsh had fulfilled her obligation. Jordie Brant had been one of her guys. You have to take care of your own, and that's what she did.

Walsh had known how she would do it since she learned Lonny Tang was in Corcoran.

A nasty little sonofabitch.

A natural-born killer.

Walsh ejected the Orbison, and decided she wanted to hear something lighter. More bouncy and upbeat. She loaded her favorite all-girl mix into the player – Pussycat Dolls, No Doubt, Rihanna, and Pink, sprinkled with classics by the Bangles, Bananarama, and the Go-Go's. She hit the play button, and cranked up the volume.

The energy filled her.

She sang with the band.

This town is my town.

She felt better already.

Those women can rock!

48

COLE FOUND THE FAMILY. They were good people, a young couple from Sierra Madre who had already adopted two children, both, coincidentally, from the former Soviet Union. Cole had checked them out thoroughly, and interviewed them several times, and Pike had watched how they related to the boy and their other children. He thought they would do a fine job.

Walsh had come through on the paperwork. Documents would be created that established the boy as a natural-born citizen of the United States, born to a fictitious couple in Independence, Louisiana, and adopted through a private attorney.

Pike held the boy for the last time on a bright sunny morning outside a federal office building in downtown Los Angeles. A private social worker employed by the attorney was going to deliver the boy to his new parents, who were currently waiting across the street.

The boy liked the sun, and he liked being outside. He flapped his arms and made the gurgling laugh.

Pike said, 'You good?'

The boy flapped his arms harder, and touched Pike's face.

Pike stroked his back, then handed him off to the social worker. Pike watched her deliver him to the young couple. The young woman took the boy in her arms, and the young man made a silly face. The baby seemed happy to see them.

Pike turned away without looking back, went into the building, and found the office. A woman there was going to generate the necessary paperwork.

She told Pike to have a seat, then faced her computer.

'I have to fill in the birth information. The name, place of birth, things like that. Most of these things will change with the adoption – like his name – but we need something right now to create his place in the system.'

'I understand.'

'I was told you're the one who has that information?'

Pike nodded.

'Okay. Let's get started. What's his first name?'

'Peter.'

'Spell it, please.'

'P-E-T-E-R.'

'Middle name?'

'No middle name.'

'Most people have a middle name.'

'I don't. Neither does he.'
'Okay. His last name?'
'Pike. P-I-K-E.'

If you have enjoyed
THE FIRST RULE

Don't miss the new thrilling
novel from Robert Crais
THE SENTRY

Available in Orion hardback
ISBN: 978-1-4091-1600-4
Price: £9.99

New Orleans
2005

MONDAY, 4:28 A.M., the narrow French Quarter room was smoky with cheap candles that smelled of honey. Daniel stared through broken shutters and shivering glass up the length of the alley, catching a thin slice of Jackson Square through curtains of gale-force rain that swirled through New Orleans like mad bats riding the storm. Daniel had never seen rain fall up before.

Daniel loved these damned hurricanes. He folded back the shutters, then opened the window. Rain hit him good. It tasted of salt and smelled of dead fish and weeds. The cat-five wind clawed through New Orleans at better than a hundred miles an hour, but back here in the alley—in a cheap one-room apart-ment over a po'boy shop—the wind was no stronger than an arrogant breeze.

The power in this part of the Quarter had gone out almost an hour ago; hence, the candles Daniel found in the manager's office. Emergency lighting fed by battery packs lit a few nearby buildings, giving a creepy blue glow to the shimmering walls. Most everyone in the surrounding buildings had gone. Not everyone, but most. The stubborn, the helpless, and the stupid had stayed.

Like Daniel's friend, Tolley.

Tolley had stayed.

Stupid.

And now here they were in an empty building surrounded by empty buildings in an outrageous storm that had forced more than a million people out of the city, but Daniel kinda dug it. All this noise and all this emptiness, no one to hear Tolley scream.

Daniel turned from the window, arching his eyebrows.

"You smell that? That's what zombies smell like, brought up from the dead with an unnatural life. You get to see a zombie?"

Tolley was between answers right now, being tied to the bed with thirty feet of nylon cord. His head just kinda hung there, all swollen and broken, though he was still breathing. Every once in a while he would lurch and shiver. Daniel didn't let Tolley's lack of responsiveness stop him.

Daniel sauntered over to the bed. Cleo and Tobey shuffled out of the way, letting him pass.

Daniel had a syringe pack in his bag, along with some poppers, meth, and other choice pharmaceuticals. He took out the kit, shot up Tolley with some crystal, then waited for it to take effect. Outside, something exploded with a muffled *whump* that wasn't quite lost in the wind. Power transformer, probably, giving up the ghost, or maybe a wall falling over.

Tolley's eyes flickered amid a sudden fury of blinks, then dialed into focus. He tried to pull away when he saw Daniel, but, really, where could he go?

Daniel said, all serious, "I asked you, you seen a zombie? They got'm here in this place, I know for a fact."

Tolley shook his head, which kinda pissed Daniel off. On his way to New Orleans six days earlier, having been sent to find Tolley based upon an absolutely spot-on lead, Daniel decided this was his one pure and good chance to see a zombie. Daniel could not abide a zombie, and found their existence offensive. The dead should stay dead, and not rise to walk again, all shamblin' and vile and slack. He didn't care for vampires, either, but zombies just rubbed him the wrong way. Daniel had it on good authority that New Orleans held quite a few zombies, and maybe a vampire or two.

"Don't be like that, Tolliver. New Orleans is supposed to have zombies, don't it, what with all this hoodoo and shit you got here, them zombies from Haiti? You musta seen something?"

Tolley's eyes were bright with meth, the one eye, the left, a glossy red ball what with the burst veins.

Daniel wiped the rain from his face, and felt all tired.

"Where is she?"

"I swear I doan know."

"You kill her? That what you been tryin' to say?"

"No!"

"She tell you where they goin'?"

"I don't know nuthin' about—"

Daniel hammered his fist straight down on Tolley's chest, and scooped up the Asp. The Asp was a collapsible steel rod almost two feet long. Daniel brought it down hard, lashing Tolley's chest, belly, thighs, and shins with a furious beating. Tolley screamed and jerked at his binds, but no one was left to hear. Daniel let him have it for a long time, then tossed aside the Asp and returned to the window. Tobey and Cleo scrambled out of his way.

"I wanna see a goddamned zombie. A zombie, vampire, *something* to make this fuckin' trip worthwhile."

The rain blew in hard, hot and salty as blood. Daniel didn't care. Here he was, come all this way, and not a zombie to be found. Anything was good, Daniel missed out. A life of miserable disappointments.

He looked at Tobey and Cleo. They were difficult to see in the flickery light, all blurry and smudged, but he could make them out well enough.

"Bet I could kill me a zombie, one on one, straight up, and I'd like to try. You think I could kill me a zombie?"

Neither Tobey nor Cleo answered.

"I ain't shittin', I could take me a zombie. Take me a vampire, too, only here we are and I gotta waste my time with this lame shit. I'd rather be huntin' zombies."

He pointed at Tolley.

"Hey, boy."

Daniel returned to the bed and shook Tolley awake.

"You think I could take me a zombie, head up, one on one?"

The red eye rolled, and blood leaked from the shattered mouth. A mushy hiss escaped, so Daniel leaned closer. Sounded like the fucker was finally openin' up.

"Say what?"

Tolley's mouth worked as he tried to speak.

Daniel smiled encouragingly.

"You hear that wind? I was a bat, I'd spread my wings and ride that sumbitch for all she was worth. Where'd they go, boy? I know she tol' ya. You tell me where they went so I can get outta here. Just say it. You're almost there. Give me a hand, and I'm out your hair."

Tolley's lips worked, and Daniel knew he was about to give it, but then what little air he had left hissed out.

"You say west? They was headed west? Over to Texas?"

Tolley was dead.

Daniel stared at the body for a moment, then drew his gun and put five bullets into Tolliver James's chest. Nasty explosions that anyone staying behind would have heard even with the lion wind. Daniel didn't give a damn. If someone came running, Daniel figured to shoot them, too, but nobody came—no police, no neighbors, no nobody. Everyone with two squirts of brain juice was hunkered down tight, trying to survive.

Daniel reloaded, tucked away his gun, then took out the satellite phone. The cell stations were out all over the city, but the sat phone worked great. He checked the time, hit the speed dial, then waited for a link. It always took a few seconds.

In that time, he stood taller, straightened himself, and resumed his normal manner.

When the connection was made, Daniel reported.

"Tolliver James is dead. He didn't provide anything useful."

Daniel listened for a moment before responding.

"No, sir, they're gone. That much is confirmed. James was a good bet, but I don't believe she told him anything."

He listened again, this time for quite a while.

"No, sir, that is not altogether true. There are three or four people here I'd still like to talk to, but the storm has turned this place to shit. They've almost certainly evacuated. I just don't know. It will take me a while to locate them."

More chatter from the other side, but then they were finished.

"Yes, sir, I understand. You get yours, I get mine. I won't let you down."

A last word from the master.

"Yes, sir. Thank you. I'll keep you informed."

Daniel shut the phone and put it away.

"Asshole."

He returned to the window, and let the rain lash him. Everything was wet now: shirt, pants, shoes, hair, all the way down to his bones. He leaned out, better to see the Square. A fifty-five-gallon oil drum tumbled past the alley's mouth, end over end, followed by a bicycle, swept along on its side, and then a shattered sheet of plywood flipping and soaring like a playing card tossed out like trash.

Daniel shouted into the wind as loud as he could.

"C'mon and get me, you fuckin' zombies! Show your true and unnatural colors."

Daniel threw back his head and howled. He barked like a dog, then howled again before turning back to the room to pack up his gear. Tobey and Cleo were gone.

Tolliver had hidden eight thousand dollars under the mattress, still vacu-packed in plastic, which Daniel found when he first searched the room. Probably a gift from the girl. Daniel stashed the money in his bag, checked to make sure Tolliver had no pulse, then went to the little bathroom where he'd left Tolliver's lady friend after he strangled her, nice and neat in the tub. A little black stream of ants had already found her, not even a day.

Cleo said, "Gotta get going, Daniel. Stop fuckin' around."

Tobey said, "Go where, a storm like this? Makes sense to stay."

Daniel decided Tobey was right. Tobey was the smart one, and usually right, even if Daniel couldn't always see him.

"Okay, I guess I should wait till the worst is over."

Tobey said, "Wait."

Cleo said, "Wait, wait."

Like echoes fading away.

Daniel returned to the window. He leaned out into the rain again, watching the mouth of the alley in case a zombie rattled past.

"C'mon, goddamnit, lemme see one. One freaky-ass zombie is all I ask."

If a zombie appeared, Daniel planned to jump out the window after it and rip its putrid, unnatural flesh to pieces with his teeth. He was, after all, a werewolf, which was why he was such a good hunter and killer. Werewolves feared nothing.

Daniel tipped back his head and howled to match the wind, then doused the candles and sat with the bodies, waiting for the storm to pass.

When it ended, Daniel would find their trail, and track them, and he would not quit until they were his. No matter how long it took or how far they ran. This was why the men down south used him for these jobs and paid him so well.

Werewolves caught their prey.

Los Angeles
Now

THE WIND DID NOT WAKE HIM. It was the dream. He heard the buffeting wind before he opened his eyes, but the dream was what woke him on that dark early morning. A cat was his witness. Hunkered at the end of the bed, ears down, a low growl in its chest, a ragged black cat was staring at him when Elvis Cole opened his eyes. Its warrior face was angry, and, in that moment, Cole knew they had shared the nightmare.

Cole woke on the bed in his loft bathed in soft moonlight, feeling his A-frame shudder as the wind tried to push it from its perch high in the Hollywood Hills. A freak weather system in the Midwest was pulling fifty- to seventy-knot winds from the sea that had hammered Los Angeles for days.

Cole sat up, awake now and wanting to shake off the dream—an ugly nightmare that left him feeling unsettled and depressed. The cat's ears stayed down. Cole held out his hand, but the cat poured off the bed like a pool of black ink.

Cole said, "Me, too."

He checked the time. Habit. Three-twelve in the A.M. He reached toward the nightstand to check his gun—habit—but stopped himself when he realized what he was doing.

"C'mon, what's the point?"

The gun was there because it was always there, sometimes needed but most times not. Living alone with only an angry cat for company, there seemed no reason to move it. Now, at three-twelve in the middle of a wind-torched night, it was a reminder of what he had lost.

Cole realized he was trembling, and pushed out of bed. The dream scared him. Muzzle flash so bright it sparkled his eyes; the charcoal smell of smokeless powder; a glittery red mist that dappled his skin; shattered sunglasses that arced through the air—images so vivid they shocked him awake.

Now he shook as his body burned off the fear.

The back of Cole's house was an A-shaped glass steeple, giving him a view of the canyon behind his house and a diamond-dust glimpse of the city beyond. Now, the canyon was blue with bright moonlight. The sleeping houses below were surrounded by blue-and-gray trees that shivered and danced in the St. Vitus wind. Cole wondered if someone down there had awakened like him. He wondered if they had suffered a similar nightmare—seeing their best friend shot to death in the dark.

Violence was part of him.

Elvis Cole did not want it, seek it, or enjoy it, but

maybe these were only things he told himself in cold moments like now. The nature of his life had cost him the woman he loved and the little boy he had grown to love, and left him alone in this house with nothing but an angry cat for company and a pistol that did not need to be put away.

Now here was this dream that left his skin crawling—so real it felt like a premonition. He looked at the phone and told himself no—no, that's silly, it's stupid, it's three in the morning.

Cole made the call.

One ring, and his call was answered. At three in the morning.

"Pike."

"Hey, man."

Cole didn't know what to say after that, feeling so stupid.

"You good?"

Pike said, "Good. You?"

"Yeah. Sorry, man, it's late."

"You okay?"

"Yeah. Just a bad feeling is all."

They lapsed into a silence Cole found embarrassing, but it was Pike who spoke first.

"You need me, I'm there."

"It's the wind. This wind is crazy."

"Uh-huh."

"Watch yourself."

He told Pike he would call again soon, then put down the phone.

Cole felt no relief after the call. He told himself he should, but he didn't. The dream should have faded, but it did not. Talking to Pike now made it feel even more real.

You need me, I'm there.

How many times had Joe Pike placed himself in harm's way to save him?

They had fought the good fight together, and won, and sometimes lost. They had shot people who had harmed or were doing harm, and been shot, and Joe Pike had saved Cole's life more than a few times like an archangel from Heaven.

Yet here was the dream and the dream did not fade—

Muzzle flashes in a dingy room. A woman's shadow cast on the wall. Dark glasses spinning into space. Joe Pike falling through a terrible red mist.

Cole crept downstairs through the dark house and stepped out onto his deck. Leaves and debris stung his face like sand on a windswept beach. Lights from the houses below glittered like fallen stars.

In low moments on nights like this when Elvis Cole thought of the woman and the boy, he told himself the violence in his life had cost him everything, but he knew that was not true. As lonely as he sometimes felt, he still had more to lose.

He could lose his best friend.

Or himself.

SHOREBIRDS

Des Thompson and Ingvar Byrkjedal

Colin Baxter Photography, Grantown-on-Spey, Scotland

SHOREBIRDS

Please return or renew this item by the last date shown.
You may renew items (unless they have been requested
by another customer) by telephoning, writing to or calling
in at any library.   100% recycled paper   *BKS 1 (5/95)*

Acknowledgments

We salute the work of hundreds of amateur and professional shorebird watchers throughout the world, and thank Theunis Piersma, David Stroud, Phil Whitfield, Colin Galbraith, Michael Usher, Paul Robertson, and the publisher for help in numerous ways.

First published in Great Britain in 2001 by
Colin Baxter Photography Ltd
Grantown-on-Spey
PH26 3NA
Scotland
www.worldlifelibrary.co.uk

Text © 2001 by Des Thompson and Ingvar Byrkjedal

WorldLife Library Series

A CIP Catalogue record for this book is available from the British Library.

ISBN 1-84107-075-0

Photography Copyright 2001 by

Front cover © Agence Nature/NHPA
Back cover © Laurie Campbell
Page 1 © Michael H. Francis
Page 3 © Derek Ratcliffe
Page 4 © Arthur Morris (Windrush Photos)
Page 6 © Arthur Morris (Windrush Photos)
Page 8 © John Cancalosi (Still Pictures)
Page 9 © Mike Cave
Page 10 © Arthur Morris (Windrush Photos)
Page 14 © Jorg & Petra Wegner (Bruce Coleman Collection)
Page 15 © Laurie Campbell
Page 17a © Jim Zipp (Ardea)
Page 17b © Geoff Trinder (Ardea)
Page 18 © Chris Knights (Ardea)
Page 21 © Chris Knights (Ardea)
Page 23 © S. Charlie Brown (FLPA)
Page 24 © Arthur Morris (Windrush Photos)
Page 27 © Chris Knights (Ardea)
Page 29 © Michael H. Francis
Page 30 © Jim Zipp (Ardea)

Page 31 © Arthur Morris (Windrush Photos)
Page 33 © Laurie Campbell
Page 34 © Pierre Petit (NHPA)
Page 38 © Tero Niemi (Bruce Coleman Collection)
Page 40 © Arthur Morris (Windrush Photos)
Page 41 © Alan Williams (NHPA)
Page 43 © Bob Glover
Page 44 © B. Moose Peterson (WRP/Ardea)
Page 47 © M. Watson (Ardea)
Page 48 © Terry Andrewartha (Survival Anglia/Oxford Scientific Films)
Page 50 © David Tipling (Windrush Photos)
Page 54 © Laurie Campbell (NHPA)
Page 57 © Tui De Roy (The Roving Tortoise)
Page 58 © Chris Knights (Ardea)
Page 59 © E.& D. Hosking (FLPA)
Page 61 © Michael H. Francis
Page 62 © Andrey Zvoznikov (Ardea)
Page 65 © Bob Gibbons (Ardea)
Page 67 © Joanna Van Grutsen (Ardea)
Page 70 © Colin Baxter

Printed in China

Contents

Photograph opposite: American oystercatcher

Page 1 photograph: Black-necked stilt   Page 3 photograph: Common greenshank eggs

Introduction

The restlessness of shorebirds, their kinship with the distance and swift seasons,
the wistful signal of their voices down the long coastlines of the world make them, for me,
the most affecting of wild creatures. I think of them as birds of the wind, as 'wind birds'. To the
traveler confounded by exotic birds, not to speak of exotic specimens of his own kind,
the voice of the wind birds may be the lone familiar note in a strange land,
and I have many times been glad to find them…

Peter Matthiessen, *The Shorebirds of North America* (1967)

There are moments in one's life when time stands still. We have experienced many of these in the company of shorebirds. Crouching on windswept mountain plateaux; exposed to the rawest elements of the arctic tundra; drenched in vast peatland plains; chilled by the bracing winds on a coastal mudflat; or merely sitting by pasture fields, we have been in contact with one of the most beautiful and enchanting forms of life on land – the shorebirds.

It's not just the color and form that excite us, for while most shorebirds are gloriously striking, some are quite drab. No, it's much more than this; our pleasure has been in absorbing their intoxicating sounds, their astonishingly varied behavior and habits on the ground and in the air, their affinity with so many faraway places, the amazing journeys they make to and from these places, and the sheer *joie de vivre* that they instil in the watcher.

We have experienced these encounters in a variety of places: on a beautiful June evening walk close to Hudson Bay, Canada, listening to Hudsonian godwits, whimbrel and American golden plovers; peering at a lone common greenshank, calling on one of thousands of boulders half a mile (800 meters) away, before he exchanges duties with his mate on the nest; marveling at the acrobatic song flights of northern lapwings accompanied by their characteristic 'wee-ip' calls; and watching tight flocks of thousands of knot and

Male American avocet on its breeding grounds hunting for invertebrates below the water.

dunlin racing overhead, as they twist and turn, up and down, propelled at breakneck speed against the backdrop of some murky, industrial conurbation. Some of these glimpses were one-offs; others are regular occurrences, seen in the fields when taking the children to school, or while walking by the sea.

Just think about where these birds have been, their adaptations to a challenging environment, and the complex lives they lead. Think about the sanderling running in and out of the waves lapping on the sandy shore; some of these nest on the lands closest to the North Pole, yet migrate to spend winter as far south as Tierra del Fuego. Other shorebirds, such as white-rumped sandpipers, curlew sandpipers and American golden plovers, also make phenomenal journeys between the two hemispheres – yet many individuals return to nest in the same spot year after year!

Eurasian golden plover signaling danger.

We have watched these birds throughout most of our lives. Ingvar's first encounter was with a flock of Eurasian golden plovers in a field in Jaeren, Norway, spied as he was cycling past. The doyen of shorebird watchers, Desmond Nethersole-Thompson, took a small boy barely able to walk (Des) across vast tracts of bogland, surrounded by high mountains, in north Scotland, to see his first nesting greenshanks, dunlins, common sandpipers and golden plovers. Much later, we met in Norway to begin work on our first book, *Tundra Plovers*.

We are utterly convinced that shorebirds are among the most interesting, puzzling and challenging of all life forms. They offer a delightful spectacle – agile, exciting, unpredictable, beautiful and tantalizing.

Mixed flock of dunlin, ringed plovers and turnstones.

Diverse Families

As a whole, the shorebirds (or 'waders', as they are popularly known in Europe) are long-legged, and tend to be associated with the shore, marshes, bogs or other predominantly wet areas. Many of them migrate over long distances – the definitive globe trotters. A close look reveals a tremendous variety of plumages, bill sizes and shapes, vocabulary and behavior patterns. Virtually all species nest on the ground, many making just a scrape, with most clutches consisting of four, cryptically patterned eggs. On hatching, the young leave the nest almost immediately, or within a couple of hours, and are cared for by both parents, though the female tends to desert before the male. Each of these aspects differs between species, however, and there are many exceptions to even the simple biological rules.

There are 199 species of shorebirds. The greatest number of nesting species occurs in Asia (90 species), followed by North America (52), Eurasia (41), South America (33) and Africa (33). Australia has only 16 species, but Central America has the fewest of all in the world's regions, with only four nesting shorebird species.

Shorebird classification

All species of animal or plant are classified into a hierarchy. If we take a particular shorebird species, such as the killdeer – common on the open agricultural plains of North America – it belongs to a class (Aves: birds), then an order (Ciconiiformes), then a family (Charadriidae: plovers), and finally a genus (*Charadrius*), within which it has the unique species name *Charadrius vociferus*, its Latin name betraying its vociferous 'kill-dee' call. Each species is classified in this way, though there can be sub-sets of some groups in the hierarchical tree, such as orders subdivided into suborders, infraorders and parvorders; superfamilies subdivided into families; and some species classified further as subspecies.

We have used a new DNA-based classification to group the shorebirds. This was published by Charles Sibley and Jon Ahlquist in their monumental tome *Phylogeny and*

Scolopacids and Charadriids – a flock of phalaropes, with stilts foraging behind nearer the shore.

Classification of Birds: a study of molecular Evolution (1990). According to this, the shorebirds belong to one of the world's largest and most complex orders of birds, the Ciconiiformes.

Going down one step, into the suborder Charadrii, we find two infraorders: one containing just four species of sandgrouse, and the other, a huge one, embracing the other 195 species of true shorebirds. The word Charadrii is derived from the Greek word *charadra*, meaning a gully – one of the coastal habitats where many shorebirds are seen. Further down the shorebird classification we find two large, species-rich lineages. The Scolopacida contains birds which have always been considered shorebirds. The Charadriida, on the other hand, includes several shorebirds, but also gulls, terns, skimmers, skuas, and auks.

Let's look at the families in detail, starting with the largest ones.

The sandpipers

The **sandpipers, snipes, dowitchers, shanks, godwits, curlews, woodcocks, phalaropes** and **turnstones** comprise the largest family (Scolopacidae, the **'sandpiper family'**) with 88 species. Most of these breed in the northern hemisphere in habitats ranging from open steppes, forests and wetlands to tundra in the far north, and most migrate over long distances. These are small to medium-sized birds, 4½ to 26 in (12 to 66 cm), bill to tail tips – the majority having long legs, slender heads and smallish eyes. Their bills tend to be long, and in some species are curved, which equips them well for hunting by touch, rather than by sight.

There are two subfamilies. The first of these, comprising the snipes and woodcocks (Scolopacinae: 25 species), have long, straight bills, fairly short legs with long toes, and constitute a small, uniform group. All of them are superbly camouflaged on the ground because of their upper plumage, consisting of pale buffish markings mixed with darker browns and blacks. Snipes are unusual in that some species perform territorial, non-vocal song flights. While circling their territories the birds regularly swoop down in whizzing dives. Spreading their outermost tail feathers in order to vibrate them in the air stream, these birds emit some of the most weird avian utterances – so-called 'drumming'.

The woodcocks are unusual also, in being birds of twilight (crepuscular) and night, with

The New Classification of Shorebirds

(family groups in bold in box on right are true shorebirds;
the number of species in each family is given on right.)

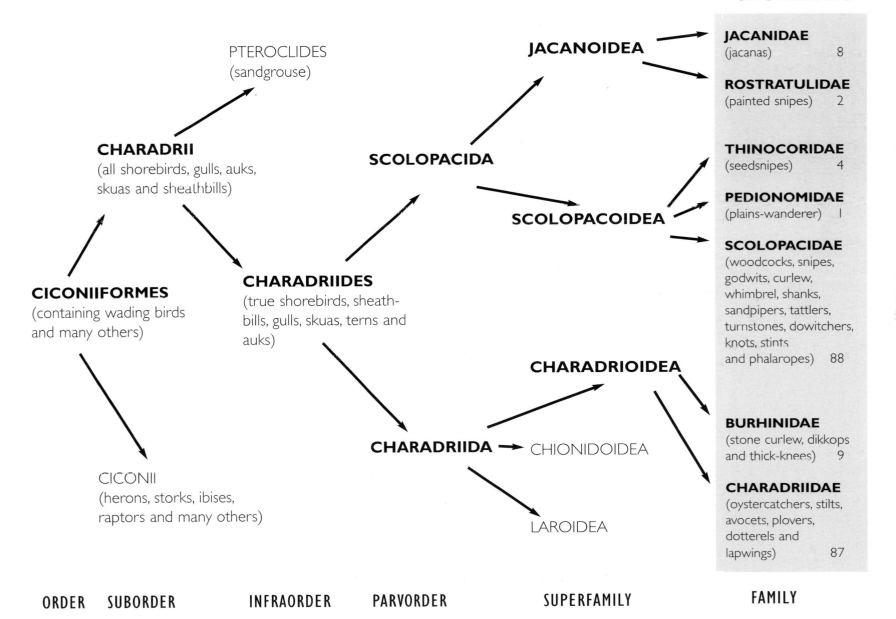

THE TRUE SHOREBIRDS

PTEROCLIDES
(sandgrouse)

CHARADRII
(all shorebirds, gulls, auks, skuas and sheathbills)

JACANOIDEA

JACANIDAE
(jacanas)   8

ROSTRATULIDAE
(painted snipes)   2

SCOLOPACIDA

SCOLOPACOIDEA

THINOCORIDAE
(seedsnipes)   4

PEDIONOMIDAE
(plains-wanderer)   I

SCOLOPACIDAE
(woodcocks, snipes, godwits, curlew, whimbrel, shanks, sandpipers, tattlers, turnstones, dowitchers, knots, stints and phalaropes)   88

CICONIIFORMES
(containing wading birds and many others)

CHARADRIIDES
(true shorebirds, sheath-bills, gulls, skuas, terns and auks)

CHARADRIIDA → CHIONIDOIDEA

CHARADRIOIDEA

BURHINIDAE
(stone curlew, dikkops and thick-knees)   9

CHARADRIIDAE
(oystercatchers, stilts, avocets, plovers, dotterels and lapwings)   87

CICONII
(herons, storks, ibises, raptors and many others)

LAROIDEA

ORDER   SUBORDER   INFRAORDER   PARVORDER   SUPERFAMILY   FAMILY

13

males of several species performing roding flights at dawn and dusk to attract females. They nest mainly in damp forests and are superbly cryptic, with reddish-brown backs streaked with black, pale, white or yellow markings, and black bands on the nape.

The other subfamily, the Tringinae, is large and diverse, with several discrete groups of birds. One of these groups has 18 sparrow- to thrush-sized species, usually referred to as sandpipers (*Calidris*). They have a distinctive non-breeding appearance – their white or pale underparts contrasting with a darker gray or brown mantle. Among these are the fascinating arctic shorebirds – great and red knots, sanderling, red-necked and little stints, and the semi-palmated, western, white-rumped, Baird's, pectoral, sharp-tailed, curlew, purple and rock sandpipers.

Another group, comprising the shanks, tattlers and close relatives (16 species), has birds with longish, brightly colored legs and long bills, and which tend to be very noisy. These are typically birds of freshwater margins. Intriguingly, at least three species nest in trees, two of them in the old nests of passerines, the third in nests built by the birds themselves.

Common greenshank.

There are five further groups. The dowitchers (three species) and godwits (four species) are readily recognized, being tall, with long, straight or slightly upturned bills. They have a more or less coppery colored breeding plumage. Curlews (eight species) are the largest of shorebirds. They are brown-spotted and have long, down-curved bills. Related to these is the upland sandpiper, a short-billed and long-tailed species found in North American prairie grasslands.

Noisy male black-tailed godwit calling to his chicks in the Netherlands.

There are two species of turnstones, small, chunky birds with short, thick legs and a wedge-like, somewhat upturned bill, deployed to flick seaweed and small pebbles on the shore. The single species of ruff is unique, with adult breeding males having distinctive head tufts and neck plumes. Finally, the three species of phalaropes spend more time on water than any of the other shorebirds, and are often seen swimming and spinning, aided by their lobed toes.

If you do a tally of the sandpiper family's species you will see we are one short. As ever, when it comes to classifying birds there is endless debate about where some birds should be placed, and the shorebirds are no exception. The now-endangered Tuamotu sandpiper, of the Pacific islands of its name, is a small shorebird, with a short, slender bill and dark-brown, almost russet appearance. It is more closely related to the tattlers than the true sandpipers. Its late cousin, the white-winged sandpiper, discovered in 1773 during Captain Cook's voyage to the Polynesian Islands, became extinct sometime over the ensuing 100 years or so; today only one specimen exists.

The plovers and allies

The other major family, the plovers and allies (Charadriidae), has a quite different group of birds. There are two subfamilies, the largest of which (Charadriinae) comprises 67 species of **lapwings, 'true' plovers** and the **Magellanic plover**. These are small to medium-sized, compactly built birds, 5¾ to 12 in (15 to 30 cm) long, with a short bill, large eyes, a thick neck and short to medium-length legs. In contrast to the sandpipers, the plovers are visual feeders, with large eyes which are well adapted for the search for food. They tend to run in bursts, pausing periodically to scan the ground, and sometimes crouch before pecking.

The lapwings (of genus *Vanellus*) comprise 24 species. These are amazing birds, with their crests, wing-spurs or wattles, in 16 species, which are always more showy in the males. Lapwings occur worldwide, except in the arctic, and most are tropical and non-migratory. The origin of the word 'lapwing' tells us something about their wonderful display. 'Hleapewince' is the Old English term for the lapwing, derived from *hleapan* (leap) and *wincian* (to jerk). And that's just what lapwings do as they tumble, roll, twist and dive to herald the advent of spring.

The true plovers number 42 species: four species of tundra plovers (the grey, and three

On their tundra breeding grounds, these golden plovers are superbly camouflaged. Adult males are much darker than females – with more black on the face, throat and belly. In winter, males and females are indistinguishable, when their upper parts are brown-gray, the breast is grayish, and the belly is pale.

Compare the female American golden plover in its breeding plumage (above, in Alaska) with the juvenile plumage of the Pacific golden plover (below, in the Galapagos Islands).

17

The unmistakable and elegant black-winged stilt. There are two subspecies,
both of which breed mainly by shallow freshwater lakes, marshes and swamps.

golden plovers), and 38 small plover species. Most of these have slender wings, well adapted for long migratory flights. The tundra plovers breed mainly in arctic and northern regions. Their golden or gray spangled upper parts contrast superbly with black underparts, from face to belly.

The small plovers are tremendously varied in their distribution, habitats, and behavior. Most have varied head and breast-band markings, which play a part in displays, and help the bird blend with the background while sitting on the nest. Among the small plovers are the 32 members of the *Charadrius* genus, including two species of ringed plovers, six sand plovers, the Kentish plover and the killdeer. There are five species of dotterel among the shorebirds, and some argue that at least two of these belong to the *Charadrius* genus.

There is no argument about the strangest of all the true plovers, the wrybill, confined to New Zealand. Its sideways-bent bill is supremely adapted for extracting small prey from the undersides of stones in its riverbed nesting grounds in South Island.

Finally there is the enigmatic Magellanic plover, found in the southernmost reaches of South America. Not yet included in any DNA comparisons, it is debatable whether this turn-stone-like bird is even a shorebird; in some ways it is more like a gull, and its pale gray and white plumage is quite unlike that of other shorebirds. It feeds its young by regurgitation, making use of its large crop for carrying food (as well as for displays, when puffed up), again more akin to the gulls.

The second subfamily within the Charadriidae is the Recurvirostrinae, containing **oystercatchers**, **avocets**, **stilts** and the rare **ibisbill** (living along high-mountain streams of Central Asia). The ten species of oystercatchers are widespread and distinctive, with their pied plumage, stocky appearance, thick orange bill, short pinkish legs, and red-orange eye rings. But there are variations on these generalized features: the American black, blackish, variable and sooty oystercatchers all have near pure-black plumages, which immediately raises questions in one's mind as to why some species are pied and others are not.

With their truly long, pink legs, straight bill, and, with the exception of one species, pied plumage, the five species of stilts are surely the most elegant of all birds — real waders – which tend to nest around saline lakes. The banded stilt, found only in Australia, nests in massive, dense colonies, sometimes consisting of more than a hundred thousand nests. These colonies are mainly found in desert regions, but only when the rains come, which can be as infrequently as only once every ten or more years. It is amazing to think that the first nest was not discovered until 1930!

The avocets (four species), with their delicate, upcurved bills and long legs, typically feed in water with a sideways sweeping action of the bill, but will regularly swim in water too deep for wading. The Andean avocet is unusual among the four avocet species in being found at high altitude, as opposed to near sea level on the coast; its relatively shorter legs and bulkier body are well adapted for local conditions.

The other shorebird families

In many ways similar to plovers, the stone curlews and thick-knees (the Burhinidae family) also occur mainly in the southern hemisphere, though the stone curlew breeds as far north as southern Britain. All nine species have large yellow eyes, long stout yellow or greenish legs, and knobbly knees, and are mainly nocturnal.

One of the most extraordinary families of birds, never mind shorebirds, comprises the eight species of jacanas (Jacanidae). With their long legs, and elongated toes and claws, these gems are supremely adapted for life on floating vegetation, and even brood and carry their young between their wings and body. But it is their mating and parental adaptations which have aroused most interest: females tend to be larger than males, and mate with several, leaving each to care for eggs and brood.

Next we have the two species of painted snipes (Rostratulidae). These birds look like exotic woodcocks and snipes, yet the DNA analysis points to a close ancestral relationship with the jacanas.

Two families of odd-looking shorebirds remain: one (Thinocoridae) containing the four species of seedsnipes of South America, and the other (Pedionomidae) with the

Stone curlew keeping a watchful eye on its brood.

Australian plains-wanderer. The seedsnipes are more like partridges, though their narrow wings render them shorebird-like.

Debatable shorebirds

Finally we are left with the group of birds which some say are shorebirds. The coursers, pratincoles and crab plover (Glareolidae) total 18 species. The amazing crab plover, with its huge black bill and habit of nesting in burrows, is well adapted to avoiding the heat of some of the hottest deserts in the world. Crab plovers are very closely related to the gulls, and whether they merit inclusion among the shorebirds is indeed debatable.

The pratincoles are very long-winged, tern-like shorebirds. They hunt for insects in the air, and nest in colonies. Coursers, as their name implies, run at speed on their long legs in predominantly arid habitats. One of the coursers, the Egyptian plover of central Africa, is the so-called 'crocodile-bird' refered to in the writings of the Greek historian Herodotus (c.485-425 BC), known as the Father of History. Well illustrated in ancient drawings within the pyramids, this plover has a chunky body, striking deep gray and black upper parts and orange-peach underparts. This really is an unusual bird, for it buries its eggs in the sand of riverbeds to protect them from the heat and from predators.

Some species, and indeed families, are clearly more shorebird-like than others. Table 1 on page 68 lists all the species of shorebirds (including three species now believed to be extinct), and gives a summary of their breeding ranges and mating systems. The debatable shorebirds are not listed because, in our view, these are more akin to gulls.

While the taxonomy of shorebirds will doubtless change in the years ahead, we have tried to provide an introduction to shorebirds as a whole. Already it is evident that we have a phenomenal variety of shapes, sizes, colors, and habits.

The crab plover – a debatable shorebird, which feeds heavily on crabs – on the Indian Ocean coast.

Appearance

Look at any shorebird, as millions of birdwatchers have done. What do you see? These, after all, are among the most challenging of birds to identify. Look at the overall shape of the bird: is it tall and slender, or small and dumpy? What about the bill, is it long, short, blunt, pointed, upturned or down-curved? What color is the bill, and is there a colored tip? What about the legs — are they long, short, thick or fine? Are they dark, yellow, orange, pink or red? And this is the easy part.

Plumage and molts

Now we come to plumage, which can tell us so much about the bird's age, sex, phases of life, and in some cases its geographical 'race' (there is great variation in some of the shorebirds, such as the dunlin). The key to recognizing the shorebird's appearance lies in knowing in which of the stages (typically six) of the plumage sequence the bird appears. Is it a downy chick, or a juvenile? Is it in its first non breeding or breeding plumage, or in its adult (second/subsequent years') non-breeding or breeding plumage? Unusually, the three golden plover species, and a few other shorebirds, have a special 'eclipse' plumage, which occurs between breeding and non-breeding plumages; scattered amongst the black breast feathers are yellowish eclipse feathers, so distinctive in golden plovers, particularly during the chick-rearing period.

All feathers suffer from wear and tear, and abrade, thus losing their strength, and they need to be replaced. At particular times of the year the shorebird sheds each of its several thousand feathers during what is known as the 'molt' (derived from the Latin word *muto*, meaning change). During each molt phase feathers are shed and replaced, but gradually and in an ordered way. On different parts of the body, such as the tail or the outer wing, one feather will be shed every few days or so as the new one pushes through. This progression of feather loss is important; if a bird were to molt all its flight feathers at once, it would be flightless and would have to find the extra resources needed to produce new ones, while

American oystercatcher, which has distinctive yellow eyes, unlike the red-eyed Eurasian oystercatcher.

also being vulnerable to predators, and unable to fly in pursuit of its own food.

Of course, when you are out in the field, you have to make snap judgements. You are looking at those parts of the body where the feathers are so distinctive, yet variable: the primary (outer) and shorter secondary (inner) wing feathers, the remaining wing 'covert' feathers (both underwing and on top), the head, tail, breast, belly, scapular, mantle and rump feathers, and so on. On each of these areas the feathers wear with time, especially those more exposed to the rigors of wind turbulence in flight or to strong sun, which can bleach the colors. They are thus molted from the body at a certain time, which helps us identify the shorebird in detail.

Let's look closely at the changing appearance of the shorebird as it develops. The downy chick has grown into a fledged juvenile. It can fly, but there are tell-tale signs such as the odd tag of down fluttering on its head. Soon, though, its appearance is fresh and clean. After a few weeks, or even months, as more feathers are replaced, the non-breeding plumage is attained. Some of these birds will now be on their wintering grounds, but others may be resident year-round. Winter ensues and the feathers endure a lot of wear. Intriguingly, as spring approaches, marked changes occur in some species, and those which breed in their first year, as many do, don a breeding plumage. The belly, breast and face, in particular, become darker and more striking; pale underparts become blackish, brown, reddish, spotted or streaked. The mantle and scapulars become blotched or streaked, and darker. In the godwits, tundra plovers, knots, stints, and shanks, the breeding plumage is stunning; they become gorgeously imposing and attractive. In some of the larger shorebirds, such as the curlews and stilts, which do not breed in their first year, the same non-breeding plumage remains into the spring, though by now many of the feathers look worn.

By its second summer, the shorebird is an adult. Its appearance is clean, sharp and fresh; after all, the body feathers are new and richly pigmented, having replaced the old, pale, frazzled and torn ones. And so the pattern of molt continues, through the key seasons, though after its first year the older adult tends to attain its non-breeding plumage later in the summer.

Adaptations in size, shape and form

What do the size and shape of the bird, and its distinctive characteristics, tell us about, for

This northern lapwing chick is only a day or so old. Yet already it is fending for itself, feeding mainly on small insects on the mud surface. At the first sign of danger it will seek cover, while its parents mob any approaching predators.

example, the northern lapwing tugging at an earthworm in the ground, or the sturdily built curlew with its massive bill deep in the mud; the stout Eurasian oystercatcher hammering at a mussel with its long, thick bill, or the trim sanderling flashing by on its narrow, compact, pointed wings? Much of what we see in the size, shape and posture of these birds has been honed by nature on the non-breeding grounds, where there can be stiff competition for food.

The bill

One of the most striking features of shorebirds is their bill. Bill size and shape, more than any other external characteristics, represent adaptations to the species' food and feeding habitat. Plovers and stone curlews possess short, conical bills with a hard and pointed tip, ideal for catching prey such as worms or mollusks in the ground. Most of the scolopacids have fairly soft bills which are more or less elongated, curved, and with a sensitive tip which is often flexible too. These birds 'feel' for their prey by touch, or snatch them at or just below the water or muddy surface. The bill length of the far eastern curlew may measure 8 in (20 cm), and in the common snipe the bill can represent over a quarter of the total body length.

The legs

The legs tell us much about the habits of shorebirds. Most species have long legs, which are perfect for two purposes: wading in water, and running on a fairly smooth surface, such as a mountain heath, a sandy beach or desert. Functionally, the bird's foot is made up by the toes alone. The visible part of the leg, above the toes, consists of tarsus and tibia, and the joint between these, looking like a knee turned backwards, is actually the heel. Long legs, primarily geared for running, such as in plovers and thick-knees, are characterized by a long tarsus and a fairly short tibia. Shorebird species finely adapted to wading have a very long tibia, readily apparent in avocets and stilts.

Some shorebirds, such as the snipes and woodcocks, have short legs but very long toes.

The American avocet's upturned bill filters out food as it scythes through water.

These birds walk on wet, mossy vegetation and do not normally run, and wade only in very shallow water. Long toes have evolved to the extreme in jacanas, enabling them to walk on floating vegetation. The length of the middle toe equals 39 per cent of the body length in the African jacana, but only eight per cent in the Eurasian oystercatcher.

Phalaropes spend most of their life swimming – on freshwater pools in their breeding grounds, and on the oceans where they spend the non-breeding season. They do not possess the familiar webbed feet found in gulls or ducks. Rather, their toes have lobes or flaps (like the coots and grebes), which extend to provide propulsion as the foot is moved backwards in the water, and when moved forwards, the lobes fold along the toes to minimize water resistance.

The semipalmated plover has semi-webbed feet.

Of all the shorebirds, avocets come closest to having traditional webbed feed, but many of the scolopacids, as well as some of the plovers, possess semipalmate or semi-webbed feet – small skin membranes in the gaps between the toes. Although most shorebirds can swim if they have to, and some do so more than occasionally, the semi-webbed toes are more likely adapted to walking on mudflats.

Wings

Strong and pointed, the wings of most shorebirds are designed for speed. The curved profile of the innermost part of the wings provides a strong lift, yet being fairly short, the wings

Red-necked phalaropes spend much of their lives swimming.

create a minimum of drag. These features provide vital advantages, not only for long-distance migration, but also in coordinated high-speed flocking flights so typical of shorebirds when avoiding attacking raptors.

The woodcocks have rather rounded wings, which they use in an explosive vertical flight when disturbed. Rounded wingtips greatly enhance maneuverability – a great advantage among dense bushes and trees. A similar wing type is characteristic of forest-living passerines and hawks. A peculiarly rounded wing is found in the northern lapwing; males, in particular, have a very broad wingtip, much more so than the females. Over their territories males perform flight displays which involve dramatic aerobatic maneuvers, and which demonstrate their prowess in fending off predators.

Display and fighting adornments

Sexual selection is apparently involved in several body structures including wings, and also in the colors of some of the shorebirds. The most remarkable example is seen in the ruff. Males are much larger than females, and possess a collar of long, seemingly broad feathers around their neck, hence the species' name. The color patterns of the birds' ruffs are unique to individuals, although they can be grouped into categories. Crests and spurs found in some lapwing species are other features that are probably sexually selected.

Some shorebirds, especially lapwings, oystercatchers and shanks, possess bright legs and bills, which probably serve a signal function. Bare wattles found in tropical lapwings and jacanas may serve signal functions too, and may also help in keeping the birds cool through heat loss.

Some species of lapwings and jacanas possess a long thorn-like spur on each wing joint. They use these spurs in territorial fights, mainly as weapons of threat. Although formidable-looking – in the Chilean lapwing the wing spurs measure almost ¾ in (18 mm) – the spurs are never used against predators. After all, lapwings would not want to get entangled with a predator.

An adult northern lapwing.

Migration and Movements

*The wind birds are strong, marvelous fliers, averaging greater distances
in their migrations than any other bird family on earth.*

Peter Matthiessen, *The Shorebirds of North America* (1967)

While we often think of the northern breeding grounds of shorebirds as their 'home', this can be misleading. Many of these birds come to the north for the huge invertebrate food supplies to sustain their chicks. They are there for a matter of only a few months, and then head south for more temperate conditions. Some of the best breeding areas for shorebirds are, for much of the year, among the harshest parts of the globe. Imagine it: in late spring, after much of the snow has thawed, the birds arrive exhausted after a long haul; they have just three months to find a mate, rear a family, and survive the daily uncertainties of where predators will appear and where food will be most accessible. And then they have to leave, before conditions deteriorate. As most of the world's shorebirds breed on tundra, heaths and inland marshes of northern and temperate regions, they have to undertake enormously long migrations south to escape the rigors of winter, and then return north the following spring.

Why migrate?

This raises a fundamental question: how did migration evolve? We know from detailed scientific studies that tens of thousands of years ago much of the central and northern globe was gripped in ice – The Ice Age. For the shorebirds, and many other birds, this posed challenges – trying to find places to feed, to breed and to survive. In many areas there will have been competition for space and food and so movement was vital. And if chance encounters led to birds settling and doing well in particular parts in the north, which were

Huge dunlin flocks perform spectacular aerial maneuvers.

35

A juvenile dunlin in a characteristic roosting pose. There are nine
subspecies, each differing in size and color of upperparts in breeding plumage.

Gulf, and yet others take the flyway along the west coast.

The East Atlantic flyway along the coast of Europe and West Africa carries shorebirds from as wide an area as the eastern Canadian Arctic right across to north central Siberia. A flyway over the Mediterranean and Black Seas partly merges with this flyway, and continues down the interior of East Africa as well as to the coast of West Africa. Further important shorebird flyways go from North Siberia to India and along the coasts of East Asia to Southeast Asia, Australia and the Pacific islands.

Who uses these flyways? Intriguingly, there are frequently large differences in the migration patterns of different populations of the same species, and there are even differences between the sexes and different age groups within these. Grey plover females and juveniles tend to migrate to the tropics and subtropics, whereas adult males winter more in the temperate zone coasts, closer to their breeding grounds. Sharp-tailed sandpiper adults leave their Siberian breeding grounds and head straight for their Australian wintering grounds in a broadfront migration over land, whereas juveniles head for the northeast Asian coast, and then proceed southwards. Purple sandpipers show remarkable differences in wintering areas, and apparently do not move south to spend the winter along the shoreline nearest to their wintering grounds. Instead, while birds from Greenland spend the winter in Iceland, Icelandic birds move to the coasts of Labrador and Britain. Purple sandpipers breeding in southern Norway overwinter in Scotland, whereas those found on the Norwegian coast in winter are from northern Russia, and those breeding in Spitsbergen go all the way to southern Sweden.

Among shorebirds, the most common pattern of migration is for the northernmost species to travel farthest, with tropical and subtropical species being, as a rule, rather sedentary. Yet even the latter can undergo substantial movements. For instance, plovers breeding in Australia, and possibly also African lapwings, can move large distances in order to track suitable feeding conditions determined by the rain seasons; these are the 'rain migrants'.

The northward journey in spring and the southward journey in autumn can be quite different. Many species use different flyways during these periods, giving rise to the term 'loop migration'. Curlew sandpipers which have bred in western Siberia frequently migrate over the Baltic to reach the East Atlantic seaboard in autumn; yet in early spring they go northeast along the Mediterranean flyway, as along this route they can exploit the many wetlands of inland Russia. American golden plovers follow the West Atlantic flyway in autumn, yet choose the inland route over South America in spring. The use of different flyways may be linked to the distribution of suitable food resources in autumn and spring, but will also be due to different seasonal weather patterns which provide shorebirds with convenient tail winds for their migration.

Wintering flock of red knots in Florida.

Helping hands and neat tricks

Tail winds can strongly enhance shorebird migration. Their own propulsion gives shorebirds an air speed of only about 35 to 42 mph (60 to 70 kmph). They need to travel much faster than this though, so in order to ride on strong winds the flocks may rise to a height of several thousand feet. This is particularly important for those species which travel long distances without resting. Red knots, for instance, may cover the distance from their West African wintering grounds to their Siberian breeding grounds in just four or five 'hops', during which they have to stay airborne for a couple of days non-stop.

Such long flights demand huge amounts of energy. The birds prepare for migration by putting on copious amounts of fat. Compared to protein, fat provides eight to nine times more energy per volume. So, in several shorebird species, before the birds take off for a migration hop, almost 40 per cent of their body mass is fat. In order to feed efficiently, they have even developed large digestive tracts to help maximize energy production on a stopover site. As departure approaches they reabsorb parts of the tract and direct the protein from this to the flight muscles. Thus, the shorebirds are supremely prepared for their long journeys, but not

The northern lapwing has the broadest wings of all lapwings.
Most flocks on migration have 30 to 50 birds, though massive flocks occur. In winter, freezing weather
can cause these birds to migrate over large distances to temporary areas of sanctuary.

surprisingly on arrival at a stopover or wintering site they are frequently exhausted. They fall asleep as soon as they land and sometimes can be caught by hand.

Having finished breeding, northern shorebirds not only hurry to get away from inhospitable areas, but also start to renew their plumage. Although they have very strong flight feathers, these get very worn during the long flights, and need to be replaced annually. This is usually done after breeding, either on special molting grounds en route to their wintering grounds, or just after arrival.

The molting of feathers, winter survival, migration, and breeding are all energy-consuming events, and for those shorebirds on the move during March to May, and then from July to October, the time schedule is perilously tight. Those wintering on the northernmost wintering grounds face yet other difficulties. Bad weather may make their feeding grounds and food difficult to get at, and they may have to migrate out of the adverse areas in mid winter. This is often seen in northern lapwings wintering in Britain, which have to move south and west to seek milder climes; or they may go into a period of fasting, an option chosen by bar-tailed godwits on British estuaries during cold spells.

While shorebirds in the tropics face the uncertainties of the rains, which vary from year to year, and over longer episodes, in creating ideal wetland conditions for nesting, those in the north have seemingly impossible challenges: when to leave, how to feed up, where to stop off, and how to trade-off time needed for feather molts and long-distance flights. Yet, amazingly, many of these birds breed in and overwinter in traditional areas – often nesting in tundra or wintering in mudflat locations just a few feet away from where they were in previous years. Clearly, familiarity with these areas is vital to the survival of the birds. That they move between these areas, across the globe, unerringly arriving at the same spots year after year is surely one of the great marvels of the natural world.

And just consider this: a 22-year-old red knot, shot in Spain, had probably traveled twice each year, back and forth, between Siberia and South Africa, notching up 700,000 air miles in the process (the distance to the moon and back). That is simply astonishing!

Wintering flock of bar-tailed godwits roosting on saltmarsh.

Mating and Social Behavior

Shorebirds show a more bewildering variety of mating and social systems than any other group of birds. Although monogamy is the most common mating system in shorebirds, as in other birds, many show different variants of polygyny (where one male is mated to more than one female), polyandry (where one female is mated to more than one male) and a strange system usually referred to as 'double-clutching' (whereby a female produces one clutch for the male to incubate and then another clutch for herself to sit on). Around 20 per cent of shorebird species are polygamous, most of these being polygynous.

Typical breeding cycle

It is difficult to generalize on the breeding season of a shorebird, as this differs between species and regions. As a rule though, in most of the monogamous species the male returns to the breeding grounds in early spring. He displays to stake out his territory and after days, or even weeks, the female arrives. Now there is intense competition, with males singing in the air or on the ground to attract a female. Their aerial flight displays are fantastic. The plovers' performances usually involve jerky, stereotyped wing beats coupled with simple rhythmic songs of one or a few syllable notes. Many of the scolopacids display with wing vibrations whilst giving buzzing and croaking sounds. Some shanks perform gliding flights accompanied by loud whistles. The flight pattern and sounds appear to underline one another, providing a marvelous sense of rhythm and synchronization.

Once paired up, often with last year's mate, the male copulates with the female, especially around the time she ovulates – a few days before egg laying. Some birds copulate dozens or even scores of times over a week or so, and during this time males tend to guard their mates closely to avoid being 'cuckolded'. The nest is a small depression in the ground, and once the four eggs (typically) are laid, the male and female share incubation. The eggs are pear-shaped and fit snugly into the nest with the pointed ends facing inwards, as this

Mating American avocets; note the longer, straighter bill of the male.

helps to minimize heat loss. The eggs are striking; background colors vary from white, brown, buff, gray, green or red, and on these are blotches, streaks and spots which are brown, black or other dark colors. Invariably they are cryptic, and it can be extraordinarily difficult to see some clutches even a few feet away. Many females lay eggs with patterns that are unique to them – blueprints which vary little from year to year over their lifespan.

In monogamous species, males and females usually share incubation duties equally. Some birds will sit for shifts of 12 hours or longer, only leaving the nest when relieved by their partner. This goes on for about three weeks (longer in larger species) until the eggs hatch. Then there can be an almighty din as the excited parents lead their chicks from the nest, often after just a few hours. Now the parents have to protect their young from predators, and lead them to safe havens for feeding. Some species stay close to the nest vicinity, but others, such as northern greenshanks, run miles in a few days. The chicks are remarkably strong and fit. If they chill, as inevitably happens in tundra regions, they are brooded by their parents, but once they warm up they are off again – to feed.

The parents' routine is extraordinary: they are sentinel for predators, giving special warning calls to the chicks to hide or to lie still (chicks have superb camouflage), and fend off predators aggressively or with an array of distraction displays. Many shorebirds rely on camouflage and a surreptitious existence for their own and their nest's protection. If a predator comes too close to the nest or young, the parent will try to lead it away by pretending to have a broken wing, and crying as if hurt. In trying to be seen as an easier meal than their nest or chicks, the parent will also scuttle along the ground with ruffled feathers, giving mouse-like squeaks. Others, notably the larger species, determinedly attack predators which venture near nest or chicks. Eurasian curlews forcefully drive away ravens from their nesting territories, and grey plovers in the arctic do not hesitate to attack raptors as large as rough-legged buzzards. Aggressive shorebirds may even act as protective umbrellas to other, more timid birds, which often nest in their vicinity.

As the chicks mature they require less brooding, and then some broods amalgamate

Superbly camouflaged red knot on the nest in NE Greenland tundra.

loosely or even into crèches, notably in some of the curlews, little stint and least sandpiper. As the chicks fledge, after around four to five weeks, the adults leave (the female days or even weeks before the male) and shortly afterwards the fledglings also quit the nesting grounds. Only one or two fledglings tend to make it from the original clutch of four eggs, and less than half of these will survive the first year. Some studies suggest that siblings stick together on the southerly migration, and even on their wintering grounds, but it is very unlikely that they meet up with their parents in winter to form family parties, as some geese do.

All of this suggests that the breeding cycle goes to plan: invariably it does not. Many nests are depredated by foxes and crows, or even deserted due to severe weather. Some pairs will try to re-nest, but others will 'divorce', with the female moving further afield to secure another mate.

Great snipe males lekking; they leap in the air with tails fanned.

Variable mating systems

Polygamy often leads to family situations in which only one of the mates takes on the parental duties. A prerequisite for this may be that the young should be able to manage without much parental help. In shorebirds this is certainly the case. Only a few, such as common snipe, woodcocks and oystercatchers, bring food to their chicks.

Entirely single-parent care is found in polygynous shorebirds with a lek system. Two such well-studied species are the ruff and the great snipe. In these, females alone incubate and raise the chicks, whereas the males do little but compete for females! On the leks, the males gather in a fairly concentrated area where they keep small individual territories of only a few square feet, from which they announce their presence. Great snipes use song and the exposure of white-patterned tail feathers, whereas ruff display their gorgeous breast feathers in total silence. The pair bond in these species lasts no longer than the few seconds it takes to copulate.

Ruffs vary enormously in their breast-feather patterns, from white to rufous spotted and glossy black. Moreover, perhaps uniquely among birds, the patterns of the display feathers are linked to behavioral traits. Dark males are the ones holding the small display territories ('resident males'), whereas white males ('satellites') appear on the territories of the resident males, where they are tolerated. Possibly, their presence helps in attracting females, and although the most dominant of the resident males are the ones which obtain most copulations, the satellites which manage to keep close to the dominant ruffs obtain some copulations too.

A less extreme polygynous system is the so-called 'resource defense polygyny', a system found in northern lapwings and pectoral sandpipers. Here, males monopolize territorial resources, such as food and breeding grounds. The males holding the most resources are the winners in competition for females. They may attract two, three, or even four mates, while inferior males remain bachelors. In this contest, male quality is in itself one of the resources: the flight display aerobatics of the lapwing males appear to mimic the birds' individual ability to chase away predators – indeed, this is bound to be a valuable piece of information for females prospecting for a mate. A male pectoral sandpiper tries to impress a female by flying over her, inflating his chest sac while making loud hooting sounds as he passes. Although male pectoral sandpipers play no part in looking after the youngsters, male lapwings at least help one of their mates.

In polyandrous shorebirds, there are systems matching those found in the polygynous species, except that the sex roles are reversed. Females are the competitive sex in polyandrous shorebirds, tend to be brighter colored and/or larger than the males, and the males take on most or all of the parental duties. In the remarkable northern jacanas, females defend territories to which males are attracted; several males can take up territories within these, which they defend against other males.

Spotted sandpiper females try to monopolize several males on their territories simultaneously. Intriguingly, Lew Oring and colleagues, working on Little Pelican Island in Minnesota, have used DNA fingerprinting to show that some males pairing early in spring with females actually cuckold these females' later mates! It seems that females store sperm from early

Male ruffs fighting at a lek site. Typically, each male defends a patch around 3 ft (1 meter) from neighbors. Females (reeves) visit the lek and are mated by one or more males; tussles between males can involve pecking and kicking.

copulations, and that when some of these get second or third mates later in the season, and put them on eggs, the poor chaps are actually incubating and raising offspring of the first male that mated with the female in early spring! In other species, notably phalaropes and the Eurasian dotterels, females attempt to mate with several males in succession. Having laid one clutch for a male to sit on, they search for the next mate. This can take the females great distances: some female dotterels can have mates in both Scotland and Norway in the same year.

Double-clutching is found in three arctic and subarctic scolopacids (Temminck's and little stints, and sanderling) and in the mountain plover. In this system, a female lays one clutch of eggs for a male to look after, and then a second clutch, fathered by the same or a different male, which she looks after.

More polyandrous and double-clutching species belong to shorebirds than to all other bird taxa combined. Why? This is one of the hardest questions to answer. Long distances between breeding and wintering grounds, differences in sex ratios on the nesting grounds, the fact that one bird only may be needed to care for a clutch of eggs have all been suggested as contributory factors. Recently, comparative studies have suggested that male-only parental care tends to be more prevalent in bird families (in taxonomic terms) that nest at low density, possibly because the risks of deserting eggs or chicks to find other matings are that much lower.

Lifetime production

We still know very little about the overall productivity of shorebirds. The work on spotted sandpipers indicates that, over a bird's lifetime (of up to nine years), females produce around five fledglings and males produce three to four. In the common sandpiper, females produce around three to four fledglings in a lifetime. As in most birds, a minority of individuals produce a disproportionate number of fledglings. In many species it may well be the case that 15 to 20 per cent of individuals produce more than half the fledglings in a population.

How long do shorebirds live? Most species have some adults that have lived to over ten years old. The oystercatchers live well into their twenties and even thirties; some of the Eurasian and African black oystercatchers do not breed until three or four years old and one was recorded as having bred for the first time aged 14.

Year in the Lives of Shorebirds

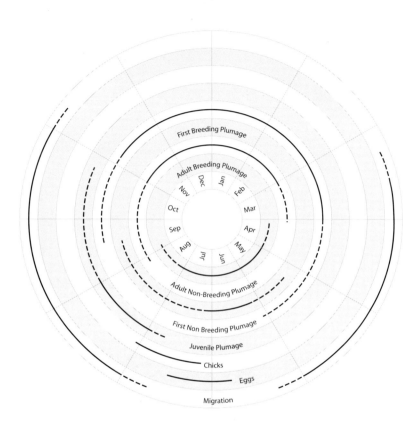

Red Knot (left)

Note how tightly squeezed the knot is in laying eggs and rearing chicks over a period of only 6-8 weeks during June-July in its far north arctic breeding grounds.

Eurasian Dotterel (right)

Nesting further south, on mountain plateaux, the breeding grounds are available to the birds from late May through to late August. In the north, though, where snow lies later in spring, they may start egg laying into late June. Females can lay several clutches, each incubated by separate males, and some may travel further north each time after they put a male down on eggs.

Each diagram shows periods of migration, egg laying, chick rearing, and development of plumages of juvenile, first year non-breeding, first year breeding, adult non-breeding and adult breeding phases of life.

Redshank (left)
Nesting in a variety of coastal and inland wetlands across the Palaearctic, redshanks can nest in early April in the south, though begin nesting as late as July in the far north.

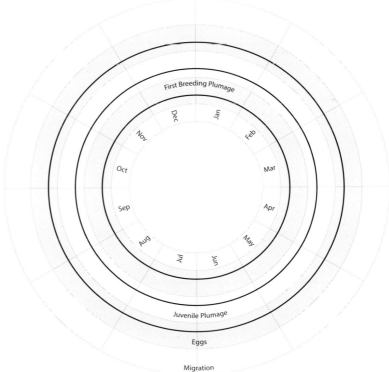

Blacksmith Lapwing (right)
Nesting in southern African wetlands, this bird is mainly sedentary. There is no nesting season; they tend to nest at the start of dry seasons. In any year they will produce two broods. Flooding and predation are the main causes of chick losses.

Food and Feeding

Shorebirds, like rats, crows, men, and other widespread and prosperous creatures, are euryphagous – partial, that is, to a variety of plant and animal food.

Peter Mathiessen, *The Shorebirds of North America* (1967)

Shorebirds feed primarily on invertebrate prey, but in some species a surprisingly high proportion of the diet consists of plant matter, notably berries. Plovers living on tundra and montane habitats are particularly prone to taking berries. Arriving there to find more or less snow-covered breeding grounds in spring, Eurasian golden plovers feed largely on crowberries, which have remained fresh and frozen in the snow since the previous fall. These berries form on plants growing on the drier ridges, and they are among the first signs of plant life to emerge above the snow in spring. The plovers gain rich supplies of carbohydrates from these berries to sustain them while they await the late spring thaw and greater access to food. Crowberries are popular food for golden plovers and several species of curlew well into late summer, and even during fall migration. Eskimo curlews, now almost extinct, were known to feed so extensively on crowberries before leaving Labrador that their plumage got blue-stained!

Of all the shorebirds, the seedsnipes are closest to vegetarians. These birds have an appearance and lifestyle more like grouse and partridges, yet have almost finch-like bills, and a basic food supply of buds, shoots, bits of leaves and seeds. Most shorebirds, however, do not feed to any great degree on vegetative matter. Instead, most feed on adult and larval insects on their breeding grounds.

Insects and worms: masses of food

In the Arctic, the huge production of insects provides the sustenance for the large shorebird populations there. Indeed, the phenomenal densities of insects may be one of the most

Bar-tailed godwit foraging; females have much longer bills than males for probing deeper in the mud.

important reasons for shorebirds finding these extreme northern areas so attractive. The larvae of midges and mosquitoes abound in the marshes and wetlands, and large cranefly larvae reside in the mossy ground. Other insects, notably beetles of various kinds, are also important. Where available in the soil, earthworms are very popular food items for many shorebirds. These worms are relatively large prey, and nutritionally extremely valuable.

Whereas plovers dig with their bills in order to get at the larvae just under the surface of the ground or vegetation, the long bills of scolopacids are equipped with numerous sensory cells so that the birds can find their prey by touch. Moreover, they can open the tip of the bill without opening the rest of it, a phenomenon known as rhynchokinesis. This enables the scolopacids to grab prey animals and swallow them with the aid of tongue movements, without having to remove the bill from the substrate – a great advantage when the bird has hit a dense clump of subterranean larvae.

The chicks hatch with relatively short beaks and are thus well adapted to feed on surface-active insects. On the tundra, the chicks hatch when there is a myriad of adult insects; clouds of midges and mosquitoes abound, and the chicks run around pecking at tiny insects on or just above the near-frozen tundra or peat.

Interestingly, the food of males and females often differs, particularly in the long-billed scolopacids, such as the bar-tailed godwit. During the days needed for egg formation, females have to feed hard to amass the necessary energy and nutrients. Godwit females probe for food in the marshes, concentrating hard on their feeding, with their bill working like a sewing machine in soft, mossy substrates. Meanwhile, their mates, who have much shorter bills, stay vigilant, only pecking occasionally at food items mainly on the ground surface. A similar division of labor is found in many shorebirds, and in the sandpipers, snipes and allies a shorter bill in males than in females is the rule.

Specialist feeding methods

Some shorebirds have very specialized modes of feeding. Avocets sweep their long upturned

American oystercatcher chick. The legs and bill are strong after just a few days.

bills back and forth while wading in shallow water, thus capturing small aquatic organisms on the move. Stilts and phalaropes, with their fine bills, exploit the water's surface tension to capture small water droplets containing tiny prey animals: as the bill is gradually opened, the droplet 'wanders' up the bill, and the prey is then ingested.

As shorebirds move from inland terrestrial and aquatic habitats, where they breed, to a salty, mainly coastal habitat in the non-breeding season, their food changes dramatically. Now they feed on mollusks such as small snails and bivalves, and on small crustaceans and polychaete worms – all living on, or in, the mud and other sediments. This poses a new problem for the shorebird: salt balance. In their brackish and marine habitats shorebirds take in a surplus of sodium chloride, which is more than their kidneys can cope with. Fortunately, they possess special salt glands to deal with this problem. These are situated above each eye, in a shallow depression in the skull, and drain salty water to the nasal cavity where it is excreted through the nostrils to finally drip from the tip of the bill.

Typically tight flock of black-tailed godwits.

Shorebirds have a constantly running nose! Similar glands are found in all birds living in marine environments. When shorebirds are on their breeding grounds in non-salty habitats, most of their salt glands atrophy, as they are not needed and it would probably take a good deal of energy to keep them functional. But as soon as the birds start feeding on marine organisms again, their salt glands grow quickly and start to function.

There has been a huge shrinkage of the world's mudflats in recent decades, and those that remain are under considerable threat from human development. This has presented shorebirds with real problems. For some, like the Eurasian oystercatcher and Eurasian curlew, earthworms are an alternative prey to mudflat invertebrates, but many fields with

Juvenile Eurasian curlew clasping one of around a quarter million worms it will consume in its lifetime.

earthworms are frozen in winter. Nevertheless, increasing use is being made of grassland habitats, not least parks and fields, by the longer-billed shorebirds. And in curlews, there is even an interesting difference in habitat use between the sexes. Females, with their longer bills, are more likely to stick to the mudflats, while the shorter-billed males feed mainly on land in pastures and fields. Farmland is a more typical non-breeding habitat for Eurasian golden plovers and northern lapwings. Often flocks of these birds are exploited by piratical (kleptoparasitic) black-headed and common gulls. The gull sits close by, watching a food-searching plover, and as an earthworm is pulled up, the gull swiftly flies in to steal it. In such situations the plovers have been found to switch from large and energetically profitable worms to smaller items which can be handled so quickly that the chances are they can be swallowed before the gulls are able to snatch them.

Some shorebirds are even predators on other birds' chicks and eggs. Stone curlews and other curlews are known to feed in this way. One shorebird, the bristle-thighed curlew, regularly feeds on eggs of seabirds while wintering on the Pacific islands. It steals eggs from terns breeding in the Austral summer and it has a special technique of cracking the eggs by using a pebble, which it swings against the egg by the tip of its bill.

Another notorious egg-eater is the ruddy turnstone. This amazing bird frequently breeds in colonies of arctic terns (which loudly and aggressively protect their territories from all predators). The ruddy turnstone exploits this 'protective umbrella', by stealing and devouring tern eggs. This bird has a huge dietary range, and on one occasion a flock of ruddy turnstones was seen feeding on a rotting human corpse which drifted ashore on the beach. In some ways this is not so surprising; in early spring they have returned after a long, arduous journey, and need to build up reserves of calcium to form the eggshell. Hence the females, in particular, of several northern shorebird species have been observed feeding on fish and other small vertebrates such as lemmings in order to derive calcium from their bones. Not so long ago one of us saw a common sandpiper feeding on a dead sheep just hours after it had arrived on its nesting grounds from central Africa.

Long-billed dowitcher about to grab its prey deep in the mud.

Conservation

What do shorebirds and dinosaurs have in common? A crisis of environmental deterioration. Not since that fateful catastrophe 65 million years ago, when a large meteor hit our planet, has there been such a major period of animal extinction – not, that is, until recent decades.

Some scientists argue that the impact of that meteor hitting Earth was so massive that the ensuing debris clouded the atmosphere, giving rise to dark, cold conditions which saw out the dinosaurs. During various periods between then and now there have been comparable losses of animals and plants due to habitat loss, hunting, disturbance and pollution. Whole continents have lost much of their natural forests, plains and coastline, and thousands of species have been wiped out in mere seconds of their evolutionary existence on land or in the sea. Shorebirds are no exception to this, and over recent centuries have experienced remorseless losses of their wetland habitats, and severe hunting pressures.

Think of the young shorebird leaving its birth place in the far north; it takes off, having at last been deserted by its parents. In all probability, the fledgling will already have coped with predators, cold and wet weather, and food shortage. Perhaps it has already been on the coast feeding up for its journey. Something triggers the beginning of an amazing journey, and the youngster is off. What lies ahead? Will the traditional 'stepping-stone' areas be undisturbed, will there be sufficient food during the short time our delicate wader lands to feed frantically, will there be yet more predators about? And what about competition for food and shelter: where should the youngster land, and for how long?

Essentially, pressures on shorebirds fall under three categories: loss of habitats used in the non-breeding and breeding seasons; hunting, predation and disturbance; and changes in the environment as a whole, such as global warming, which impact on food availability as well as some of the rudiments of the life cycle of the birds themselves.

A ringed plover, alone in a barren waste of tundra in Russia, settling on its clutch of three eggs.

Habitat losses

Coastal wetlands have shrunk throughout the world. Even in the more developed countries, such as Britain, up to 90 per cent of some estuaries have been developed largely for industry, agriculture and housing. The ensuing contraction of mudflats has imposed a tight squeeze on space available to over-wintering shorebirds. For us, though, the greatest shock has been the statistics on losses of mudflats and other coastal habitats along the East Asian-Australasian flyway. Here, along the coasts of the Philippines, Indonesia, China, Taiwan, Korea and Japan, up to 70 per cent of habitats used by shorebirds stopping off on migration have been lost in the past 20 years. Think of the birds as they fly south searching out vital patches where they can bolster their reserves on the long journey. If the tidal flats are gone the birds risk starvation or exhaustion. Many hundreds of thousands of shorebirds must have perished because of this. In South Korea alone, the government proposes to 'reclaim' almost a million acres (half a million hectares) of mudflat, including over 150 estuaries. This could be catastrophic for some shorebird species.

The changes in agricultural practices throughout the world are also giving rise to losses of grassland and steppe habitats. Pastureland, in particular, has declined rapidly, affecting breeding and non-breeding populations. Then there is the problem of pesticide applications and pollution, which reduce the invertebrate food supplies. Disturbance from people, notably on beaches, and hunting are additional problems.

Hunting

When we look at some of the shorebirds themselves we begin to appreciate the crisis they face. One of the classic cases is the Eskimo curlew. Once an abundant bird in northern Canada, it was almost exterminated through being shot on migration, mainly over the U.S.A. In 1926 it was declared extinct, but in 1945 two birds were found in Texas, and today there may be as many as 20 birds. Yet back in the early twentieth century there are descriptions of huge flocks. E.H. Forbush mentioned in his classic tome *Game Birds, Wildfowl and Shorebirds* (1912) that Eskimo curlews and golden plovers appeared in such massive flocks that they appeared to 'almost darken the sun'. The American golden plovers were equally harried, with almost fifty thousand killed in one day. Now, both golden plover species are protected in the American continent.

Extinctions and threatened species

Recently, Theunis Piersma and colleagues based in the Netherlands produced a valuable overview of the conservation status of some of the shorebirds. We have added to this by listing all endangered shorebird species (Table 2, page 71). Three species have gone extinct, and the black stilt will possibly become extinct soon. The Eskimo curlew and the southwest Siberian-nesting slender-billed curlew are teetering on extinction, the latter due to hunting and probably losses of its Mediterranean wintering grounds. In fact, the slender-billed curlew is now Europe's rarest bird; no breeding record exists since the last record, timed some time between 1914 and 1924.

Black-tailed godwits, dunlin and others foraging in Poole Harbour, UK.

65

Nordmann's greenshank of eastern Russia is endangered for broadly similar reasons, and probably numbers fewer than a thousand birds. Some species have declined rapidly in recent years: the sociable lapwing, spoon-billed sandpiper and black-banded plover, for instance, may soon be endangered. And for some of the populations of the world's smallest islands, predator introductions are invariably cited as culprits. In all, around 40 species, almost a quarter of the world's shorebirds, are declining or at risk.

Global changes

Today, global warming, desertification and coastal habitat loss are the most significant threats. The former is the big unknown, though scientific predictions seem to agree that by the end of this century the climate may be up to 8°F (4°C) warmer. It is predicted that the largest effects on habitats will occur on the arctic tundra-breeding grounds presently used by millions of shorebirds. The extent of tundra is bound to contract, and sea-level rise will overwhelm many of the existing tidal flats throughout the world.

But it is not all gloom. There is terrific international cooperation in surveying and monitoring these birds. Important African-Eurasian and Asian-Pacific flyway protection strategies have been developed. The African-Eurasian governments' Flyway Conservation Treaty is now being implemented. Global networks of protected sites have been established. In the western hemisphere there is the real prospect of protecting almost 30 million shorebirds through the conservation and management of over 3 million acres (1.5 million hectares) of wetlands. And there are plans, and indeed actions, under way to recreate the equivalent of some of the mudflats already lost to sea-level rise. It remains an open question, however, as to whether these laudable actions are sufficient to reverse the negative impacts and trends.

All this is a far cry from where we started out – in the field marveling at the beauty, diversity and behavior of shorebirds. Still, it is a huge consolation that the sheer enjoyment of watching these birds motivates so many people to join forces to study and care for shorebirds and their habitats.

Table 1: Shorebird Species of the World (199 species)

English name	Latin name	Breeding region	Mating system	English name	Latin name	Breeding region	Mating system
Family-Jacanidae				Fuegian Snipe	*Gallinago stricklandii*	SA	—
African Jacana	*Actophilornis africanus*	Af	Pa	Imperial Snipe	*Gallinago imperialis*	SA	—
Madagascar Jacana	*Actophilornis albinucha*	Af	—	Jack Snipe	*Lymnocryptes minimus*	Eu, As	Mo
Lesser Jacana	*Microparra capensis*	Af	Mo	Chatham Snipe	*Coenocorypha pusilla*	Oc	Mo
Comb-crested Jacana	*Irediparra gallinacea*	As, Au	Pa	Subantarctic Snipe	*Coenocorypha aucklandica*	Oc	Mo (Pg)
Pheasant-tailed Jacana	*Hydrophasianus chirurgus*	As	Pa	Black-tailed Godwit	*Limosa limosa*	Eu, As	Mo
Bronze-winged Jacana	*Metopidius indicus*	As	Pa	Hudsonian Godwit	*Limosa haemastica*	NA	Mo
Northern Jacana	*Jacana spinosa*	CA	Pa	Bar-tailed Godwit	*Limosa lapponica*	Eu, As	Mo
Wattled Jacana	*Jacana jacana*	SA	Pa	Marbled Godwit	*Limosa fedoa*	NA	Mo
				Little Curlew	*Numenius minutus*	As	Mo
Family-Rostratulidae				Eskimo Curlew	*Numenius borealis*	NA	—
Painted Snipe	*Rostratula benghalensis*	Af, As, Au	Pa	Whimbrel	*Numenius phaeopus*	NA, Eu, As	Mo
South American Painted Snipe	*Rostratula semicollaris*	SA	Mo	Bristle-thighed Curlew	*Numenius tahitiensis*	NA	Mo
				Slender-billed Curlew	*Numenius tenuirostris*	As	—
Family-Thinocoridae				Eurasian Curlew	*Numenius arquata*	Eu, As	Mo
Rufous-bellied Seedsnipe	*Attagis gayi*	SA	Mo	Long-billed Curlew	*Numenius americanus*	NA	Mo
White-bellied Seedsnipe	*Attagis malouinus*	SA	—	Far Eastern Curlew	*Numenius madagascariensis*	As	—
Grey-breasted Seedsnipe	*Thinocorus orbignyianus*	SA	—	Upland Sandpiper	*Bartramia longicauda*	NA	Mo
Least Seedsnipe	*Thinocorus rumicivorus*	SA	Mo	Spotted Redshank	*Tringa erythropus*	Eu, As	Mo (Pa)
				Common Redshank	*Tringa totanus*	Eu, As	Mo
Family-Pedionomidae				Marsh Sandpiper	*Tringa stagnatilis*	Eu, As	Mo
Plains-wanderer	*Pedionomus torquatus*	Au	Pa	Common Greenshank	*Tringa nebularia*	Eu, As	Mo
				Nordmann's Greenshank	*Tringa guttifer*	As	Mo
Family-Scolopacidae				Greater Yellowlegs	*Tringa melanoleuca*	NA	—
Eurasian Woodcock	*Scolopax rusticola*	Eu, As	Pg	Lesser Yellowlegs	*Tringa flavipes*	NA	Mo
Amami Woodcock	*Scolopax mira*	As	—	Solitary Sandpiper	*Tringa solitaria*	NA	Mo
Rufous Woodcock	*Scolopax saturata*	As	—	Green Sandpiper	*Tringa ochropus*	Eu, As	Mo
Sulawesi Woodcock	*Scolopax celebensis*	As	—	Wood Sandpiper	*Tringa glareola*	Eu, As	Mo
Moluccan Woodcock	*Scolopax rochussenii*	As	—	Terek's Sandpiper	*Tringa cinerea (Xenus cinereus)*	Eu, As	—
American Woodcock	*Scolopax minor*	NA	Pg	Common Sandpiper	*Actitis hypoleucos (Tringa hygoleucos)*	Eu, As	Mo
Solitary Snipe	*Gallinago solitaria*	As	—	Spotted Sandpiper	*Actitis macularia (Tringa macularia)*	NA	Pa
Latham's Snipe	*Gallinago hardwickiii*	As	Mo	Grey-tailed Tattler	*Heteroscelus brevipes (Tringa brevipes)*	As	Mo
Wood Snipe	*Gallinago nemoricola*	As	—	Wandering Tattler	*Heteroscelus incana (Tringa incana)*	As, NA	Mo
Pintail Snipe	*Gallinago stenura*	As	Mo	Willet	*Catoptrophorus semipalmatus*	NA	Mo
Swinhoe's Snipe	*Gallinago megala*	As	Mo	Tuamotu Sandpiper	*Prosobonia cancellata*	Oc	—
Great Snipe	*Gallinago media*	Eu, As	Pg	White-winged Sandpiper	*Prosobonia leucoptera (extinct)*	Oc	
Common Snipe	*Gallinago gallinago*	NA, Eu, As	Mo			NA, Eu, As	
African Snipe	*Gallinago nigripennis*	Af	Mo	Ruddy Turnstone	*Arenaria interpres*		Mo
Madagascar Snipe	*Gallinago macrodactyla*	Af	—	Black Turnstone	*Arenaria melanocephala*	NA	—
South American Snipe	*Gallinago paraguaiae*	SA	—				
Puna Snipe	*Gallinago andina*	SA	—				
Noble Snipe	*Gallinago nobilis*	SA	—				
Giant Snipe	*Gallinago undulata*	SA	—				
Andean Snipe	*Gallinago jamesoni*	SA	—				

The breeding region is given for each as Eu = Europe (including Greenland), Af = Africa, As = Asia, Au = Australia, Oc = Oceania, NA = North America, SA = South America, and CA = Central America.

Mating system is given for each as Mo = monogamy (recorded/suspected), Pg = polygyny, Pa = Polyandry, Dc = double-clutching, – = no information

English name	Latin name	Breeding region	Mating system
Short-billed Dowitcher	Limnodromus griseus	NA,As	Mo
Long-billed Dowitcher	Limnodromus scolopaceus	NA	Mo
Asian Dowitcher	Limnodromus semipalmatus	As	Mo
Surfbird	Aphriza virgata	NA	Mo
Great Knot	Calidris tenuirostris	As	Mo
Red Knot	Calidris canutus	NA, Eu, As	Mo
Sanderling	Calidris alba	Na, Eu, As	Mo, Dc
Semipalmated Sandpiper	Calidris pusilla	NA	Mo
Western Sandpiper	Calidris mauri	As, NA	Mo
Little Stint	Calidris minuta	Eu, As	Dc
Red-necked Stint	Calidris ruficollis	As	Mo
Temminck's Stint	Calidris temminckii	Eu, As	Dc
Long-toed Stint	Calidris subminuta	As	Mo
Least Sandpiper	Calidris minutilla	NA	Mo
White-rumped Sandpiper	Calidris fuscicollis	NA	Pg
Baird's Sandpiper	Calidris bairdii	As, NA	Mo
Pectoral Sandpiper	Calidris melanotos	As, NA	Pg
Sharp-tailed Sandpiper	Calidris acuminata	As	Pg
Purple Sandpiper	Calidris maritima	NA, Eu	Mo
Rock Sandpiper	Calidris ptilocnemis	As, NA	Mo
Dunlin	Calidris alpina	NA, Eu, As	Mo
Curlew Sandpiper	Calidris ferruginea	As, Na	Pg
Stilt Sandpiper	Micropalama himantopus	NA	Mo
Buff-breasted Sandpiper	Tryngites subruficollis	As, NA	Pg
Spoon-billed Sandpiper	Furynorhynchus pygmaeus	As	Mo
Broad-billed Sandpiper	Limicola falcinellus	Eu, As	Mo
Ruff	Philomachus pugnax	Eu, As	Pg
Wilson's Phalarope	Phalaropus tricolor (Steganopus tricolor)	NA	Pa
Red-necked Phalarope	Phalaropus lobatus	NA, Eu, As	Pa
Red Phalarope	Phalaropus fulicaria	NA, Eu, As	Pa
Family-Burhinidae			
Stone-curlew	Burhinus oedicnemus	Eu, Af, As	Mo
Senegal Thick-knee	Burhinus senegalensis	Af	Mo
Water Dikkop	Burhinus vermicularis	Af	Mo
Spotted Dikkop	Burhinus capensis	Af	Mo
Double-striped Thick-knee	Burhinus bistriatus	CA, SA	Mo
Peruvian Thick-knee	Burhinus superciliaris	SA	—
Bush Thick-knee	Burhinus grallarius	Au	Mo
Great Thick-knee	Burhinus recurvirostris	As	Mo
Beach Thick-knee	Burhinus giganteus (Esacus magnirostris)	Au, Oc	Mo
Family-Charadriidae			
Eurasian Oystercatcher	Haematopus ostralegus	Eu, As	Mo

English name	Latin name	Breeding region	Mating system
Canarian Black Oystercatcher (extinct)	Haematopus meadewaldoi	Af	—
African Black Oystercatcher	Haematopus moquini	Af	Mo
American Black Oystercatcher	Haematopus bachmani	NA	Mo
American Oystercatcher	Haematopus palliatus	NA, CA, SA	Mo
Pied Oystercatcher	Haematopus longirostris	Au, Oc	Mo
Variable Oystercatcher	Haematopus unicolor	Oc	Mo
Sooty Oystercatcher	Haematopus fuliginosus	As	Mo
Blackish Oystercatcher	Haematopus ater	SA	Mo
Magellanic Oystercatcher	Haematopus leucopodus	SA	Mo
Ibisbill	Ibidorhyncha struthersii	As	Mo
Black-winged Stilt	Himantopus himantopus	Eu, Af, As	Mo
White-headed Stilt	Himantopus leucocephalus	As, Au, Oc	Mo
Black Stilt	Himantopus novaezelandiae	Oc	Mo
Black-necked Stilt	Himantopus mexicanus	NA, CA, SA, Oc	Mo
White-backed Stilt	Himantopus melanurus	SA	Mo
Pied Avocet	Recurvirostra avosetta	Af, Eu, As	Mo
American Avocet	Recurvirostra americana	NA	Mo
Red-necked Avocet	Recurvirostra novaehollandiae	As	Mo
Andean Avocet	Recurvirostra andina	SA	—
Eurasian Golden Plover	Pluvialis apricaria	Eu, As	Mo
Pacific Golden Plover	Pluvialis fulva	As, NA	Mo
American Golden Plover	Pluvialis dominica	NA	Mo
Grey Plover	Pluvialis squatarola	NA, Eu, As	Mo
Red-breasted Plover	Charadrius obscurus	Oc	Mo
Common Ringed Plover	Charadrius hiaticula	NA, Eu, As	Mo
Semipalmated Plover	Charadrius semipalmatus	NA	Mo
Long-billed Plover	Charadrius placidus	As	—
Little Ringed Plover	Charadrius dubius	Eu, As	Mo
Wilson's Plover	Charadrius wilsonia	NA, SA	Mo
Killdeer	Charadrius vociferus	NA, SA	Mo
Black-banded Plover	Charadrius thoracicus	Af	Mo
St Helena Plover	Charadrius sanctaehelenae	Af	Mo
Kittlitz's Plover	Charadrius pecuarius	Af	Mo
Three-banded Plover	Charadrius tricollaris	Af	Mo
Forbes Plover	Charadrius forbesi	Af	Mo
Piping Plover	Charadrius melodus	NA	Mo (Pa)
Chestnut-banded Plover	Charadrius pallidus	Af	Mo
Kentish Plover	Charadrius alexandrinus	NA, Eu, As, Af	Mo (Pa, Pg)
White-fronted Plover	Charadrius marginatus	Af	Mo
Red-capped Plover	Charadrius ruficapillus	Au	Mo
Malaysian Plover	Charadrius peronii	As	—
Javan Plover	Charadrius javanicus	As	—

English name	Latin name	Breeding region	Mating system	English name	Latin name	Breeding region	Mating system
Collared Plover	Charadrius collaris	NA, SA	–	Javanese Wattled Lapwing	Vanellus macropterus (extinct)	As	–
Double-banded Plover	Charadrius bicinctus	Oc	Mo				
Puna Plover	Charadrius alticola	SA	–	Masked Lapwing	Vanellus miles	Au, Oc	Mo
Two-banded Plover	Charadrius falklandicus	SA	–	Blacksmith Plover	Vanellus armatus	Af	Mo
Lesser Sandplover	Charadrius mongolus	As	Mo	Spur-winged Plover	Vanellus spinosus	Af, As, Eu	Mo
Greater Sandplover	Charadrius leschenaultii	As	Mo	River Lapwing	Vanellus duvaucelli	As	–
Caspian Plover	Charadrius asiaticus	As	Mo	Black-headed Lapwing	Vanellus tectus	Af	Mo
Oriental Plover	Charadrius veredus	As	–	Spot-breasted Lapwing	Vanellus melanocephalus	Af	–
Mountain Plover	Charadrius montanus	NA	Mo, Dc	Grey-headed Lapwing	Vanellus cinereus	As	Mo
Rufous-chested Dotterel	Charadrius modestus	SA	Mo	Red-wattled Lapwing	Vanellus indicus	As	Mo
Hooded Plover	Charadrius rubricollis	Au	Mo	White-headed Lapwing	Vanellus albiceps	Af	Mo
Shore Plover	Charadrius novaeseelandiae	Oc	Mo	African Wattled Lapwing	Vanellus senegallus	Af	Mo
Eurasian Dotterel	Charadrius morinellus	Eu, As	Pa	Lesser Black-winged Lapwing	Vanellus lugubris	Af	Mo
Red-kneed Dotterel	Erythrogonys cinctus	Au	Mo				
Tawny-throated Dotterel	Oreopholus ruficollis	SA	–	Greater Black-winged Lapwing	Vanellus melanopterus	Af	Mo
Wrybill	Anarhynchus frontalis	Oc	Mo				
Diademed Plover	Phegornis mitchellii	SA	–	Crowned Lapwing	Vanellus coronatus	Af	Mo
Inland Dotterel	Peltohyas australis	Au	Mo	Brown-chested Lapwing	Vanellus superciliosus	Af	Mo
Magellanic Plover	Pluvianellus socialis	SA	Mo	Sociable Lapwing	Vanellus gregarius	Eu, As	Mo
Black-fronted Dotterel	Elseyornis melanops	Au, Oc	Mo	White-tailed Lapwing	Vanellus leucurus	Eu, As	Mo
Northern Lapwing	Vanellus vanellus	Eu, As	Pg	Pied Lapwing	Vanellus cayanus	SA	–
Long-toed Lapwing	Vanellus crassirostris	Af	Mo	Southern Lapwing	Vanellus chilensis	SA	Mo
Yellow-wattled Lapwing	Vanellus malabaricus	As	Mo	Andean Lapwing	Vanellus resplendens	SA	–
Banded Lapwing	Vanellus tricolor	Au	Mo				

Table 2: The Extinct, Critical, Endangered, and Vulnerable Shorebirds of the World (26 species).

A further 12 species are threatened.

English name	Latin name	Breeding area	Population Size (number of adults)	Conservation status
Canarian Black Oystercatcher	*Haematopus meadewaldoi*	Africa	-	Extinct
White-winged Sandpiper	*Prosobonia leucoptera*	Oceania	-	Extinct
Javanese Wattled Lapwing	*Vanellus macropterus*	Asia	-	Extinct
Eskimo Curlew	*Numenius borealis*	North America	c.50	Critical
Slender-billed Curlew	*Numenius tenuirostris*	Asia	c.50	Critical
Black Stilt	*Himantopus novaezelandiae*	New Zealand	c.60	Critical
Nordmann's Greenshank	*Tringa guttifer*	Asia	c.1,000	Endangered
Tuamotu Sandpiper	*Prosobonia cancellata*	Oceania	190-250	Endangered
Red-breasted Plover	*Charadrius obscurus*	Oceania	c. 60	Endangered
St Helena Plover	*Charadrius sanctaehelenae*	Africa	c.315	Endangered
Shore Plover	*Charadrius novaeseelandiae*	Oceania	c.130	Endangered
Plains-wanderer	*Pedionomus torquatus*	Australia	11,000	Vulnerable
Amami Woodcock	*Scolopax mira*	Asia	< 10,000	Vulnerable
Moluccan Woodcock	*Scolopax rochussenii*	Asia	?	Vulnerable
Solitary Snipe	*Gallinago solitaria*	Asia	?	Vulnerable
Wood Snipe	*Gallinago nemoricola*	Asia	?	Vulnerable
Chatham Snipe	*Coenocorypha pusilla*	Oceania	c.1,000	Vulnerable
Bristle-thighed Curlew	*Numenius tahitiensis*	North America	< 10,000	Vulnerable
Spoon-billed Sandpiper	*Eurynorhynchus pygmaeus*	Asia	2,000-2,800	Vulnerable
Broad-billed Sandpiper	*Limicola falcinellus*	Europe, Asia	26,000-44,000	Vulnerable
Black-banded Plover	*Charadrius thoracicus*	Africa	< 1,000	Vulnerable
Piping Plover	*Charadrius melodus*	North America	c.3,000	Vulnerable
Mountain Plover	*Charadrius montanus*	North America	5,000-10,000	Vulnerable
Hooded Plover	*Charadrius rubricollis*	Australia	> 5,000	Vulnerable
Wrybill	*Anarhynchus frontalis*	Oceania	c.5,000	Vulnerable
Sociable Lapwing	*Vanellus gregarius*	Europe, Asia	(< 5,000?)	Vulnerable

Conservation Status:
Critical - (verging on extinction);
Endangered - (global population in large decline and fewer than 10,000 breeding pairs);
Vulnerable - (global population in large decline with more than 10,000 pairs, or in moderate decline and fewer than 10,000 pairs).
Near threatened species (declining in many parts of their range): Sulawesi woodcock, Latham's snipe, great snipe, Fuegian snipe, imperial snipe, subantartic snipe, Hudsonian godwit, far eastern curlew, Asian dowitcher, African black oystercatcher, diademed plover and Magellanic plover
Population size: ? = not known

Index

Entries in **bold** *indicate pictures*

Recommended Reading and Biographical Note

Hayman, P., Marchant, J., & Prater, T. (1998, reprint). *Shorebirds. An identification guide to the Waders of the World.* London and Boston. A superb guide to identification, distribution and habits.

Hoyo, del, J., Elliott, A., & Sargatal, J. (eds) (1996). *Handbook of the Birds of the World.* Vol. 3. Hoatzin to Auks. Barcelona. An up-to-date standard general reference (821 pages), with much of the shorebird text written by Theunis Piersma and Popko Wiersma.

Matthiessen, Peter. (1967). *The Shorebirds of North America.* (edited by G.D. Stout). New York. An evocative text, with magnificent paintings by Robert Verity Clem.

Piersma, T., Wiersma, P., and van Gils, J. (1997). The many unknowns about plovers and sandpipers of the world: introduction to a wealth of research opportunities highly relevant for shorebird conservation. *Wader Study Group Bulletin*, 82: 22-33. An important paper.

Wader Study Group Bulletin and *International Wader Studies*, produced by the Wader Study Group, an association of amateurs and professionals from all over the world. Details from: WSG, c/o National Centre for Ornithology, The Nunnery, Thetford, Norfolk IP24 2PU, UK. www.uct.ac.za/depts/stats/adu/wsg

This is the authors' second book, following their highly acclaimed *Tundra Plovers*, published in the Poyser/Academic Press series in 1998.

Prof Des Thompson is with Scottish Natural Heritage, where he works on upland and conservation issues. He has produced six books, and is an Associate Editor of *Ibis* (one of the leading scientific journals on birds). Dr Ingvar Byrkjedal is Curator of Vertebrates at the Zoological Museum, University of Bergen, Norway. He has researched shorebirds in the new and old worlds, especially in tundra regions, and is the world expert on several of these. The authors share a passion for shorebirds, and especially their northern haunts.